MYSTERIOUS GIRLF

by the same author
Disappearer
Colin Cleveland and the End of the World
Girl's Rock
The Eternal Prisoner
Rogue Males

Mark Hunter series
Beautiful Chaos
Sixty-Six Curses
Trouble at School
Mysterious Girlfriend
The Beasts of Bellend
Countdown to Zero

Mysterious Girlfriend

Chris Johnson

Samurai West

Published by Samurai West
disappearer007@gmail.com

Story and Art © Chris Johnson 2020
All rights reserved

This paperback edition published 2025
ISBN-13: 9798294504656

The Linton featured in this story is fictitious and bears no resemblance to any actual
Linton, living or dead.

I was crossing over to Jersey on a ferry and as we pulled out, there was another ferry pulling in. And on it there was a girl waiting to get off. A white dress she had on; and she was carrying a white parasol. I only saw her for one second, and she just looked at me and said, 'What are you gawping at?' ... I'll bet a month hasn't gone by since that I haven't thought of that girl.

Citizen Kane (kind of)

'This is Alpha One to Vesta Control. I have the cloud on visual. Am closing in.'

'Roger that, Alpha One. Are you getting any readings, Frank?'

'Negative. It's like my signals are just bouncing off the damn thing.'

'Well, we know the thing has defied electronic analysis. We could be dealing with unknown elements here.'

'It's just a gas cloud, Julie. Don't make a big mystery out of it.'

'It *is* a big mystery, lunkhead. That cloud just showed up out of nowhere.'

'Nah. It just drifted into the asteroid belt.'

'It didn't just drift in. Our astronomers would have tracked it.'

'Maybe they didn't see it. You said yourself it can't be analysed.'

'Yeah, so it's an anomaly. Anomalies can still be detected, even if they can't be analysed.'

'Well, if it didn't just drift in, then where the hell did it come from, Einstein?'

'Well, we don't know, do we? One theory is that it may have been ejected by one of the asteroids.'

'Great! So it's an asteroid fart.'

'You sure have a way with words, Frank. But yeah, that's what it could be.'

'So which asteroid did it come from? I guess it couldn't have been one of the ones we're mining…'

'No. If it happened on an inhabited asteroid, it would have been detected. Something like that would have to have been a pretty big seismological event.'

'Maybe an asteroid is slowly releasing the gas; y'know,

like Mars is losing its atmosphere as it goes along…'

'Negative. If it was anything like that, the gas would be forming a trail; and the trail would lead us right back to the point of origin. How are the readings?'

'Still nothing. I'm closing in. I guess we won't know what we're dealing with until I've collected a sample of this stuff and brought it back to base.'

'Well, we hope so. And remember, you're to just drift right through the cloud. Don't use your navigation rockets until you're safely out of it. Not unless you run into an obstacle and you have to use 'em.'

'Yeah, I know. We don't know what the cloud's made of and if it's combustible, my rockets could ignite it. I'm not gunna forget that, am I?'

'Yeah, but you kind of have this history of taking stupid risks, Frank.'

'"He who dares…" baby.'

'Yeah, whatever. Just make it back in one piece, okay?'

'Julie! Honey! I didn't know you cared!' 'I just have a bad feeling about this…'

'Oh, c'mon! It's just a gas cloud!

'But where did it come from? If it didn't come from one of the asteroids, then where did it come from?'

'You're not gunna get all sci-fi on me, are you, Julie? Start talking about rifts in space and parallel universes and that kind of crap?'

'I dunno… Like I said, I just got a bad feeling…'

'That'll be your imagination, Julie. Fortunately, I don't have one. I'm the one who's here, all alone in my tin-can, and I'm just fine… Here we go, Julie, I'm starting to enter the cloud.'

'Readings?'

'Still nothing.'

'Visual?'

'Just a lot of green gas.'

'Nothing else?'

'What do you want? A hidden space-fleet? Not much room for one of those, is there? Okay, I might as well collect my sample of this stuff. I'm switching on the vacuum pump.'

'Roger that.'

'Okay... The tank's full. Switching off the pump. I got what I came here for. Piece of cake.'

'Okay, Frank. Just drift on through the cloud. Then you can turn round and get your sorry ass back here to Vesta.'

'Sure thing, honey. Say, how about you and me get together tonight?'

'Yeah, Frank, could you wait until you're not on an open channel before you start hitting on me? I've got people laughing at me here.'

'Who cares! We got no secrets, have we? Say—What the hell...?'

'What is it, Frank? Talk to me!'

'I swear I just saw something! Right ahead of me, through the cloud...'

'Saw what, Frank? Is it a meteor? If you think you're gunna hit something you'll have to use your rockets to—'

'It wasn't a meteor, Julie. It was—I dunno, but I could've sworn... No, I must've just imagined it...'

'Frank, you just said you don't have an imagination. If you saw something, you saw it. Give me a description!'

'Well, it was—Oh, crap! There must be a leak in the containment cylinder! The green gas: it's getting into the cockpit!'

'Put your helmet on, Frank! Stat! That stuff could be lethal! Do you hear me, Frank? Do you hear me?'

'Oh my God. It's there again! On the screen. Oh, Christ! Oh, Jesus fucking Christ! Those eyes!'

'Eyes? What is it, Frank? What do you see?'

'I can't look away! Those eyes! Those eyes!'

'What's the situation, dammit, Frank! What do you see? Have you got your helmet on? Frank? Speak to me, Frank! Vesta Control to Alpha One, do you read me? Do you read me, Alpha One...?'

Chapter One
Mysterious Transfer Student

It was love at first sight.

The first time Murray saw Eve Chandler he fell madly in love with her.

His divinity stands before the class, next to the teacher's desk. She's smiling, she has just introduced herself. Eve Chandler. Just moved down from Rotherham. There's something about this girl. Yes, she's beautiful, even if she does have short black hair and not the long blonde tresses Murray has always thought he preferred in the opposite sex. Yes, she's beautiful, but it's not just that. There's something else, something else that thrilled Murray to the core from the very moment she walked into the room. The way she moves, the way she smiles. It's her confidence, Murray realises—her supreme self-assurance. He reads it in her posture, her expression: here is a girl who knows her own mind, who controls her own life, who faces every new situation without a tremor.

Completely lacking in these qualities himself, it's small wonder that Murray Leinster should find himself attracted to them.

She's a tall girl, his goddess, elegant in her school uniform. Strong arms and legs, hands and feet. There is nothing delicate or fragile about her figure, everything is bold and well-defined. The same boldness marks her facial features: from the arched brows over her shrewd brown eyes, to the long nose, wide, full-lipped mouth and the emphatic curve of her jaw.

The eyes of class 9-C study this addition to their ranks, appraising, assessing. The girls measure her looks against their own, the boys against their personal preferences. There are perhaps feelings of desire, of physical attraction in some of those eyes, but not love, not the overwhelming once in a lifetime feeling of love that has surged over Murray Leinster.

'There's a spare desk at the back there,' says form teacher Miss Forbes. 'Is that alright for you? You don't mind sitting near the back? If you do, I suppose we could move the desk forward... Or maybe you could swap places... Not with me of course! But maybe someone else...'

'Sitting at the back is fine,' says Eve, and without further parley she moves to take her place at the vacant desk.

Her course takes her along the centre aisle and right past Murray Leinster's desk.

Is it that Murray catches her eye as she passes? Does she read that look of bashful adoration on his face? Or is there something more subtle at play? Something subconscious, something pheromonal? Whatever the cause, her eyes do indeed lock with his and she favours him with a smile; a bountiful smile, a dazzling smile, a smile that lights up her face. Murray's heart performs somersaults. He blushes, grinning stupidly.

She noticed him! She noticed him! And that smile! That display of strong, healthy teeth; it seemed to promise him everything. No girl has ever smiled at Murray like that before!

His face burns even more when he sees that many of his classmates have witnessed this non-verbal exchange. People are grinning at him. Murray is not the kind of boy who usually receives this kind of attention from girls. The boys of class 9-C, like any other secondary school class, are divided into those boys who always have girlfriends, the boys who sometimes have girlfriends and boys who never have girlfriends. Murray is firmly entrenched in the last of these categories. Hence all of these ironic grins directed upon him.

Both embarrassed and elated, Murray turns to his friend Spacey, seated on his left. Spacey also smiles at Murray, but his is a genuine smile of congratulation, a smile accompanied by a slow, approving nod of the head.

Next to Spacey's desk, in the row beside the windows, sits Pornboy. His eyes are likewise fixed on Murray, but he is not smiling. No, Pornboy is glaring at him with concentrated, bespectacled, chubby-faced malice.

Eve Chandler has taken her seat at the last-from-back row. The class is chattering.

'Okay class, let's take roll-call...' says Miss Forbes. 'If you could just stop talking for a minute...'

Miss Forbes' voice does not carry well and she is anyway ignored by her students. She is a meek, bespectacled educator, blandly good-looking.

'Really, class, this will only take a minute... So if you could just quiet down... It would be really nice if you could... do that...' The chattering persists.

'Didn't you clowns hear?' breaks in a new voice from the back of the class—male, strident. 'Miss Forbes wants to take roll-call. So shut your bloody racket.' Silence.

Lassiter, 9-C's alpha male has spoken. His word is law.

Miss Forbes proceeds to take the register. Murray, still high as a kite, drifts off into fantasies of his new inamorata. He imagines himself talking to her—yes, actually talking to her—while she looks at him with her sparkling eyes, smiles at him with her dazzling smile... So lost in these innocent fantasies is Murray, that he does not hear Miss Forbes calling out his name in her quiet, hesitant voice. Only when others start to echo the call in louder and increasingly sarcastic tones does Murray surface from his own thoughts, snapping back to reality.

'Here!' he calls out, red with embarrassment.

Everybody laughs.

After this hold-up, roll-call proceeds to its end in an orderly, alphabetical manner.

Miss Forbes closes the register.

'You didn't call Vanessa's name!' shouts somebody.

(Vanessa Young; the last name on the register.)

'She's not here, you mongoloid!' says someone else.

'I know she's not here! But teacher's still supposed to call out her name!'

'Maybe Miss Forbes already knows why she's not here,' suggests Lassiter. 'Is that it? Do you know why Vanessa's not here, Miss?' Miss Forbes' response is to burst into tears.

'Poor Vanessa!' she sobs. 'Poor child!'

The class becomes electrified. What? Has something happened to her? Is she dead?

Comes a chorus of demands for information.

'Poor, poor girl!' continues Miss Forbes, loudly blowing her nose into an embroidered handkerchief. 'To be raped at her age!'

Raped! That loaded word ricochets around the classroom. Vanessa Young: Raped!

Miss Forbes suddenly looks alarmed. 'Oh no! It's supposed to be secret—Class, please forget what I just said! I wasn't supposed to tell you! Vanessa's just... She's just poorly. That's it! She's just poorly! So please forget anything I said about... about...'

By first break it's all over the school: Vanessa Young of class 9-C has been raped! Prurient speculation spreads like wildfire.

When did it happen? Must have been Friday night! Or Saturday night! Nah, it was last night! So she's not in school today? 'Course not! She's at home! No, she's in hospital! Why, was it a violent rape? Must have been!

Who did it? Was it her dirty uncle? Nah, she was grabbed in the street, wasn't she? Dragged into some bushes! What was Vanessa doing out at night? She's a bookworm! She doesn't go out! She stays in her room, doesn't she? Maybe it happened on her way home from school! In broad daylight? Right in the middle of town? Yeah, why not? It happens, doesn't it?

Maybe it happened at home! So, it was her uncle! Or her brother! Don't be stupid! She hasn't got a brother! Can't have been a date-rape! Who'd date her? Must have been a stranger, one of those sexual predators!

Have they got him, then? Not likely! Have they got a description? Nah! Did her from behind, didn't he? She never saw his face! But they'll have his DNA, won't they? They can trace the guy from that! Unless he used a condom! Fuck off! Rapists don't use condoms! They always shoot their wads, don't they? Must have been her first time an' all! And her last! That's the only way *she'll* ever get any!

'So what does raped mean?'
    So asks Murray Leinster.
    Sniggers from Spacey and Pornboy.
    They stand in a corner of the playground; their usual spot, away from the noise and movement. A blue sky looks down on the drab school buildings.
    'That's a joke, right?' says Spacey.
    'He's just stupid,' sneers Pornboy.
    Fourteen going on ten, Murray Leinster is a youth of medium height, skinny, tousled blond hair; he looks upon the world through ingenuous blue eyes, a permanent look of bewilderment on his cherub face.
    Innocent for his age, but as for being stupid... Well, it's a fact that his grades haven't been good, his concentration is poor, but no, let's not say stupid.
    Spacey is acid-head mellow. Twin curtains of centre-parted hair, a relaxed smile, at ease with the world. At school Spacey hangs with the likes of Murray and Pornboy. Out of school he hangs with older kids, clubbing and tripping.
    Pornboy is the fat, bespectacled computer geek. Grounded in the nuts and bolts of the technology, Pornboy might have had a bright future in computer programming; but then somebody went and filled cyberspace with pornography and now he's become hopelessly addicted to the stuff.
    'So, what is it?' repeats Murray.
    'Rape is like sex,' says Spacey. 'But it's like sex without

permission. Taking without asking. Using force.'

'Don't you watch the news?' demands Pornboy. 'You always hear about women getting raped. Attacked in the street.'

'Yeah, but I thought,' says Murray, 'that they just get their clothes torn and hurt a bit.'

'There's that,' says Spacey. 'But there's also the sex.'

'So, did Vanessa get attacked in the street?'

'Musta' been. Wouldn't have been a date-rape. That girl never goes on dates.'

'Never mind that,' says Pornboy. 'What about you and that new girl, then? Couldn't keep your eyes off her, could you?' Murray blushes.

'You're well in there, friend,' Spacey tells him. 'That girl likes you.'

'What?' sneers Pornboy. 'Just cuz she smiled at him?'

'Sure.'

'Huh! She only smiled at him cuz she saw he was gawping at her.'

'A lot of people were looking at her, man. Murray was the only one she smiled at.'

'Huh! He hasn't got a chance!' declares Pornboy. 'She's sitting at the back near Lassiter. He started chatting her up straight away. You watch: she'll be Lassiter's girlfriend before home time. Murray hasn't got a chance.'

Murray's heart sinks. He is the type to be easily discouraged and Pornboy's prediction sounds all too plausible.

Spacey, sympathetic, sees his dejection.

'Don't listen to him,' he urges Murray. 'Not all chicks go for Lassiter. He might not be her type.'

'Yeah, right. Lassiter can talk the knickers off any girl he wants. Where's your precious Eve Chandler right now? If she was interested in you, she would have come looking for you, wouldn't she?' Pornboy looks around with exaggerated emphasis. 'Nope, I don't see her here. I bet you she's with

Lassiter right now! Bet you she is!'

Actually, Pornboy is right. Lassiter has cornered Eve by her locker.

'Do I want to hang out with you?'

'Yeah,' says Lassiter. '"Us" is Malcolm, Sasha, Scarlette and my good self. We sit at the back, just behind you. You should join up with us. We've got the keys to the school garden.'

'So you're the Gardening Club?'

'Er, no,' says Lassiter, offering her his film-star smile. 'We just hang out there. It's a handy place for smoking and... well, all kinds of things...'

'Well, that's really nice of you,' replies Eve. 'But, y'know, I've only just got here. I reckon I'll check out the rest of the attractions first. No offence, like!'

'None taken, our kid!' Lassiter assures her, mimicking Eve's accent. 'But I tell you, in 9-C, there isn't much to choose from. There's Tracy and her crowd, but they're the download charts townies. Then you've got Linda and those other girls at the front, but they're the retards who still like sweets in paper bags. Then there're the swats including the sadly raped and absent Vanessa, but they're pretty boring... So that's about it!'

'That's the lasses taken care of,' says Eve. 'But maybe I'd rather hang out with some of the lads.'

'You'll find most of them playing football in the yard. So, if you wanna stand on the sidelines and cheer them on, knock yourself out. Otherwise, it's back to us.'

'You're pretty sure of yourself, aren't you?' Eve tells him. 'But you've missed out one clique. What about Murray Leinster? Lads like him don't look like the football type.'

'Well, yeah. But frankly I didn't think the geeks were even worth mentioning.'

'Why not? I like Murray. He looks cute.'

'Yes, I saw that he caught your eye. But trust me, even if

you like his looks, he wouldn't be your type. I tell you, that kid's still in primary school.'

'Well…' says Eve, 'maybe I could help him grow up.'

She gives Lassiter a challenging smile.

In spite of himself, Lassiter is staggered. Is she…? Would she really…? Well, it happens. Even geeks and losers can get laid if an obliging girl comes along…

But he can't let that happen…!

'Look, I'm telling you here, Eve, if you hang around with Murray Leinster your reputation at this school is down the tubes. Either that or people will think you're just dating him out of pity. Trust me on this.'

'I'm not really bothered about what other people think,' says Eve. 'Besides, I've only just got here.'

'I can see you're going to do your own thing, whatever I say,' sighs Lassiter, affecting the tone of someone who has tried his best. 'Well, knock yourself out. But, if ever you change your mind you can come and hang out with us…'

'Ta. I'll be sure and remember that…'

North Linton High School is not the nicest high school in Linton. It's only the second nicest.

Out of two.

In plain language, North Linton is a shit-hole of a school. This is because the other comprehensive, South Linton High School always gets the lion's share of the yearly budget allocation. The city council claim this inequality of funding is on account of South Linton having the higher achievement level in terms of exam results; this, they claim, entitles them to a greater share of the budget. Cynics argue that is more to do with the fact that South Linton High happens to be in a nicer part of town, a more middle-class part of town, and the school to which more town councillors send their own kids. The buildings of South Linton High are newer. Originally, they were older, but then back in the '90s the existing buildings were levelled and new ones built in their place.

And the 1990s were an enlightened time when planners had finally realised that attractive-looking school buildings actually did a hell of a lot for the morale of the students. Prisons look grim because they're supposed to look grim.

People aren't sent to prisons to have a good time. But schools are not supposed to be prisons. They are seats of learning. And students are much more receptive to learning when their surroundings are pleasant looking.

The buildings of North Linton High were constructed in the '60s. They are drab and functional; grey, glazed boxes badly in need of a lick of paint. There is nothing appealing or inspiring about the appearance of this school. Additionally, a rampant litter problem has made the school grounds a rendezvous for seagulls. And to top it off, all of the other problems that can beset a state secondary school can be found at North Linton: drugs; bullying and violence; sexual harassment; truancy; poor exam results; shortage of funds and equipment and a staff composed of mainly jaded, unmotivated teachers. North Linton has all of these in spades.

Now, you would have thought that a milksop like Murray Leinster would get eaten alive in an environment like North Linton High School. But somehow he manages to hang on.

Lunchtime finds Murray despondent. It's not that the flame of his love for Eve Chandler has died out; even for a teenager, intense feelings like these don't evaporate in the space of a few hours. Murray is still in love with Eve Chandler, but it has become a hopeless love. Pornboy's earlier words have hit home, and he has decided his love will never be requited; a girl like Eve Chandler is way out of his league.

Yes, she smiled at him. But that didn't really mean anything, did it? It felt like it did; yes, it felt like it at the time. That smile had seemed to promise so much... But that could have been all in Murray's head, couldn't it? He could have misread the signals, couldn't he? Seen something in those eyes, in that smile, something that wasn't really there. Maybe she had just smiled at him out of charity, because she'd pegged straight away what a loser he was.

Yes, it was probably just that.

And there's the awful and undeniable fact that Eve hasn't spoken to him since homeroom. (But then, she didn't speak to him then, did she? A look and a smile, but not a word had been exchanged.) He hasn't even seen her since then. She has been assigned to none of the same classes as Murray, thus far. Murray is not surprised at this. Eve Chandler is obviously a smart girl; she will have been put straight into the top classes for all the subjects.

As for Murray, he is on the intermediate track, even sinking as low as foundation level for subjects like Maths and Science. Murray does not excel academically. In fact, his grades and performance have been steadily slipping since Year Seven. For a while he had been propped up by the excellence of his homework, and teachers were beginning to surmise he was one of those students who could better apply themselves to their studies outside of, rather than within, the classroom environment. But then they had called Murray's mum in for a conference, and from this conference it had emerged that she had been the one doing her son's homework for him! Murray is alone this lunchtime. Spacey has disappeared. He often does. (Murray is never sure if on these occasions Spacey just wanders off in an acid haze, or if the drugs in his system actually give him the ability to teleport.) And Pornboy has been summoned to see Lassiter for some reason. Probably a computer-related reason. People will often make use of Pornboy's expertise in this area, generally treating him like a handy, but disposable, computer technician.

So Murray is alone, and as he usually does when he's alone, he wanders aimlessly around the quieter parts of the school grounds. Wandering, and of course thinking about Eve Chandler. As I've said, his mood is low, pessimistic...

He has no idea. He has no idea he is about to have an

encounter that will signal a change in the pattern of his life. A monumental change that will open his eyes and reshape his world.

Of course he has no idea: Murray can't see into the future. Only omniscient third person narrators can do this!

And so our Murray walks listlessly along, berating himself for his stupidity in ever imagining that a girl like Eve Chandler could love a boy like him; and thinking that she's probably already Lassiter's girlfriend by now.

Murray is behind the Science building. Ahead a row of firs mark the boundary of the staff car park. A figure appears through those trees, a tall girl with short black hair, her striped school tie vivid against a background of white cotton blouse.

It's Eve Chandler! Murray's heart bounds. Yes, it's her! And there she is alone and walking directly towards him! Does she just happen to be passing this way? Perhaps she— No! She's looking right at him! She's smiling at him!

'So this is where you've been hiding yourself!' she greets him. 'Lone Ranger, are you?'

She stops before him, a radiant divinity. The feeling floods over Murray anew, that overwhelming sense of her intense presence. She is taller than him, her lines are strong; hers is no vague presence, she positively glows!

And her words suggest she was looking for him. Actually looking for him.

'You're Murray, right?' says Eve.

She's just spoken his name! And in her wonderful Northern accent!

So carried away is Murray that he immediately makes a mistake. He attempts to confirm her query.

'Yes, I'm Mu-Mu-Mu-Mu-Murray.'

Murray is afflicted with a nervous stutter. It usually manifests itself in the presence of girls, especially girls he finds attractive. And when this speech impediment is upon him, he finds it particularly difficult to form words that begin with the letter M. Murray's name begins with the letter M. So you can see the problem here.

Murray is very self-conscious of his stutter. And of course his classmates will mock him on account of it, which makes it even worse. Right now, he feels like he's making a poor show of himself in front of Eve, and right from the very first sentence he's ever spoken to her.

But Eve doesn't comment on his impediment.

'I'm Eve,' she says. 'Eve Chandler.'

'I know,' says Murray. 'You introduced yourself this m-morning.'

'Yeah, I did. But y'know, I wasn't sure if you'd have remembered.' 'I rem-em-em-em-embered,' affirms Murray.

'Made a good impression, did I?' asks Eve. 'That's good. I liked you an' all. You just kind of caught my eye, y'know?' Murray turns scarlet.

Eve grins, puts a hand on his shoulder.

'So, what are y'doing all on your own, Lone Ranger?' she asks. 'Not got many friends?'

'Not really... Spacey... Pornboy...'

'Shy lad, aren't you? Well, don't worry. You just need the right person to give you a hand. Help you come out of your shell, like.'

The hand moves from Murray's shoulder to the side of his face. A strong hand but warm and soft, a kind hand.

'Yeah, I'll look after you from here on,' she continues, musingly. 'You stick with me. Y'need to get out more. That's what it is. You need to see more of life. With you it's like just your school and your home, isn't it? And your home's just down the road, right? Only takes you five minutes. Five minutes to get here, five minutes back. That's not much of a world, is it?'

'How did you know where I live?' wonders Murray.

'Oh, I know a lot of things,' archly. 'What you need is an Adventure. Something new. Something to take you out of yourself.'

'An adventure?' echoes Murray. 'You mean like a quest?'

A shrug. 'A quest. A mystery. A rescue. Summat like that.'

'But things like that only happen on TV,' says Murray, confused.

'Says you.'

'Or on computer games.'

'Says you. Adventures happen in real life as well, y'know. You just have to know where to find them.'

'But don't adventures usually happen to people when they're not expecting them?'

'Yeah, sometimes. But sometimes even when you go out looking for one you can still find one. Like I said, it's about knowing where to look.'

'And do you know where to look?'

'Oh yeah. I know.'

'How come?'

'I told you. I know lots of things.'

She means it, Murray realises. She's so matter-of-fact about it, but she's not joking. She's serious! It starts to seep into Murray's being— this feeling, this feeling of some imminent change; like a door being opened, a door he didn't even know was there before. And this amazing, beautiful girl in front of him, she's the one who's going to take him by the hand and lead him through that door!

This dawning realisation must be visible on Murray's face. Eve nods. 'That's right,' she says. 'You stick with me.'

Chapter Two
Mysterious Manor House

Linton Hall sits comfortably in leafy surroundings just outside the town of the same name. An imposing Georgian edifice, the Hall is the ancestral home to a long line of hereditary peers.

At least, it used to be.

If we look into the Hall's sumptuous master bedroom, we

see the bed therein occupied by someone who does not look like most people's idea of a hereditary English peer. For one thing, she's Japanese, and for another, she cannot be more than eighteen years of age.

It would seem that Linton Hall has changed hands.

The girl in bed is Misaki Morishita, just emerging from the arms of Morpheus, lazily wiping the drool from her face with a silk pyjama sleeve. The time is three o'clock in the afternoon, which might seem like an odd time to be waking up: Last bell has just rung at North Linton High, and the students are pouring through the gates like liberated convicts. The parents of these kids, working in shops, factories, offices, will be looking at their watches, waiting for their shifts to end... Yes, it's an odd time for someone to be waking up.

But Misaki Morishita is an odd young lady. For one thing, she is a night owl. (A silly expression really, as most owls operate at night.) Misaki always rises as the working day is drawing to a close, lives her life through the hours of darkness and then retires to bed at sunrise and sleeps through the day. This is the invariable pattern of her existence.

The door opens and a maid enters, wheeling a breakfast trolley. This is part of the routine. Misaki always enjoys her breakfast in bed. The maid is young, blonde, English. Her name is Harriet. She wheels the trolley up to the side of the bed, then stands to attention, hands folded across the apron of her full-skirted uniform.

Misaki sits up in bed, stretches. She is an elegant girl, languid, unruffled. She has narrow, sensual eyes, bobbed raven hair, razor-fringed. Misaki turns her eyes to Harriet, looking at her as though expecting something from her. Harriet looks alarmed.

'Is something wrong, your ladyship?' she inquires.
'Yes,' answers Misaki.
'What would that be, your ladyship?'
Misaki frowns. 'Can't you tell?'

The maid's alarm increases. 'I'm afraid I—If you could just—'

'The pillows, stupid!'

'Of course!'

Harriet springs forward, vigorously plumps Misaki's pillows. The operation completed, Misaki sits back, satisfied.

'You may pour the tea.'

Harriet complies. The teapot is silver, very English, but the tea inside it is the green tea favoured by the Japanese. Harriet pours the brew into a china teacup with matching saucer—also very English—and passes it to her mistress.

She takes a sip.

'Is the tea to your satisfaction, your ladyship?'

'Yes, it's all right.'

Harriet looks relieved.

'Where's Ren?' inquires Misaki, sipping her tea.

'I believe she will be here presently, your ladyship,' answers Harriet. 'She said something about just having completed another stage of her computer game.'

'Hm. Doesn't that girl ever sleep?'

'I believe not, your ladyship.'

Misaki hands back the cup and saucer.

'I'm ready to eat now.'

'Of course, your ladyship.'

Harriet takes a breakfast tray bearing a covered dish from the trolley and sets it down before her mistress. She removes the silver dish cover and reveals—a hamburger. Yes, a hamburger—but not some grubby hamburger from a fast-food joint or kebab stall—this is a princely hamburger, the kind you would expect from a gourmet burger emporium. (In actuality, this particular burger has been prepared right here in the kitchens of Linton Hall, the work of the resident five-star head chef.)

Tucking a napkin into the collar of her pyjama-shirt, Misaki takes up a silver knife and fork and cuts a neat slice from the burger.

She consumes her breakfast with satisfaction and grace combined, and doesn't miss a beat when the door bangs open and a second young Japanese girl barges into the room on large, heavy feet.

This is the previously advertised Ren. Ren Hoshino is Misaki's friend, her lover, her secretary, her sidekick, or perhaps all of these. Her exact position in Misaki's household and in Misaki's affections is undefined and a matter for speculation amongst the staff. Ren is ungainly while Misaki is graceful; Ren is excitable while Misaki is placid; Ren is plebeian while Misaki is patrician. Stocky, but not obese in build, Ren's has hair very long and very straight, adorned with a white band; her large eyes framed by thick-lensed glasses.

Ren's advent inspires contrasting reactions: Misaki looks delighted, while Harriet's lip curls with mute contempt.

'Hiya!' says Ren to Misaki, affecting to ignore the maid's disdainful looks.

'You look happy,' observes Misaki, speaking in Japanese. 'Did the game go well?'

'Oh yeah! It was Ritsuko. She's a super-cute girl and I like really gave it to her!'

(Ren is one of those girls who likes to play dating games and being the male protagonist.)

'I'm happy for you.'

Misaki dabs her face with the napkin, throws it onto the now empty plate. On cue, Harriet removes the breakfast tray.

'You can go now.'

'Very good, your ladyship.'

Harriet steers her trolley from the room, briefly glaring at Ren as she passes her.

'She doesn't like me,' says Ren, when the doors have closed.

'She doesn't have to like you, she just has to obey you,' Misaki tells her. 'Does she do that?'

Ren shrugs. 'I guess so… But she always looks like she'd

rather not... Makes me feel guilty for telling her what to do...'

'Harriet is a domestic, Ren,' says Misaki. 'It's her job to do what she's told. If you think she's being insubordinate, slap her back into line.'

Ren looks at the pile carpet. 'I'm not real good at that...'

A sigh. 'Then *I'll* have a word with her.'

'Yeah, but that might make things worse...'

Another sigh. 'I wish you hadn't given up on that online assertiveness course...'

'It was boring.'

'Putting that aside,' proceeds Misaki. 'Any news today?'

'Oh yeah!' Ren produces a tablet, apparently from thin air, starts scrolling down the screen. 'The big news is there was a rape in town last night!'

Misaki looks unimpressed. 'There are always rapes. Is there anything special about this one?'

'Sure!' Dancing lights of joy illuminate Ren's triple-thinned lenses. 'It was a schoolgirl rape!'

Still unimpressed. 'That would be more your area of interest than mine, Ren.'

'Okay,' agrees Ren. 'But there's even more to it than that! It's a locked room mystery!'

'Now that is interesting,' concurs Misaki, sparks of interest glinting in her tapered eyes. 'Give me the details.'

'Sure. Girl's name is Vanessa Young, age fourteen, goes to North Linton High. She was attacked in her own bedroom, at around 01:00 this morning. And here's the thing: there's no sign of forced entry. Into the *house* I mean!' She releases a prurient chuckle. 'Forced entry! That's good! Didn't see that one coming!' Another explosion of mirth. 'Coming!'

Misaki sighs. 'Could you control yourself and get on with the report, Ren-chan?'

Ren collects herself. 'Sure. Where was I...? Oh yeah. The house is a detached property. The alarm system hadn't been tripped, and there was no sign it had been overridden, either.

No doors or windows forced open. Like I said, real locked room mystery.'

'And who was in the house apart from the girl?'

'Just her folks.'

'Well that's it then. Daddy must have paid a nocturnal visit to his little girl.'

'Yeah, that's what the cops thought, too. But apparently Daddy was all riled up about being under suspicion and he even volunteered for a DNA test—insisted on it.'

'And...?'

'They gave him a DNA test.'

'And...?'

'He's clear. Daddy didn't do it.'

'Hm. Interesting,' muses Misaki. 'So someone managed to break in without tripping the alarm system or leaving any traces... There's nothing random about this. The victim here must have been specifically targeted. Any suspects?'

'Apparently the girl herself can't even think of one. She's a swat at school, doesn't hang out with guys or anything.'

'And do we have a description of the rapist?'

'Nah, not much of one. Cops didn't give out all the juicy details, but I'm figuring she must have been done from behind. Facedown, or something. All she can say is the guy was big and strong. A grown man, not a kid.'

'And this happened last night?'

'Yep.'

'And how is Vanessa today?'

'Shook up, I guess. Leastways, she's absent from school—Oh! That reminds me! She's in class 9-C!'

'Murray Leinster's homeroom class!' exclaims Misaki, sitting up. 'Are they friends at school?'

'Doesn't seem like it. Murray's only spoken to her a few times in his life. She's smarter than him academically, so they're in different classes for most subjects.'

'And what about Murray? What's in his report today?'

'Main news is he's got a new classmate. A transfer

student just arrived today. Name's Eve Chandler. Seems she just shipped in from some Northern prefecture.'

'They call them counties here.'

'Right. Northern county.'

'Anything else?'

'Yeah. Word is Murray's really smitten with the girl.'

Misaki's eyes widen. 'He's fallen in love with her?'

'Could be.'

'Then we need to find out more about this girl. Get Kondou to run a full background check.'

'Will do.'

'And what did Murray have for breakfast this morning?'

Ren consults her tablet. 'Erm... Cheerios!'

'Cheerios. That's three days running, isn't it?'

'Yep.'

'Hm...' Misaki ponders this useful piece of information. 'Anything else to report this afternoon?'

'Nope. That rape's the main buzz today.'

'Okay. I'm getting up now. We'll head into Linton at the usual time. Go'n see about that background check.'

'Sure thing.'

Exit Ren, noisily.

Chapter Three
One Angel: Fallen Already?

Lassiter serves as both 9-C's class comedian and alpha male. He has the height, build and looks of a male model, a ready wit and is a master of that inconsequential small talk that constitutes agreeable conversation. (Unlike those unfortunates who *think* they are great conversationalists, but who in fact do nothing but bombard their listeners with information.)

He is good at sports, although has no real interest in them, and to support his alpha male status, he can boast of as notches in his belt a good many of the girls in his year, not to mention a fair few from the years above him. Lassiter gets through a lot of girlfriends, not because he is prone to arguing and falling out with them, but usually because after he has 'dated' (i.e. 'had sex with') any one girl five or six times, he gets bored and wants to move on to the next one.

The elite group he presides over consists of just three of his classmates, two girls, one boy. It's lunchtime and the group occupy their usual spot in the school gardens. (Yes, we've gone back to lunchtime; I never said this was going to be a completely linear novel.) The gardens are fenced off and, apart from on strictly supervised occasions, are out-of-bounds to students, to prevent the flowers from being trampled and whole place being used, like the rest of the campus, as a litter bin. But Lassiter has somehow acquired a gate key and has made the gardens the exclusive rendezvous for his little coterie.

Their 'spot' in the garden is outside the greenhouse. Lassiter, Malcolm and Sasha stand smoking tobacco products while awaiting the arrival of Scarlette, who has gone on an errand.

Malcolm is Lassiter's male crony, his right-hand man. He is of that tall, loose-limbed build which gives the impression of him being physically awkward, but in fact he isn't. His deep voice and intellectual bearing make you think of pipe-smoking middle-aged men in tweeds. (The tweed suit may be yet to come, but as for the pipe, he has one clamped in his mouth even as we speak.)

Smoking a king-size menthol cigarette is Sasha Distel. Sasha is both the class beauty (democratically elected) of 9-C and also the class girl-with-glasses. Academic skill and immaculate blonde good looks combine themselves in Sasha.

Scarlette appears at a turn in the path ahead. An American import, Scarlette is also a good-looker, smaller and curvier than Sasha, hair dark and chin-length.

She turns to speak to someone as yet hidden from the others by intervening shrubbery.

'Come on, then,' she says. 'We're not gunna bite.'

Grinning at her friends she advances along the path. The rotund form of Pornboy appears, following hesitantly in her wake.

'Pornboy!' welcomes Lassiter. 'Glad you could join us! Just a quick word with you if I may? Won't keep you for long.'

Scarlette joins Sasha and Pornboy finds himself surrounded by four encouraging smiles. He stands awkwardly, fingering the strap of his school bag, feeling ill at ease, out of his element amongst these attractive, socially gifted, elite members of his class. His eyes are wide behind his glasses, his thick lips pursed.

'I can see you're wondering why I called you here,' proceeds Lassiter. 'You are, aren't you? You're wondering, yes?'

'Is it to do with computers?' asks Pornboy, hesitant.

Lassiter trades looks of admiration with his three friends. 'He's sharp, this one, isn't he? I knew this lad was sharp.' To Pornboy: 'You've got it one, my man. You have hit the nail right on the head. Yes, the reason I asked you here *is* to do with computers. You are sharp, Pornboy. That is one of the qualities I most admire about you.'

'You want me to show you how to do something?' ventures Pornboy.

'Not exactly that,' demurs Lassiter. 'It's more in the way of online research.'

'Research?'

'That's right. Research. I want you to do some digging around for me and then to report back to me with what you've got. And as a reward: well, you're gunna like this, my man. Sasha here has found some very hot new porn sites; really hardcore stuff, you know? And she can't wait to tell you about them. Isn't that right, Sasha?'

'That's right,' confirms Sasha. 'Really yummy stuff. None of that tame crap. I'll give you the web addresses.'

Pornboy looks at Sasha like he's never seen her before.

'I can see your surprise there,' chuckles Lassiter. 'Didn't know Sasha here shared your keen interest in that particular art-form, did you? Well, she does. She may not look like it, but Sasha's as into that hardcore stuff as you. She just laps it up! Don't you, Sasha?'

'Can't get enough of it,' affirms Sasha, tipping a wink at Pornboy. 'Every night, after I've done my homework, I'm in my room flicking my bean to some red-hot hardcore action.'

'But I thought your dad was a vicar...' hazards Pornboy.

'Well, yes he is,' says Sasha. 'But I always make sure he's not in the room when I'm wanking off to porn.'

'Sasha is a Conscientious Objector,' explains Lassiter. 'She Conscientiously Objects to all those silly, outdated Christian morals. So, obviously she has to keep that a secret from her dear old dad. We all keep things from our folks, don't we? I'm guessing your mum doesn't know about your interests either, eh?'

'No, she doesn't,' admits Pornboy. Turning back to Sasha: 'What are those web addresses?'

'Ah-ah! Hold your horses!' cautions Lassiter. 'He's eager, isn't he?' 'Champing at the bit,' concurs Malcolm.

Pornboy looks at Lassiter.

'The research,' Lassiter reminds him. 'I want you to do some research for me. *Then* you get your reward. Payment for services rendered.'

'Oh yeah,' says Pornboy. 'What is it, this research?'

'Well, this may seem a funny thing to ask, but it's our transfer student, Eve Chandler. I would very much like to have a bit more information about her.'

'Like what?'

Lassiter spreads his hands. 'Anything, really. Whatever you can find out.'

'She's from Rotherham,' says Pornboy.

'She is,' agrees Lassiter. 'She is from Rotherham. You make a very good point there, Pornboy. But you see, the thing is, Eve told us she was from Rotherham when she introduced herself to the class this morning; so that information, you see, that information is already what you would call public domain.'

'Public domain,' confirms Malcolm, between pipe-clenched teeth.

'So, you see, what I'm hoping to get from you, Pornboy, is information about Eve that is a bit more private.'

'Privileged information,' suggests Scarlette.

Lassiter pounces on this. 'Exactly! Privileged information. The kind of information that can only be dug up by a computer genius such as yourself.'

'You mean you want me to hack her computer files?' asks Pornboy. 'School records and stuff?'

'That's it exactly!' exclaims Lassiter. 'Once again you've gone and hit the nail right on the head. I knew you would understand. And who better to ask?'

'No,' says Pornboy.

'Sorry?'

'No,' repeats Pornboy. 'I'm not doing that. I could get into trouble.'

'Trouble? Don't be daft! This is a walk in the park to someone like you!'

'I'm not doing it,' insists Pornboy.

'But the porn sites Sasha has found for you!' protests Lassiter. 'You don't want to miss this stuff, I'm telling you!'

'Don't care,' doggedly. 'Still not doing it.'

Lassiter turns to Malcolm. 'I don't think I'm getting through to him. And here I thought we all were on the same wavelength. You've got the highest IQ here, Malcolm. Do you think you can make him understand?' Malcolm looks thoughtful.

'Yes,' he decides. 'Yes, I think I might be able to get through to him.'

Clamping his pipe in his mouth, Malcolm takes hold of Pornboy's right arm and twists it savagely behind his back.

Pornboy howls, sagging to his knees.

Lassiter hunkers down, looks into Pornboy's pain-racked purple face. 'I'll tell you how it is, Pornboy. I need to know everything you can find out about Eve Chandler. I want to know what she was like at her old school. Was she expelled? Or did she just leave cuz her family was moving? I want to know if she has a bad record. Was she doing drugs or turning tricks behind the bike-sheds? Was she a bully? Was she being bullied? Was the headmaster banging her? I want every bit of dirt you can find on that girl. You see? Simple as that. Now, all you have to do is say "yes" to my request, and Malcolm here won't make it so that you can't operate a keyboard for the next few months. So, what do you say, Pornboy? What do you say?'

'Yes...' squeaks Pornboy.

Lassiter frowns. 'I'm sorry? What was that? Didn't quite catch it.' 'Yes...!' gasps Pornboy.

Lassiter looks at Malcolm. 'He just said "yes" didn't he?'

'I believe he did,' confirms Malcolm.

'Well, in that case you can let go of him.'

Malcolm releases the armlock. Pornboy collapses to the gravel path.

'What?'

'Y-y-y-y-y-you!'

'Me?'

'Y-y-y-y-y-you're—'

'I'm?'

'Sm-sm-sm-sm-sm-sm-smoking!'

Such is the sight that greets Murray Leinster on passing through the school gates: Eve Chandler, leaning against a gatepost smoking a cigarette! The vision clashes violently with Murray's idealised image of his new love. To him, Eve Chandler is a model of perfection, and models of perfection should not be smokers.

Smoking is bad for you.

Murray lowers the arm he has rather impolitely been pointing at Eve. He looks around. Students are drifting out of the school grounds, the cyclists weaving around the pedestrians.

'Yeah? So what? You don't approve?' asks smiling Eve, blowing a cloud.

'No,' says Murray. 'And anyway, you shouldn't sm-smoke so near the school. A teacher might see you.'

'I know that,' answers Eve. 'But I was waiting for you, weren't I?'

'You were waiting for m-m-me?'

'Aye.'

Waiting for him! She was waiting for him!

So what if she smokes! decides Murray, suddenly reconciled. That just makes her more grown-up, doesn't it?

She was waiting for him!

'Are we going on an Adventure?'

'Nah. Not yet. I just wanted to walk home with you.'

'Okay...'

They set off, Eve walking on Murray's left, keeping close, giving him the full benefit of her secondary smoke.

He's walking home with a girl! He, Murray Leinster, is walking home with a girl!

They walk along in silence for a while. Murray looks at Eve, looks away, looks back again.

'You look like you wanna say something,' says perceptive Eve.

'Well... I...' hesitates Murray.

'Go on, spit it out!' encourages Eve. 'You can say what you like to me, y'know. I'm not gunna laugh at you or 'out.'

'Well, I was wondering...' says Murray.

'Yeah? What were you wondering?'

'I was w-wondering if we were...' still hesitating, 'if we were like...' he takes the plunge: '...going out...'

'Oh!' says Eve, understanding. 'You mean, are we an item? Are we girlfriend and boyfriend? Well, let me see... "Going out," "an item," they're just, like, names, aren't they? Official titles. Me, I don't go for official titles like that.'

Her words send Murray's hopes plunging like a doomed airliner. 'So, we're just... just friends, are we...?' he says.

'No, I'm not saying that, silly!' returns Eve brightly. ''Course we're more than just friends! But, like, saying we're dating, or we're an item: they're just labels. They're just so's the rest of the school knows what's what.' Transferring her cigarette to her left hand, Eve puts her arm round Murray's shoulders. 'See, here's your first lesson from me, Murray: Don't go through life worrying about how you look to other people, about what other people might be thinking about you. That ain't no way to live your life, that ain't.'

'But...'

'Look, you don't just want me for a trophy girlfriend, do you? I mean right, I know it must make you feel pretty good, this walking home with a smokin' hot babe like me, knowing that everyone can see you. But don't get too hung up on that. That's just appearances, that is. That's just superficial.' She leans in, breathing ashtray breath over Murray. 'And you're not superficial, are you, love?'

'I don't think so...' replies Murray, relishing the ashtray breath because it's hers.

'Right. So don't worry about if people think we're an item or not. People can see us together now; they'll see us together a lot. Well, they can work it out for themselves, right?'

'I guess...' says Murray. 'But then... I'm still not sure myself...'

Eve squeezes his shoulder. 'Okay! If you want it all cut and dried, then yep, we're an item. I'm you girlfriend, your squeeze, your woman. But, I'm not your ordinary, run-of-the-mill girlfriend, remember? Cuz I'm the girl who's just dropped out of the sky and I'm gunna take you out on

Adventures. Adventures! So there you go! That's a bit more exciting than just going to the pictures, in't it?'

They have turned into Meredith Way, a quiet street of small, detached bungalows. This is where Murray has lived for most of his life. He stops outside the bungalow which is his home.

'I live here,' he announces.

Eve surveys the premises. 'It's just you and your mam, in't it?' 'Yes,' says Murray. 'What about you? Have you got far to go?'

'To go where?'

'To where you live…'

'No, I should be home in about ten seconds.'

'Ten seconds?' Murray is confused.

Eve points to the bungalow across the road, the one with the estate agent's 'sold' sign planted conspicuously in the front garden.

Murray's eyes widen. Eve grins at his surprise. 'You're the people who just moved in over there?'

'Aye.'

His new girlfriend lives right across the road!

'So who do you live with?' he asks. 'Are your mum and dad still together?'

'Yeah, they are. Well, we'd both better show ourselves indoors, eh? But I'll see you soon.'

'How soon?'

Eve makes a show of looking thoughtful. 'Hmm…. How soon? Well, it could be anytime, couldn't it? Like I say, Adventures can come along at any time. Expect me when you see me!'

She winks at him and crosses the road.

It occurs to me that, thus far, I haven't really described any rooms that have featured in this chronicle. I don't think I said anything about the appearance of 9-C's classroom, or anything about Misaki Morishita's bedroom. Am I being negligent here? I think most of us know what a school classroom looks like and most of us can probably conjure up a mental image of a bedroom in an English stately home. But, even so...

I know there are authors who will describe in meticulous detail every character and every location in their opus, and they do this because they are determined to make the reader visualise every scene exactly as they themselves perceive it. Now this is not only a lost cause, but it goes a long way towards confirming the popular theory that all creative writers are psychopaths!

But on the other hand, if I don't include any descriptive detail at all, I might be open to accusations of being a lazy, half-hearted author. Right now, the room we are looking into is the front room of Murray Leinster's house. If I wanted to set myself up as a modern Balzac, I would at this point launch into a tedious and minute description of the room's fixtures and fittings; but even his best friends admit that Balzac had his faults as a writer, and his furniture catalogues were one of them.

As for the living room, I could mention that the room is airy, the walls are of a pastel shade, the furniture modern, nothing chintzy or antique-looking and that a large LED TV is the room's inevitable centrepiece... but it wouldn't be very exciting, would it? Rooms are like faces:
Only the interesting or unusual ones are worth describing.

Murray sits watching cartoons when his mum sashays into the room, dressed in lacy underwear and wafting expensive perfume. She drops elegantly onto the sofa beside her son, crossing her long legs.

'Mum!' Murray's tone is one of weary protest. 'I thought you were going to stop doing that!'

'Doing what, dear?' inquires Mum, her voice rich and caressing.

Mary Leinster's long, luxuriant hair is of the same fair shade as her son's; she also has the same blue eyes. She is much taller than her son, and a Freudian might observe that her body is built upon those same strong lines that Murray instantly admired in Eve Chandler's figure. (But I'm not a Freudian, so I'm not even going to go there.) All in all, Mary Leinster has the striking looks of a more mature fashion model.

'Walking around the house in your underwear!' replies Murray to his mother's innocent question. 'It's embarrassing!'

'You shouldn't be embarrassed, dear,' Mum tells him. 'What's come over you? I remember when you were little you didn't mind at all!'

'That's cuz when I was little, I used to think that all mums walked around the house looking like that! But now I know that they don't!'

'It doesn't matter what other mums do, Murray,' says Mum. 'Everyone's different. Anyway, I'm working tonight, and I don't want to get dressed until I've made your dinner, sweetie; I might get food down my clothes.'

'You could wear an apron over your clothes.'

'I can wear an apron over this.'

'That'll look silly!' declares Murray, clearly not up to speed with current fetishes.

'Look, stop worrying about appearances, silly,' says Mum. She folds an arm around her son's shoulders, leaning close. Murray breathes in the familiar scent of his mother's perfume; a comfortable, reassuring smell. 'Now, what do you want for dinner? How about pasta with your favourite sauce and parmesan cheese? Is that what my little man would like?'

'Yes, please,' says Murray, meekly.

Miss Leinster gives her son a noisy kiss on his peach-fuzz cheek and repairs to the kitchen.

So there you have it! A charming snapshot of daily life within the Leinster household!

Mrs Young quietly opens the bedroom door.

Vanessa is sleeping at last. The woman steps into the darkened room, crosses to the bed, looks down at her sleeping daughter. She studies the girl's face, dimly visible in the light intruding into the room from the landing. The features are relaxed, the breathing steady; Vanessa appears to be in a deep, untroubled sleep.

Today has been an ordeal for all of them; and now they have finally found haven at the house of Mrs Young's sister, Vanessa's aunt, here in a village adjacent to Linton. Vanessa and her mother will remain here tonight. Mr Young has remained in Linton. A rift has occurred. Mr Young had at first been a suspect in the assault upon his daughter, and Mrs Young herself had even cast looks of doubt upon him.

But what else could she have thought at the time? Vanessa was assaulted in her own bedroom. The police forensic team insisted there was no sign that any intruder had affected entry into the house. What else was she to think? It wasn't that she had always been suspicious of her husband's moral probity; their marriage was a comfortable one and she had never had cause to doubt him. But when the police had made it clear to her that there only appeared to be one suspect, she had suddenly looked at her husband with new eyes (as the saying goes); started thinking that perhaps the man she had been married to for fifteen years was a stranger after all.

Then had followed the indignation, the official caution, the DNA test, and finally her husband's exoneration. Mrs Young could almost have wished the test results had been otherwise; then at least her suspicions would have been justified, the mystery resolved; but now she has been left with this barrier between herself and her husband, and an impossible mystery surrounding the rape of her daughter.

The steady, uneventful course of this family's lives has now been violently interrupted, directed into this new and unknown channel.

Vanessa begins to grow restless in her sleep. Her body

begins to twitch, incoherent sounds pass her lips.

Mrs Young feels her bowels clench. Is she reliving the assault? Is her ordeal being played back to her in her dreams? Vanessa has been dull and apathetic all day; and Mrs Young just can't tell how traumatised she might be. Everyone reacts differently to these things.

The sleeping girl's motions become more violent; she is now writhing in her bed. Her voice becomes louder, the words discernible.

'Those eyes!' she cries out. 'Oh my God! I can't look away! Those eyes! Those eyes!' Those eyes.

Mrs Young will report these words. Words that echo a voice from across the solar system. A connection will be made, and alarm bells will start to ring.

Chapter Four
Mysterious Night Out

Murray is sitting at his bedroom desk, trying to concentrate on his homework, when Eve Chandler makes an unexpected entrance through the open window.

Attracted by the noise, Murray swings round in his chair. 'What are you—' he begins.

'Shhh!' hisses Eve, finger to lips.

'But you—'

'Keep your voice down!' urgently whispers Eve.

'Okay,' complies Murray in the same tone. 'But what are you doing?

Why did you climb in through the window? The front door—' 'Because it's time,' whispers Eve.

'Time for what?' whispers Murray.

'Time for your first Adventure!' whispers Eve.

'But it's getting late,' whispers Murray.

'So what?' whispers Eve. 'Adventures often happen at

night! Come on. Get your shoes on and we'll sneak out through the window.'

'Why do we need to sneak out through the window?' whispers Murray.

'So your mam doesn't know you've gone, of course!' whispers Eve.

'But my mum's not in,' whispers Murray.

'You what?' demands Eve, speaking normally.

'She's working tonight,' whispers Murray.

'Yeah, you can stop whispering,' says Eve.

'But it was you that said we had to whisper!' whispers Murray.

'Yeah, because I thought your mam was in the next room, you divot,' says Eve.

'No, she's gone to work,' reiterates Murray, speaking normally.

Eve sighs. 'You could have said so. Why did you think I was making us whisper like that?'

'I thought it was cuz it was a secret conversation we were having,' says Murray, contrite.

Another sigh. 'You daft sod. Well, never mind. Just get some shoes on and we'll be off then.'

'Off where?'

'Just into town.'

'Where in town?'

'Everywhere. A quick guided tour. Now stop asking questions and get your shoes on.'

Shod, Murray sets off with Eve Chandler.

Night has fallen, and Murray feels completely out of his element treading the lamp-lit streets of his home town. He hardly ever ventures out after dark. He has never had any reason to. Eve, on the other hand, walking by his side in jeans and hooded top, looks completely in her element. He can feel her easy confidence, it warms him like a comfort blanket. Murray feels like he could go anywhere with Eve Chandler by his side.

'So, where does your mam work?' asks Eve.
'At the science park,' answers Murray.
'Where at the science park?'
'Some research place.'
'Researching what?'
'Physics. Mum did physics at university.'
'Did she now? And she works nights?'
'Sometimes. Not always.'
'And why do they have to do nights at a physics lab?'
'Don't know. Experiments, or something.'
'You get on with your mam?'
'Yeah, but she can be a bit…'
'A bit what?'

'Nothing,' backtracks Murray, not wishing to go into his mum's more embarrassing character traits. 'We get on.'

'And what about your dad? Do you see him at all?'

'No. I've never seen him.'

Eve looks at him, surprised. 'You've never seen him? Were your folks never married?'

'No, they were married,' says Murray. 'But they split up when I was really little, so I don't remember my dad.'

'But why don't you see him at all?' persists Eve. 'Has he left the country or summat?'

'Don't know.'

'You don't know? Do you know if he's still alive?'

'I think he is. Mum would have mentioned it if he was dead.'

'So, you don't know anything about him? You must know what he looks like, at least. Your mam must have some pictures of him?' 'She's never shown me any,' says Murray.

'So, you don't know anythin' about him? And haven't you ever wondered? Wondered where your old man is and what he's up to?'

'Not really,' says Murray. 'It's just me and Mum. It's always been like that.'

'Okay then,' says Eve. 'I won't keep on at you about it.'

They emerge from the residential streets of North Linton and continue along one of the main thoroughfares to and from the town centre. The traffic is heavier here and they pass more pedestrians.

'So where are we going?' asks Murray. 'Is something happening somewhere?'

'Summat's always happening in a town like this at night,' answers Eve. 'You just have to know where to look for it.'

'But we're heading towards town centre,' protests Murray. 'There won't be anything happening there in the evening. All the shops will be closed.'

'Shops,' echoes Eve, tonally rolling her eyes. 'Just shows you don't get out much. Town Centre may about shops during the day, but lots of other stuff happens at night.'

'Like what? And anyway!' with the voice of someone belatedly remembering something. 'How can you know what goes on in Linton? You only just moved here this weekend!'

'Ah, well, I've got a bit of a confession to make about that,' says Eve, airily apologetic. 'It's true I only moved in over the road from you this weekend, but I've actually been in Linton a little bit longer than that.'

Murray is suspicious. 'How much longer?'

'About a week.'

'You came here a week ago?' says Murray. 'Where were you sleeping?'

'I had somewhere to crash,' says Eve, vaguely. 'A kind of hostel. Just for girls.'

'But why pretend?' persists Murray. 'Why did you have to pretend you only just got here?'

'Ah, well, I've got me reasons. But they're a bit secret,' replies Eve. 'I'm not just a schoolie, y'know! I do other things an' all.' 'What do you mean? Are you a spy?'

'Well yeah, you could say that I'm a spy,' confirms Eve. 'A kind of spy, at any rate. That's how I know about having Adventures. And that's why I'm here: to help you have some Adventures!'

Murray looks at Eve with renewed awe. A spy! A girl with a double life! And she has come here just for him! To be his Mysterious Girlfriend and take him on Adventures!

Eve catches his look, grins at him.

The door opens and Norma slips into her sister's bedroom.

Norma is a girl in her late teens. She has anxious, haunted eyes and moves with an alert wariness. By contrast, her sister Fiona looks completely placid and at ease with the world. Beneath silky bangs she displays the flawless, expressionless face of the prepubescent child she is. Both girls have the same honey blonde hair: Norma's chin-length and rather dishevelled, while Fiona's tresses descend to her waist like a silken waterfall.

Sitting on her bed, Fiona breaks off the conversation she has been holding with the large teddy bear seated beside her. She looks at her sister inquiringly.

'Oh, hello! Have you come for that talk you said you wanted to have with me?' she asks. Her tone is calm; she does not seem to register her sister's visible anxiety.

'Keep your voice down,' hisses Norma. 'And yes, this is it; but we're not just going to talk. I'm getting you out of here!'

Fiona looks mildly perplexed. 'What? You want me to go downstairs with you?'

'Not just downstairs!' urgently whispers Norma. 'I mean out of this house! Out of this prison we're in! We've got to get away!'

The dimple between the eyebrows deepens. 'What for, Norma dear? This is our family home. Why would you want to leave?'

Norma looks pityingly at her sister. 'Oh, you poor kid, Fee. You don't understand what they're doing to you, do you? How can you? You're too young. But listen, you have to realise... Your brother, your father, they're both monsters!'

Fiona giggles. 'Don't be silly! Daddy and big brother aren't monsters. They're just Daddy and big brother.'

'Not when they're doing what they do!'

'But they just do what daddies and big brothers always do!'

'They don't, Fee; they don't. Other fathers, other brothers, they don't do the things ours do. You think it's normal, but it's not. You just don't know any different. That's why I've got to get you out of here, Fee. I've got to get you safely away and then we can get help. We'll go to the police and they'll come and rescue mother.'

'Why does Mummy need rescuing?'

'She's locked in that room, Fee! Locked in there all day every day! Haven't you ever wondered why you haven't seen Mum for so long?'

'Because she's poorly, that's all.'

'That's just what they're saying! If she really is bedridden, they must be doing something to keep her poorly all the time. She might even be— we might even be too late right now!'

'Too late for what?'

'To save her!'

Fiona looks unconvinced. 'You really think we need to get out of this house and go to the police?'

'Yes!'

'Because Mummy's being kept locked in her room?'

'Yes!'

'And Daddy and big brother are doing bad things to you and to me although I'm too young and innocent to realise the things they do are bad?'

'Yes!'

'But even if all that's true, how do you plan to get out of the house? It won't be easy. You know how worried Daddy always is about robbers breaking in: that's why he has all those locks and bolts on the doors and why he's super-glued all the windows shut.'

'Fiona,' groans Norma. 'The doors are locked and bolted

and the windows are glued shut to keep us *in*, not to keep burglars *out*. Can't you see that?'

'Not really,' sighs Fiona, frankly confessing her fault. 'But just for now I'll believe you, shall I? But to return to my last question: How do you plan to get out of the house?'

'I've found a way,' announces Norma, grimly satisfied.

Little Fee's eyes open wide. 'You've found an escape route?'

'Yes,' confirms Norma. 'I've *made* one.'

'You've made an escape route?' still wide-eyed and impressed. 'Oh, tell me how you've done it! Tell me! Have you tunnelled under the floorboards?'

'Keep it down!' hisses Norma. 'No, I haven't made a tunnel; I've managed to get one of the windows open.'

'That's amazing, Norma!' enthuses Fiona. 'Which one is it? Which one?'

'It's my bedroom window,' is the reply. 'It took a long time to cut through all that glue. I couldn't make any noise, so I've had to work very slowly. My bedroom window was the only one I could work on for long enough without being caught.'

'Yes, I suppose it would have to be your bedroom window,' ruminates Fiona. 'What have you used to get the window open?'

'Just a table knife I managed to palm. I didn't dare take one of the sharp knives in case they noticed it was gone. That's another reason why it's taken me so long.'

'Yes, it must have been quite a job, working away with a blunt knife like that,' says Fiona, still in reflective tones. 'How long did it take?'

'A week.'

'Goodness!' exclaims Fiona. 'But, wait a minute! I've just thought of a problem! Your bedroom is upstairs like all the other bedrooms; how do you hope for us to escape out of an upstairs window? If we jump from that high up, we might hurt ourselves!'

'We won't have to jump,' says Norma. 'I've made a rope.'

'You've made a rope?' echoes Fiona. 'You *have* worked hard!'

'That's because I'm desperate, Fiona,' Norma tells her. 'Desperate for you and me and Mum. If I don't get out of here now, I'll...'

'How did you make the rope?'

'I just knotted some clothes and bed sheets together. I've already tied the rope to the leg of my bed. All we've got to do is open the window, throw the rope out, and we climb down it. Or I could tie the rope round your waist and lower you first, if climbing down is too scary for you.'

'No... No, I don't think it would be too scary for me,' decides Fiona.

'Come on, then!' urges Norma. 'Now's the time! We've got to get out of here while we can!'

She turns to the door.

'Wait a minute!' says Fiona.

Norma stops, looks round.

'You've worked really hard, Norma, and this is a very good plan, but you see you've made just one teensy-weensy mistake.'

Norma looks alarmed. 'Mistake? What mistake? Quickly!'

'Don't worry,' says Fiona. 'There's nothing to panic about because it's oh, *much* too late to correct this mistake. You see, your mistake is that you thought you could trust me.'

Norma stares at her sister. Fiona meets her gaze with a placid smile. A freezing sensation in the pit of Norma's stomach as her instincts— reprehensibly late—tell her that this is all too true, that her younger sister is not someone she can trust.

'Yes,' says Fiona. 'I can see the truth dawning on your stupid face. You should have escaped on your own while you had the chance.' She turns to address the built-in wardrobe behind her. 'You can come out now.'

The wardrobe responds by opening and disgorging our friend Lassiter of class 9-C, with a big grin ready for his elder sister.

'Surprise!' he says.

Norma looks totally crushed.

Little Fee crosses the room to the door. 'Daddy!' she calls out across the landing. 'You can come and get her now!'

Tears stream down Norma's face.

'Please...' she sobs. 'For Christ's sake, please... just let me go...'

'No can do, sis,' responds Lassiter, shaking his head. 'We're big on family values in this domicile. If you upped sticks and left that would destroy our perfect family unit, wouldn't it? Where would the Lassiter family be without its ever-practical eldest sister?'

'For God's sake, please...' moans Norma. 'I won't go to the police... I won't tell anyone... I promise... Just let me...'

The Lassiter patriarch appears in the doorway. He looks rather like a middle-aged version of his son, except for some extra pounds and his hair being dark (the children's flaxen hair presumably having come from the mother's side of the gene-pool.)

'Has that daughter of mine been misbehaving again?' he inquires, speaking in the manly tones and smiling the engaging smile that have secured him many a role on stage and screen. The name of Frank Lassiter is known chiefly for his appearance in the cult film *Shadbolt & I* (his one starring role), the royalties from which serve to keep the household pot boiling.

'Just a bit,' answers the son of the house. 'She's only forced open the window in her bedroom, made herself a rope and was planning to make an escape.'

Mr Lassiter looks at his daughter reproachfully. 'Escape? Anyone would you think were a prisoner! This is your family home, Norma, not the state penitentiary!'

A sullen resignation has settled over Norma's features. 'No, this isn't a prison,' she says, 'because even convicted criminals still have some of their human rights. This place is Auschwitz.'

'Dear, dear me,' sighs Mr Lassiter. 'We have to be so dramatic, don't we? "Human rights" indeed.'

And he drives his fist into his daughter's stomach.

Norma jackknifes, gasping in agony. Her sister claps her hands and giggles.

'Serves you right,' says her brother.

'Now, now; don't be too hard on her,' adjures Mr Lassiter. 'She only needs a lesson to remind her of her place in this family unit. And you know, I think I will see to that at once. No time like the present, is there?'

And grabbing her by the hair, he drags the screaming girl from the room.

'And make sure to give her a lesson she won't forget,' advises Fiona.

The screams diminish across the landing, before being sealed behind the paternal bedroom door.

Little Fee throws herself at her brother, hugging his waist.

'Oh, big brother,' she coos. 'She said all those nasty things about you. It was hard for me not to start hurting her, it really was! But I knew you were here, and I knew you wanted me to keep pretending, right till the very end.'

'And you did a lovely job,' Lassiter tells her, stroking her silken hair. 'Lovely.'

'And am I going to get a reward from my dearest brother?' asks Fee.

'Of course you are, my little angel,' says Lassiter.

'And when will that be?' asks Fee.

'Why, right now, of course...' says Lassiter.

Chapter Five
A Walk in the Park

'What about the countryside? Do you ever get out into the countryside?' 'No,' says Murray firmly. 'I don't like the countryside.'

And then the man appears. A thin-faced, lank-haired man with sharp features. His clothes are very 1970s: polo-neck jumper, wide-lapelled brown leather jacket, flared jeans. Their paths cross just as they are under one of the park's streetlamps. Murray happens to glance at the man. The man happens to glance at Murray. The man's eyes widen with... what is it? Surprise? Recognition? Alarm?

Murray's heart somersaults. It's like he has received a sudden major shock, only he doesn't know the cause. The man is a stranger to him, but yet...

And then the man has walked past. The spell is broken. The moment becomes a memory, leaving behind it a strange feeling of unease, of something elusive, out of reach... Eve is by his side.

'What was all that about?' she asks. 'You know that feller?'

'No,' answers Murray. 'I mean... I don't think so...'

'Well, it sure looked like he knew you,' avers Eve. 'Moment he saw you he looked like he'd seen a ghost or summat.'

'I dunno...' says Murray, still confused. 'I know I haven't seen him before, but...'

'Friend of your mam's, maybe?' suggests Eve. 'Y'know, someone you've only seen like once or twice.'

'Can't be that,' says Murray. 'Mum doesn't know any men.'

'Your mam doesn't know any men?' echoes Eve, incredulous. '"Course she does! What about boyfriends? She must have had a boyfriend now and then.'

'No, she hasn't!' hotly, from Murray. 'Only girls have boyfriends. Mums don't have them.'

'They do if they've split-up with their husbands, like your mam has,' insists Eve.

'They don't!' equally insistent.

'It is allowed, y'know,' says Eve, smiling. 'So, your mam never has fellers round the house?'

'No!'

'Okay. Guess she's too taken up with you, eh?'

They walk on across the park. Crossing Fairview Park is a shortcut into town.

''Ello,' says Eve. 'Two people necking on that bench up ahead. Right under a streetlight, an' all. Must want the whole world to see.'

'You hear people talking about this park at school,' says Murray. 'I think a lot of them must come here for kissing.'

'You really don't get out much, do you?' sighs Eve. 'Kids like us come here for a lot more than just snogging, love. Boozin'. Drugs. Making out in the bushes. These parks are made for us kids.'

They are drawing closer to the lovers on the bench. Murray looks at them, arms entwined, faces pressed together, kissing hungrily...

And then he realises something— 'They're both girls!'

'Oh, yeah!' says Eve. 'It's Rose and Jenny. I should have guessed it were them.'

Rose and Jenny are two girls from Murray's year at school, although not in class 9-C.

'Hey up, you two!' Eve greets them as they reach the bench.

The girls disengage, greeting Eve with smiles of recognition.

'Hello there,' says Rose. Rose Gardener is short-haired like Eve, but more compact in build. She's a saucy minx, a caustic comedienne with a razor wit feared even by the teachers.

Rose turns an inquiring face to Murray. 'Who's this, then? Don't know you, good sir. You do look a bit like this boy at school, but you can't be him cuz he's one of those stay-at-home types.' 'Not tonight he's not,' says Eve.

'You've managed to extract him from his house, then,' observes Jenny. An academic prodigy, Jenny Jones, blonde-bobbed and bespectacled, is known at school as "Kettle-head" on account of her ample expanse of burnished forehead.

'You managed to sneak him out past his mum?' asks Rose.

'Didn't have to in the end; she was out,' says Eve. 'Y'know we could see you two necking a mile off. You're right under the spotlight. You playing to an audience tonight?'

Jenny snorts. 'Matter of fact, we were,' she says. 'An ironic performance. Look over there.'

The 'over there' indicated is further along the path. The next bench along is on the other side of the path, and although not directly under a lamp, two seated figures are dimly visible.

'Anyone we know?' asks Eve.

'Can't you guess?' replies Rose. 'It's our old pal the Wheezer, of course!'

'Oh aye. I should've guessed. And who's that with him?'

'Stavro.'

'Oh, that sourpuss.'

'Who's this?' Murray, completely at sea, asks Eve. 'And you're talking like you've known these two longer than just today.'

'Sorry, love,' says Eve. 'Yeah, you're right, I met Rose and Jenny here before I started at school today. They're night-birds like me. As for those two,' she indicates the nearby figures with an inclination of her head, 'the Wheezer's this park's resident perv. Folks call him the Wheezer cuz of the way he laughs. You could be necking on a bench like these two, or making out in the bushes, an' then if you hear this wheezy dirty laugh you know you've got an audience. He's the fat one. The thin one is Stavro. He's this real misanthropic type.'

'Misan...?'

'Misanthropic. Means he doesn't like anyone. A real cynic.' 'Got any fags?' asks Rose, deftly changing the subject.

'Sure,' says Eve.

She produces cigarettes and lighter. Rose and Jenny take one each and the three girls are soon puffing away.

'What about Murray?' asks Rose.

'Murray doesn't smoke,' says Eve.

'You could start him off,' says Rose.

'I don't really want to get him smoking,' says Eve.

Rose turns to Murray. 'What do you say? You wanna try a ciggie?' 'Not really,' says Murray.

'Go on!' urges Rose. 'Be a man!'

'Don't make him!' remonstrates Eve.

'Just let him have a drag on yours,' suggests Jenny.

'Yeah, I suppose that won't hurt,' decides Eve. She holds out her cigarette. 'Wanna try?'

'O-okay,' says Murray.

So, Murray takes a pull and his inevitable fit of coughing provokes the inevitable outbreak of laughter from the girls.

Murray hands back the offensive weed.

'Not for you, eh?' says Eve.

Murray, mouth scrunched with distaste, shakes his head.

'So where are you off to with him?' asks Rose. 'Taking him to a pub?'

'Nah, not tonight,' replies Eve. 'We're just gunna have a look around town. Any'ow, I don't fancy drinkin' on a school night.'

'Yes,' agrees Jenny. 'Getting through the school day burdened with a hangover can be an ordeal.'

'Still, the teachers always manage it somehow!' says

Rose.

'We couldn't go to a pub!' protests Murray. 'We're too young!'

'Well, yeah we are, technically,' agrees Eve. 'But there's some pubs as aren't too strict about asking you for ID. You just have to know which ones to go to. But like I said, we won't be doin' that tonight.' 'I don't really want to drink,' says Murray, half-ashamed.

'Why not?' demands Rose. 'It's a rite of passage! Your first night getting hammered. And then your first trip to the hospital to get your stomach pumped. It's all part of the growing process!'

'I don't really like drunk people,' mumbles Murray.

'Yeah, but it's not so bad when you're one of them,' says Rose.

'You had some bad experience with drunk people?' inquires Eve. 'I wouldn't have thought so, seeing as you've never gone out at night before today.'

Murray looks uncomfortable.

'Yeah, but there's my mum,' he says. 'Sometimes she gets a bit drunk.'

The girls burst out laughing at this.

'Bit of a handful, is she?' grins Eve.

'What does she do?' Rose wants to know. 'Does she start stripping off and coming on to you?'

'Yeah, and then I have to drag her to bed,' says Murray. 'And she's heavy.'

More laughter.

Eve places a consoling hand on Murray's shoulder. 'Well, remember you've got me just over the road from you now. If you ever need to get away from your mam, my door's always open for you.'

'"Me legs are always open for yer!"' mimics Rose, in her best Sheffield dialect.

'Shurrup, you!' grins Eve.

'Well, he is your new boyfriend, isn't he?' Rose reminds

her.

'Yes, this is your first date,' says Jenny, scrutinising Eve's appearance. 'You haven't really dressed up for the occasion, have you? Just your usual jeans.'

'Nothin' wrong with jeans. Any'ow, I'm wearing me thong knickers!' Eve pats her buttocks in confirmation of this fact.

'You always wear thongs with jeans though, don't you?' counters Jenny.

'Well, yeah...' admits Eve.

Rose aims a dirty smile at Murray. 'Thong knickers! Major Wedgy! Right up between her cheeks. Fancy peeling them off and having a whiff of that delicious smell of female arse! Yummy-yummy!'

'*Female* arse?' echoes Jenny. 'Do our posteriors smell any different to those of the males?'

''Course they do,' answers Rose, with feminine pride. 'Ours smell much nicer.'

'Shall we be getting a shift on?' says Eve to Murray. 'We don't wanna be out too late on a school night.'

'We'll come with you,' says Jenny. 'Across the park, anyway.' 'Yeah, we ought to be getting home,' agrees Rose.

The two girls rise from the bench.

'Which way are we going?' asks Murray.

'This way, o' course,' replies Eve, pointing.

'But then w-we'd have to pass those two dodgy blokes,' says Murray.

'That doesn't matter!' Eve assures him. 'They just sad. Nothing to be scared of.'

They set off. As they near the next bench its two tenants become more visible. The first man is fat, with a bristly double-chin. This is the voyeuristic Wheezer. The grin he directs at the approaching youngsters is at once salacious and vacuous. His companion is taller, thinner, dark haired and bearded. His expression is sour. This is the misanthrope named Stavro. Both men look ragged and seedy.

'Get your money's worth, did you?' asks Rose brightly, as they pass the two men, unhurriedly but without stopping.

Wheezing laughter from the fat man.

Stavro neither laughs nor smiles. He says: 'If you don't want an audience, then don't bloody do it in public, you little tarts.'

'Fuck you, granddad,' replies Rose, grinning as she gives him the finger.

Murray Leinster!

It was him, wasn't it? It must have been! He was older, he was taller; well, he would be, wouldn't he? But he still looked the same. The same as back then...

Carson is a small-time crook; the pettiest of petty crooks. The simple truth is he is one of those shiftless people who lack motivation; he can no more persevere with any criminal enterprise than he can with more legitimate work. As a result, he is always in and out of employment and in and out of trouble.

Having left Fairview Park, he makes his way into the labyrinthine residential area that exists on its borders, street after street of semidetached monotony.

Reaching a particular house, one of more than a few in this neighbourhood whose overgrown front garden is used by its own residents for the disposal of unwanted furniture and appliances, Carson advances up the path, knocks on the paint-peeling front door and then without further ceremony, walks in.

The living room is in-keeping with the exterior of the house in terms of spruceness. A man with unkempt light brown hair whose thickness emphasises its recession from the forehead, slouches on a settee watching an LCD TV. The modernity of the television contrasts with the mish-mash of decades-old furniture. The air is heavy with dust and the odours of beer and tobacco. The man on the sofa looks to be in his late twenties, the same age as Carson, and like him also has a long face, albeit with features soft and lumpy while Carson's are thin and sharp.

This man, the owner of the house, is named Drubble.

'Alright,' he greets Carson. He makes no comment on the latter's uninvited entrance; clearly this is customary.

'Alright,' returns Carson. He drops into an armchair.

'Help yourself to a beer,' invites Drubble, indicating the three unopened cans on the cluttered coffee table.

Carson takes a can, pulls the tab, swigs.

'Anything happening tonight?' asks Drubble.

'Nah,' replies Carson. 'Nothing that I've been told about.'

'Think something might be going down what you *haven't* been told about?'

'Probably. There's always *something* going down.'

'Maybe we should split with Piggy,' suggests Drubble. 'Y'know, go our own way.'

'You don't just "split" with Piggy,' Carson tells him. 'Not if you wanna stay healthy. Still, there's nothin' to stop us pulling something on our own account…'

Drubble perks up at this. 'That's great then cuz I've got this idea—'

'Well, you know what you can do with your fucking ideas,' cuts in Carson. He regards his friend sourly. 'I know all about your "ideas", don't I? That last one of yours ended with us nearly gettin' collared.' Drubble. 'Wasn't—'

'And don't say it wasn't your fault!' snaps Carson. 'Not your fault. Who else's fuckin' fault was it?'

'Yeah, but—'

'Look, just keep your ideas to yourself,' Carson tells him. 'Leave the thinkin' to them who's got more than a half a fuckin' brain.'

'Alright,' capitulates Drubble.

He takes a cigarette from a packet on the table, offers one to Carson.

'What about that Jap bird?' inquires Drubble. 'Heard

anything from her?'

'Nope.'

The 'Jap bird' in question is none other than our mansion-dwelling friend Misaki Morishita! Her formidable intelligence-gathering network extends itself even to embrace such worthies as Carson and Drubble.

The sound of floorboards above and then a pair of legs balanced on stiletto heels appear, descending the open staircase at the far end of the room. A mini-skirt and a striped, long-sleeved top follow, and then a peroxide-blonde head completes the picture.

'Alright, Liz?' greets Carson.

'Alright,' is the lackadaisical reply.

Liz is Drubble's kid sister. She had been ejected from the family domicile as soon as she'd failed her GCSEs, and Drubble had taken her in. Now eighteen, Liz is an attractive girl, but her glow of youth has made way for a hollow-eyed, faded look.

She crosses the room, picks up the cigarette box from the table, takes one, lights in, and then absently stuffs the packet into her shoulder bag.

'Off for another night on the tiles?' smiles the indulgent big brother.

'That's right,' answers Liz, carelessly.

'She's a real party animal, isn't she?' chuckles Drubble to Carson. 'Always out painting the town red. Never home to the small hours, she isn't.'

'Yeah, it's like she does it for a living,' says Carson dryly.

'You two clowns planning a heist or something?' asks Liz, nervously sucking on the cigarette.

'Nah, not tonight,' answers Drubble.

'Work's slow at the moment,' explains Carson.

'Oh,' says Liz. 'Well, I'm off out then.' 'Have a good time,' says Drubble.

'Take care of yourself,' says Carson.

'Yeah. Ta.'

The front door closes behind Liz.

'Don't you ever worry about Liz going out every night like that?' demands Carson.

An unconcerned shrug. 'Gotta enjoy yourself while you're young.'

Carson shakes his head sadly. He still finds it hard to believe how blind Drubble is to that which is going on right under his nose. The simple truth of the matter is that Liz is a smackhead prostitute. Carson knows that Liz is a smackhead prostitute. Friends and cronies know that Liz is a smackhead prostitute. The neighbours know that Liz is a smackhead prostitute. The local stray cat population knows that Liz is a smackhead prostitute. It is only Drubble himself, Drubble the doting brother, is blissfully unaware of the fact.

Carson doesn't know whether to laugh or cry. Either way, he has never had the heart to enlighten his friend.

Drubble absently stretches an arm out to the coffee table. 'Here, where have my fags gone?'

What'll happen to Murray when he gets laid by Eve? wonders Rose. Would he still be the same shy, stuttering boy? Or would he walk into school the next morning suddenly all confidence and charisma, acting more like Lassiter, Year Nine's alpha male?

Rose and Jenny had parted from Eve and Murray just outside the park, the latter turning towards the town centre, while she and Jenny headed homewards. Rose has said goodbye to Jenny at the end of the street in which she lives, and now wends her solitary way towards her own family home.

As for Eve, reflects Rose, it'll be no change for her; she's obviously already handed in her V-card. Eve has never said anything to Rose about having been with boys, but Rose knows she must have had her ticket punched more than once: with girls their age, you can always spot the ones who have gone all the way with boys: they have this kind of 'knowing' look about them.

It is a source of annoyance to Rose that by 'official' standards, she's still classed by society as being a virgin. Even after all those afternoon bedroom sessions with Jenny... Apparently you can have whatever you like shoved up your fanny, but if it hasn't got a man attached to it, then you're still a virgin!

It's like the way there's no age of consent for lesbians: It's like they think lesbian sex isn't worth making any rules about!

Fine, then. If the laws of the land say she's a virgin, then a virgin she will be. She has Jenny; she doesn't want or need to be penetrated by any man; the only thing she needs between her legs is sweet Jenny's face. She sings to herself:

*'Wanna hold her, wanna hold her tight,
Get teenage dykes right through the night...'*

It's just a phase, Rose's mum keeps telling her. Lots of girls your age play around with each other. Sooner or later you'll still end up wanting a boyfriend.

Hmph. People don't say that about teenage boys when they come out, do they? protested Rose to her mother. No one says it's just a phase when boys start buggering each other.

Don't they? Mum had snorted. Just go and find any married man who went to a boys' boarding school and ask him about what he and his mates used to get up to in the dorms at night.

These arguments aside, Rose has had no trouble with her mum about her going out with Jenny. Her mum makes a show of being cynical, but she's basically unprejudiced.

Not so easy for poor Jenny, though. Her mum and dad are really old-fashioned. Even though Jenny hasn't confessed anything, her parents have already become suspicious that something 'inappropriate' might be going on between her and Rose. As a result, Rose has been barred from the Jones family domicile. Mr and Mrs Jones do not want their Straight-A daughter going down a crooked path. This is why Rose and Jenny had parted company at the end of the street rather than in front of Jenny's house and in full view of twitching curtains.

Rose knows it's not just a phase, her and Jenny. She'll prove her mum's cynical predictions wrong! Unavoidably, this process is going to have to take several years, but she will persevere!

Turning into Church Lane, Rose repeats her paraphrase of the old punk classic:

'Wanna hold her, wanna hold her tight,
Get teenage dykes right through the night...'

She doesn't hear anything. No sound alerts her. But somehow Rose suddenly knows she is being followed. Some instinct warns her, sets alarm bells ringing in her head.

The song dies on her lips.

She stops. She looks back.

A dark figure, clearly male, is walking purposefully towards her.

Rose resists the impulse to run. There's nothing wrong; he's not out to get you; he's just walking in the same direction as you, is all. Just step back and let him pass. That's what you're supposed to do, isn't it?

The man continues to advance, still walking in that decided manner. As he draws nearer, Rose realises there's something odd about the man's clothing. What is that he's wearing? A uniform? Overalls?

And then she sees the man's face as it comes within the radius of a streetlight and she realises something is very wrong indeed.

She turns and runs.

She knows she's too late. She knows that her pursuer will break into a run as well and that he is going to be a faster runner than she is.

And he *is* running! She can hear him!

And then it happens, just as she comes to the churchyard. The fear that lurks in a corner of a girl's mind when she is walking alone at night: the fatal embrace. Powerful arms encircle Rose, drag her into the churchyard. She screams and swears, of course. She struggles. She struggles wildly until a fist smashes into her jaw, stunning her. Lights explode before her eyes; she is forced to the ground; she feels her jeans and underwear being roughly pulled down her legs.

And she now knows that, in spite of all those good resolutions, she is going to experience being penetrated by a man after all.

Chapter Six
Mysterious First Kiss

Wearing a thong! Just like Mum wears around the house sometimes!

Her choice of underwear makes Eve Chandler seem very mature to Murray. To him a thong is a very grown-up undergarment.

She is some kind of spy who has pretended she only arrived in Linton over the weekend, but she has actually been here for more than a week. She is wise beyond her years, talking more like a teacher than a student. She is the embodiment of energy and confidence. And she wears a thong.

And she is his, Murray Leinster's, Mysterious Girlfriend!

Murray already feels himself growing, although he's still nowhere near Eve Chandler's lofty stature. Here he is, out on an Adventure with her; out after dark and without his mum's knowledge or consent. He already feels the change; like he's leaving his old life, his old self behind and moving into some new and unknown realm, with his Mysterious Girlfriend by his side.

But there is a lot more to an Adventure than just being out and about after dark. Murray's night of adventure has hardly begun and it's not all going to be exactly to his liking.

Having parted company with Rose and Jenny, the two continue on their way towards the centre of town.

'So, you've already been hanging out with those two?' asks Murray. 'I mean Rose and Jenny.'

'Yep. We met at a gig,' replies Eve.

'A gig?'

'Yeah. At the Windmill. You know the place?'

'I've walked past it. It's a pub, isn't it?'

'Not just a pub. It's a live music venue. I wanted to check out the music scene around here, so I went there; and that's where I met Rose and Jenny.'

'The music scene? Have we got one here?'

'Of course you have, silly!'

'What sort of music?'

'Rock music.'

'Rock music?'

'Yeah. Electric guitars, like. You won't have heard them before if you only listen to the download charts.'

'Is it good, that kind of music?'

'Yeah. Well, I reckon it is, anyhow.'

'Is that where we're going now? The Windmill, I mean.'

'Nope. *That's* where we're going.'

Eve points. Murray looks. She appears to be indicating the skyline.

'Where's where we're going?' he asks.

She points again. '*There*. Can't you see it? It's big enough.'

'What's big enough?'

'That bloody building!'

'You mean the one that's taller than all the others?'

'Aye, the one that's taller than all the others. It's right smack in the centre of town. Haven't you even noticed it before?'

'I suppose I have,' says Murray. 'I'm not really sure...'

Eve sighs. 'No; I guess when you're in town, you never look any higher than the signs over the shop doors, do you? Linton's an old town, y'know? And the oldest buildings are there in the town centre. I know the shops all look dead new, but if you look up, you'll see that the buildings they're in are way older.'

Murray looks up at the tower, seeing it with new eyes. Yes, he guesses he must have seen that tower before, but he'd always sort of seen it without seeing it, as it were. It was always there, but he had never previously given it a second thought.

'You mean we're going right up to the top?' he asks.

'Yeah. There's like this observation platform on top. You get a smashing view. You can look out over the town in any direction.'

'And how do you get up there? Do we have to pay? Cuz I haven't got any—'

'We don't have to pay, silly!' cuts in Eve. 'Fact is, you're not really supposed to go up there at all. But there's a way up for people who're in the know.'

'We're not supposed to go up there?' Murray, alarmed. 'You mean we'll be trespassing? What if we get caught?'

Eve hooks an arm round Murray, pulls him close. 'Listen, you. You can't have an Adventure without taking a few risks. As for us getting caught, we'll just have to make sure we *don't* get caught, won't we? An' I happen to be an expert at not getting caught.' She gives him an extra squeeze of encouragement. 'Okay?' 'Okay,' agrees Murray readily.

Of course, it's okay. With Eve Chandler, he can go anywhere. Right up to the top of the world.

They come to the shopping district of Linton. Murray has

never been here before at night. He has never seen the shops as they are now, closed and shuttered under the artificial lights. Recalling Eve's words, Murray raises his eyes and yes, above the paving-stones of pedestrianisation and the corporate logos, the buildings do indeed look much older, displaying the fussy, ornate architecture of another time. And looming above all else, the tower, the tower that Murray has always seen but never seen, the tower they are going to ascend together.

An incongruous sight brings Murray's vision back down to street-level. They are crossing the paved central square of Linton Town Centre, the square with its benches and illuminated fountain; and right in the middle of the mosaic pavement stands a small tent, a circular, gaudily coloured canvas structure with a conical roof; a tent that would have looked more at home at the scene of a medieval festival.

The presence of this anachronism here in a modern shopping district is so out of place it inexplicably alarms Murray.

'W-w-what's that?' he stammers.

'Oh, that's just Madam Rulenska's tent,' is the unconcerned reply.

'Madam Rulenska...' repeats Murray. 'Should I know her?'

'Actually, I guess you wouldn't know her,' admits Eve. 'She's a gipsy fortune teller. She's famous around these parts, at least she is with people who actually get out a bit. She always pitches her tent here at nights, she does. Never in the same place twice. And the funny thing is no-one ever seems to see her setting-up or packing up. It's like her tent just appears. And like I said, in a different spot every night.'

'And she's like one of those people who predict the future for you?'

'Yep, that's what she does.'

'And do people actually go to her tent to have their fortunes told?'

Eve shrugs. 'I suppose they must do. If she didn't have customers, you'd have thought she would've moved on to some other town by now.'

They pass close to the tent. The entrance flaps face them, but nothing can be seen save a faint glow issuing from within. Murray wonders what this Madam Rulenska looks like… He has never seen a genuine gipsy fortune teller at any circus or carnival he has been to; he has only ever seen them on TV.

'Boy!' croaks a voice; the voice of an old woman.

Murray and Eve both stop in their tracks. Their heads turn to face the tent.

'Yes, you!' continues the voice. 'Cross the portal, enter my sanctum.

I have much to tell you, boy. There are many things you need to know.' Murray looks at Eve.

'Does she mean me?' he asks breathlessly.

'Of course I mean you!' snaps the voice from within the tent. 'Do you see any other boys around here? Enter, I say! There is much you need to know.'

'W-what shall we do?' asks Murray.

'Go in, I suppose,' answers Eve. 'If you wanna know what she's got to say, at any rate.'

Murray looks nervously towards the wedge of eerie light.

'Can you come in w-with me?' he asks Eve.

'Yes, the girl may accompany you if you wish it.'

They lift the flap of the tent and step inside. Everything is as it should be: a wizened old crone—hawkish forbidding features, bandanna knotted over grizzled locks, bangle earrings, jewelled fingers—sits at a small round table draped with a cloth, and on the table the source of the eerie light, a glowing crystal ball.

Her eyes are fixed on the newcomers.

'Step forward into the light,' she commands.

Murray and Eve step forward.

Rulenska's eyes pinion Murray.

'Yes...' says Madam Rulenska, her voice quiet now. 'Yes, boy... You are the one... The focal point of all things...My glass sees many things concerning you...'

Her glass? Has she got a magic mirror as well? Murray doesn't see one.

'Cross my palm with silver and I will tell you that which you need to know...'

'I haven't got any silver on me,' confesses Murray.

A shutter seems to drop down over Madam Rulenska's face. 'Then go forth. You must face your destiny blindfold!'

'Look, I'll pay for him,' interposes Eve, extracting a coin purse from her jeans pocket.

Rulenska extends a claw. Eve deposits a fifty pence coin. Rulenska looks as though something unpleasant has just landed on her open palm.

'Half price for kids?' suggests Eve, hopefully.

'This is a lot less than half price,' retorts Rulenska. She sighs. 'So be it. I am feeling generous tonight.' To Murray: 'Take one step closer, boy. Let yourself be bathed in the light from my crystal.'

Murray steps forward. He looks at the glowing sphere. He can see nothing; just a milky white light.

Madam Rulenska fixes her own gaze on the crystal ball, sweeping her hands over its surface as though coaxing it into life.

'Yes...' she says. 'A time of great confusion fast approaches... Yes... You are at the centre of things... There is a stranger, a stranger who will enter your life... The stranger will take you by the hand and lead you to new experiences... But you will face danger, also... There is great danger... Dark forces are gathering, cosmic forces, gathering over this town...'

'He's already met that stranger,' cuts in Eve. 'That'll be me. And yeah, I'll be showing him a thing or two. And as for all that stuff about danger and dark forces, that could mean anything.' She turns to Murray. 'Come on, love. We've had our money's worth.'

'Don't be so impatient, girl!' snaps Madam Rulenska. 'This future I foretell involves yourself as well. Wherever he goes you will be with him. You will face the same perils.'

'Then I'll be around to look after him, won't I?'

'You are conceited, girl. There's more to this than you think you know...'

'Well, tell us more about those cosmic forces that are gathering,' suggests Eve.

'I can't, girl! You're asking me to stare into the abyss! There are things that cannot be gazed upon for long, without bringing on death or insanity.'

'And all this has to do with Murray?'

'Yes. The boy will have his part to play... The images are fading. I can't see...' She glares at Eve as though this loss of reception is somehow her fault. 'I have nothing more to say. Leave me.'

'But—'

'Begone, I say!'

They exit the tent.

'I didn't understand most of that,' confesses Murray.

'Wasn't much to understand,' says Eve. 'But don't you worry. Even if what she says is true and things are gunna start happening, I'll be here to look out for you.'

'Okay.'

They move on and come to the building from which the tower rises. Murray now sees that the building itself, which houses Claverings, a multi-level department store, is not the base of the tower; rather the tower emerges from the roof of the building.

'I didn't realise the tower was right here,' he says. 'I've been in this shop loads of times.'

'This hasn't always been a Claverings store,' Eve tells him. 'It used to be the town cinema back in the day; but it closed down back in the 1980s.'

'Why did the cinema close down?'

'Ah, well y'see, going to the pictures started to go out of fashion for a while in the '80s. People weren't going to the pictures as much and cinemas all over the country started shutting down. Y'see, this was when what they call "home entertainment" first turned up. It was videotapes first, before they invented DVDs and blu-rays, and people reckoned that this "home entertainment" was gunna kill off the pictures for good an' all. But then in the '90s, going out to the pictures came back in, and cuz a lot of the old cinemas had already closed, that was why they started building these new multiplex cinemas, like the one we've got here on the outskirts of town.' She pats Murray on the back. 'Anyway, forget the history lesson: time we were moving. Onwards and upwards!'

'How do we get up? Do we have to get into the shop?'

'Not exactly,' says Eve. 'We have to go round the back. Come on!'

She leads Murray past the department store and to a narrow alley between the shop and its neighbour. The mouth of the alley is blocked with wheelie bins and piles of empty cardboard boxes. With Murray following, Eve worms her way past these obstructions, and they find themselves in a pitch-black alleyway.

'Keep right behind me,' says Eve. 'I'll lead the way.'

The paving beneath their feet is uneven, and the passage they thread twists and turns, narrow and inky black. They stop at a door, set back in the wall. Eve opens the door and they pass through, not into a building, but another passage, an offshoot of the main alleyway.

Through a second door and they emerge into a courtyard, a confined courtyard, but still open to the night sky. On three sides rise a crazy mass of pipes, gutters, projecting windows and projecting roofs. And there, above this backstage architecture, the tower points at the night sky.

'This is where we have to do a bit of climbing,' she announces.

Without a further word, she climbs onto a coal bunker positioned against the wall. She reaches one hand up to the thick projecting ledge of a small window, and, with the other hand round the bracket of a pipe fixed to the wall, she deftly climbs up onto the flat roof above the recessed window.

Crouched on the roof, Eve looks down at Murray. 'Now, it's your turn,' she tells him. 'Up you come!'

'But I can't do that!' protests Murray.

'Course you can!' Eve tells him. 'You just have to do exactly what I did. Come on! I'll tell you what you have to do. You can't go wrong!'

Murray is unconvinced. 'Isn't there an easier way up?'

'If there was, I wouldn't have just done all that climbing, would I?' says Eve. 'Now come on!'

'I don't think I can do it,' says Murray. He's not very good with heights and even worse when it comes to taking risks.

''Course you can do it!' Eve assures him. 'It's as easy as pie for kids like us! Come on, it's part of the Adventure, in't it?' 'Can't you help me up the wall?' asks Murray.

A sigh from the rooftops. 'You want me to get you in a fireman's lift and carry you up here? No can do, love. Like I said, I'll help you by telling you what to do. I know I said I'd look out for you, Murray, and I will, but I can't be holdin' your hand every single minute. You've got to do some things for yourself. Otherwise, we'll just have to pack up and go home. Now that's not what you want, is it?'

No, it isn't what Murray wants. He can't back out now. If he backs out, he knows he'll spend the rest of his life regretting it.

He climbs up onto the coal bunker.

'Right! First get hold of the window ledge with your left hand...'

And following Eve's instructions, Murray climbs up the wall. Eve takes his arm and helps him over the top and he is on the flat roof.

He's made it!

He smiles at Eve and she smiles back.

'Nice one!' she congratulates him. 'And that was the hardest part! The rest of the way up is dead easy!'

And easy it proves to be. Up one fire ladder, across another flat roof, an easy climb over a projecting roof and they are at the base of the tower, standing before a door.

'There's a camera!' squeaks Murray, spotting the device bracketed to the wall above the door.

'Don't worry! It's a dummy,' Eve assures him. 'So's that alarm box over the door. It's not wired to anything.'

'The door's not locked, then?'

'Ah! Well y'see, anyone who came up here and didn't know any better would think it was,' says Eve. 'See: I grab the handle, turn it, pull: door doesn't open. But there's a trick to it; you just have to know what it is.'

'A trick?'

'Yeah. What you have to do is twist the knob the wrong way like this. And you have to be pushing on the door while you're doin' it, like you're trying to open the door the wrong way. Then you turn the knob back the right way, still pushing and then you hear a click. There! And now you can pull open the door.'

And Eve does just this; the door opens to reveal a gloomy stairwell.

'How did you know how to do that?'

'Rose and Jenny showed me. I first come up here with them.'

'And where did they find out?'

'Dunno. You'll have to ask them.'

They walk inside, Eve closing the door behind them. Murray is surprised to find that where they stand is not the base of the tower, after all. They are on a switchback landing, with stairs both ascending and descending. Landing and stairs are both of rough concrete, guarded by rusty metal railings. The air is cold, musty and the lights fixed to the walls shed a dull, orange light.

'So the tower goes on down through the building, then?' says Murray.

'Yep.'

'Then a security guard from Claverings might come up here!'

'No chance of that,' replies Eve. 'Those stairs'll take you down about five floors, which must be to sub-basement level. But there're no doors. No doors on the landings and no door at the bottom, either. There's only the two doors into the tower: this one here and the one that'll let us out at the top. So you don't need to worry about security guards or 'out. Come on.'

They begin their ascent.

'But if no one from the shop can get in here, who's switched the lights on?' asks Murray.

'Good question, that,' says Eve. 'I reckon they must be on the same circuit as some other lights: Claverings' storerooms or summat. So it's like when they turn on their lights, they don't know it but they're turning on the lights in here an' all! And paying for them too! Funny that.'

'But then, that would mean this tower must belong to Claverings.'

'It probably does, technically. It's all part of the same building.'

'But then you'd have thought there would be a way for them to get in here from the rest of the building.'

'Well yeah, there probably were more doors here once upon a time. One on the ground floor, one right at the bottom of the stairs. They must have just been bricked off.'

'Why would someone do that?'

'Dunno. Maybe it was part of the refurbishment when this place first became a fleapit.'

Their footsteps echo as they climb the tower; diagonal ascent, right-angle turn, diagonal ascent... Not infrequently Murray sees graffiti on the walls, evidence of previous visitors. A procession of names, slogans, affirmations of love, phallic artwork... Testaments left behind by those who have found their way into this exclusive location.

'Like I said,' continues Eve. 'It's weird that this tower's even here. It'd make sense if it had a clock on it; but it doesn't and there's no sign that it ever did have one.'

At last they reach the top of the stairs. Here they are confronted with another drab, unassuming door. Apparently this door does not require any occult ritual in order to be enticed to open: Eve just turns the handle and pulls. The door obligingly opens.

Eve grins. 'Here we are: Top of the World!'

They step outside. The platform surrounds the stairwell housing on all sides, offering them an uninterrupted view from all points of the compass. Above the stairwell housing the metal spire, the pinnacle of the tower, lances into the starry firmament. The air is colder this high up, the sky more vast.

Murray and Eve cross to the edge of the platform, and, resting their forearms on the parapet, they feast their eyes on the view. The town stretches out below and before them; a vast landscape of light and shadow. The course of the roads marked by the headlights and taillights passing along them; tiny squares of lights, curtain-tinted; hundreds and hundreds of them, delineating homes and people and lives; streetlights picking out the dark shapes of trees, those structures of nature's landscape that we try to harmonise with the artificial landscapes with which we overwrite nature.

Murray stands spellbound. He has lived in this town all the fourteen years of his existence, yet he feels like he has never really seen the place until tonight. The town he has always known, or thought he knew, now presents a different aspect to him, a glorious spectacle only to be seen from this spot, its highest vantage-point, and only at this time of day, when the sun has dropped below the horizon and the town perforce provides its own illumination.

'Pretty amazing, eh?' comes Eve's voice.

Murray glances sideways at Eve's profile. 'Yeah,' he says. 'It is.' Her eyes meet his.

'So how do you feel? Right now; how do you feel?'

'I dunno, I...' Murray gropes for words. How does he feel? Something courses through him, energising him, invigorating him, promising endless possibilities. How can he describe it...?

'Can't find the words?' says Eve. 'How about alive? Is that how you feel: more alive?'

'Yes!' agrees Murray. 'That's it! More alive.'

'Yeah... That's how I feel, an' all. We all do. We're kids and it's night; kids always feel more alive at night. There's something about the night: it's our air, it's our freedom, the night is. I mean yeah, the night can be dangerous, and sometimes it can kill you; but you have to take that risk if you wanna get this buzz we're feeling now. Spend all your time shut up in your room, you'll never get to feel this, never feel properly alive. And then before you know it you've wasted your youth and you're a grown-up, and grown-ups, they lose what we've got; they just get scared of the night, and they stay indoors and close the curtains to keep it out.

'Just look at it. This is your town, Murray. Your town at night. It's different at night. The rules are different. The people *are* different. The day people are behind all those lighted windows you can see. They're watching the telly and stuff. A different crowd comes out at night. Mad people, bad people; all kinds of people. People who live in the gaps. And us young 'uns.'

Eve turns to face Murray. He looks at her beautiful face in the dim light. Eve Chandler. His Mysterious Girlfriend. This goddess of the night. He feels a renewed wave of admiration for her—admiration, and its more earthy cousin, physical attraction.

'You know so much...' he hesitates. 'It's like you know everything...'

'I don't know everything,' grins Eve. 'And knowledge

isn't everything, anyway. It's what you do with what you know; that's what counts.'

'What you do with what you know…?'

'Aye, application of knowledge,' says Eve. And then suddenly: 'Look, forget the fucking social philosophy. C'mere.'

She grabs Murray in a tight embrace, crushes her mouth against his.

His first kiss!

Murray's feelings spike; his heart races, his blood courses. Suddenly confident, he returns the embrace, returns the kiss.

His first kiss!

Eve's mouth tastes of cigarettes, but that's fine, cuz it's Eve's mouth, Eve's lips fixed to his lips, Eve's tongue curling around his tongue, Eve's spit merging with his spit. Here on this illicit rooftop, high above the town, an epiphany, a first kiss.

Speaking in tongues.

Finally, they surface for air.

'You snog good for a first-timer,' Eve tells him. 'And I can tell that you're pleased to see me.'

She rubs her crotch against his in emphasis of this last point.

Murray blushes in the darkness. 'Sorry about that…'

'Don't be sorry, you wally!' smiles Eve. 'I'd be pissed off if you didn't have a hard-on. Us lasses take that as an insult, we do.' 'Is it normal, then?' asks Murray.

''Course it is!' replies Eve, rubbing his nose with hers. 'Did you fall asleep in sex education class or summat?'

'No, I…'

'Look, you have wet dreams, don't you?'

'No! I've never wet my bed!'

'I don't mean bed-wetting, silly. I'm talking about when you wake up with a hard-on and a sticky mess in your pyjamas.'

'Sticky mess?'

'Aye. White and gooey.'

'No, that never happens…' says Murray, puzzled.

'It must do!' protests Eve. 'You know when you wake up hard like you are now…?'

'Yes, that happens sometimes…'

'And there's gooey stuff on your pyjamas…?'

'No. Nothing like that.'

'There must be! Or maybe it's on the bedclothes, on your duvet or whatever…'

'No. When I wake up like that, the duvet's always come off me…'

'Always? You sure?'

'Yes…'

Eve gives him a quizzical look. 'Let me get this straight: so when you wake up with a boner, the duvet's always been pulled back and there's not a drop of jism to be seen?'

'Ye-es,' says Murray, unsure of what 'jism' might be.

Eve runs a tongue across her teeth. 'O-kay… And when you wake up these times; do you ever hear a sound?'

'A sound?'

'Yeah, like the sound of your door closing…'

A dirty laugh issues from the darkness.

Eve and Murray spring round, alert. They are no longer alone.

Two figures emerge from the shadows around the stairwell door. 'Sound like someone getting a helping hand…'

Chapter Seven
Linton Rock

The newcomers are both Oriental girls, one with bobbed hair and calculating eyes, the other taller and bespectacled, a white band in her hair. They are both strangers to Eve and to Murray, but not to anyone who remembers the second chapter of this history. The girls are none other than Misaki Morishita, tenant of Linton House, and her loyal sidekick Ren Hoshino.

Both girls have smiles on their faces: Misaki's ironic, Ren's lascivious.

Eve's rapid threat-assessment of these newcomers judges them to be no immediate threat. She relaxes and becomes annoyed instead.

'And how long have you two been standing there?' she inquires.

'We came in during the kissing scene,' replies Misaki smoothly.

'Should have been fireworks,' chuckles Ren.

'Well, I guess you've got as much right to be up here as we have,' allows Eve. 'But you could've announced yourselves a bit sooner.'

'And interrupt Murray Leinster's first kiss?' says Misaki. 'We couldn't do that. In fact, we were honoured to be witnesses of such a momentous event.'

Eve, back on the alert: 'How do you know Murray?' To that worthy: 'They friends of yours?'

'No, I've never seen them before,' says Murray.

Murray's mood also has been deflated by this unwelcome intrusion. From the ecstasy of experiencing his first kiss with Eve (and a proper kiss with tongues!), the arrival of these newcomers just makes him feel like he has been caught doing something dirty. The precious moment has been irretrievably ruined.

'Please don't be alarmed by my knowledge,' says Misaki. 'I make it my business to know everyone in this town. I know who you are as well, Eve Chandler.'

'Well, I don't know you,' says Eve firmly. 'So how about some introductions?'

'Of course,' is the ready reply. 'My name is Misaki Morishita and this is my good friend Ren Hoshino. We both come from Tokyo, Japan.'

'Yeah, but you said you know everyone in Linton,' Eve reminds her. 'Does that mean you've moved to this country? Or are you exchange students or summat?'

'No, we are not emigrants,' says Misaki. 'And nor are we students. This is more of an extended vacation for us. We have been staying here precisely two months, two weeks and three days I believe.'

'And that's long enough for you to get to know everyone?' asks sceptical Eve.

'Knowing people doesn't always involve having to meet them socially,' Misaki tells her. 'For instance, I know of both of you, but I hadn't actually met either of you until this moment.'

'And so where do you get all this information about people? Have you got a team of spies or summat?'

'Yes, I have an information-gathering network,' is the ready response. Misaki crosses to the parapet, looks out over the town. 'An interesting town, don't you think? It's unique and yet it's the same as everywhere else. This is just as you will find wherever you go in this world: everywhere is different and everywhere is the same. Take our two countries for example, our two cultures. On the surface we could be described as very similar to one another in terms of our popular culture and entertainment forms; but these are just superficial trappings: underneath, we couldn't be more different. Our two country's respective histories, our national identities, our worldviews; these are entirely dissimilar.'

'Well yeah, people are different wherever you go,' says Eve. 'Even in just this country people are different. I mean I'm from the North and folk up there are different to the folk down here in the South. You doing some sort of social study?'

'Yes, you could call it that,' says Misaki. 'I'm just interested in people, and at the moment I'm interested in English people. Some of the things you do I really don't understand at all. Your outlook on life is very strange to me, also many of your customs. In England, you are known for your "stiff upper lip," for containing your feelings; but in Japan we seek to conceal our emotions even more than you English. We avoid argument and confrontation. We do not like to upset or anger anyone. We, and especially us females, are taught to smile at the world because it is considered impolite to appear downcast…'

She brightens. 'But then, we also believe that the tomb of the prophet Moses is located in Japan and that he travelled to our country on a flying saucer.'

'Now that one you just made up,' declares Eve.

'Not at all,' insists Misaki. 'I am perfectly serious. Am I not, Ren-chan?'

'Yes, is true,' confirms Ren.

'Ren-chan's English is not as good as mine,' says Misaki. 'Her habits are somewhat like yours, Murray Leinster. Ren also would spend all her time amusing herself within doors if I were not here to take her out into the world. This is your first night out, isn't it, Murray Leinster? How are you finding the experience?'

'You know a lot, don't you?' accuses Eve. 'Just how did you even know Murray was coming out tonight? I didn't even tell him myself until I turned up at his house a couple of hours ago.'

Misaki shrugs. 'I know because I see you both here.'

'And did you know we'd be up here right now?'

'This I did not. Ren-chan and I came up here on our own

account; meeting with you two has been a pleasant surprise. I often like to come up here to look down on this town at night. I see all those lighted windows and wonder about all the lives they conceal. Yes, there will be much that is mundane: the families gathered around the television set; but there will be other things besides…

'It's the dark side that fascinates me. To think that behind some of those innocent façades small acts of rebellion are being carried out: the girl who laughs as her boyfriend ejaculates over the infant she is babysitting; the father who conceals surveillance devices in the bedrooms of his daughters; the child, precocious in evil, who psychologically torments her parents…

'And then there are the people plotting evil, people who are driven to explore the darkest corners of their minds, those dark corners we all possess. Some of those people just plan; they fantasise about taking over the world, performing obscene acts of self-gratification, perpetrating motiveless atrocities. They live comfortably in a world of harmless fantasy… But then there are others who dare to go further, to bring their dark fantasies out into the real world. They take positive steps to raise themselves to the state of supremacy they yearn for, to satisfy the unnatural urges which torture them, to express their misanthropy in violent action…

'Those are the people I want to know about. I applaud the pro-active approach. I want to watch people as they trample over the rules and conventions of society.'

The urgent wailing of sirens pierces the air. Misaki points to several flashing blue lights moving at speed. 'The emergency services responding to an alert. I see several vehicles; one is a van, but I cannot tell whether a police van or ambulance. Someone out there has just taken a bold step, performed a small act of rebellion. Perhaps they have chopped a corpse into small pieces… Perhaps they have thrown a brick at a moving car…'

(In fact, the emergency services here are rushing to the

scene of the assault upon Rose Gardener.)

'So many people, so many possibilities...' purrs Misaki.

'Well, ta for giving us the benefit of your ...er, unique outlook on life,' says Eve; 'but you won't mind if we leave you to it? We've got things to do.' Eve folds an arm round Murray. 'Come on, love. Let's have us another look at things from street-level.'

'I hope we're not driving you away,' says Misaki.

'Actually you are, but don't worry about it,' Eve tells her.

Ren suddenly jumps in front of them as they make for the door, a galvanic, awkward movement. She grins toothily.

'You gunna fuck him?' she challenges.

'Excuse me?' from Eve.

'You want him to tear your clothes off and rape you,' declares Ren. 'You want him to fuck you up and down the street.'

'Do I, now?'

'Yeah, and you want him to pump you full of his love-custard. You want it all over you.'

She giggles gleefully.

'You know how big he is? How big Murray Leinster? I do! I know!' 'And how the hell do you know that?' demands Eve.

'Twenty-two centimetres.' The Japanese are always metric. 'Or is it—must check.'

Ren whips out her tablet, starts bringing up files. Eve takes advantage of this to guide Murray and herself past this prurient obstruction.

'I apologise for my friend,' says Misaki. 'Her mind is locked in a particular groove. She spends all her time playing dating sims. It has this effect on her.'

'What're dating sims?' asks Murray.

'They're these porny computer games from Japan,' supplies Eve.

'When it comes to sex, Ren-Chan prefers 2D to 3D,' proceeds Misaki. 'She has never known the real thing.

Although I'm sure she would enjoy watching you two perform.'

'Ta, but we won't be doing it in front of an audience,' demurs Eve. 'Nice to meet you and all that. See you around.'

Murray and Eve exit down the stairs.

A dingy office, curtained, lamp-lit.

The old man sits at a desk, scratching away with a quill. His limp, thin hair is white, as is his goatee beard. He wears pebble-lensed, wireframed spectacles. His black suit is rusty with age. Neatly arranged piles of paper surround him on the desk. The man appears to be working his way through these, copying data, calculating totals. He works diligently, but without enthusiasm.

Having finished working through one pile of receipts, he turns to the next, heaving a weary sigh.

'I 'eard that,' says a voice behind him.

The voice belongs to the Boy.

The old man turns round in his chair.

'I only sighed,' is his weary protest.

'I know you did,' says the Boy. 'And I don't like it.'

The Boy sits on a sofa at the back of the room, toying with a flick-knife. He is nine years of age, brittle and bristling in appearance. He wears a suit and tie that, on any other child of his age, would seem like fancy-dress or a visual gag, but with the Boy, the suit is worn in all solemnity, and no one would think of even smiling, let alone laughing.

The old man is known to his associates as the Accountant, while the Boy goes under the appellation of Piggy. Two theories exist as to how Piggy came by this name: One theory says that it is on account of Piggy's *retroussé* nose, which bears a passing resemblance to the snout of a pig; the other theory contends that the name derives from the fact that Piggy snorts like a pig when he laughs.

Now the undeniable fact is, the Boy, being completely bereft of anything remotely resembling a sense of humour, never laughs. Never.

So it must be the nose.

'Can you blame me?' asks the Accountant, still on the subject of that sigh. 'I've been wading through these accounts for hours. I'm always wading through accounts. As soon as I've cleared one pile, another lot get dumped on my desk. It's a never-ending cycle.'

'Well, that's your job, innit?' says the Boy. 'You're the Accountant. You do the bleedin' accounts.'

'Yes, but if we had a computer, these things could be calculated in seconds,' says the Accountant.

Now it's the Boy's turn to sigh. 'Not that one again. What 'ave I told yer?' he demands. 'Go on: What've I told yer?'

'You don't like trees,' tiredly.

'Tha's right. I don't like bleedin' trees. An' tha's why I like to see more of 'em being chopped down an' mashed up an' doin' somethin' useful.'

'The paperous office,' says the Accountant with a bleak smile.

'You what?'

'I said the paperous office. Instead of the paperless office.'

'That's right,' concurs the Boy. 'That's what I like to see: lots of paper. Big piles of it. Lets you know that your business is tickin' along nicely and that the money's rollin' in.'

'All right, but what about *this?*' The Accountant holds aloft his quill pen. 'Why do I have to write with *this* damned thing?' 'I don't like pigeons, either,' is the unanswerable reply.

Another sigh.

'Pack it in,' snaps the Boy. 'Remember where you'd be if it wasn't for me. Remember 'oo it was what got those charges against you dropped. You'd be in the clink, wouldn't yer? Stuck in one room all day long. 'Avin' to do borin' jobs...'

'I *am* stuck in one room all day long. I *am* forced to do

boring jobs!'

'Yeah, but you got yer liberty, ain't yer? You know that you can walk out of this 'ere room any time you want.'

'Except that *you* won't let me!'

'You can go out when the work's done.'

'But the work's *never* done! And I need breaks. I need fresh air. I would like to walk in the park, hear the singing of the birds and breathe the fragrance of the flowers...'

'Yeah, but you an' parks don't get along very well,' says the Boy. 'Parks 'as swings and roundabouts an' little kids playin' on 'em; and tha's what gives you bad ideas. Tha's what you nearly ended up in the jug for. So I'm akcherlly doin' you a favour, keepin' you out of them parks. You should be thankin' me. An' any'ow, 'oo needs parks? Parks is full of trees.'

'You're the one who has issues with trees; *I* do not.'

A derisive snort. 'Name one thing trees is good for, apart from bein' turned into wood an' paper?'

'They generate oxygen,' says the Accountant. 'We need oxygen to breathe.'

At this point a heavy knock on the door interrupts this interesting dialogue, and what the Boy's response might have been is unfortunately lost to history. Would he have disputed the trees' ability to produce oxygen? Dismissed it as an urban legend? Or would he instead have contested humanity's reputed need to inhale that particular gas compound? Sadly, we shall never know.

In response to the Boy's 'It's open!' the door, previously closed, does now open and in walk two thugs in black suits escorting between them a third individual covered in a hessian sack, secured with rope, leaving only the legs free for ambulation.

The Boy rises from his seat to greet these newcomers, and the sack-clad prisoner is thrown to the floor in front of him.

'You got one of 'em, then?' he observes with satisfaction. 'Nice one. Where'd you find 'er?'

'At the tower, Boss,' says the first thug, large and stupid-looking. 'We spotted 'em and we followed 'em to the tower, an' they went up to the top. So we jus' waited at the bottom of the stairs for 'em to come back down, an' then we grabbed one of them, jus' like you wanted.'

'Very sensible,' approves the Boy, his tone suggesting 'sensible' as not being something he normally associates with these two minions. 'What about the other one? Did she give you any trouble?'

'Nah,' replies the second goon, this one small and stupid-looking. 'Alf grabs the first one when she comes through the door and I slams the door "wham!" into the second girl when she tries to come out. Proberly knocked some of 'er goofy teeth in for 'er!'

Small and stupid chuckles at this prospect.

'Alright, get 'er out, then,' orders the Boy. 'So's we can 'ave us a nice cosy chat. Japanese birds.' He shakes his head. 'In London they got Albanians movin' in on their turf, and 'ere in Linton we've got the bloody Triads!'

'Yakuza,' corrects the Accountant.

'You what?'

'Yakuza. That's the name of the Japanese organised crime syndicate. The Triads are Chinese.'

'Yeah, thanks for that, Professor Know-it-all. All I know is we've got these Jap birds pokin' their yeller noses inter other people's business, and I don't like that. So now we're gunna find out what their bleedin' game is.'

The ropes untied; the supine prisoner is released from the hessian sack.

Everyone stares.

'What the bloody 'ell is this?' explodes the Boy. 'This ain't no fuckin' Japanese bird! She ain't Japanese, and she ain't even a bird!'

This is true; the revealed prisoner, looking suitably alarmed and bewildered, is none other than Murray Leinster.

''Oo are you?' roars the Boy, menacing him with his

flick-knife. 'M-M-Murray!' whimpers Murray.

'Murray 'oo?'

'M-Murray Leinster!'

'Never 'eard of yer.'

The Boy transfers his accusing expression to the two dumbstruck thugs.

'Is this some joke?' he demands, dangerous. 'Cuz I don't like jokes. I've never liked jokes and I ain't abaht to start likin 'em. I thought I'd made that clear to every bastard what works for me!'

'Honest, Boss,' says Alf. 'This ain't a joke, honest it ain't!'

'Then what the fuck is it?' is the reasonable rejoinder. 'Cuz this ain't the Jap bird I asked you to pick up for me, is it? This 'ere is some snotnosed, wet-be'ind-the-ears schoolboy! 'Ow could you mistake 'im for a bloody Jap girl?'

'Honest, Boss,' says Alf once again. 'We's as surprised as you! It 'appened just like we said. We saw the two Nips go up the tower, we waited for 'em to come down, an' we grabbed the first one what came out! I don't get 'ow this boy got there! Me an' Fred was stood outside the tower the 'ole time. No one else went up there after the Jap girls, I swear they didn't!'

'Then 'e went up there *before* the Jap girls, you stupid pricks! Ain't you got eyes?'

'But, Boss, it's dark up on that roof!' speaks up Fred. ''Ow was we ter know there was someone else up there?'

The Boy switches his gaze back to Murray. 'Yeah, what *were* you doin' up there? You don't look the type to be aht at night. You look like you ought ter be at 'ome tucked up in bed. You a friend of those Jap girls? Did ya arrange ter meet 'em up there or somethin'?'

'No, I d-don't know those girls at all,' says Murray, hoping this is the right answer. 'I'd n-never seen them b-before tonight.'

Apparently this is *not* the right answer, as Murray finds the point of the Boy's knife-blade under his chin.

'Never seen 'em before, eh?' says the boy. 'Just 'appened ter meet by accident in a place what most people don't even know 'ow ter get to.' Pause. 'But you came back down with 'em, didn't yer? Why would yer do that if you weren't chummy with 'em?'

'But, I didn't come down with them! I was—'

''E's lyin', Boss!' cuts in Fred. 'Them girls was right be'ind 'im! Like Fred said, he smashed the door right inter one of 'em!'

The interrogative knife returns to Murray's under-jaw. 'Now we know yer lyin', sunshine,' says the Boy. 'Them birds was with you!' 'No, it wasn't them!' insists Murray.

'Then 'oo the 'ell was it?'

'It was me, Piggy.'

Eve Chandler stands in the doorway, a bloody nose in support of her claim.

'You?' says the Boy. 'You mean you know this pipsqueak?' 'Yeah, he's my boyfriend,' says Eve.

The Boy looks as though he doesn't think much of Eve's taste in male companionship. He looks from Eve to Murray, back to Eve.

'Lemme get this straight: You an' lover-boy was already up on the tower when the two Jap birds showed up?'

'Correct.'

'An' you didn't arrange ter meet 'em there?'

'Nope. Never saw them before tonight. Murray and me were having a romantic moment—'

'What, you was shaggin' 'im?'

'No, just snogging. Then those two girls showed up, spoiled the mood and we left. End of story.'

Sighing, the Boy looks round for someone to blame, remembers his goons. 'You pair of tits. You shoulda made sure you 'ad the right person!' To Eve: 'Them girls still up there?'

Eve shrugs. 'As far as I know.'

To the goons: 'Well, don't jus' stand there: Go'n grab 'em! Like I said before: one of 'em or both of 'em, just bleedin' bring 'em 'ere!' Alf and Fred make noises of assent, move towards the door.

'Why are you so interested in those girls?' inquires Eve.

''Cuz they're bleedin'—' He turns to the Accountant. 'What was it?' 'Yakuza,' supplies the Accountant.

'Cuz they're bleedin' Yakuza,' says the Boy. 'And I wanna know what their racket is.'

'They haven't got a racket,' Eve tells him. 'We spoke to them for a bit. I'm pretty sure they're not gangsters; they're just nosy like me. Taking an interest in everything that goes on in Linton.'

'Izzat what they said?'

'Yes.'

'An' you believe 'em?'

'Yeah. Didn't have any reason not to.'

'Gorblimey!' groans the Boy. 'You'd think I was runnin' a bloody side-show 'ere! Why can't people mind their own bleedin' business? This ain't one o' them reality TV shows!'

'So, do we still go get those girls?' asks Fred.

'No!' snaps the Boy, exasperated. 'Yer know what? I've 'ad enough of this! So you two idiots can make yerselves scarce, and you, Eve Chandler, can take yer milksop boyfriend and do the same. I'm going ter bed!'

'And I shall depart as well?' asks the Accountant eagerly.

'No!' roars the Boy. 'You can finish those fuckin' accounts!'

The office proves to be above a nightclub.

Eve leads Murray along a corridor, down a narrow flight of stairs and along another corridor to a side entrance guarded by a bouncer who lets them out into the street.

'How was that for an Adventure?' says Eve. 'A bit more than I'd planned for you for tonight, I'll admit.'

Murray pouts. He doesn't see anything to be so pleased about.

Eve reads his look, interprets it. She lays a hand on Murray's shoulder. 'I get it,' she sighs. 'You're pissed off that I let you get grabbed like that. Well, I didn't do it on purpose, did I?'

'You said you'd always look out for me,' sulks Murray.

'I am lookin' out for you!' protests Eve. 'I just got you out of that mess, didn't I? And before you say I should've stopped you getting in that mess in the first place, remember that I got a door whacked in me face.' She indicates her bloodstained visage. 'I was stunned, y'know? Seeing stars. But as soon as I was on me feet again, I was on your trail. Finding you turned out to be easy, cuz those two idiots Alf and Fred marched you right through the town centre, and I met this feller I know who told me they were Piggy's men. Soon as I heard that I came straight here. So it wasn't so bad, was it?'

'I suppose not,' says Murray, unconvinced.

Eve sighs. 'Listen, Murray. You're mollycoddled; that's your problem. It's like you expect to be protected all the time. You expect it from your mam, and now you expect it from me. I told you all along that you can't have Adventures without danger. You need to learn to stand on your own two feet a bit more. I mean I can help you with that, but like I said before, I can't be holding your hand every minute of the day.' She pats Murray's semi-consoled back.

'Anyway, let's be getting home,' she says. 'I reckon we've had enough adventure for your first night out.' They set off through the streets.

'So who was that boy with the knife?' asks Murray.

'What, Piggy? He's the local crime boss. I thought you would have worked that out.'

'What do you mean, crime? Like the Mafia? There's nothing like that in Linton! There can't be!'

'Shows how much you know,' counters Eve. 'Any town

has its crime boss, and the boss around here is Piggy. All the rackets are run by his mob; everything from drugs to dog fights, brothels to bootleg booze.'

'But how can he be the boss?' protests Murray. 'He's only a little kid!'

Eve shrugs. 'Kids are always getting into crime young these days,' she says. 'You should watch the news more.'

'And how come you know him?' demands Murray. 'Do you work for him?'

''Course not, silly!' says Eve. 'I've just run into him once or twice since I've been here. That's how I know him.'

'You shouldn't be friends with someone like that,' remonstrates Murray. 'You should just call the police and have him arrested.'

Eve hugs Murray as they walk along. 'Bless your heart! Y'know, I almost don't like to shatter all these illusions of yours. Well, for starters, Piggy is not my friend; just an acquaintance. Right? And secondly, getting him arrested isn't as easy as just dialling 999. The cops around here know about Piggy and his gang, but they can't just arrest him. Criminal gangs carry a lot of clout.'

'Clout?'

'Yeah. They've got connections, influence. Y'know, you tonight reminds me of something: You ever seen *Blue Velvet*? No, I don't suppose you will have. Well, it's this old David Lynch film. It's set in this small American town where everything seems peaceful like. But the hero, this teenage lad, finds a severed ear when he's out for a walk.'

'An ear?'

'Aye, a human ear. Just lying in a field on the edge of town. So this lad, he decides to start playing detective, find out where the ear came from; an' this leads him into the criminal underworld and he finds out his hometown isn't all apple pies and picket fences. Bit like you tonight, in't it? Well, except that the lad in the film gets in a lot deeper than you did just now. You were just a case of mistaken identity.'

'This Piggy won't come after me again, will he?' wonders Murray.

''Course he won't,' Eve assures him, squeezing him again. 'He's most likely already forgotten you exist. If you're not a threat or someone he can squeeze money out of, he's not interested.'

By now they are leaving the town centre behind, nearing the park where they had met Rose and Jenny.

'So you've had your first official Adventure,' says Eve. 'Not a bad start, really. And tomorrow it's back to school, and we act like nothin's even happened.'

'Back to school...' echoes Murray. 'It's a different world from all this...'

Just one day has passed, and within that day Murray Leinster has met the girl of his dreams, that girl has become his Mysterious Girlfriend, and his Mysterious Girlfriend has taken him on a nocturnal adventure which has led to him seeing his native town from a different perspective, experiencing his first snog, being treated to twisted philosophy from a Japanese girl and has ended with a brief but terrifying interlude on the local crime lord's carpet.

He has a lot to process.

Let us return to Madam Rulenska, the fortune teller whose vague but portentous predictions hinted at events of a cosmic nature occurring here in Linton, events in which Murray will find himself deeply concerned.

We won't be seeing her again.

Even mysterious gipsy fortune tellers need sustenance, and Madam Rulenska has just returned from a trip to a nearby kebab stall to supply her bodily needs. (If I was a writer of what Aldous Huxley described as 'the whole truth', I could also mention that she stopped off along the way to satisfy another bodily need; although she has had to use a 'pay on the door' facility, as all the free to use ones get locked up at night!)

Madam Rulenska seats herself to consume her meal. Had any potential client walked in at this juncture, they would probably have felt disillusioned at the sight of those polystyrene fast-food containers sharing the table with the fortune teller's crystal ball, the odour of kebab meat doing battle with the ambient incense which normally pervades the air of the tent. In fact, these signs of the commonplace in the abode of an apparent mystic may have been so discouraging as to make this hypothetical client turn right about on his or her heel and exit the tent.

No such client does appear, however, and as Madam Rulenska's crystal ball, aside from its primary function of divining the future, seems also to perform the duties of a closed-circuit television system, perhaps no potential customer *could* have approached the tent without the prognosticator being alerted to the fact.

Whatever the case, Madam Rulenska rapidly devours her meal, seemingly unconcerned at the possibility of any interruption from without.

Interruption from within however, as events are about to demonstrate, seems to be one possibility even the fortune-teller cannot anticipate.

Repast consumed, Madam Rulenska returns the cartons to the plastic bag provided for their transport, and she drops the bag behind the chair out of sight of any forthcoming customers. She then produces a crystal bottle with a rubber bulb and renews the mystic incense in the air, eliminating the olfactory evidence of the takeaway meal.

She has just seated herself when her crystal ball, which until now has been emitting the gentle light indicative of a crystal ball on stand-by— starts to glow, and it starts to glow with *darkness*. This paradoxical phenomenon increases in intensity, until the sphere becomes a void of blackness.

Fear distorts the gipsy's wizened features. Her eyes are fixed on that black void. And within the crystal, within that dark light, a pair of eyes appear to look right back at her.

Yellow eyes, tapered, unspeakably malignant. The eyes begin to grow in size.

'You...' gasps the fortune teller. 'It was you... You're the...'

The crystal ball cracks open and the black haze, released into the air quickly fills the tent; and those eyes, those awful eyes, become huge, fixed on the helpless fortune teller.

'No...' she croaks. 'It's not possible... You can't—'

A seizure grips Madam Rulenska, freezing her face, her words and her heart.

Chapter Eight
Mostly About Rape

Opening Rose Gardener's bedroom door, Eve finds herself confronted by a wall of flowers.

'I'm here if you can find me,' comes Rose's voice.

Eve pushes her way through the floor-to-ceiling flora and emerges into a clearing around Rose's bed and on which the girl sits cross-legged. Beside her is a huge pile of cards, which Rose appears to be working her way through: opening, perfunctorily reading, tossing aside. A subdued Rose, with left cheek bruised and swollen, stitched lower lip.

'Condolence cards?' says Eve, after greetings have been exchanged.

'Yep,' confirms Rose. 'And the flowers to go with 'em. Take a pew.' Rose flings aside a pile of cards to make room for Eve on the bed.

The girls embrace.

Bouquets of flowers surround them, piled one on top of another. All the colours and varieties of nature represented, the cloying scent eased by the introduction of fresh air from an open window, out of view.

'This is a stupid amount of flowers,' says Eve.

'Tell me about it,' says Rose. 'You'd think I'd just won

an Oscar. And they're not just from Linton people, either. They've been sent from all over the bloody country. Just because they heard about me on the news...'

'It's cuz you're a schoolgirl,' says Eve. 'If you were ten years older you wouldn't have got so many flowers.'

'Yeah, but it's stupid,' declares Rose. 'I mean, all these people who don't even know me... For all they know I could be bullshitting about this and I wasn't raped at all. They don't fucking know, do they?'

Eve shrugs. 'People are quick to believe bad news,' she says. 'And the cards and flowers: that's just people wanting to show that they're with you on this.'

'Yeah, but some of the things they say...' Rose searches for a particular card. 'Listen to this: "My heart goes out to you. This horrific event will haunt you for the rest of your life. You will never get over this." Now is that supposed to make me feel better or worse?'

'Yeah, not really what they should be saying to you,' agrees Eve. She strokes Rose's face. 'How *do* you feel?'

'I'm okay. I'm strong!' Rose imitates a bicep-flexing pose, smiling through her injuries. 'This isn't gunna beat me!'

Eve returns her smile. 'Good for you, girl. Wanna talk about it? About what happened?'

'Sure,' says Rose. 'It's not much of a story: I was walking home; this guy grabbed me and dragged me into the churchyard; I tried to stop him but he was too strong and he raped me. When he'd shot his load he just got up and left. Didn't say a word. Not so much as a "thank you, ma'am".'

'What sort of feller was he?'

'Creepy. Fucking creepy. He was like a robot or something. He didn't speak. He didn't make any sounds at all. Not even a grunt while he was fucking me. And his face, it was like a concrete mask, y'know? No expression. All the time he was looking at me, but it was a kind of blank stare. He didn't look angry, he didn't look horny... Like I said, a robot.'

'I think men do go like that sometimes. Y'know, when they go into predator mode.'

'Yeah, but with this guy... I really felt like he wasn't even enjoying it. It was mechanical; like he was doing a job he had to do.'

'And what was he like? I mean, to look at?'

'He looked about thirty, I'd guess. Short dark hair. Strong, but strong like an athlete, not a body-builder. Weirdest thing about him was his clothes. It was some kind of jumpsuit, but it looked like it was military or something. I'm sure it had—what d'you call it?—insignia on it.'

'What kind of insignia?'

'That's what the fuzz keep asking me, but it was dark; I couldn't see any details.'

'D'you think the guy looked like he was military?'

'Yeah, I'd say he did.'

Eve ponders. 'So we've got a military guy who's targeting schoolgirls... At least, it was definitely the same cunt who raped Vanessa Young. Don't think they've said if Rachel Ryder—'

'That was him too,' affirms Rose. 'My mum got that straight from the fuzz. Rachel's description of her attacker is the same as mine. Vanessa; she never saw the guy's face; guess he did her from behind; but the DNA matches, so we know it's him.'

'So if Rachel is number three, then we've got a pattern here, haven't we? All girls from our school. And our year, an' all. The rapist is a stranger; none of you know the guy... You and Rachel were both jumped in the street after dark, but he actually broke into Vanessa's house to get at her; that means he can't be just an opportunist; he's choosing his targets.'

'Yeah, seems like it,' agrees Rose. 'I mean, he went out of his way to break into Vanessa's house, and the cops reckon he must have been following me for a while the night he got me. They reckon he waited till I was near the church cuz that was a good place for him to rape me without being seen by anyone.'

'Maybe he was already watching you when Murray and me met you in the park... But we didn't see anyone, did we? Just Stavro and the Wheezer...'

'Yeah, and it wasn't either of them,' says Rose. 'When I told the cops about those two, they were ready to drag them in on suspicion, but I kept telling them the guy didn't look anything like either of them; they finally got the message. They still pulled them both in for questioning, though; just to see if they saw the guy.'

'And they hadn't seen him?'

'Nope.'

'What about Jenny? Did she notice anything when you two were walking home together?'

'No, she didn't,' Rose smiles sadly. 'Poor Jenny. She's more cut up about this than I am, bless her!'

'She would be,' says Eve. 'I bet your mam is, too.'

'Jenny's been crying a lot, but Mum's just angry. She's all fired-up! Says she wants to find the guy and rip off his wedding tackle with her bare hands!'

'Yeah, that's what I'd like to do,' says Eve. 'If we just had some clue who he was... I mean how does he even know you girls...?' 'Fuck knows,' says Rose.

She absently picks up another condolence card, opens it.

'What the fuck?' she suddenly exclaims.

'What is it?' asks Eve.

'This is the weirdest one yet! Have a look.' Eve takes the card. The message reads:

Just pretend you were bitten by a dog and forget about it! Best wishes, Misaki and Ren.

Beneath this a cartoon drawing of a girl's smiling face and one raised hand displaying the peace sign.

Dodo Dupont!

The TV psychologist who also does porny modelling, right here at North Linton High School! And she's about to give some 'special class' here in 9-C!

She stands facing the class, leaning casually against the unoccupied teacher's desk. One leg crossed in front of the other, she verily oozes charisma and animal vitality. A six-foot amazon dressed in boots, cargo pants and t-shirt; all designer brands. Her short hair is black, her eyes grey. And with that wry smile tugging at the corners of her wide mouth, she has more the demeanour of a stand-up comedienne than a professor of psychology.

The students silently assess her, unspoken opinions invisibly crosshatching the air. She's hot! Look at that rack! Nice legs. Too mannish. Too tall. Fat arse. Make-up looks good. Expensive perfume.

As a popular psychologist, who combines her qualifications in psychology with an observational sociology and presents her particular worldview in the form of television documentaries and accessible books, Professor Dodo Dupont enjoys an equivocal reputation. On the one hand she has gained a loyal following who revere her as 'the voice of reason', applauding her humanity and objectivity, her obvious love of life; but she also has her detractors who throw her privileged background in her face, or who choose to interpret her objective stance as concealing a dubious morality. Some, jealous of her success, label her a media whore and accuse her of 'trivialising' the study of psychology.

It really hit the fan when Dodo posed naked for Japanese photographer Mayumi Takahashi. The publication of the first photobook (which has since been joined by another) ironically drew derision from both male chauvinists and the more tight-arsed end of the feminist spectrum. How were people supposed to take her seriously as an intellectual woman when she starts flaunting herself for the camera with no clothes on? (This in spite of the mitigating fact that she had defied convention by displaying an abundance of armpit hair.)

Dodo, who detests pointless verbal sparring, merely responds to these attacks with a dismissive shrug of the shoulders.

And now here she is: Dodo Dupont, the controversial celebrity, standing before class 9-C in the shit-hole that is North Linton High School!

'So,' she says brightly. 'How do you all feel about rape?'

A bland, hazy afternoon.

Carson, toolbox at his side, squats beside the motorbike standing on the driveway. This particular motorbike spends all its time either on the driveway or in the garage, or being guided between these two locations.

Because this motorbike doesn't bloody work.

It worked when Carson bought it, cash in hand, but then it stopped working, and it has been not working ever since, for over a year now. He can't get his money back. Bastard says Carson must have done something to the bike; says it was working fine when he sold it to Carson.

Yeah, but it didn't work for long, did it? Ever since then, for more than a year, Carson has—between fits of dejection—been tinkering with the engine in an effort to coax the machine back to life. He has loosened and tightened, he has scrubbed and oiled, he has taken apart and reassembled. All to no avail. In his efforts Carson is handicapped by one major obstacle: he knows nothing about motorcycles or internal combustion engines and has absolutely no idea what he is doing.

But Carson is possessed of this fixed idea that what has become faulty can be made to work again, and that if he tweaks and tinkers for long enough, sooner or later things must come right, and the engine will burst into throbbing life, allowing Carson to fulfil his dreams of freedom and take to the road. In this belief Carson shows himself less of the mechanic and more of the African witch-doctor, searching for that right propitious alignment of the bones and entrails.

Carson is engrossed in this never-ending task when he hears a car pull up. He looks. The word 'POLICE' looks back at him. Two officers step out of the squad car, adjusting peaked caps. Carson is unsurprised to see that one of the officers is a man of his acquaintance, one Sergeant Brent. The second officer remains by the car while Brent ambles up the drive, affecting the air of a man who just happened to be passing.

'Still messin' around with that heap of junk?' is his greeting, favouring Carson with a sardonic smile.

'Looks like it, doesn't it?' is Carson's surly reply.

'Why don't you just give up and send it to the scrap heap?' suggests Brent.

'Why don't you just mind your own fucking business?' suggests Carson.

'You wanna watch your mouth,' advises Brent, scowling. 'In case you've forgotten, I happen to be an officer of the law.'

'You're a public servant,' counters Carson. 'So why don't you do me a service and piss off?'

He turns his attention back to the machine.

'Maybe I'm here on official business,' suggests Brent.

Carson looks at him. 'What official business?' he demands. 'I ain't done nothin'.'

'Haven't you now?' says Sergeant Brent. 'What about them schoolgirls gettin' raped, eh? Maybe you know somethin' about that? That sketch they've drawn of the rapist, the one that's in all the papers: looks a lot like you I reckon.'

Carson glares. 'He does *not* look a lot like me,' he says firmly. 'His hair's shorter than mine, and his face is wider. He *doesn't* look like me.'

'Maybe the artist got them bits wrong,' says Brent. 'Maybe we ought to bring you into the station...'

'Look, don't bullshit me,' growls Carson. 'I've been through the copshop before; the whole bloody circus. You've got my DNA on record; so all you've gotta do is compare it with that rapist's, and it won't bloody match, will it? Cuz I didn't do it.'

'Yeah, maybe you didn't,' agrees Brent, musingly. 'Them girls: bit old for your tastes, ain't they? Yeah, I seem to recall...' He ruminates. '...Yeah, you like 'em a bit younger, don't you? Oh, and you like 'em to be boys, not girls, don't you?'

Carson's wrench clatters to the ground.

'Just you shut-up,' he warns Brent, lips pursed. 'You don't know nothin—'

'I know that restraining order's still in place,' says Brent.

'I ain't been anywhere near him...' Carson trails off, recalling a brief meeting in the park a few nights before. 'And I never did nothin' anyhow. It was all a fuss over nothin'.'

'A fuss over nothin' with a restraining order attached to it,' retorts Brent. 'Look at you. Still livin' with your old lady, no job to go to. And you thought you was so much better than me back at school, didn't you? Ha! Well, look at us both now.' He indicates himself with gloved hands.

'Well, you just went over to the other side, didn't you?' says Carson. 'If you've finished gloating, how about you do me a favour an' piss off.'

'I'm goin',' Brent tells him. 'Not cuz you told me to, but cuz I'm too busy to stand around all day talkin' to a loser like you.'

He turns, takes a step down the drive and looks back. 'And watch yourself, mate. Cuz I'll be watching you too.'

And with that parting shot, he returns to his colleague. They climb back into the car and drive off.

'So why do men commit rape? Any ideas?'

'Cuz they're animals!'

(Laughter)

'No, they just get carried away sometimes!'

'Like that's an excuse!'

'Well, it's true that men do get carried away by their reproductive instincts, the sexual imperative; but yes, that's not an excuse. We're all still responsible for our actions, aren't we?'

'But sometimes men just get the signals wrong!'

'Yeah, but if the girl's saying "no" then they should fucking stop, shouldn't they?' (Agreement)

'Good point. A lot of date rapes happen because the man doesn't believe the girl means it when she says "no". These men seem to think that by forcing themselves on the girl they can also force her to enjoy the experience. But what about the serial rapists like the one who has attacked some of your classmates? Are his motivations the same?'

'Yeah. They're just sad blokes who can't get it any other way!'

'No, they're not! Them serial rapists are men who've got issues with women. They're motivated by hate more than lust.'

'Oh, listen to you! Professor Eve Chandler!'

'No, actually she's right. These serial attackers usually don't expect their victims to enjoy the experience; in fact they may want it as unpleasant for them as possible.'

'Yeah, it'd hurt like fuck if you're not turned on!'

'Well, if you are turned on, then that means you're liking it!'

'No it doesn't, you fucking moron!'

'What about the rapist here in Linton? Who can tell me why he's targeting schoolgirls?'

'Cuz he's a perv, like all men are!'

(Laughter)

'Cuz they're weaker than grown-up women.'

'No we're not! I could deck you any day!'

'I reckon it's the school uniforms they wear. They're asking for it dressed like that!'

(Uproar)

'I don't think we can blame school uniform. Those girls were all attacked at night; none of them were wearing their school clothes.'

'I think men like girls our age cuz we look better.'

'And why do you think you look better?'

'Pretty obvious, isn't it? We've got all the curves and everything, but we're still young and fresh.'

'You mean you've still got that "glow of youth"?'

'Yes. That's why grown men all fancy us and grown women are all jealous of us.'

'Oh, are we now? So you think *I'm* jealous of you, then?'

''Course you are. I mean you may look pretty good for thirty, but it's not gunna last much longer, is it?'

'You know, I'm going to come over there and slap you.'

(Laughter)

The man behind the desk looks to be in his thirties, well-groomed and affable, side-parted brown hair and a smart brown suit. Murray Leinster and Eve Chandler have just taken the chairs facing him. Eve looks relaxed, Murray anything but.

'Eve Chandler and Murray Leinster? Thank you for coming here.'

'We didn't have much choice,' says Eve. 'We were summoned.'

The man shrugs, smiling ruefully. 'Well, there's always a choice, isn't there? Yes, there was a summons, but you didn't have to obey it, did you? But you're here, so we don't need to follow that avenue of speculation. You look worried, Murray, so let me start by saying the two of you are not in any kind of trouble; I just want to ask you a few questions.'

'And who are you?' demands Eve. 'Are you with the fuzz?'

'Patience, my dear; I was just about to introduce myself. My name's Mark Hunter, and no, I'm not a policeman. I've come here to Linton from London. I'm with what we call the intelligence community.' 'So you're a spy?' says Eve. She laughs.

'And what's so funny about that?' demands Mark, affecting an offended tone. 'We may have been done to death in fiction, but we still exist in real life.'

'And have got any proof that you're a spy?'

'How about the fact that I'm sitting here? I hardly think your principal would have loaned me the use of her office or allowed me to interview two of her students if she wasn't satisfied with my credentials.'

'Okay, so you're a spy,' accepts Eve. 'I just wouldn't have thought you'd be interested in a rape case.'

'Who says I am?' returns Mark.

Eve looks surprised. 'I thought that was what you wanted to see us about? Because we saw Rose Gardener that night, before she got attacked?'

'No, it's not quite that I'm concerned with,' Mark tells her. 'It's somebody else you saw that same evening I want to talk to you about: a gipsy fortune teller, name of Madam Rulenska. You paid her a visit that night, didn't you?'

'Yeah, we did,' admits Eve, surprised at the line of inquiry. 'What about it?'

'You know that she's dead, I assume?'

Murray and Eve exchange looks strongly suggestive of their having known nothing of the sort.

Eve confirms this: 'No, we didn't know.'

'You didn't? Well, maybe I shouldn't be surprised about that. Her death was reported in your local rag, the *Linton Evening News,* but it was only a couple of paragraphs. The demise of an elderly gipsy is not quite as newsworthy as the rape of a schoolgirl.'

'So you mean she died that same day we saw her?'

'Within hours of you seeing her, although the death

wasn't discovered until the next morning. It seems she always packed up her tent and departed before daybreak, but the morning after you saw her, her tent was still there, in the town square. A curious council worker took a look inside the tent and found Madam Rulenska sitting in her chair, stone dead.'

'And she'd been murdered?'

'Nope. Natural causes, as far as the coroner can tell. A fatal heart attack. No indications of foul play.'

'I don't get it then,' says Eve. 'What do you need to talk to us about, and why is a spy from London even interested in the death of a fortune teller? Were we the last ones to see her alive?'

'To answer your last question first, no you weren't,' is the reply. 'Madam Rulenska's tent was in full view of a CCTV camera—that's how we know you were there—and no, she had several other clients after yourselves. In fact she left her tent herself to buy herself a takeaway meal, at around midnight. The coroner places the time of death at around that time, so she must have died not long after she returned to her tent and ate her meal.'

'And you think she might have been poisoned?'

'Not at all. The autopsy would have revealed any poisoning.'

'Then I don't get it,' says Eve. 'An old lady has a heart attack and dies; what do you want us for?'

'Well, I'd just like to know what passed between yourselves and Madam Rulenska. From the CCTV footage it looks like you were all set to walk right on past her tent without stopping, but then it seems you changed your minds and went in. Why was that?'

'Cuz she called out to us,' answers Eve. 'Said she had something to tell us. Well, to tell Murray, really. So we went in and she read Murray's fortune.'

Mark turns to look at Murray. 'So, she singled you out for her prognostications, did she?'

'Prog-nosta—' Murray struggles with the word, surrenders.

'Her fortune telling,' supplies Eve.

'Oh. Yes,' answers Murray. 'She called out to me. She knew my name and I'd never even seen her before.'

'And what did she tell you about your future?'

'That's his business,' interjects Eve. 'Why should he tell you that?'

'There are one or two question marks surrounding Madam Rulenska's death. I'm trying to clear them up, so anything you can tell me might help.' To Murray: 'I mean, if there was anything deeply personal to yourself in what she predicted to you, of course you don't have to repeat it—'

'There was nothing private like that,' Eve tells him. 'It were all general stuff. Said there'd be a lot of stuff happening soon and that Murray would be right in the middle of it all.'

'Really? That's interesting. What sort of things would be happening?'

A shrug. 'Like I said, it was all vague. Cosmic events, I think she said.'

'Cosmic?' echoes Mark. 'She actually used that word?'

'Yeah, I think she did.' Eve turns to Murray who nods confirmation. To Mark: 'That's the kind of thing fortune tellers say. Everything's cosmic to them, written in the stars.'

'Crystal ball fortune telling isn't related to astrology,' Mark advises her. 'If Rulenska spoke of cosmic events, she may have been speaking more literally than you seem to think. I should tell you, although Madam Rulenska died from a heart attack, she was found with a look of complete terror frozen on her face. And her crystal ball was shattered. It hadn't fallen on the floor; it was still on the table, but it had broken into pieces. Now that's a puzzler, isn't it? How could her crystal ball have shattered like that without being dropped?'

'So, what are you saying? Madam Rulenska saw something in her crystal ball that was so terrifying the ball exploded and she had a heart attack?'

Mark Hunter sits back in the principal's upholstered chair, smiles softly.

'It's a theory, isn't it?'

Chapter Nine
Mysterious Garden

The second Adventure is to be tonight!

This time Eve has given Murray advanced notice of the planned excursion. Get yourself round mine at eight this evening, were her instructions, given after school that day. And don't bring your phone with you.

Murray isn't sure why he's not supposed to bring his phone with him, but he has no problems with this prohibition. Like most kids whose families are not living in actual poverty, Murray owns a smartphone, but he doesn't use it much. Before the advent of his Mysterious Girlfriend, Murray had never been very mobile as a person and had, therefore, never had much need for a mobile phone.

Eight o'clock has almost arrived, and Murray sits on his bed lacing up his trainers. His mum is at home tonight, so he will have to sneak out the window. He has no way of locking his bedroom door, but he hopes, by leaving the light switched off, that if his mum calls out to him and receiving no reply decides to put her head round the door, she will just assume he has gone to bed early and is already asleep. To this end he has added padding to make the bed appear occupied.

Yes, for the first time in his young life, Murray Leinster is attempting to pull the wool over the eyes of his devoted and all-powerful Mum. And for the first time in his life he has a secret he is keeping from that same over-affectionate parent. The apron strings are being stretched to their very limits!

He has told his mum that there exists a girl named Eve Chandler, who has just transferred to his school, and that she resides in the house right across the road; but he has not told her that this girl is his Mysterious Girlfriend. He has spoken of her as nothing more than a classmate. And this withholding of information is Murray's own decision; Eve has never requested that Murray not tell his mum that the two of them are an item. So why hasn't he told his mum? It's not as though he's ashamed of his Mysterious Girlfriend; quite the reverse... But he's just not sure how his mum will take the news. His mum is a bit on the possessive side; always has been. Would she approve of Eve Chandler? Would she approve of Murray having a girlfriend at all?

These are just some of the questions Murray has avoided putting to the test by keeping the relevant information to himself.

He is ready now. He switches off the light, satisfies himself that the padding under his duvet will fool anyone, and climbs out through his bedroom window. At least he attempts to climb out, but never having performed this manoeuvre before, he loses his balance and falls headfirst into the garden, knocking the casement right back on its hinges in the process.

Recovering from his fall, Murray springs upright and peers over the windowsill into his bedroom, fearfully expecting his mum to come bursting into the room to ascertain what all the noise was about. Thankfully, this does not happen. Watching TV in the living room, his parent obviously hasn't heard anything.

Closing the window as far as he can, Murray crosses the garden to the street. The living room curtains are drawn so he doesn't have to worry about being seen from that direction. He crosses the road and approaches Eve Chandler's bungalow. This will be his first visit to Eve's home. As yet, he hasn't even seen, let alone been introduced to, Eve's mum and dad. Are they in on the secret of Eve's double life and her nocturnal activities? Or does Eve always sneak out of the house unbeknownst to them? Murray isn't sure. Eve never talks about her parents and Murray has never thought to ask.

Either way, his visit must be expected by the entire household because Eve has told him to just come right up and ring the front doorbell.

Murray does just this and the door is promptly opened by Eve herself.

'Hiya,' she greets him. 'Come on in.'

The door closed, Eve folds Murray in her arms and presses her lips to his. Murray immediately voices stifled protests and attempts to break from the embrace.

Eve looks understandably put out by this reaction.

'What's wrong wi' you?' she demands.

'We can't do it here!' hisses Murray, urgently. 'Your parents might catch us!'

'My parents aren't here, you daft sod,' Eve tells him.

'You mean they're out?' asks Murray.

'No, I mean they're not here,' says Eve. 'They don't live here. It's just me. I live on me own.'

Murray looks incredulous. 'No, you don't!'

'I ruddy do.'

'But you can't live on your own!'

'Can't I?' says Eve. 'Come on.'

Taking Murray by the hand, she conducts him on a quick tour of the house. Sure enough, there are no parents, no other inhabitants at all; and only one bedroom is in use, this clearly belonging to Eve.

'Y'see?' says Eve, when the tour has brought them back to the living room. 'It's just me.'

Murray switches from amazed to aggrieved. 'That means you lied to me!' he accuses.

'Lied to you? When?'

'On Monday!' insists Murray. 'When you first told me you lived here. You definitely told me you lived with your parents! You did!'

Eve casts her mind back. 'No... What it was you asked me if me mam and dad were still together, and I said they were, which is true; they are still together. It's just that I don't happen to live with them.'

Murray scratches his head in bewilderment. 'But, isn't it against the law for people our age to be living on their own?'

Eve shrugs. 'It might be, but I get away with it.'

'Is it... to do with your secret job?'

'I s'pose it is really,' says Eve. 'But you could say I've still got some guardians who look out for me. In fact, it's them who we're going to meet tonight.'

'What, are they coming here...?'

'No, we're going to see them,' Eve tells him. 'They've got this place: it's right in the middle of town but no one knows about it and no one can get into it. It's a secret place. But you're gunna be allowed in, y'see; cuz I'll be taking you there. So that's our Adventure for tonight. It won't be a dangerous Adventure, but it'll be an exciting one for you.'

Excitement without any attendant danger: this sounds very agreeable to Murray.

Once again, they commence their journey on foot. Apparently you don't catch the bus when you're heading out on an Adventure. Murray is still assimilating this latest revelation concerning his Mysterious Girlfriend: she lives on her own! Fourteen years old and completely self-sufficient! She cooks her own meals. She performs the housework all by herself. She understands the mysteries of how to operate a washing machine... Is there nothing this girl can't do?

Self-sufficient, but apparently not without any grown-ups to turn to in a crisis...

'So are they part of your spy group?' asks Murray. 'These people we're going to see?'

'Aye, they are,' confirms Eve.

'And they're grown-ups. Are they men or women or—'

'They're both women,' Eve tells him. 'In fact, place

we're meeting them, only women are allowed. But we're making an exception for you tonight. So, be grateful!'

'A place where only women are allowed...' ponders Murray. 'So any woman can go there?'

'Course not, you pudding-head!' returns Eve. 'I told you this place is dead secret. Only members of our group, people in the know, can get into this place.'

'So there won't be a lot of women there?'

'No, just the two we're going to meet and maybe the caretaker. No one else is there.'

'And what are they like? I mean—'

'No more questions, you!' commands Eve. 'You'll be meeting them soon enough; you have to wait till then to see what they're like! It's part of the Adventure.'

They proceed, Eve smoking a cigarette.

Presently: 'Can I ask another question?' from Murray. 'It's not to do with where we're going.'

'Go on, then. Let's hear it.'

'Why did you tell me I couldn't bring my phone when I came out tonight?'

'Ah, yes!' says Eve, remembering. 'You're right, I do owe you an explanation there. I didn't want you bringing your phone cuz I don't want anyone being able to trace us.'

Murray frowns. 'Trace us? What, you mean like if my mum found out I was out and rang me on my phone?'

'No, not your mam! I mean people tracing us by satellite,' clarifies Eve.

'People can trace us by satellite?' queries Murray. 'With our phones?'

'That they can. Walking around with a smartphone on you is pretty much like walking around with a tracking device. Anyone with access to the right technology can find out exactly where you are. That's why I never use a smartphone.'

And as she says this, Murray realises for the first time that, yes, he has never once seen Eve with a phone in her hands. Unheard of amongst modern youth!

He asks: 'But what if you need help in an emergency?'

'I'm covered there,' Eve assures him. 'In an emergency I've got this.' She pulls back her left sleeve, revealing a wristwatch.

'The watch?'

'Yep. It's also a communicator. I only use it for emergencies. The rest of the time, when it's inactive, no one can track me with it. It might as well be just a normal watch.'

'So, do you all have those?'

'Aye.'

'Do all spies have them?' wonders Murray. 'What about that spy we met today, Mark Hunter? Will he have—'

'He's nothing to do with me,' Eve tells him. 'He won't have one of these watches.'

The duo are now threading a street of ethnic grocery stores, charity shops, eateries of various kinds. The shops are mostly shuttered but the eating houses are still open for business. There are a fair number of pedestrians. Amongst these, a small woman who appears to be the worse for drink. She sways and totters towards Murray and Eve.

'Isn't that—' begins Eve. And then: 'Christ; it is! It's Miss Forbes!'

And it is indeed class 9-C's homeroom teacher; the timid, bespectacled Miss Forbes, but not as she usually appears to her students! Her modest skirt-suit is still in place, but looking somewhat dishevelled, the blouse unbuttoned to cleavage level. Her hair is disordered, her glasses askew, make-up smudged.

She stops before Eve and stands there swaying, eyeing the girl belligerently.

'I know you,' she declares, her voice slurred but much more audible than her usual classroom squeak. 'You're that new girl who thinks she's sho hot.' She transfers her bleary gaze to Murray. 'And it's the milkshop mummy's boy. Shurprised your mummy let you out of the housh.' 'Erm, are you okay, Miss?' asks Eve.

Miss Forbes rounds on her. 'Coursh I'm okay! Why shouldn't I be okay? Don't you judge me, you... you... fatarshed piesh of jailbait! I can have a drink or two if I wanna! I'm a resphon...reshponshible adult! If I wanna have a drink I'll have a drink, and the resht of you can fuck off! And like you kidsh never get drunk when you can get holda the shtuff! Ha! Leasht I'm over eighteen. Old enough to drink reshpon...reshponshibly! Not like you little turdsh who always end up in A and E having your pumachs shtumped! Ha!'

Miss Forbes leans her face in close to Murray's, breathing beer fumes all over him.

'And you,' she says, dropping her voice. 'Don't think I don't know what you're up to, you little shit. You don't fool me, you milkshop. I've got my eye on you, I have. I've got my eye on you.'

She taps the side of her nose to indicate her visual alertness.

To both of them, louder again: 'Now get outta the way the both of yer! I gotta get home! Shome of ush have jobs to go to in the morning! Lazy little shitsh!'

Eve and Murray step aside; Miss Forbes staggers past them.

'And don't you be late for shchool!' she throws back at them. 'Or I'll tark you as mardy!'

'Well, that was an eye-opener,' says Eve to Murray. 'Come on.' 'Will she be alright?' hesitates Murray.

'Don't worry,' says Eve. 'Drunk people always somehow make it back home safe and sound. They say there's a guardian angel or summat for drunks.'

'I'll feel a bit funny seeing Miss Forbes at school, now,' confesses Murray, as they resume their journey. 'I mean, won't she be embarrassed...?'

'Don't sweat it,' advises Eve. 'Come homeroom tomorrow morning, she either won't remember seeing us or she'll pretend she doesn't remember. Either way, we just go along with it and we don't say a word about it.'

'Okay.'

Eve leads Murray further into town and finally down a rutted gravel access road between the looming walls of warehouses. There are no streetlights here, and Eve takes Murray's hand as they proceed through the darkness.

'Not much further,' she assures him.

She brings Murray to a halt at what Murray can dimly see is a door in the middle of a wide expanse of brick wall. Looking upward he sees that the wall here is not the side of a building but a boundary wall of some kind, very tall and topped with spikes and barbed-wire. Both the door and the wall look very old.

Murray cannot see what Eve does at the door, but he thinks he hears a sound, an electronic bleep of some kind, and then comes a loud click and Eve opens the door. She takes Murray by the hand once more.

'This is a bit tricky in the dark,' she says. ''Specially for someone who's not been here before.'

'What's tricky?' asks Murray.

'Basically, this wall is about three times as high other side of the door,' explains Eve. 'The ground's like thirty feet down or summat. So we'll be walking onto a platform at the top of some stairs. There's a guard rail but it's not much of one, so I don't want you falling over it.'

'Okay,' says Murray, tightening his grip on Eve's hand. 'And is this the only way into wherever it is we're going?'

'It's the only way in I can show you,' is the reply.

Eve leads Murray across the threshold. They squeeze around the inward-opening door, which Eve then closes.

Murray finds himself standing on a narrow stone platform guarded by a low wooden railing. He gazes, astonished, upon an unexpected view.

It is a vast sunken garden, like a section of some enchanted woodland transplanted from a fairy dream into the centre of a modern town; and yet hidden from all eyes by a surrounding wall rising higher than the crowns of the most venerable of the trees. No building can be seen, and there is no electric lighting, no artificial pathway or cultivated flowerbed or rustic bench. A garden for nymphs and dryads is this, not a place for vulgar human beings.

'Pretty amazing, isn't it?' speaks Eve, having let pass an appropriate interval of silence.

'How did it get here?' says Murray, voicing his continued disbelief at what he sees.

'I dunno,' confesses Eve. 'Maybe it was here all the time, before anything else. Maybe the whole town was built around this place…' She squeezes Murray's hand. 'Come on. Let's go down. You haven't seen the half of it yet.'

On their left, a stone staircase descends from the platform to the level of the sunken garden, flush with the wall and guarded on the right by a continuation of the wooden railing. Eve leads Murray to this descent.

'The stairs are steep and there's a lot of 'em,' says Eve, 'but it's not wide enough for us to walk next to each other, so I reckon we might manage better not holding hands. I'll go first and I'll walk slowly; you just keep right behind me and keep your hand on the rail. You'll be alright.'

'Okay.'

In the murky light the descent looks alarming. But Murray is eager to get down to that enchanted garden; he wants to know that this vision won't just disappear when he reaches the foot of the stairs, that it won't fade away like a mist or a dream.

They begin the descent. Eve advises Murray to keep his eyes forward. He does this, resisting the temptation to turn his head and watch the garden drawing nearer, trying to ignore the vague feeling that the landscape might evaporate if he doesn't keep his eyes fixed upon it.

'You haven't seen half of it yet,' were Eve's words. What other wonders could be waiting down there…?

Finally, they reach the foot of the stairs. The perspective has changed but the garden is still here and maintains its enchantment. The ground slopes down from the enclosing wall on all sides, a rich pasture dotted with wild flowers and shrubs, sweeping down towards the groups of trees. The trees stand most densely in the very centre of the garden, forming an impenetrable fairy grove.

'Do you see anything?' asks Eve.

'What should I be seeing?'

'Anything moving.'

'No, I can't see anything moving…'

'You will. Come on.'

Taking his hand once again Eve leads Murray down the sloping bank.

'It's like a crater, isn't it?' says Eve. 'No one seems to know for sure, but maybe that's what it really is. Maybe something landed here like thousands and thousands of years back, and maybe this garden grew here from out of whatever it was. Who knows what the world was really like back then? Those people who dig things up; they talk like they know it all, but they don't. They find a few bones and an arrow-head and they reckon they can work it all out, but they're just guessing. They don't really know the half of it…'

The trees loom closer, the ground starts to level out. Murray's heart beats fast; his eyes dart around, scanning the trees, the foliage. Look for something moving… But what?

And then he does see movement. Quick darting movements at first; shadows darting from cover to cover. Shapes. Small, lithe shapes. To the left. And to the right. All around them. And then the shapes start to appear in the open and there are eyes, dozens of pairs of small, luminous eyes. The eyes move towards these two intruders on their domain.

Eve and Murray stop walking.

Cats. A multitude of cats, a feline colony. Cats of all shapes and sizes, all breeds and colours. All of them slowly mincing their way towards Eve and Murray. For a moment

Murray panics, but he quickly senses that these cats are not feral, that they are as tame as any house cat, and that they advance not with fear or hostility, but just with simple feline curiosity and desire for attention.

Eve hunkers down to greet the cats. Murray joins her. Soon the cats are milling around them, circling the two crouching humans, rubbing against them, purring, raising their heads for petting. Short-haired, longhaired, young cats and old cats, tabbies and tortoiseshells, all vying for their share of attention.

Murray strokes the fluffy hides as they mill around him, tails upraised. The cats rub their wet mouths and their scent-secreting temples against his hand... Are they claiming all of Murray Leinster as their property, or just that affectionate hand? 'You like cats, then?' asks Eve.

'Yes, I've always liked them.'

'Thought so. Didn't think you were a dog person.'

'We used to have a cat,' says Murray. 'But he got run over.'

'Yeah, their traffic sense can be pretty lousy,' admits Eve. 'At least this lot don't have to worry about that. No roads down here.'

'They never leave this garden then?'

'No. Why should they? This garden's big enough for them. Cats are territorial. They like enough space to move around in but they don't need too much. Down here they've got everything they want and without the dangers like cars and bad people that most other cats have to put up with. This place is a haven for them.'

'Is that what this garden's for then?' inquires Murray. 'A cat sanctuary?'

'Well, not really,' says Eve. 'This garden is a special place belonging to the people I'm with. And our people are lasses. Like I said before, no fellers are allowed in here. 'Cept for very rare exceptions like you tonight. As for the moggies, no one seems to know how long they've been here, or who first put them here. We just look after them; it's a tradition. They fit in here, anyway, the cats. This is a female place and cats are feminine; dogs are masculine.'

'Where are the two women I'm going to be meeting?' wonders Murray. 'Are they the people who feed the cats?'

'No, the caretaker does that. The ladies we're meeting are waiting for us at the house.'

'House?' echoes Murray. 'Is there a house here?'

Eve smiles. 'I know what you mean. When you first look at this place, you'd think there can't be anything like a house here; but there is a house,' she points. 'It's hidden away, right in the middle of that big clump of trees. I guess it's meant to be hidden away, cuz it's not a part of nature like everything else here is. Come on.'

Eve and Murray rise to their feet, eliciting some mews of protest from the cats, who obviously understand that this signals the end of their quota of attention. The two teenagers move forward, the cats coiling around their ankles, attempting to impede their progress. But they soon desist, some of the cats moving off to find something else to interest them, while others trot along in their wake, either still curious or perhaps hopeful of some more attention.

Chapter Ten
Thar She Blows!

As promised, in a clearing at the centre of that copse of trees, stands a house. The Pavilion, as Eve calls it. A many-sided wooden structure, the first floor raised above the ground, surrounded by a veranda to which a short flight of steps give access. Above this roofed veranda, a gabled upper storey, while beneath it there appears to be another floor, far too low in height for human habitation and accessible via a number of small doorways. The entire Pavilion, painted white from top to bottom, glows pale and ghostly under the night sky.

The riddle of the truncated lower floor is soon explained when two cats appear from the trees, pad across the clearing, pass under the veranda and disappear through one of the miniature doorways.

'So that's where the cats live,' remarks Murray.

'Yep, they've got a whole floor to themselves,' confirms Eve.

'And is their food in there?'

'Yep. Food, water, lots of cushions to sleep on; it's like in a miniature hostel. No litter trays, though. They don't need 'em; they just come out here to do their business, and that's okay cuz cats are tidy like and always bury their doings.'

'So the two women live here,' says Murray. 'And they live with the caretaker who looks after the cats and garden?'

'Not quite. Only the caretaker lives here all the time. The rest of us, we just come here sometimes for a break, or for meetings; and maybe if one of us needs somewhere to hide out for a while; or if you just want to spend some quality time with the moggies. It's an open house for us. A shelter. Come on.'

They climb the veranda steps. Curtains are drawn across all the first floor windows; not a chink of light is visible. Eve advances to a pair of French windows and after tapping on the glass to announce her presence, opens them. She steps inside, lifts the curtain.

'Come on,' she invites Murray.

Murray passes through the uplifted curtain and steps into what looks to him like an Arab chieftain's palace. He has little time to assimilate the vista because, with a cry of 'What an adorable boy!' a pink and yellow blur slams into him, and he finds himself flat on a Turkish carpet, straddled by an auburn-haired woman in diaphanous peach-coloured negligee, who proceeds to plaster his face with wet, noisy kisses.

'Oh, he's so adorable!' she coos between salvoes. 'I could just gobble him up!'

'Er, yeah, he's my feller, remember,' comes Eve Chandler's voice. 'I didn't bring him here for you to pounce on.'

'Oh, but we're all girls together here,' says the woman coaxingly. 'Share and share alike. That's our motto, isn't it?'

'Up to a point,' allows Eve. 'But I don't want you doin' anything with him that I haven't done with him yet. And can you let him get up? He's only just got here.'

The woman pouts but complies. Eve helps Murray to his feet.

'Sorry about that,' she says to him. 'This is Fifi, and as you can tell, she keeps her brains in her knickers.'

'That's right,' confirms Fifi, brightly. 'I keep my PhD down there.'

Fifi's affectionate nature and her state of déshabillé remind Murray of his mum. And she looks to be about the same age, as well. Her long thick hair is of a more golden hue than that of his parent, and she exhibits an air of childlike eagerness; her blue eyes are wide and in constant motion. A gauzy, peach-coloured baby doll and matching lacy knickers form her raiment. (And if I was George WM Reynolds I would probably at this point start waxing lyrical about the admirable 'symmetry' of her figure.)

'Erm... pleased to meet you,' says Murray.

'Oh, and he's so polite!' enthuses Fifi. 'He's just too divine! I could get wet just looking at him!'

'Yeah, you look like you already are,' remarks Eve.

'Oh, you know I can't help it!' protests Fifi. 'The love just flows out of me!'

'Yeah, you should go and see a gynaecologist about that one,' advises Eve. To Murray: 'Come on. Let's say hello to Jane.'

A second woman, seated on a divan across the room, has been silently observing the proceedings. Eve takes Murray by the arm and escorts him to her. Murray now has a chance to take in the details of the room. The vast chamber seems occupy most of this floor of the Pavilion, and it has been fitted out in an Eastern style: brightly-patterned Turkish carpets cover the floor; the walls are concealed by rich, heavy hangings; the furniture composed of low divans and tables, nests of cushions on which to recline. Huge, ornately painted vases decorate the room; a massive chandelier hangs from the ceiling and the air is heavy with a heady, feminine incense. The room's centrepiece is an ornamental fountain. (And surprisingly, there is not a single cat to be seen!)

'Like the place?' asks Eve.

'It's like an Arab's palace,' says Murray.

'Yeah, or more specifically it's meant to be like a harem,' explains Eve. 'Y'know, the place where an Arab prince keeps all his women. 'Cept that ours is a harem with no master and no rules. Just us women, and no one to tell us what to do.'

The woman seated on the couch looks also to be in her thirties. There is something polished and executive about her; she wears a skirt-suit of expensive cut; her brown hair neatly clipped in place, make-up immaculate; to Murray she seems to radiate a relentless efficiency as she studies him coolly through her gold-framed glasses.

'And this is Jane Richmond,' introduces Eve. 'Although we call her Lady Jane.'

'Lady Jane is my professional name,' the woman explains. She extends a well-manicured hand to Murray. 'Pleased to meet you.'

'Me too,' mumbles Murray. 'I mean, you too…'

He trails off, unsure. Our Murray has never been very good with these formal introductions!

Meanwhile, baby doll Fifi has joined them.

'Lady Jane' is a euphemism for pussy,' she informs Murray. 'It's an appropriate name when you consider what her job is!'

'Is it?' frowns Murray, uncomprehending. 'Does she look after the cats, then?'

'No, darling. Not that kind of pussy. Jane's a prostitute.' Murray still looks blank.

Eve helps him out. 'A prostitute is someone who sells sex for money.'

'The world's oldest profession, they call it,' says Lady Jane. 'The oldest profession for women, at any rate. The oldest profession for men is assassination. Women's first commercial notions were to sell pleasure; men's were to sell death.'

'True, but women's career opportunities have opened right up since then,' says Fifi. 'Take me, for instance, Murray darling (and please do take me whenever you want!): I happen to be both a company director and a scientist! Both at once!'

Murray's face reflects his reaction to this news.

'I know,' sighs Fifi. '"How can a girl as young and fresh-looking be the head of an entire company? Surely she must be still at Sixth-form College?" That's what you're thinking, isn't it?'

'No, you look about the same age as my mum,' says Murray, completely oblivious. 'I was just thinking that you don't look like a business-woman dressed like that.'

'I don't go to work dressed like this, darling,' replies Fifi, smiling through clenched teeth.

'It's true about that Ph.D. she says she keeps in her knickers,' says Eve. 'She runs her own lab over at the science park.'

'The science park?' echoes Murray. 'That's where my mum works!' 'Really? Which company does she work for?' asks Fifi.

'It's a place called Fleetwood Laboratories,' says Murray.

Silence.

Confused, Murray looks from one face to another. Has he said something wrong? Everyone looks dumbstruck.

And then Eve and Lady Jane turn accusing eyes towards

Fifi.

Fifi, uncomfortable, looks at Murray. 'Are you sure about that, my love?'

'Sure about what?'

'That your mumsie works at Fleetwood Labs? You're sure it's not some other place?'

'No, it's definitely Fleetwood,' Murray assures her. 'Why? Is there something wrong about that place?'

'Not at all,' answers Fifi. 'In fact, that happens to be *my* laboratory. Fleetwood is *my* surname. Silly Eve should have told you that before.'

'Never mind silly Eve,' retorts Eve. 'How come is it Murray's mam works for your company and you didn't even know it?'

'Well, what about you?' fires back Fifi. 'How come you never asked Murray where his mum worked?'

'I did!' declares Eve. 'Leastways, Murray told me she worked at the science park. I mean yeah, I didn't actually ask him what lab it was...' her voice trails off.

'Ha!' says Fifi triumphantly. 'Then you're just as bad as me, aren't you?'

And she sticks out her tongue to settle the argument.

'Let's stick to the point here,' speaks up Lady Jane. 'Fifi, I'm having a hard time believing you didn't even know that Murray's mother works for you. Your staff at the lab isn't that large, is it?' To Murray: 'Clear this up for me, Murray: is Leinster your mother or your father's surname?'

'It's mum's.'

'And what's her first name?'

'Mary.'

Lady Jane favours Fifi with a look of annihilating scorn. '"Mary Leinster",' she growls, her voice matching her expression. 'Her name sounds practically the same as his. How, by all that's holy could you have not—'

'Oh, *Mary* Leinster!' exclaims Fifi, in the tone of someone suddenly recalling one of the vast number of

Leinsters currently in her employ. 'Oh yes, I know her! Lovely lady! Wonderful in the lab! Wicked sense of humour! Big juicy bum!'

'So you know my mum?' says Murray eagerly, instantly recognising his parent from the foregoing description.

'Yes, sweetie, I do!' replies Fifi. 'In fact, I'm the one who pays her her very generous wage-packet! Only you mustn't tell her you've seen me here tonight!'

'Murray knows he's not supposed to talk about this place,' says Eve.

'Now that we've got this settled, how about some tea for our guest?' suggests Lady Jane. 'It's your turn in the kitchen, Fifi.'

'Yes, tea for our darling guest! Where are our manners?'

'I think yours are in the same place you keep your Ph.D.'

Fifi skips off across the room, disappears behind a curtain and almost immediately returns, bearing a tray with four steaming mugs.

'It had just been made,' she announces, before anyone can praise her promptitude at bringing water to the boil.

'Must have been the caretaker,' adduces Lady Jane.

'Well, it wasn't one of the cats,' retorts Fifi, revenging herself for before.

Armed with a mug each they sit down, Eve and Murray side by side on the cushions, Fifi similarly seated, Lady Jane presiding on her couch.

'So, Murray,' she begins. 'Eve has told you precisely who we are, what we represent, what we do, our goals, etc...?'

'No,' says Murray, alarmed Eve might be punished for this oversight. 'She didn't tell me any of that.'

'Good,' replies Lady Jane. 'Because then we would have to have killed you.'

'Which would be a shame, because he's such a sweet little boy,' adds Fifi, as one anticipating the loss of a cherished plaything.

'They're just pullin' your leg, love,' Eve tells him.

'We're just a loose society of like-minded women,' proceeds Lady Jane. 'That's all you really need to know.'

'So... Are you like those #MeToo people?' ventures Murray.

Fifi sprays a mouthful of tea.

'We're not directly affiliated,' replies Lady Jane, straight-faced.

'Okay...'

Jane turns to Eve: 'I believe you've got something to tell us, haven't you?'

'Yeah, it's summat that happened at school today,' says Eve. 'Me an' Murray got called to the principal's office to meet this guy who's come here from London. And he's a spy. Least, that's what he says he is. I thought maybe you should know about this.'

'Yes... What was this spy's name?'

'Mark Hunter.'

Fifi and Lady Jane trade easily interpreted looks.

'So you've heard of him?'

'Yes, we have,' says Lady Jane.

'Is he like a problem, then?'

'No, not at all. I've never met him but apparently he's a very nice person,' says Lady Jane. 'I don't think he'll be any bother to us. But why is he here? What did he want to see you and Murray about?'

'About this fortune teller me and Murray saw a few nights back,' and Eve proceeds to relate the story of Madam Rulenska and her untimely demise.

'Hmm,' ponders Lady Jane. 'Why would a spy from London be interested in the only slightly suspicious death of a gipsy fortune teller?'

'Yes, but when you think about those things she said to Murray—' begins Fifi.

'Which *he* didn't know about until this afternoon!'

'Oh yes! Silly me!'

'There must be more to it than just that,' pursues Lady Jane. 'There has to be something else to have brought Mark Hunter here. He has a reputation for tackling all the most bizarre assignments.'

Her eyes settle on Murray, her expression thoughtful. Then she turns to Eve. 'He was on his own when he saw you, was he?' An affirmative. 'I ask because he often works with a partner. You might know her: Dodo Dupont, the TV psychologist.'

'She was in school as well!' exclaims Eve. 'You telling me she's really a spy?'

'Not officially, but Mark Hunter is her friend and she has been known to work with him on his assignments. And she was at your school? Doing what?'

'She was giving our class a talk about sexual violence and all that,' says Eve. 'Y'know, because of the rapes that have been happening.'

'Giving talks won't be the only reason she's here,' Lady Jane tells her. 'She'll be working with Mark Hunter. I wonder... Perhaps it's the serial attacker that's brought them here... But then that would suggest that there's some connection between the assaults and the death of that fortune teller, as Hunter was interested in that as well...'

'That's just silly!' declares Fifi. 'Why would a spy be interested in a rape case? That's just police business.'

'There might be something,' says Eve. 'Something not normal about the attacks. My mate Rose Gardener was one of the girls who got raped; she said there was summat weird about the guy who did it; said he seemed more like a robot; no expression, an' he never spoke, never made a sound.'

'Yes, if there's something abnormal or inexplicable about what's been going on, that would be enough to bring Mark Hunter here.'

'And Rose also said the rapist was wearing a jumpsuit and it looked like it might have been military. Said it had insignia on it.'

'Really? The newspapers didn't mention that. I wonder if Mark Hunter is making them keep quiet about some of the details...'

'And what about young Murray here?' wonders Fifi. 'The fortune teller said he was going to be at the centre of everything. What's it all got to do with you, Murray?'

'I don't know,' confesses blushing Murray. 'I don't get it. I'm nobody special.'

'Well, I'd say your mumsie thinks you're pretty special,' says Fifi. 'She's always going on about you at the lab.'

'And how come you didn't work out she was Murray's mum if she's always talking about Murray?' inquires Lady Jane.

'It's not my fault!' protests Fifi. 'She always just calls him "my boy" or "my little man". How was I to know who she was talking about? I don't think she's ever mentioned Murray by name.'

Lady Jane places her mug on the table beside her divan. She leans forward, gazing intently at Murray.

'So just how "special" are you, Murray Leinster?' she demands. 'Just special to your mother and to Eve here? Or are you special to everyone?' 'There's all different kinds of special,' advises Fifi.

'Yes... In what ways are you so special, Murray Leinster? What is it that you've got?' She appraises him speculatively, then turns questioning eyes to Eve.

'Can't help you there,' says Eve. 'We've only got to second base so far.'

'Hmm... But we need to know,' says Lady Jane, eyes back on Murray. 'This could be important.'

'Very important, I'd say,' agrees Fifi. 'Demanding immediate investigation.'

'I concur,' says Jane. 'Standard Examination Number One, I think.'

The three women look at each other, exchange nods.

Murray feels the change in the atmosphere. Three pairs of

eyes now regard him with differing, yet equally covetous, expressions.

'I should probably be heading back home now...' ventures Murray.

This feeble protest is treated with the contempt it deserves. The three women pounce on our hero and he finds himself flat on the carpet, pinned down with gentle firmness; Eve holding one arm, Fifi the other, Lady Jane straddling his legs.

'Oh, you three are worse than my mum!' groans Murray.

'Now let us see what we have,' says Lady Jane. And with the air of a surgeon who has just snapped on her rubber gloves, she unzips Murray's fly, and assisted by unbuttoned boxer shorts beneath, easily extracts his penis. And clearly less bashful than its owner, this organ promptly announces itself to be pleased at making Lady Jane's acquaintance.

Three pairs of eyes light up.

'My! He *is* special,' says Fifi.

'A very special boy,' agrees Lady Jane. Eve just smiles her pride of ownership.

'Do you want to do the honours?' asks Lady Jane generously.

'I'd kind of like our first time to be without an audience,' replies Eve. 'But I do wanna be his first, so can you just...?'

'Yes, I won't mount him,' promises Lady Jane. 'But if you're agreeable, I will however bring about a crisis manually.'

'Yeah, that's alright,' says Eve. 'I reckon I'm already too late to be the first one to do that for him.' Lady Jane sets to work.

'Why are you doing this!' wails Murray.

'It's alright, sweetheart,' soothes Eve, stroking his heated cheek. 'It's okay. It's just a little test. Nothing bad. You're safe here. None of us would ever do anything to hurt you, Murray...'

Her soothing tones pacify Murray. He has nothing to fear.

He should just lie back...

'Something's happening...' he says to Eve presently. 'I think I'm going to...'

He starts to squirm again.

'It's fine, love,' coos Eve. 'You're not going to pee. It's your orgasm. You can feel it building up, yeah? That's good. Don't fight it, love; just go with it.'

And it comes. For the first time Murray experiences the full force of something he has only previously perceived on the borders of sleep. Eve gazes into his face as he features contort with the intensity of the feeling.

Fifi's eyes, with a similar look of adoration, are glued to the source of the eruption.

'Thar she blows!'

Murray subsides, overwhelmed by the new sensation. But there is an attendant feeling of shame.

'I've wet myself...'

'You haven't wet yourself, silly!' reassures Eve. 'I told you before: it's semen! Nothing to be embarrassed about!'

'Silly boy,' says Fifi. 'That's just what we wanted to see; and you were marvellous, darling; marvellous.'

Lady Jane licks her hand. 'Has he not been through sex education? He seems remarkably naïve.'

'Well, he was there in the classroom during sex ed,' answers Eve. 'But I'm not sure on how much of it he took in.' She strokes Murray's face. 'But he's starting to get the picture now.'

'You've got some in your hair, darling,' Fifi advises Lady Jane.

The evening is not quite over for Murray Leinster.

The return journey to Meredith Way is performed without incident. But, having parted company with Eve, and gained his bedroom by climbing in through the window, he is brought up in his tracks by the alarming presence of a human figure. The figure, cloaked in darkness, sits on his desk chair, the chair turned towards him.

'And just where have you been, young man?' inquires the voice of his mum.

Chapter Eleven
Mysterious Nightmares

Vanessa Young was the first to experience the nightmares. Her words 'Those eyes! Those eyes!' echoed a cry from outer space and had reverberated around Whitehall, bringing Mark Hunter and Dodo Dupont to the environs of Linton.

And now the infection seems to be spreading. Rose Gardener and Rachel Ryder, the second and third victims of the mysterious rapist, have reported experiencing similar bad dreams. Identical, in fact. The same pair of eyes: yellow, tapering, unspeakably malignant. Eyes that stand large on some formless entity, like a black flame, or a teardrop; the only features it possesses. All three girls see this same creature in their dreams. The context may differ: sometimes it appears against a cloud of green smoke; sometimes against an alien landscape of barren rocks in an eternal twilight; and sometimes it appears against scenes familiar to the dreamer: a landscape from childhood memory, a familiar street, and, most terrifyingly, in the very room in which she slumbers.

In every scenario the creature faces the dreamer, glaring at her with a palpable, unfathomable, malevolence.

And each of the three girls describes having being left with the same feeling, the feeling of having been in the presence of something totally alien, something completely outside of human experience or comprehension.

But what is this creature? And why should these three girls be the ones to be plagued by it in their dreams? Yes, they have all been attacked by the same man, a strange man like a human automaton, but a man in no way resembling the nightmare entity with the blazing eyes.

'It's like we've all been infected,' says Rose Gardener to Dodo Dupont. 'Can you have such a thing as a sexually-transmitted nightmare?'

'Normally, I would say no,' replies Dodo, 'but then there's nothing normal about this case.'

'You're just sore because she totally shot you down!' crows Sasha Distel, neatly illustrating how we often love to gloat over the misfortunes of our friends.

'And if that didn't bruise your ego enough,' she persists, 'now she's going out with that little drip Murray Leinster!'

Lassiter and his cronies—Sasha, Malcolm and Scarlette, in case you've forgotten—loiter in their usual break-time rendezvous of the school gardens, outside the greenhouse.

'Yes, I'll admit that I'm pissed off about that one,' answers Lassiter, 'But I fully intend to get my revenge; on him as well as her.'

'Don't they say that revenge is the refuge of the weak?' challenges Sasha.

Malcolm removes his pipe from his mouth. 'Lassiter here favours the Oriental attitude to revenge,' he informs Sasha. 'He sees its inherent nobility.'

'Yeah, and so do the Mafia,' retorts Sasha.

'For them revenge is just a matter of policy,' counters Malcolm.

'Look, revenge is just a basic human instinct,' cuts in Lassiter. 'It's about making yourself feel better when you've been wronged, and I freely admit that once I get my revenge on Eve Chandler and Murray fucking Leinster, I will feel a whole lot better. That's what it's all about. No need to dress it up.'

'And how are you gunna go about getting your revenge?' demands Sasha. 'Pornboy was a dead loss. He didn't dig up anything useful about Eve, did he?'

(Pornboy had located the Rotherham secondary school

Eve Chandler had attended and had managed to pull up her personal file. There had been a disappointing lack of information. No extra notes appended by the principal, no juicy stories of sexual delinquency; no juvenile crime record. In short, no lever for Lassiter to use against Eve. Now Pornboy had been in no way to blame for this disappointingly spotless and uninformative school record, but nevertheless he had been duly punished with another arm-twisting from Malcolm and the denial of that promised treasure-trove of online porn.)

'Yeah, that was a wash-out,' admits Lassiter.

'Still, you've made him your spy now,' points out Malcolm. 'He's keeping an eye on Chandler and Lassiter for you.'

'Yes, but I don't expect to get much out of that, either,' responds Lassiter. 'He's a useless little shit, and those two won't say anything worth repeating while he's around them, playing gooseberry.' 'So, what're you going to do?' persists Sasha.

'I don't bloody know, okay?' snaps Lassiter. 'What I'd really like to do is beat the living shit out of Murray Leinster, but I don't wanna land myself in it and get expelled.'

'You could get someone else to work him over,' suggests Malcolm.

'Someone Leinster doesn't know and who can't be traced back to you...' 'Yes, that might be an idea,' agrees Lassiter, thoughtfully.

Sasha suddenly turns to Scarlette. 'And what's wrong with you today?' she demands.

'Whaddaya mean what's wrong with me?' replies Scarlette.

'"Whaddaya mean what's wrong with me?"' parrots Sasha, mimicking the transatlantic accent. 'You're not saying much is what I mean. You've been like this all week. Like you've got something important on your mind. So, what is it? Why don't you let us in on it?'

'Why don't you mind your own god-damn business?' retorts Scarlette.

'What's with the fucking attitude?' flares up Sasha.

'The child is fractious,' observes Malcolm. 'She needs a good raping to calm her down.'

Scarlette bristles. 'Just you try,' she warns him.

'I wouldn't want to sully myself,' is the haughty reply.

'Fuck you.'

'You know, you need to do something about that attitude, Scarlette,' speaks up Lassiter. 'Here's Sasha and Malcolm only showing concern and trying to help you out, and you throw it back in their faces. I don't like it. I do not like it. In fact, I'm dismissing you for the day. Go'n have a wank or get laid or something, and then come back when you've remembered how to keep a civil tongue in your head.'

Scarlette turns and leaves, accepting her dismissal without a word.

This isn't going well, thinks Murray. It has hardly begun but already it isn't going well. His worst fears are being realised; he had worried from the start that it wouldn't go well, this meeting between his mum and his Mysterious Girlfriend.

And it isn't.

The obligatory coffee has been made, and the three of them sit with their mugs on their laps in the Leinster front room. Even the very process of seating themselves had become a source of dissension. Murray had sat down first and he had sat himself in his usual place on the sofa. This had led to an immediate contest between the two women to gain possession of the other space on the sofa and by proximity also gain possession of Murray himself. Eve had won the race, but Murray thinks it might have been better if she'd just let Mum win, because now Mum, sitting in the adjacent armchair, just glares at Eve.

Eve breaks the uncomfortable silence.

'Nice coffee,' she says.

'It's instant,' replies Mum.

Another awkward silence.

Begins Eve: 'Look, Mrs Leinster—'

'It's *Miss* Leinster,' corrects Mum. 'I was married once but I've taken back my family name.'

'Then shouldn't it be *Ms* Leinster?' suggests Eve.

'It might be, but I don't happen to like "Ms",' says Mum. 'It's a bit...'

'Yeah, it is a bit,' smiles Eve. 'Well, what the heck? They're all short for the same word.'

'True,' agrees Mum, also smiling.

Murray starts to relax; the tension seems to be easing.

'Well, Miss Leinster,' resumes Eve. 'Since I feel more like I was ordered rather than invited round here today, do you wanna tell me what it is you want? Cuz, anything you want to know: just ask away. I'm easy.'

'Alright,' says Mum. 'Let me get a few things clear in my head. You've only just moved to Linton? You started school on Monday and that's when you met my boy? And now you consider yourselves an item?'

'Yes to all of those.'

'Okay,' says Mum. 'Fair enough. You seem a nice, intelligent girl, and if I had to choose a girlfriend for Murray, it would probably be someone like you.' (Eve nods her acknowledgement of the compliment.) 'But what's with these furtive trips out at night? Why make my boy climb out through the window and not tell me where he's going?'

Eve looks suitably contrite. 'Well, y'see, I wanted to make it all seem more like an adventure for Murray. Y'know, not just "going out". And I guess also, well, I weren't sure if you'd let him out at night. I mean, seeing as he never used to go out like...'

'Okay, I see what you mean,' allows Mum. 'But I wouldn't have stopped him going out. Much as I love my little boy, I don't want to hold him back. I can't keep him forever...' A sigh. 'But no, I'm glad that he's got himself a girl and a social life. I mean it's always been nice to have him at home with me, but I've never wanted him to grow up into one of those bedroom-dwelling recluses, and I have been worried he might be heading in that direction.'

Better and better! Murray feels a weight lifting from his shoulders. Mum doesn't mind him having a girlfriend! She wants him to get out more!

'It was just a big shock,' continues Mum. 'When I went in his room and found out that he had snuck out of the house, I didn't know what to think. I know you kids like to go out after dark, but, well it's not always safe out there, is it?'

'Yeah, but he's not on his own,' says Eve. 'He's got me looking out for him.'

'Yes, you look strong,' agrees Mum, studying Eve thoughtfully. 'And you obviously know your way around. Just keep him safe, will you?' 'I will,' promises Eve.

Mum brightens up. 'Good! Now just a few more questions. I assume you've already deflowered my boy, so—'

'Uh, no, we haven't actually done that yet,' cuts in Eve. (Strictly speaking, as a euphemism for taking someone's virginity, "deflowering" is really a gender-specific term; but Eve does not take issue with this. Perhaps she just doesn't want to seem pedantic.)

'You haven't?' Mum looks surprised. 'And why not? My boy not good enough for you, or something? Because I can tell you, he may not look like an Adonis, but under—'

'No, it's nothing like that,' Eve quickly assures her. 'Honest; I think he looks great. It's just that we just haven't gone all the way yet.'

'So when will you be doing that?' demands Mum. 'How about this weekend? You could come round for dinner and—'

'Mum!' Murray breaks his silence to voice this protest.

'This weekend's not so good,' says Eve, hesitantly.

'Why not?' Mum's tone is still interrogative. 'Have you made other plans? Got something more important to do than making a man of my little boy?'

'No,' says Eve quickly. 'It's just that it's not the right time of the month…'

Right time of month? Murray is confused. Can you only have sex at certain specific times? Are there laws about that? He's never heard about this before.

Mum, however, does not share her son's befuddlement.

'Oh, I see!' she says. 'Yes, let's wait, then. We don't want his first time to be all messy. Although it'll be messy anyway if you've still got—'

'No, I haven't still got that,' says Eve.

Messy? Still got what? They might as well be talking in Etruscan for all Murray can understand.

'What are we talking about?' he asks. 'What's all this about the time of the month and it being messy and if Eve's still got something or not?' 'Oh, isn't he sweet?' sighs Mum, adoringly.

'He's lovely,' agrees Eve. 'I just wish he'd stayed awake more in biology class.'

The two women laugh, but this time Murray is not so happy. They've developed a rapport alright: they're already having a laugh at his expense!

Chapter Twelve
Don't Feed the Plumber!

Stavro knew the plumber was bad news from the moment he let him into his flat.

The man was giving off signals; bad signals.

As human beings, we are always sending and receiving these nonverbal signals. They are a gift from our ancestors and one that we share with the rest of the animal kingdom. Signals of attraction or repulsion, signals of warning or of promise… But, unlike the rest of the animal kingdom, human beings can often misconstrue these signals. With animals, for whom these signals are in constant use, they are a key form of communication; but us human beings have developed and come to rely on spoken language; what started out as simple noises to express emotions have now evolved into a complicated system of expressing our thoughts and ideas, as well as for deceiving and misleading our enemies. Proud of this system which sets us apart from the brute beasts, we have come to rely on language, and as a result our skills with those primitive, non-verbal, forms of communication have become a bit rusty. We often misread signals, sensing dislike where there is none, attraction where there is none...

Stavro, a man who spends far too much time reflecting upon things of this nature, knows all about this, knows that signals can be misread, especially by a person whose state of mind is less than sound... He knows all this, but he is still certain that the man with the toolbox engaged in repairing the leaking radiator, is very bad news.

Do you remember Stavro? Of course you don't! Let me refresh your memory. He appeared back in Chapter Five, sitting on a bench in Fairview Park with that mentally challenged Peeping-Tom the Wheezer. A bearded, down-at-the-heels middle-aged man with a jaded air about him, is our Stavro. What? That boring minor character, you cry? Did you have to bring him back?

Unfortunately yes; everyone has their part to play in this chronicle.

'Yeah, this won't take long,' the plumber, McKearney by name, is saying. 'Just a washer what's rusted through; needs replacing, that's all. 'Course really you want your whole central heating system replacing. Whole thing's rusting over.'

'Try telling that to the landlord,' invites Stavro.

Stavro stands, awkward, watching over McKearney as he works on the radiator. Had it been any other room in his flat—bedroom, bathroom, kitchen—he would have just left him to it, but the living room is where Stavro passes most of his existence, and he feels like he can't just vacate the place and consign himself to his own kitchen while the plumber is at work. So he looks at the grey stubble on top of the plumber's head as he squats before the radiator, turning a wrench to disconnect the pipe.

He cannot see them right at the moment, but it was the plumber's eyes that had first set the alarm bells ringing; hungry, shifty eyes that seem to betray their owner's true nature. Stavro senses that this man is capable of any evil, and, in spite of a jowly flabbiness, that he is a hard man, as solid and unyielding as a concrete block.

This being the case, Stavro wonders if he should extend the hand of friendship to him.

Stavro makes a point of only choosing for his friends the worst examples of humanity he can find. Acquaintances would be a better word, as he doesn't consider that he has any actual friends. From half-witted voyeurs like the Wheezer, to the drunks, the down-and-outs, the mentally ill, guilt-ridden paedophiles; these are the kind of people Stavro gathers around himself. And not because he has any sympathy for these individuals; he just considers them to be the only fit company for one such as he.

Bitterness and self-loathing are Stavro's guiding stars. A disastrous life has led him to this point, and his condition is aggravated by the fact that things had originally started so well for him. He had emerged through childhood and adolescence an average, well-adjusted adult; he had found himself a job and a wife, and Stavro had felt happy both at work and at home. But then his formerly happy marriage had broken down and not long after the separation, internal office politics had lost him his job. From that point on, things had just carried on downhill. He felt betrayed by both his spouse and his co-workers, and he became increasingly bitter. His inability to recover his career and to form any new relationships had chipped away at his self-esteem. He started drinking. He felt that people now regarded him as a loser and a hopeless case; that they were even wary of him. And so, one day he had decided that if people thought him so bad, then he would be that bad; at least he would hang around with all the worst social outcasts he could find; the people shunned by society, as he felt himself being shunned.

The net result of this shift in lifestyle was only to be expected: in spite of never actually breaking the law or committing any offence, Stavro soon began to earn himself a very bad reputation. The police had their eye on him and he was often to be found 'helping them with their inquiries.' If any sick or sordid crimes were committed locally, Stavro would be sure to be dragged in for questioning. He had been dragged in for questioning just this week, over the assault on Rose Gardener; but as always, he had been released without charge.

Even Stavro's name is a reflection of his jaded personality. Stavro is not the Greek given name people assume it to be; it isn't even his real name. 'Stavro' is short for 'Stavrogin' and he takes the name of Stavrogin from the tortured, occasional child-rapist, anti-hero of Fyodor Dostoevsky's novel *Devils*. (Or *The Demons*, or *The Possessed*, depending on which translation you happen to have.)

So yes, Stavro collects bad people, sad people, rejects. But he really doesn't know if he ought to add McKearney to his collection. A voice inside tells him that this guy is too bad; that he is one to be avoided.

But then, should he even listen to that voice? That voice belongs to another time, another life.

Finally, McKearney finishes repairing the radiator. With a grunt, he hauls himself to his feet, faces Stavro, and Stavro sees those eyes again, those eyes that scream warning signals.

'There you go, all done,' says McKearney, pointedly adding: 'Thirsty work, that.'

'Sorry,' says Stavro. 'I should have offered you a cup of tea.'

'Tea's nice, tea's nice,' agrees McKearney. 'But d'you know what'd be even nicer? A nice cold beer. I could murder one of them right now... You got any beer in the fridge?'

'Yes, I have,' admits Stavro. 'But shouldn't you... I mean while you're working...'

The plumber waves a dismissive hand. 'Oh, don't worry about that. You're my last job this afternoon. I got nothin' on now. Yeah, I could just sit meself down, put me feet up and watch the telly, I could,' glancing round the room at Stavro's armchairs, Stavro's television set. 'How about it?'

The alarm bell eyes fix themselves on Stavro.

'Sure, we can do that,' says Stavro, taking that step deeper into the mire.

'I can't take this much longer!'

'Do you think I like it, girl? Do you think I like having to wait hand and foot on that sadist? That gangster's daughter?'

'It's her vulgar friend that I can't stand! That four-eyed—'

'Oh, I wish you'd shut up about your petty squabble with that Hoshino girl! She's just Morishita's pet, her creature. It's Morishita herself we've got to worry about. She's the one calling all the shots. She's the enemy.'

Our location is the butler's pantry at Linton Hall, and the speakers are Harriet, the young maid we have met before, and Parker the head butler, whom we have not met. Parker, a man in his fifties with grey hair and moustache, is the father of Harriet. They sit in private conference at the table in the pantry.

'Can't we just escape, Pa? I mean just run for it?'

'It isn't worth the risk, I tell you! Those Yakuza thugs patrolling the grounds would shoot us without a second thought! They're trained killers, every one of them!'

'But this is England—'

'You think that matters to them? They've taken over this

place, and so as far as they're concerned this is now their territory. They'll do whatever they please.'

'It's like a nightmare...' Harriet rubs her forehead in frustration.

'I know it is, girl. And who have we got to thank for this? Who invited that girl here?'

'Oh, stop it, father! I didn't know, did I? I didn't know what she was really like!'

Parker sighs. 'Alright. I'm sorry, child. Let's both try and keep calm. We need to keep calm if we want to find a way out of this mess. The main trouble is that man Kondou, Morishita's bodyguard or head of security or whatever he is; he watches us like a hawk. He's always there just when you don't want him to be.'

'Do you think he suspects?'

'Of course he does! He'd be a fool not to suspect us of planning something or at the very least waiting for the opportunity to make a break for it. Yes, he'll be taking that for granted. That's why he's always—'

The parlour door opens and in walks a tall, broad-shouldered Japanese man. He wears an immaculate black suit; dark glasses add to the inscrutability of his square-jawed face. This is Kondou, right on cue.

'Can we help you?' inquires Parker.

'Just doing my rounds,' answers Kondou, making a slow circuit of the room.

'We're just—'

'I know what you're doing,' says Kondou.

Harriet and Parker exchange sickly looks.

'We all have our roles to play here,' says Kondou. 'I advise you both to stick to the script.'

'Until when?' demands Parker.

'Until the last curtain.'

Exit Kondou.

While all this is going on, Misaki and Ren are outside. The

day is warm and clear, and the two girls are sunning themselves on loungers in the gardens of Linton Hall. Misaki wears a very daring bikini, while the less body-confident Ren has settled for baggy shorts and a t-shirt. Between the loungers, on a small table, the ice-cubes quietly melt in two tall glasses.

'Nothing looks cute in this country,' complains Ren.

'They do not share our *moe* culture,' says Misaki. 'They don't even understand it. They think that cute things are just for kids, like they think comics and cartoons are just for kids.'

'I had a look at some English comics,' says Ren. 'They look ugly.'

'And what do you think of the English girls?'

'Okay, I guess,' is the reply. 'They seem more brazen than Japanese girls. But the school uniforms aren't very cute.'

'That's because they don't want schoolgirls to look cute in this country,' Misaki tells her. 'They don't accept your reverence for schoolgirls. That reminds me of something: back home the most popular junior idols are middle-schoolers, twelve- to fifteen-year-olds, right?'

'Sure. Girls look cutest that age.'

'That's what we think in Japan. But there's an interesting parallel in *The 120 Days of Sodom*, a novel by the Marquis de Sade—'

'Your favourite author!'

'Correct. Well, in this story, there are these four libertines who want to build a harem of beautiful girls, so they send out their lackeys to scour the countryside, search out the twelve most beautiful girls they can find and bring them back to their castle. And guess what?'

'What?'

'The twelve most beautiful girls they abduct are all aged between twelve and fifteen!'

'Wow!' says Ren, suitably impressed. 'So Marquis de

Sade invented middle-school girls!'

This mismatched couple have been friends since their first year at high school. Both had been accepted into the same prestigious Tokyo girls' school. Misaki, being the only daughter of a high-ranking Yakuza member (so Eve was wrong about that!), who had known luxury all her young life, and Ren being from a blue-collar household with too many kids and not enough bedrooms, their respective backgrounds couldn't have been more unalike.

The two girls were not in the same class at the school they attended, and if things had been different they might never have met, but Misaki was a girl who always relished entering any new environment and would take a keen interest in the people around her with a view to causing as much mischief amongst them as possible. Now it happened that Ren had been singled out for victimisation by the school's bullies. Her crimes were twofold: she was not only a scholarship student, but was an otaku to boot! Contrary to popular belief, not everyone in Japan watches anime, and its most dedicated fans—the otaku—are a despised race, and there is no-one who despises them more than the trendy schoolgirl set. Yuna Koyama was the alpha-female of this set and had become Ren's chief persecutor.

When Misaki had discovered this situation, she had at first remained in the wings, a mere observer. She was eager to see just how this campaign of bullying would escalate. Would the victim be driven to leave the school? Would she be driven to end her own life? Or would it end, as some previous cases of bullying had, in the murder of the victim herself? Relishing these possibilities, Misaki watched events with eager eyes. But she soon came to realise that the crisis of events she anticipated was not going to occur. Yuna Koyama proved herself to be the most predictable and unimaginative of school bullies. She had the perseverance, the right amount of senseless hatred, but her cruelty was mundane and pedestrian. She clearly lacked the courage to take her bullying to the higher levels. In short, Yuna was a bitter disappointment to Misaki; not nearly entertaining enough. And so Misaki decided it was time to intervene; and transferring her allegiance to the unfortunate victim, she intervened on Ren's behalf.

All it took was a quiet word in Yuna's ear as to which 'family' she belonged and what its representatives, at a word from Misaki, might do to *her* family, and Yuna was annihilated, all her arrogance crushed on the spot. Much to Misaki's delight, the girl literally wet herself! It streamed down her legs and soaked her designer knee socks. And as for Ren Hoshino—well, her response was to develop an immediate and intense infatuation with her saviour. She began to stick to her like a limpet. Misaki had not anticipated this development, and she might have been annoyed into some kind of retaliation, but instead, flattered by this idol-worshipping adoration, she found herself starting to fall in love with Ren. (At least in as far as an individual like Misaki was capable of feeling love towards anyone other than herself.)

And so the Yakuza daughter and the working-class otaku had become friends and lovers, with Misaki the one firmly holding the whip hand.

And Ren, lustful but submissive, wouldn't have had it any other way! Misaki turns over onto her stomach. 'Oil my back, please.'

Eyes lighting up behind her chunky glasses, Ren jumps up from her own recliner and drops to her knees beside Misaki's. She reaches for the bottle of oil. Misaki unties her bikini top. Drooling at the sight—Ren possessing a back fetish, along with just about every other body fetish you can think of—she starts to spread the oil over Misaki's soft skin.

'Any news about Murray Leinster?' inquires Misaki. 'Is he still a virgin?'

'Yep,' confirms Ren. 'They still haven't gone all the way yet.'

'Anything new about her?'

'No. We still can't find anything. Apart from her living on her own, there's nothing unusual.'

'I'm sure there *is* something unusual,' responds Misaki. 'It's just buried too deeply, whatever it is. And what about the serial rapist affair? No new incident?'

'No, he's been quiet the past couple of days,' says Ren. 'There is something, though. You know that artist's sketch they've released of the guy?'

'Yes.'

'Well, I used a software comparison programme to run a check on it. See whatever faces it could dig up that looked like this one.'

'And? I should imagine there were quite a lot of matches.'

'Yeah, there were. But one of them was *ve-ry* interesting.'

'In what way? You think this person could be the culprit?'

'Well, that's just it. This guy just *couldn't* be the culprit; it's not possible. But there's a connection, a connection with Linton.'

'He was born here?'

'No, not born here. But there is a definite family connection.'

Misaki turns her head so that she can look back at her friend. 'Okay, Ren you've tantalised me enough. I'm interested. Tell me who this man is…'

Chapter Thirteen
Saturday Night's Alright for Fighting!

'I think we're being followed.'
 The speaker is Eve Chandler and the person spoken to, Murray Leinster. It's Saturday night and the two are walking into town, and this time with the excursion officially countenanced by Murray's mum. ('Don't let him smoke any of your filthy cigarettes or take any drugs, and if he comes home blind drunk, I'll slap you.') They are going into town to check out the nightlife, so it will be something of a wildlife expedition.
 Murray looks back down the lamp-lit street.
 'I can't see anyone,' he says.
 'That's because they don't want to be seen,' replies Eve.
 'How long have they been following us?'
 'Pretty much since we set out. At least, if there *is* anyone following us.'
 'But how did you first know about it? I never saw or heard anything.'
 'That's because you didn't look back. Most people don't look behind them when they're walking along, but I do.'
 'Is that part of your spy training?'
 'Yeah, kind of,' says Eve. 'Tell you what; let's see if I'm right or not. See that turning on the left coming up? We'll turn down there. As soon as we're round that corner we'll be out of sight of anyone tailing us. Then we start running.'
 'Okay,' says Murray.
 Round the corner and they break into a run. Another corner, a gravel access road, offers itself ahead. They duck into this and then stop, flattening themselves against the wall.
 At first nothing happens. The street is residential, quiet. Then they hear footsteps. Someone approaching. Just one

person.

A figure appears. Eve steps out from the shadows. 'Can we help you?'

The man literally jumps.

'What the bloody—'

'It's you!'

The newcomer, his features picked out by the streetlight, is Carson. Eve recognises him from that other night in Fairview Park.

Murray recognises him too. And when Carson sees the boy standing there, his thin face assumes a look of something like horror.

'Why are you following us?' demands Eve.

Carson drags his eyes away from Murray.

'I wasn't bloody following you!'

'Yeah, sure you weren't,' retorts Eve. 'Who are you and how do you know Murray?'

'Who says I know him?'

'Your face does.'

'He just reminded me of someone is all. But I was wrong; it's not him.'

Eve turns to Murray and receives a shock. His face looks more horror-stricken than even Carson's. He literally trembles.

'Murray!' She grabs his shoulders. 'Are you alright? What's up?' 'I'm out of here,' announces Carson.

He departs hurriedly.

'Hey!' calls out Eve.

She hasn't finished with Carson, but she can't leave Murray like this.

'What's up, love?' she asks, turning back to him. 'It's that feller, isn't it? Have you remembered him now?'

Murray's eyes focus on Eve's concerned face. 'No, I... I don't remember, not properly... But his voice... When I heard it, it was like I knew it from somewhere... I started feeling really scared, but I don't know why...'

Eve squeezes his shoulders. 'You must know him from somewhere. Can't you remember when it was?'

'No...'

'Must have been a long time ago,' surmises Eve. 'Something bad happened, maybe, when you met that guy. Something you don't want to remember...'

She embraces Murray, soothes away his anxiety.

While her vicar father sits downstairs in his study fine-tuning tomorrow morning's sermon, Sasha Distel reclines on her bed, laptop open for business, talking dirty on Facebook; one of her favourite recreations

It makes her laugh when she hears those stories on the news about all those paedos using social media for grooming, and that sixty percent of teenage girls with Facebook accounts have been sexually harassed online.

Well, duh. If you spread yourself around on social media, accept friend requests from complete strangers from all over the fucking world, of course you're gunna pick up some perverts! Lots of them! That other forty percent of teenage girls in those surveys are probably just the ones who don't call it harassment cuz they're into all that stuff!

And those men, they all have to send you their dick-pics on Messenger! And that's cuz the losers are all so in love with their dicks, and they can't wait to show 'em off! They think that just one look at their hard-on and you'll be all over them.

Sasha likes to talk dirty with the older guys most of all cuz the bigger the age difference, the better, cuz then the more wrong it seems. Whether they're South American guys, Middle-Eastern guys, East Asian guys, or local pervs from the next town over, there are always plenty of guys who like them young and fresh. (Especially if their wives are starting to look a bit rough!) Sure they're all perverts, but they know when girls look their best. (That's just what she told that Dodo Dupont woman at school. She's not getting any younger!)

And the grown-ups think we're too stupid to know that it's wrong and that those guys are dangerous. So fucking what? Wrong is the new Right in Sasha's personal bible, and as for them being dangerous, well any bloke can be dangerous; he doesn't have to be middle-aged. Just look at Lassiter and Malcolm, her best friends at school. Those two are about as dangerous as it gets. Most internet pervs will be walkovers compared to those two psychos!

But this is what Sasha likes. Internet pervs are not 'nice' people; Lassiter and Malcolm are not 'nice' people. Good! Sasha doesn't go for 'nice' people; 'nice' people are twats who just get taken for a ride. Case in point: Sasha's dear Daddy is a 'nice' person and for this crime she despises him. Being 'nice' means he actually believes all that Jesus crap he spouts in church every Sunday; being 'nice' means he has no idea that Mum is fucking the married guy from next door; being 'nice' means he is completely taken in by his daughter Sasha's pretence of being a good little girl. Sasha can never forgive him for these offences.

Right now Sasha is 'chatting' with one of her local admirers. He's a bald, fat forty-seven-year-old horn-dog, but he's married and Sasha likes the idea of seducing a man into cheating on his past-it wife, even if it is only an online seduction and the guy doesn't actually require much seducing. Right now they're sketching out a sex-scene in pornographic detail. Sasha doesn't get off fantasising about the sex they're describing; she just gets off thinking about the guy at the other end, picturing him typing one-handed as he pulls on the fat cock he can hardly see cuz his hairy beer gut's in the way. And she's the one making him do this, the sad old fart! It's a real power-trip.

Come on, you old fart. Let's hear that you've spunked all over your own hairy gut.

Right now she is interrupted by a message window popping up: It's from Scarlette.

What does that moody cow want?

She opens the message:

Hey! Sorry for being a bitch at school. It was just one of those days, I guess. Wanna come over to my place tonight? We can steal some of my mom's liquor and watch a movie! If you're cool, you can head over right now!

Having read the message, Sasha weighs up the pros and cons. Should she accept the invitation? Or should she punish Scarlette by not even deigning to reply? That girl's attitude problem is still annoying her…

Deciding that the booze sounds good, she magnanimously elects to accept the offer.

'No, I'm never gunna have any babies,' pronounces Eve Chandler. The subject of offspring has been prompted by the squalling of an infant issuing from an open window they've just passed.

'Is that cuz you don't like babies?'

'Well, I'm not mad about 'em, but it's more than just that. Do you know how seriously overpopulated the world is? I just don't want to add to that, y'know.'

'Is the world overpopulated?'

'Course it is, love! Didn't they tell you that in Humanities? There's like zillions more people on the planet right now than there's really room for. Over the last hundred years or so the number of people's gone up from being two billion to over seven billion. That means it's more than tripled.'

'Why's that? I'd've thought the number of people would always stay the same.'

'Doesn't work like that. The world's population has always been getting bigger, but it's only recently that it's like shot up so much that it's getting out of hand.'

'Why's that?'

'It's basically cuz less babies are dying and more people are living much longer than they used to. And this is cuz we've got better medicine than we used to have. We've got cures for lots of diseases that they didn't used to have cures for, and we've got better living conditions, cuz it's bad living conditions that used to help diseases spread. So yeah, basically we're healthier than we used to be so we live longer.'

'And why's that bad then?'

'Well, like I said: it means there's more people than there's really room for on the planet. It means you get overcrowding; it means there aren't enough houses for everyone, so you get more and more countryside being covered up with new houses and new towns. In a lot of places there's not enough food for all the people. So basically you've got the environment being destroyed, all those fossil fuels being used up, and it's only going to get worse unless the population starts getting smaller.'

'And how do you make that happen?'

'By having less babies, of course!'

'Did people used to have less babies in the past?'

'No. If anything I reckon they used to have more. But there was higher infant mortality, which means that more babies died. Like I said, they didn't have the medicine to save them. And then people would be killed off in the thousands by wars, epidemics and natural disasters. These days we still have wars and natural disasters but we've learned how to cure a lot of the diseases and to stop them spreading in the first place. Some people say we're going against nature and that if we didn't interfere, nature would keep the population from getting too big. But it's a bit mean to want people to drop dead from epidemics and earthquakes, so the only other answer is, people should have less babies.'

'Then why don't people just do that?'

'Ah, well, that's easier said than done, love. It's cuz we've all got reproductive urge built into us, and it's really strong cuz nature wants us to keep having babies. Reproductive urge is basically the sex urge. A lot of people like sex without the babies, an' that's why we've got birth control and whatnot, but it's all part of the same instinct. With women it's a bit different though, cuz women can have this maternal instinct, and want to have kids and bring them up, which is kind of separate from just the sex urge. Men don't get anything like that. They only like doing the thing that makes women pregnant, after that they're not interested. They'd rather go off and leave it to the woman to bring up the sprogs.'

'But there are lots of dads who stay there to bring up their kids! I know mine didn't, but—'

'Yeah, they're there, those dads, but they don't need to be there. All that talk about kids needing a father or a father figure is just crap. You only need a mother to bring up her kids right. That's how it is with animals, and that's how it should be with us.'

'Then why do we always have families with dads as well as mums?'

'Well, that's partly to do with religion and partly to do with men wanting to control everything. But really they should just keep out of the way. Kids will grow up right without any help from them. As long as the woman's a good mother, anyway; not all of 'em are.'

'Is my mum a good mother?'

'Yeah, I guess she is. She's maybe mollycoddled you too much, but yeah, she knows what's what. And she stopped with just one kid, an' all! More women should do that. There's too many couples who just keep on having kids, like they do it on automatic pilot. They don't think about how they're adding to the overpopulation problem. Mind you, there are lots of places in the world where women still don't have much to do *besides* starting families... So there you go! That's why I'm not gunna have any kids and why lots more people shouldn't have any, either. You got all that?'

Murray's face is a picture.

'Oh, I'm sorry, love! That was like total information-

overload for you, wasn't it? I shouldn't give you so much to process in one go... One thing I will tell you, though...'
'What's that?'
'I think we're still being followed.'

Sasha still doesn't know what she's going to do with her life. Academically, she excels, but she has no career goals. She guesses that after she's breezed through her GCSEs she'll follow the usual Sixth Form and then University route. And at uni she'll have the usual gap year and see a bit of the world. Yeah, that sounds best. It puts off the pain of looking for a job for another six years after you've finished school, and there'll be plenty of opportunities for getting laid and getting high. But after all that... Finding herself a sugar daddy, some rich older man to live off... Yeah, that would be nice...

But, dreams of luxury and indolence aside, Sasha doesn't really know what she's going to do with her life.

Fortunately, this lack of forward planning is not going to affect Sasha's future. As she is not going to survive this evening, she has no future.

Clipping the lights onto her bicycle, she wheels the machine down the gravelled vicarage drive. The vicarage is adjacent to the church, and the church in question happens to be the very one in whose precincts Rose Gardener was raped earlier this week.

Poor old Daddy, thinks Sasha, as she cycles past the house of worship. He was really cut up about that rape happening in his own churchyard; what with it being consecrated ground and all. He probably went out armed with a flask of holy water to cleanse the crime scene, the site of the desecration!

Funny it should have been that dyke Rose Gardener who got herself raped. Maybe she'll stop being such a smart-mouthed bitch now.

The route from Sasha's house to Scarlette's takes her through quiet, residential streets. Both girls have followed the same journey countless times, when calling on each other.

Good thing about hanging out round Scarlette's is that there's always going to be a supply of booze. Scarlette's mum, a woman in her fifties, is a complete alcoholic. She sits around the house all day in her dressing gown and wearing heavy make-up, boozing and smoking like some washed-up Hollywood queen. Scarlette always helps herself to her mum's supply when she's entertaining friends, and her mum is either too drunk to notice the deficit, or else she just doesn't care.

Sasha has decided she'll forgive Scarlette for her arsiness in school yesterday. It'll be fun to just kick back and watch a film together; just the two of them, no Lassiter or Malcolm. What film will they watch tonight? A comedy would be best. Sasha likes the films that make her laugh. They take you out of yourself.

She remembers a previous time around Scarlette's, another occasion when it had just been the two of them in her room with a bottle to share. They were watching that old film *The Naked Gun*. There was that scene at the press conference where Leslie Nielsen goes to the bog to have a huge pee, and he's forgotten to take off the microphone clipped to his jacket. Everyone in the press conference could hear him having this massive piss! Sasha had laughed so much it'd made her ribs ache!

This might just be Sasha's happiest memory. And why not? A happy memory doesn't have to be some major event, some cosy family moment, a childhood holiday... Just having a good time with a friend and laughing at a funny film...

And then, out of nowhere, something slams into Sasha's side, hurling her from her bicycle and sending her rolling across the road. The initial shock turns quickly to anger and Sasha, bruised and grazed, springs to her feet, straightening her glasses, eyes searching for her antagonist.

Where is he? One of those drunken pricks who thinks it's funny to knock a passing cyclist off her bike! Bastard!

And then she sees the man, just standing there at the edge of the road. She sees the expressionless face whose pencilled likeness has appeared in all the newspapers, and she realises it isn't just some drunken prick; it's something much much worse.

Pint in hand, Carson weaves his way through the tables of the crowded pub. This establishment, Dirty Dick's, is the meeting place for Linton's criminal fraternity and is located in a back street right in the centre of town. The saloon is a great square room, dimly lit, filled with tables and chairs. An aisle runs from the entrance doors at one end of the room to the bar counter at the other.

The pub, appropriately enough considering the fact that it's a den of thieves, is named after the infamous highwayman Dick Turpin. According to local legend, Turpin passed through Linton during his famous (and entirely fictitious) overnight ride from London to York, a fact which is all the more gratifying for the prestige of Linton when you consider that the highwayman had to have ridden considerably out of his way in order to do this.

Carson has work to do tonight, but that encounter with Murray Leinster keeps intruding into his mind. Why now? Why does he have to see him now, after all this time…? First it was him in Fairview Park. He wasn't sure if it was Murray, but there was enough of a resemblance to startle him. And now, tonight, he has run into him again and that girl with him has confirmed Murray's identity.

And who is that girl, anyway? Murray's girlfriend? Nah. A tough girl like her wouldn't date a wuss like him… But then again, maybe she would…

His pal Drubble sits at their usual corner table. Carson pulls out a chair and sits down. Plonking down his pint he nods to Drubble's glass. 'Is that your first pint?'

'Yeah.'
'Make it your last. We got a job on.'
'When.'
'Tonight.'
'That's a bit short notice!'
Carson shrugs. 'Only got the word from Piggy this afternoon. It's an easy job. Everything arranged. Piggy says even we can't mess this one up.'
Drubble smiles at this. 'Knows we won't mess it up. Looks like he's startin' to have some faith in us!'
Carson looks at his friend. 'No, Drubble. It means he thinks we're a couple of fucking idiots who can only handle the easy jobs.'
Drubble frowns. 'Why's that?'
'In your case, it's because you *are* a fucking idiot,' growls Carson. 'And just by being with you, they think I'm one an' all.'
'Yeah, but—'
'Look, let's not get into an argument about that,' says Carson. 'This is the job, so just shut up and listen: It's a warehouse in Kenton Lane. Pharmaceutical place. We're gunna pick up a consignment of drugs.'
'What, like Es or somethin'?'
'No, you pillock. This is a prescription drug. It's called Serotonin Plus; it's an antidepressant, but a really strong one; y'know, for them that's *really* down in the dumps. But for people who ain't depressed, if you swallow a load of 'em at once, you can get a real buzz from 'em.'
'No!' scoffs Drubble. 'You can't get high from a chemist's drug!'
'Shows how much you don't know,' retorts Carson. 'Haven't you heard all that stuff in the news about that painkiller drug, Fenta… Fentasomethin'-or-other. It's got opium in it and it packs more of a wallop than an armful of heroin.' Shooting up makes Carson think of Drubble's sister, so he quickly moves on. 'Anyway, never mind what the

stuff's for; we've just to pick it up and shift it to Piggy's depot.'

From his pocket Carson produces a single key, fresh from the locksmith's. 'This 'ere's a duplicate key to the van in the warehouse. Keep hold of it.'

Drubble takes the key. 'So we're nicking their van?'

'Yeah, their keys for the van will be locked up somewhere, so they'll think we must have hot-wired it. We don't want 'em to know it was an inside job, see?'

Drubble looks confused. 'But it's not an inside job if we're doing it.'

'Pillock. We've got inside help. There'll be a window left open for us to get in and inside there'll be just one security guard. He's the inside man, but he doesn't want to be fingered so we've got to make it look good; we'll give him a couple of lumps and tie him up. I got the rope here.' He taps his jacket. 'Once we've done that, all we have to do is load the boxes into the van and away we go. Simple, see?'

'Should be a doddle,' agrees Drubble. 'When are we going?'

'Soon as we've finished our pints...'

'Busted!'

Eve Chandler points. Murray Leinster looks. He sees Mark Hunter, the Spy in the Brown Suit from school, in conversation with a skinny blonde girl in fishnets (who is in fact none other than Liz Drubble.)

'"Spy from London, supposedly on assignment in Linton, caught in the act of soliciting prostitutes!"' announces Eve, with audible quotation marks.

Eve and Murray come to a halt before Mark and Liz.

'I am not soliciting,' Mark informs Eve. 'And I would be very grateful if you didn't go shouting out my job description to the entire street. We are meant to be secret agents, you know.'

'You're a spy then? Not a cop?' asks Liz, vaguely

interested.

'Not exactly James Bond, though,' remarks impudent Eve. 'You never catch *him* paying for it.'

Mark pointedly holds out a copy of the now familiar artist's sketch of the serial rapist. 'I was just asking this young lady whether she or any of her colleagues had seen this man.' 'Ha!' says Eve triumphantly.

'Now what?' inquires Mark.

'So, you *are* here about the rapist. It's not just the death of that fortune teller you're here about.'

'I never said it was just that.'

'So the two things are connected then?' eagerly.

'I never said that, either,' smoothly.

Eve turns to Liz. 'And have you seen that feller? You had him as a client?'

'Excuse me—' begins Mark.

'No, I ain't seen him,' answers Liz readily. 'Like I told him,' nodding at Mark; 'none of us girls have seen 'im. An' if we did catch the bastard we'd mess up his face for 'im. We don't like his sort.'

'Do you mind leaving the questioning to me?' says Mark to Eve.

'Knock yourself out.'

Eve and Murray proceed into the town centre. They are surprised to see that Waterstone's, Linton's last remaining bookshop, is lit up and apparently still open for business. A large queue of people are lined up outside the shop.

'What's going on?' wonders Murray.

'Dunno,' says Eve. 'Maybe a writer giving a talk or summat. Let's have a nosey.'

They approach the bookshop.

'Hello, Murray Leinster, Eve Chandler,' a voice greets them.

Amongst the queue are Misaki and Ren, the two Japanese girls they had met on the viewing platform of the tower.

Eve and Murray join them.

'What's going on?' asks Eve.

'A signing session,' replies Misaki. 'A countrywoman of ours, Mayumi Takahashi.'

'Is she a Japanese author, then?'

'No, she's a photographer,' says Misaki.

'Oh yeah? what kind?' Ren sniggers salaciously.

'Oh, that kind,' says Eve.

'Yes, she photographs females,' says Misaki. 'Nude or semi-nude. Her latest book has caused a degree of controversy in the art world.'

'Oh yeah? What's in it, then?'

'We can show you,' says Misaki. 'Ren is a big fan of Takahashi-san. She already owns the book and has brought her copy for signing. Show them, Ren.'

'Sure.'

Ren holds out a very large, slim, hardback volume. Eve takes the book and examines the cover in the light of the display window behind them. Murray looks as well. The title of the book is *Multitask Lady*. The dust-jacket photograph shows a Japanese woman seated on a toilet, knickers round ankles, typing on a laptop.

'The cover is not actually representative of the book's content,' Misaki informs them. 'I suggest you look inside to fully appreciate the theme.'

Ren sniggers her approval of this advice.

Eve opens the book. A singular sight greets her eyes. As she leaves through the pages she laughs, both with surprise and delight, while Murray's eyes bulge with something approaching total disbelief. The 'multitasking' referred to in the title involves Japanese women casually defecating while performing other tasks. A school-teacher leaning over her desk; a grieving mother kneeling in prayer at the altar of her deceased child; a female CEO holding forth at the boardroom table; a woman in traditional dress engaged in flower-arranging; a policewoman on her haunches comforting a crying boy; a waitress in maid café, taking down an order; a schoolgirl hunkered down to stroke a neighbourhood cat... Women at work, at play, all looking very natural in their poses except that in each case the buttocks are bare and the turtle's head is peeping out!

'This is great!' is Eve's verdict. She returns the book to its owner. 'Totally outrageous but great! Not surprised it's controversial.'

'This is European edition,' Ren tells her. 'Japanese edition is censored.'

'Censored?' echoes Eve. 'What, have they covered up the turtle's heads?'

'No,' says Ren. 'Japanese censor only censor pussy, not shit.'

'Get away!'

'This is so.'

'So, your censors reckon a woman's fanny is more obscene than her bum-hole and her poop?'

'This is so.'

'That's...' Eve pauses, ponders. '...I was gunna say that was daft, looking at it that way; but maybe it does make a kind of make sense...' 'We have no taboos about excrement in Japan,' says Misaki.

'What you think of book, Murray Leinster?' Ren challenges Murray.

Murray turns red. 'Well, it's a bit rude...'

'You like it,' declares Ren, informing Murray of his preferences. 'You wanna watch your girlfriend shit.' She chuckles.

'Yeah, and you'd probably want to watch him watching,' counters Eve. 'Well, if ever I did decide to go "Multitask Lady", you wouldn't be getting an invite.'

Ren looks suitably crestfallen.

A woman of striking appearance, tall, with short hair, walks past them and into the shop.

'Dodo Dupont!' exclaims Murray.

'Wonder what she's doing here?' says Eve.

'There is no surprise about that,' answers Misaki. 'Dodo Dupont is Mayumi Takahashi's lover.'

'Oh, right!' says Eve. 'I mean I knew she'd done some nudie photobooks; so was the photographer your Mayumi... whatshername...?'

'Takahashi,' supplies Misaki. 'Yes, she is the photographer and also her lover.'

'She was in our school this week; Dodo, I mean.'

'So I heard,' says Misaki. 'Giving talks with reference to the attacks on some of your classmates. Speaking of which, have you heard the latest rumour?'

'Don't think so,' replies Eve. 'What rumour?'

'Well, it appears that the serial rapist bears a striking resemblance to an American astronaut named Frank Hanson.'

'An astronaut?' echoes Eve with disbelief. 'What would an astronaut be doing raping schoolgirls in England?'

'His identity is not confirmed, but the resemblance is very strong,' says Misaki. 'And it could perhaps explain the overalls the rapist is described as wearing; they could be an astronaut's flight suit.'

'Yeah...' says Eve, ruminating. 'Our mate Rose is one of the girls he's raped, and she said she thought there was some sort of military insignia on the overalls... An astronaut...'

'However,' resumes Misaki, 'in spite of these factors it would appear to be impossible for Frank Hanson to be the assailant.'

'Why? Is he up in orbit?'

'Much further than that. He is attached to the mining programme in the asteroid belt. And the asteroid belt is over 200 million miles from Earth.'

The light grows stronger as Carson and Drubble make their way through the towering stacks of boxes towards the illuminated front part of the warehouse.

'Where's that bloody security guard?' mutters Carson. 'He's supposed to be expecting us; he shouldn't be hiding himself.' 'Maybe he's asleep on the job,' suggests Drubble.

Carson grunts. 'The amount of noise you made gettin' in through that window was enough to wake up fifty security guards.'

(Apparently the waking up of fifty security guards is more of a challenge than to disturb the sleep of just one.)

They arrive at the loading area at the front of the warehouse. A van is parked before the shutter door. One stack of boxes stands conspicuously clear of the others, close to the van's rear doors.

'Here we are,' says Carson. 'There's the van, there's the stuff. Just like it should be. But where's that bloody guard? Maybe he is asleep or he's pretending to be.'

'Why would he do that?' asks Drubble.

'Maybe he's chickened out cuz he thinks we'll hit him too hard or somethin',' answers Carson. 'But saying he was asleep when the place was robbed is gunna be a piss-poor alibi for him.' He shrugs. 'Well, that's his lookout. Let's start loading the boxes into the van.'

One box is unsealed. Carson opens the flaps; inside are neat rows of plastic containers. He takes out one of the tubs (they are unlabelled)) and shakes it.

'Pills. Yeah, this is the right stuff. Come on.'

They start loading the boxes into the back of the van.

They have almost finished loading when they hear the sound of approaching footsteps. A uniformed security guard, substantial and stolid, appears. He stares at the two crooks.

'Well, you took your bleedin' time,' sighs Carson, advancing to meet him. 'Now look, we'll be as easy on you as we can; but we got to make this look good if you don't wanna be a suspect, right? So I'll just—'

The guard's fist smashes into Carson's face, sending him staggering.

Carson, bleeding and disbelieving, stares at his assailant.

'What the 'ell did you do that for?' he demands. '*I* don't need to look injured, you twat!'

Fists raised, the guard advances towards him.

'Oh, *I* get it! You wanna pay me back in advance, do you?' deduces Carson. 'Well, alright then, the gloves is off. We *won't* go easy on you! Let's get 'im, Drubble!'

The two crooks fall on the guard. The man resists with all his might, but the odds are against him. Carson and Drubble pummel him soundly, then bind and gag him.

Carson pauses to catch his breath, looking down at the trussed guard. 'What a twat,' he says. 'Well, leastways no one's gunna suspect him of being in on the job. Not after that working over.'

'Maybe he wanted to provoke us just so's we wouldn't go easy,' suggests Drubble.

'Well, that's his lookout. I hope he thinks his cut is worth that pounding we've just given him,' says Carson. 'Come on, let's finish up and get out of here.'

The remaining cartons are loaded into the van.

Carson slams the doors with satisfaction. 'Right. You start her up, I'll open the doors.'

Drubble climbs into the driver's seat of the van. He reaches into a pocket. He frowns. His fingers have clearly not found what they were searching for. He tries all his other pockets, jeans and jacket. None of them bear fruit.

'I can't find the key!' he calls out.

Carson, halfway to the door controls, spins on his heel.

'What?' he demands.

'I can't find the key!' repeats Drubble helplessly.

'You fuckin—' begins Carson. 'I give you one lousy key to look after...! You must've dropped it when you fell in through that window. Oh, Christ. We'll have to go back and—'

'No, it's alright! It's alright!' cuts in Drubble, elated. 'The key's here! They've left it in the ignition!'

'Well, thank Christ for that,' sighs Carson, relieved. And

then, 'Bit sloppy of 'em. And after our lot going to the trouble of making a duplicate. Lucky for us, though. Start 'er up, then; I'll get the doors.'

First they hear sirens, lots of them. And then the word, first just a murmur, strengthens like a mistral across a summer plain. It spreads from mouth to mouth around the town centre—Another girl has been raped! Some say there has been murder done this time. The rumours say the crime has occurred over near Fairview Park.

The rumours reach the ears of Eve and Murray. 'Let's check this out,' says Eve. 'Come on.'

They set off across the town square, quick-pace.

Murray spots someone he knows up ahead. It's Spacey! Walking along arm-in-arm with some older boy. (Spacey, Murray's acid-head classmate, hasn't appeared in this history since Chapter One: a lamentably neglected secondary character.)

'Hello, Spacey,' Murray greets him, feeling rather proud to be seen out on the town at night in the company of his Mysterious Girlfriend.

'Hey there, Murray,' returns Spacey. His smile becomes a look of puzzlement. 'No, wait. No, it can't be... Sorry, dude; mistook you for a pal of mine, Murray Leinster. A great guy, Murray, but kinda square, y'know? Doesn't go out at nights...'

'No, Spacey. It is me. It's Murray,' Murray assures him.

Spacey chuckles. '...Yeah, you sure do look like him... Had me there for a second, you did... Catch you later, man!'

And he passes on, without having either introduced his companion or appearing to have registered Eve's presence.

'Why didn't he know it was me?' wonders Murray, somewhat aggrieved.

'Well, he was tripping, wasn't he?' replies Eve. 'They get like that.' 'Yeah, but he's often tripping when he's at school,' argues Murray. 'He knows who I am then.'

'Yeah, but at school he expects to see you,' says Eve. 'Right here and now you were out of context, and I guess his fuzzy brain couldn't process it… I wonder who that lad was who was with him?'

'Just one of his friends,' says Murray. 'He hangs around with older kids outside of school.'

'They kind of looked like they might've been more than just friends,' opines Eve. 'Anyway, let's get a shift on.'

They leave the town centre heading north, taking the most direct route to Fairview Park. They turn into deserted Factory Street. A man appears on the pavement ahead of them; a young man dressed in a pinstripe suit and a bowler hat. He raises his hat to Eve and Murray. Other young men, identically dressed, emerge from the shadows, forming a rough semi-circle behind their leader.

'Oh crap,' says Eve, stopping in her tracks.

'What is it?' asks Murray, alarmed.

'A local gang,' replies Eve. 'They call themselves the Gentlemen.'

The first Gentleman, followed respectfully by his five minions, swaggers forward, stopping a few paces from Eve and Murray. An ironic smile on his lips, the Gentleman's eyes, sardonically assessing, range first over Eve and then settle on Murray.

'Well, young man,' says the Gentleman. 'And what have you got to say for yourself?'

Eve steps forward.

'Are you the ones who've been following us all night?' she demands.

The Gentleman sighs. 'A lady should always know her place,' he says, not even bothering to look directly at Eve. 'She adorns the drawing room and she speaks when she is spoken to.'

'Look, we're in a hurry, so—'

'I was speaking to the young man,' cuts in the Gentleman. He looks at Murray. 'You appear to be hiding behind a woman's skirts, old fellow. This is very bad form. Very bad.'

'Leave him alone,' says Eve, belligerent.

'Step forward like a man,' says the Gentleman to Murray. 'Can't you see that your very manhood is in peril here? Your dignity, your honour, your standing in society… This is a test, old chap; a test to determine your worthiness to be called an English Gentleman. You must show yourself fit to protect this lady, my man. You must fight, not for her honour, but your own. Because if you cannot successfully defend the lady, then the lady will be assiduously raped right before your eyes by myself and my esteemed colleagues. The humiliation you will thus endure will be your condign punishment, as you will have proven yourself to be unworthy to call yourself a gentleman.

'Now step forward.'

Murray quakes in his casual footwear. He feels dizzy. His bladder has betrayed him… The Gentleman's words have struck him like a hail of arrows. A voice inside him tells him that this man is right; at least in so far as it being his duty as a man to protect his Mysterious Girlfriend. And this is something new for poor Murray. Murray has always previously considered it other people's business to protect *him*. His Mum; teachers at school; now Eve… He has always looked to women for protection.

But…

These words, these taunts, have awoken a new feeling in Murray Leinster; a feeling that maybe it is his job to protect his Mysterious Girlfriend. He doesn't know how he is going to manage this: his opponents are six in number and all of them much bigger and stronger than himself… He doesn't know how, but that voice is telling him he has to try.

And so, and in spite of feeling literally sick with trepidation, he steps forward in front of Eve and faces his antagonists.

'Very good, very good,' says the Gentleman, in a tone of ironic admiration. 'You at least know your duty as a man.

Well, sir, prepare to do battle. If you can successfully fight off myself and my esteemed colleagues—we shall attack simultaneously, it goes without saying—you will have indeed proven yourself worthy to call yourself an English Gentleman.'

'Six against one's not very fair, is it?' remarks Eve.

'A true gentleman is never deterred by overwhelming odds.'

Eve steps in front of Murray. 'Tell you what, I'll take you on instead.'

'Out of the question. A Gentleman cannot fight a Lady. It is beneath his dignity.'

'Yeah, but I didn't say I was giving you a choice, did I?' And Eve launches herself at her opponents.

Murray can only stand and watch, dumbfounded. It's not that he is surprised at all to discover that Eve is so proficient in the art of unarmed combat; it's entirely in character; and in this enlightened age kick-ass heroines are ten-a-penny on film and TV. But what *does* surprise him, witnessing this real-life, un-choreographed fight scene, is the sheer unrelenting ferocity of Eve's attack. She moves like a whirlwind, striking again and again. But with so many opponents to neutralise, she has to strike fast and hard; to give a fraction of an inch could be to shift the balance in the enemy's favour. And she doesn't give them that chance; she kicks and punches until all six of the Gentlemen are down for the count, bodies battered, senses reeling.

'Come on!'

Eve grabs Murray's hand and they race down the street, stopping only when they are a safe distance from the scene of the combat.

'Phew!' gasps Eve, catching her breath. 'Wish I hadn't had to do that during me period!'

Murray looks at her; she is flushed, breathing hard. Her eyes, once again sparkling with good nature, meet his.

'What's up, love?'

'I...'

A sympathetic smile. 'You still a bit shook-up, eh? C'mere!' She steps forward to embrace him.

'Don't!' cries Murray, stepping back.

An injured look appears on Eve's face. 'What wrong, love?'

'I don't want you to touch me,' says Murray wretchedly. 'I'm... I'm wet...'

Eve is momentarily confused but then sees the darkened crotch of his jeans.

'Is that all?' she says, her smile back in place. 'Y'think I'm bothered about that?'

She grabs him and hugs him. Murray starts to cry, and Eve comforts him with those soothing words and sounds that flow naturally from a woman. This is Murray's second hug from Eve tonight; he wishes it could last forever; that he could just remain like this, feeling Eve's powerful body against his, his nerves relaxing under the spell of those soothing words and sounds, breathing in the comforting smell of her sweat...

Eve loosens her embrace so that she can look Murray in the face.

'Thank you,' she says.

'Me?' says Murray. 'I didn't do anything. You—'

'You stepped in front of me cuz you wanted to protect me,' says Eve. She halts Murray's verbal protest with a finger to his lips. 'That just makes me feel so fucking grateful, Murray. I don't think anyone's ever made me feel like that before...'

A long, lingering kiss, and the embrace is raised to a level of equality.

They have no trouble locating the crime scene; a road close to Fairview Park, ablaze with flashing lights and cordoned off with tape and hurdles.

'Get away from there!' snarls a policeman as they

approach the barrier.

'Oh, it's you two.' A figure steps forward from the confusion of light: Mark Hunter.

'So is it another attack? That guy again?' asks Eve. 'That's what the rumours are saying.'

'Yes, we're pretty sure it's him.'

'And is it another lass from our school?'

'That we don't know. We've yet to formally identify the victim.'

'Identify? Can't you just ask her? Or is she injured?'

'Worse; I'm afraid she's dead. Strangled. Our serial rapist has become a murderer.'

Chapter Fourteen
Diarrhoea

As is always the case with these things, no-one (except us) knew where the story originated, but once it got out, it spread rapidly like wildfire, although without involving the disastrous effects on the environment occasioned by an actual forest conflagration; the Linton serial rapist is actually astronaut Frank Hanson! The descriptions from the victims, the artist's impression drawn from these, even the clothes he is said to be wearing; they all point the finger at Frank Hanson!

The story is now all over the cyber world, speculation is rife, and the conspiracy theorists are having a field day. And in the corridors of power, in the infrastructure of the establishment, people grind their teeth and wish that they could put a lid on the story; but like our metaphorical wildfire, rumours, once they have gained ground, are all but impossible to extinguish. The only option is to just wait until they lose momentum and expire of their own accord.

Attempts to refute the story, to prove it false, have all

failed. First comes an official announcement from NASA—Astronaut Frank Hanson cannot be raping girls in some piss-ant English town, because astronaut Frank Hanson is 200 million miles away from said piss-ant English town, right in the middle of a two-year tour of duty in the asteroid belt, goddammit!

The response comes swiftly: Well, obviously Frank Hanson isn't in the asteroid belt. It might be that he *should* be there, but clearly he is not; clearly he must have gone AWOL and returned to Earth on the last transporter, and NASA, for unscrupulous reasons of its own, is covering up this desertion.

Baloney! Frank Hanson appeared on a live broadcast from Vega Station only two weeks ago! The broadcast was screened and streamed all over the world! This proves categorically that Hanson was in the asteroid belt two weeks ago, and if he was in the asteroid belt two weeks ago he cannot be back on Earth right now, because, quote: 'No propulsion system known to man can traverse that distance in such a brief space of time,' goddammit!

The response to this one: Well, obviously that broadcast was faked. In fact, it's obvious that the whole Asteroid Belt Mining Project is faked! We've never even *been* to the asteroid belt! No manned space flight has ever gotten that far! The Mining Project is one big *Mission: Impossible* style deception. All that alleged footage sent from the asteroid belt is actually being produced right here on Earth! The interiors of the bases are studio sets, the mine tunnels are really terrestrial caves or else also studio sets. And as for the footage of the spaceships and mining vehicles—all miniature model-work worthy of a Gerry Anderson production. (CGI effects would have been too easily seen through.) To think that Earth's space project could actually have advanced as far as mining the asteroid belt by only the twenty-first century? Who would swallow that? Even *Red Dwarf* realised how far-fetched the idea was and retconned it to the twenty-third century. No way are we really mining the asteroid belt. Christ, we only landed on the moon in 1969! (And that was faked as well.)

This idea, long entertained by the conspiracy theorists, starts to gain ground. It would certainly explain how Frank Hanson was able to seemingly traverse the impossible distance from the asteroid belt to Earth if he never *was* in the asteroid belt! But then how did he get to the UK? Hanson is an American citizen. Oh, come on! Don't sweat the small stuff! If we've eliminated space travel from the equation, travelling from one country to another here on Earth is pretty small beer. For that matter, maybe the secret facility that houses the fake Asteroid Belt Mining Project is located in the UK. It would explain his being in England, if he had been in England all along!

Fair enough. But that still leaves one big question: Why is a trained astronaut, one who's up to his ears in a top-level conspiracy, going around raping schoolgirls?

You might have thought this one would have them stumped; but never underestimate the creative ingenuity of the conspiracy theorists! A solution is put forward: Brainwashing! Yes! By being subjected to drugs and psychological conditioning, the astronauts and engineers involved in the faked Asteroid Belt Mining Project don't even know themselves that they are participating in a deception! They have been brainwashed into believing that they really are in outer space, millions of miles from Earth and part of a genuine Asteroid Belt Mining Project! It makes sense! The fewer people who actually know the truth about the Big Lie, the less chance of it ever leaking out! Brainwashing someone is more secure than just buying them off.

But how does this account for his schoolgirl-raping activities?

Simple! Hanson must have somehow escaped from the facility housing the fake asteroid belt colony. He must have crawled through a vent or opened a door that should have been kept locked, and he found himself literally behind the scenes. And if the shock of this wasn't enough to scramble his drugged and conditioned mind, imagine what must have happened when he managed to get out in the open air and was confronted with the realisation that he was still on Earth? It must have driven the guy insane! And now he's out of control, stalking the countryside more beast than man, committing rape and murder. Yeah, but why is he only attacking schoolgirls? Well, maybe he's always liked 'em young.

And as if this isn't enough to keep the social media networks buzzing, yet another factor starts to creep in; additional information which, if it happens to be true, provides a solid connection between American astronaut Frank Hanson and the English town of Linton. This new account says that Frank Hanson's mother and kid sister happen to be living in Linton…

Scarlette Hanson can tell that something is wrong the moment she walks into the classroom.

Conversation drops to a whisper and all eyes are upon her. For an instant Scarlette feels a surge of guilt, but then she relaxes. Sure, people will be looking at her. Her best pal, the girl she sat beside in nearly every class, has been raped and murdered. People will be looking at her to see how she's taking it. Yeah, that's all it is.

She walks to the back row of desks and takes her usual place, beside Sasha's now vacant desk. Lassiter and Malcolm sit to her left. Scarlette seats herself self-consciously, aware that she is still the cynosure of attention. Even Lassiter looks at her, regards her with a wry, calculating smile.

'And how are we today?' he inquires. Scarlette smiles weakly.

'Hanging on, I guess.'

Lassiter nods, digesting this information.

'Still trying to cope with what's happened to Sasha, eh?'
'Sure. It's a lot to process.'
Another ruminative nod of the head.
And then: 'And how's that big brother of yours?'
Scarlette freezes. 'Brother?' she echoes weakly. 'I never said I had one.'
'No, you didn't,' confirms Lassiter. 'You *didn't* say you had one. But it turns out you *do* have one. He's an astronaut, isn't he? Although it seems that recently he's branched out into rape and murder.'
Scarlette just stares at him.
'I can tell you haven't been online much this weekend,' proceeds Lassiter. 'Or you wouldn't be so surprised about me knowing all this. It's all over town, Scarlette. I'm only saying what everyone else is saying. Your brother's big news.'
Scarlette fiddles with her bracelets. 'Who's saying?'
'Everyone. The whole bloody world's talking about it.'
'Then folks have got it wrong,' says Scarlette, after another pause. 'Yeah, I know that rapist guy *looks* like my brother; I noticed that the first time I saw that artist's sketch of the guy. But that's just a coincidence, y'know? Lots of people look like other people. And Frank, well he can't be the rapist, cuz he's not here, he's stationed at the asteroid belt.'
She smiles, looking more confident.
'I know he is, I know he is,' concurs Lassiter. '200 million miles away or whatever it is. But then the rumours say that he's come back, or even that he wasn't ever out there in the first place... Well, that's just rumours. Nothing's been proven yet; not a thing. Thing that puzzles me though, and it's puzzling old Malcolm here an' all—'
Malcolm, thus far a silent auditor to the conversation, grunts confirmation of this fact.
'—Thing that's puzzling us,' continues Lassiter. 'Is how come is it you never told us you had this astronaut big brother. Most people would be proud about having a

celebrity like that in the family. Wouldn't they, Malcolm, old son?'

'They would,' confirms Malcolm.

'Oh, that's easy enough,' replies Scarlette, visibly relaxing. 'My mom and dad separated a few years back. And when mom and me moved here to England, she didn't want people knowing who she was. We're kind of an astronaut family cuz Dad was an astronaut too, y'see? So yeah, mom just didn't want me telling anyone about that side of the family; so I didn't tell anyone. I'm sorry if you guys are pissed at me keeping secrets.'

'No, Malcolm and I are not pissed off with you,' Lassiter assures her. 'Even if we were, your explanation has cleared the matter up. Let's say no more about it. Let's put this one to bed. Change the channel. Still...' Lassiter pauses, tapping his mouth with a thoughtful forefinger. 'Still... If the rapist *was* your astronaut brother—and yes! I know it isn't him—but if it *was* him, y'know it could almost explain his choice of victims, couldn't it?'

Scarlette's smile has vanished. 'What do you mean?'

'Well, I mean look at the first three: Vanessa Young, Rose Gardener, Rachel Ryder; all girls that you couldn't stand... You know how you get all worked up when you're talking about people you hate; those three girls were always at the top of your bitch-list, weren't they? So, like I say, if the rapist was your dear brother, it would have almost seemed like he was doing it for his sister, wouldn't it? Y'know, teaching those bitches a lesson...'

'That's crazy,' says Scarlette, looking at her desk.

'...And then there's Sasha. The latest victim and one of our own. And not just raped this time; she gets murdered too. Someone really had it in for her... And you'd just had that bust-up with Sasha, hadn't you...?'

'...Yeah, but it wasn't just her; I was mad at all you guys that day. And I'm sorry. I was in a bitchy mood. And y'know, Sasha and me, we'd just made-up. I mean, when it happened, she was coming over to my place to chill and watch a movie…'

Lassiter looks at her. 'Yes. She *was* just coming over to your place, wasn't she?'

Scarlette, pale as death, is saved from having to respond to this by the arrival of Miss Forbes with the register.

In a small, untidy kitchen, a mother and son share a sullen breakfast. The air is redolent with the smell of the food heaped on the plates before the two diners. The full English breakfast, but presented here in its greasy-spoon café rather than its luxury hotel variant.

You can see that the two are mother and son. The facial resemblance is pronounced; the same sharp, sullen features, the same long nose. The mother's face is rounder than that of the son and heavily lined. Her uncombed hair is grey and grizzled. You might estimate her age as sixty, but it's actually an unkind fifty. The son, with lank brown hair, is in his late twenties, and we already know him. It is our old friend Carson.

Mother and son sit facing each other at the table which occupies much of the available space in this modest kitchen. A steaming mug of tea stands beside each plate of food. The table, covered with a dirty cloth, is also adorned with a nest of condiments and a chipped glass ashtray.

It is Mrs Carson who breaks the silence.

'Don't suppose you've got any work this week?' she asks.

'Better than that,' replies her son, smugly. 'I got some money coming in from some work I did *last* week.'

Mrs Carson looks gratifyingly mystified. 'Work you did last week? You weren't working last week.'

'Shows how much you know,' replies her complacent son. 'It was a bit of work I did on Saturday night. Just a one-off.' He takes a noisy mouthful of tea.

'Yeah, I know about those Saturday night jobs of yours,'

says Mrs Carson. 'It won't be anything on the level.'

'And like you care about that,' retorts Carson. 'As long as it puts some money in the pot.'

'How much?' demands Mrs Carson.

'Five hundred.'

'Cash in hand?'

'Yeah. I don't take cheques.'

'And when are you getting this windfall?'

'Should be today.'

Mrs Carson studies her son. 'This job. Was it for Piggy's lot?' 'What if it was?' challenges Carson.

'He's a vicious little bastard,' pronounces Mrs Carson. 'I don't like 'im.'

'Well, *I* don't like 'im, if it comes to that. But he always pays up.'

'Yeah, I suppose,' mutters the mother, shovelling a greasy slither of fried egg into her mouth. 'I know these jobs can land you in trouble, but at least it's not *that* kind of trouble; not like what happened—'

'Oh, don't you go bringing that up!' roars Carson. 'That was years ago!'

'I know, but—'

'But nothing! I didn't do nothing! It was all a misunderstanding!'

'A misunderstanding with a restraining order stuck on the end of it!' retorts Mrs Carson. 'It was 'umiliating, it was! The looks I got from the neighbours and everyone…'

'It's ancient bloody history, now, ain't it? I haven't even seen 'im—' he breaks off.

His mother's eyes lock on him, suspicious, interrogative.

The telephone in the hallway starts to ring.

'That'll be for me,' says Carson, rising quickly to his feet. 'About picking up that pony.'

Carson exits the kitchen, followed by his mother's suspicious gaze.

Carson's mood has recovered by the time he, having been joined by Drubble, reaches the paymaster's office; in other words that room above the nightclub. In they walk, and there's the Accountant, sitting at his desk, with his quill and his ink-well.

A thousand smackers! Five hundred each!

''Ello mates,' says a voice, stage left.

Carson freezes. Piggy! What's he doing here?

The office doors close firmly and Carson looks round to see big and stupid Alf and small and stupid Fred standing sentinel.

Carson's good mood collapses into debris. Piggy wouldn't be here this early in the morning unless there was something wrong. He wouldn't come in just to supervise a wage payment.

'Alright Piggy,' says Carson nervously. 'Anything wrong?'

'Yeah,' is the unwelcome reply. 'Unfortunately, there is somethink wrong.'

'About the job on Saturday?' asks Carson, knowing it can't be anything else. 'Shouldn't be any problems there. Went like clockwork, it did. Didn't it, Drubble?'

'Like clockwork,' confirms the faithful echo.

'Like clockwork, did it? All very nice,' says the Boy. 'But, thing is, when we examined the merchandise what you brought back to us, we found out there was somethink wrong with it.'

'Something wrong with it?'

'Yeah.' The Boy takes a container from an adjacent table. Carson recognises it as one of the plain grey cartons contained in the boxes they had stolen from the warehouse. The Boy pours a few of the tablets into his palm, holds it out. 'Now, what d'yer think these are?' 'That's the Serotonin Plus, ain't it?' says Carson.

'No, it ain't Serotonin Plus,' the Boy tells him, his voice dangerously calm. 'It ain't that at all. Y'see, what we 'ave 'ere is Vitamin C tablets. Tha's what they are: Vitamin C.'

The Boy hurls the container across the room, scattering its contents. Carson and Drubble flinch.

'Now y'see, I can't do much with them pills,' proceeds the Boy. 'Those Serotonin pills, scoff a load of them an' you get high. But scoff a load of Vitamin C pills, an' all you get is the shits. The messy kind.' 'Diarrhoea,' supplies the Accountant helpfully.

'Yeah, diarrhoea,' says the Boy. 'Now, there ain't much of a demand on the streets for diarrhoea pills. So, what I'm wonderin' is, why the fuck did you two pillocks bring me a van-load of vitamin pills what I can't do nothink with?'

The anger is starting to emerge in the Boy's voice.

'But we just did the job like you ordered, Boss,' pleads Carson. 'Into the warehouse through the back window, take the stack of boxes nearest to the van. That's what we did! We followed your instructions to the letter. If they was the wrong boxes then it must have been the inside man's fault. We didn't do nothing wrong!'

'You did do somethink wrong,' snaps the Boy. 'Because you was in *the wrong fuckin' ware'ouse!*'

Carson is the first to recover from this bombshell. 'But it can't have been the wrong one,' he says weakly. 'I mean, everything was just like you said it'd be.' (But even as he says this he can't help thinking of the curiously uncooperative security guard and the keys being in the ignition of the van.) 'And any'ow, you drew us a map...'

'Yes, I *did* draw you a map,' agrees the Boy. 'But you still fuckin' managed to read it wrong, didn't yer?'

Carson grasps at a straw. 'You want us to go back?' he offers. 'Lift the right stuff for you? We can go tonight—'

'Shut it!' snarls the Boy. 'It's too fuckin' late, ain't it? That shipment's gone out.' He shakes his head. 'Yer know, I underestimated you two, I really did. I said that even you two couldn't mess up this job. Well, I was wrong. I admit it.'

'You failed to anticipate the sheer extent of their resource and ingenuity,' offers the Accountant.

'Yeah I did,' confirms the Boy, not having understood a word. He walks up to Carson and Drubble, glares up at them. The two men look down at him and quail.

'I'll tell yer what I'm gunna do,' says the Boy. 'Even though I can't sell them pills, I 'ate to see all your 'ard work going ter waste; so what I'm gunna do is give 'em all to you.'

Looks of relief. 'Fair enough, Boss,' agrees Carson readily. 'We'll take 'em off your hands, no worries. We can store the boxes round Drubble's place. Just lend us a van—'

'No no no.' The Boy shakes his head. 'Alf! Fred!'

The two goons step forward, each bearing a silver tray. On each tray stands a tall glass of water and a large pile of tablets.

''Ere's yer first dose,' announces the Boy. 'These should make yer nice an' regular, these should. You can come back for yer next lot tommorer.'

'Oh but, Piggy...!' protests Carson, helplessly.

'Now now, take yer medicine,' says the Boy. 'An' in case either of you's the type what finds it 'ard to swallow pills, Alf and Fred are 'ere to 'elp yer. Alf and Fred is really good at 'elping people take their medicine.'

The two goons present the silver trays under Carson and Drubble's noses.

Chapter Fifteen
Mysterious Journey

And suddenly Murray is literally dragged off upon another Adventure.

He's in schoolyard, talking with Spacey and Pornboy. Eve appears as if out of nowhere, grabs Murray by the sleeve and with nothing more than a 'Come on,' compels him to fall into step beside her as she marches briskly towards the school's main entrance. Further down the road leading to the gates, walks another student, a girl.

'What's going on?' demands Murray.

'We're following her,' Eve tells him.

'Who is it? I can't tell.'

'It's Scarlette Hanson.'

'She's walking out the gates!' exclaims Murray. 'Has she been sent home?'

'No. She's doing a bunk.'

'But we can't follow her! Break's nearly over!'

'Then we'll have to miss a lesson or two,' replies Eve, unconcerned. 'Some things are more important than lessons.'

Skiving off school! Playing hookey! Playing truant! This is an enormity that Murray has never even dared contemplate before! Only 'bad' people skive off school, and Murray has always perceived himself a 'good' person. But here is Eve Chandler, his Mysterious Girlfriend, casually breaking the rules; taking him out of school and forcing him along with her!

Does this make Eve Chandler a 'bad' girl?

'Good', 'bad' or just 'Mysterious'?

The moment they actually pass through the school gates, pass beyond the precincts of the school, Murray experiences a feeling of having taken an irrevocable step. But he also feels liberated, feels like a weight has been lifted from him. Outside the school gates and during school hours, the air somehow tastes sweeter.

'Why are we following Scarlette?' he asks, as they proceed along the street, keeping their quarry in sight.

'Cuz I saw her sneaking out and I'd like to know where she's going,' replies Eve. 'You've heard what everyone's saying, right? About her brother being the serial rapist?'

'Yes. You think her skiving off school is to do with that?'

'Yeah... She might just have walked out cuz she's fed up of everyone talking about her; but maybe, if the story about her brother's true, then she might be going to warn him.'

'You think it is true, then?' asks Murray. 'About her brother?'

'I dunno,' confesses Eve. 'I mean it seems far-fetched an' all; but then there's a lot of circumstantial evidence.'

'Circum....?'

'Circumstantial. A lot of things that back up the idea that her brother is the rapist.'

They walk on, staying in Scarlette Hanson's footsteps. Murray, feeling very conspicuous in his school uniform, keeps expecting to be challenged by passers-by; but this does not happen. If people they pass realise Eve and him are playing truant, they do not say anything.

But what if they run into a policeman? *He's* not going to turn a blind eye!

'Y'know, the way we're going, I think she might be heading home,' says Eve presently.

'Could that be where her brother is?'

'I dunno. I know Scarlette lives with her mam, and it's a pretty big house they've got... I mean yeah, they could both be in on it; he's her
lad just as much as he's Scarlette's brother...'

'Maybe they don't know he's the attacker,' suggests Murray.

'They must have heard the stories by now,' says Eve. 'And there's one version says Scarlette is the one putting him up to raping those girls, and if that were true, then the mam would have to be in on it... But on the other hand, maybe her brother's hiding out somewhere else, and Scarlette's just going home now to change out of her school things, so she can go'n meet him.'

They turn the corner onto Scarlette's home street and immediately see that something is transpiring. A sizeable crowd and a number of vehicles are blocking the road in front of Scarlette's house. There are a couple of police cars, but most of the vehicles are vans and trucks emblazoned with the logos of television and radio news networks. Scarlette has concealed herself behind a tree to survey this scene.

'We're too late!' exclaims Murray. 'They must have raided the house and arrested Scarlette's brother!'

'I'm not so sure it's that,' counters Eve. 'If it were a raid there'd be a lot more coppers around. Look at 'em, that crowd's mostly reporters and film crews. I reckon the press have got wind of all the rumours and now they're besieging the house. I wonder if that's cuz they think Frank Hanson might be in there, or if they're just after a statement from his mam.'

At this moment, Scarlette turns from her vantage-point behind the tree and, breaking into a run, retraces her steps back up the street. There is no time for Murray and Eve to move or conceal themselves. They can only stand there while the girl rushes past them. Staring straight ahead and with a scowling expression on her face, she does not appear to register the presence of her classmates.

'Did she see us?' wonders Murray, after she has turned the corner.

'I dunno, but come on!'

Murray and Eve run after her. Turning onto the next street, they see that Scarlette has slowed to a brisk walking pace. Her direction is towards the town centre, so she is clearly not returning to school.

'Now where's she going?' asks Murray.

'Maybe to wherever her brother's holed up,' suggests Eve. 'Let's keep following, but we'll have to be careful now. All those reporters outside her house must have spooked her. She'll be suspicious now.'

And so, exercising caution, they stay on Scarlette's tail. They continue towards the centre of town, threading housing estates, crossing parks. Scarlette seems to be avoiding main roads as much as possible.

'I asked Mum about Dad,' announces Murray, at length.

'Oh, yeah?' says Eve. 'What did she say?'

'She thinks he might still be here,' answers Murray.

'Living in Linton.'

'He is, is he? So how come you never see him?'

'Mum didn't say. She says she hasn't spoken to him since they divorced.'

'And when was that? You said it was when you were little, didn't you?'

'Yeah. Mum says it was when I was only one.'

'Ah! Not surprising you don't remember him then.'

'Yeah. I asked Mum if I could see a picture of him, but she said she's got rid of them all.'

'All of 'em? Even her wedding photos?'

'Yeah. So I don't know what he looks like.'

'And do you want to find out or summat?'

'Well, it's… I think I might have seen him…'

'Yeah? When?'

'That man. That man from the park; the one we thought was following us… I thought it might be him…'

Eve can't help but laugh at this. 'I'm sorry, love! But you're not very good at judging how old grown-ups are, are you? That guy was way too young to be your dad! He would've had to have married your mam when he was still at school!'

'Oh,' says Murray, crestfallen.

Eve puts a hand on his shoulder. 'I'm sorry, love. Why did you think that feller might've been your old man?'

'I thought that might be why I had that funny feeling when I saw him. I thought maybe part of me remembered him from when I was little.'

'I think part of you *does* remember that guy from when you were little. But he's not your dad, I can tell you that. You couldn't have remembered anyone you only saw when you were a baby. Did your mam say why they split up?'

'She just said they didn't get along.'

'Was that all?'

'Yeah, Mum didn't seem like she wanted to talk about him, really. She said I didn't need a dad and that he wouldn't be bothered about me, anyway.'

'Well yeah, she's right there. If he'd wanted to see you, he could've seen you; 'specially if he still lives local. It's thirteen years, remember. He probably remarried ages ago and has got a new family now.'

'Yeah…'

'I mean, if you're dead set on tracking him down I could—'

'No, no!' interrupts Murray. 'That's okay. I probably shouldn't…'

'Aye. Let sleeping dogs lie. That's probably for the best.'

While this dialogue unfolds they are still keeping Scarlette in sight. Apparently the town centre is not her final destination. Avoiding the busiest streets, she leads her pursuers on to the park behind the modern polytechnic building and over a pedestrian bridge spanning the River Lint. They are now in South Linton, an area for the most part unfamiliar to Murray. He vaguely recalls venturing south of the river when out playing with other kids when he was very young; but aside from this he has never had any call to visit this part of town.

'You'd've thought she'd catch the bus, if she was coming this far,' he complains.

'Yeah, this a long old trek,' agrees Eve. 'I dunno if Scarlette has a bike, but if she does, maybe that's what she was going home for; but then she had to change her plans when she saw all the reporters there.' They continue southwards, passing through residential streets.

'I'm feeling hungry,' says Murray.

'Well eat your lunch,' Eve tells him. 'It's in your bag, isn't it?'

Murray looks at his watch. 'It's not lunch hour yet.'

Eve rolls her eyes. 'Yeah, well I think we can relax the rules about that just this once. We're not in school now, remember?'

'Yeah! We'll get into trouble for this!'

'So, we'll get into trouble. At least we'll be in trouble together. I keep telling you, you can't have Adventures without a bit of risk. And that includes the risk of getting an earful from your teacher.'

On and on they walk. Murray starts eating his lunch. Eve smokes a cigarette.

'I don't know this end of town so well,' says Eve. 'But if she carries on much further, I reckon we're going to be outside Linton completely.'

This soon proves to be the case. On a quiet street, Scarlette turns into a public footpath between two houses; Murray and Eve follow and emerge into open countryside; a wilderness of trees, thickets and tall grass which constitutes Linton's greenbelt. Scarlette still walks ahead of them, following a well-defined path through the wild grass.

'Looks like her brother's hiding out in the countryside,' remarks Eve.

'You still think it's her brother she's going to see?' asks Murray.

'Sure,' replies Eve. 'I can't think of any other reason why she'd ditch school and come all the way out here.'

'So you really think that her brother really is the attacker? But they say he couldn't have got back to Earth from space so quickly.'

Eve shrugs. 'Then maybe the whole space mining thing is a big fat lie, like they're saying.'

'Do you believe that story?'

'I didn't used to; but now…'

'But why is he going around attacking people?'

'Like they say; the guy must be off his head.'

'But then, what about Scarlette? Wouldn't he be dangerous to her as well?'

'Not if she's got some kind of control over him.'

'How could she do that?'

'I dunno. It's all fucking weird, isn't it? The whole thing is.'

The backs of that last row of houses are already out of sight; all around them now is the countryside: the tall grass, the shrubbery, the stands of trees; tranquil nature beneath a hazy sky. To all appearances, they could be miles from any human habitation. The birdsong here does not have to compete with the sound of mechanical traffic: no motorway runs close to the southern boundary of Linton.

Murray, looking about him and taking in this sight, feels a strange sense of unease beginning to assert itself; a growing feeling of being out of his element. This feeling is reflected on his face, and is read by Eve.

'What's wrong, Murray?' asks Eve.

'I don't like the countryside,' he replies. 'I dunno why; I just don't.'

'You said that before,' recalls Eve. 'It's kinda strange you don't like the countryside. Have you got some problem with open spaces? Is that what it is?'

'No, it's not that. It just gets me feeling nervous, out here. I'm not sure why...'

'Will you be okay, love? I don't wanna—' She breaks off. 'Where's she going?'

Her attention on Murray, Eve has taken her eyes from their quarry, but now looking back, she sees that Scarlette has left the footpath and has struck off through the tall grass.

Even as they watch, she reaches a tall thicket of brambles and, stooping, disappears within.

'Where's she gone?' wonders Eve, pulling up in her tracks.

'Maybe she's just gone behind the bushes, to... you know...'

'Answering the call of nature. Yeah, it could be that.' Crouching down, they wait.

A minute passes. Another. Scarlette does not reappear.

'Come on,' says Eve tersely. 'This ain't just a toilet break.'

She runs for the thicket, ploughing through the tall grass,

with Murray close behind.

'How could she have got into this lot?' wonders Eve, when they reach the thicket. 'Where was it she went in...?'

They walk along the border of the thicket and the mystery is explained when they come upon a small gap in the prickly foliage, the entrance to a tunnel into the briers, narrow and just tall enough for a stooping person to pass through.

'Here we are,' says Eve. 'Look, you can see the flattened grass where she came through. She must have already known this tunnel was here; you couldn't just spot it from the path... Come on.'

Eve stoops to enter the tunnel. And then, realising Murray is not following, looks round. Murray hangs back.

'I don't think we should go in there,' he says, looking nervous.

'Why not?' asks Eve, rejoining him. 'D'you know this place or summat?'

'No, I... I'm not sure. I've just got a bad feeling...'

Eve strokes his arm. 'Look,' she says. 'D'you wanna stay here while I go in and have a quick look and see where the tunnel leads to? I'll just have a look and come right back!'

'No... No, I'll come with you...'

'You're sure?'

Murray manages a weak smile. 'Yeah...'

'That's the stuff!'

They enter the tunnel. A dense twilight engulfs them, and as they move forward, they have to keep their heads low to avoid having their hair snagged by the grasping brambles. The narrowness of the passage forces them to proceed in single file. The tunnel stretches onwards for a surprising length.

But then they emerge and find themselves looking into a green twilit hollow; a hollow clothed in grass and moss, bordered and partially roofed-over by the trees growing densely on either side. One particular tree stands isolated, rising from the declivity of the hollow; standing out all the more for being dead, the victim of a past lightning strike; a leafless, crownless skeleton, with limbs contorted, petrified.

Murray stares at the tree. He has seen it before. A forgotten memory that brings fear with it.

Eve sees Murray's fixed expression.

'What's wrong?' she asks.

Murray snaps out of his trance, looks at her.

'I've been here before,' he says. 'It's that tree, as soon as I saw it I remembered it... I'm sure I've been here before... I think... I dunno... I think something bad may have happened here...'

'Oh, Murray...' says Eve, folding her arms around him. 'That's probably why you've forgotten for so long; your mind must've blocked it out... Come on, pet; let's go back. We can come back another time. We've probably lost the trail, anyway; no sign of Scarlette.'

'Perhaps she's gone to the ruins,' says Murray; and immediately looks puzzled at his own words.

'Ruins?' says Eve. She looks around. 'Where?'

'You have to go on a bit further,' says Murray, still perplexed.

'Looks like you're starting to remember more. Shall we see if you're right?'

'Yes. I want to see...'

'Okay!'

Eve takes Murray's hand and they enter the hollow. The course of the depression curves off to the left, and soon the hand of man comes into sight. At the furthest extremity of the hollow stands a venerable stone wall, festooned with creepers, and in the centre of the wall an arched doorway.

Murray's heart beats faster. Vague memories, formless feelings of unease.

'The ruins are through that doorway,' he says.

'Looks kind of churchy,' remarks Eve.

'I think it's an abbey or something.'

Eve lowers her voice. 'A place like this would be a good

hide-out for Scarlette's brother. We'll need to be quiet. She could be here.'

'I don't think the building's got any roof,' replies Murray in the same tone. 'Just the walls.'

'Still... We know Scarlette came this way...'

Through the doorway, the ground, rank with undergrowth, rises towards what are indeed the remains of a religious building. The grey stonework matches that of the outer wall and arched window embrasures can be seen.

Eve and Murray wade through the undergrowth and, climbing through a gap in the wall, enter the building. The interior space is one vast area littered with fallen masonry; in many places weeds and nettles have found a purchase. As Murray has predicted, the building is completely roofless, open to the heavens at all points.

'You're right; there's no shelter in this place,' says Eve. 'Not unless—'

She breaks off. Murray suddenly looks terrified. Alert, Eve spins round, looking for danger. But the ruins remain still and silent.

'What's wrong?'

'I can't stay here...' says Murray, shaking his head. 'I can't!'

He turns and runs. He jumps through the broken wall and scrambles down the incline. Eve follows him out through the arched doorway and catches up with him in the hollow. She stops him, hugs him, soothes him.

'What is it, love?' she coos. 'What have you remembered?'

'I don't know,' replies Murray wretchedly, tears streaming down his face. 'I just know I was here a long time ago. And Carson; he was here as well!'

'Carson? Who's Carson, Murray?'

'That man! The one we first saw in the park and then when we thought he was following us. That's Carson!'

'His name's Carson, is it? You've remembered

something! Can you remember anything else?'

'He's bad,' says Murray. 'When I think of him I feel scared. Really scared...'

Eve strokes his face. 'Alright, sweetheart. That's enough for now. Let's be getting back...'

And with her arm around him, she leads Murray away.

Their departure does not go unobserved.

Chapter Sixteen
It's Only a Phase!

And then the house of cards comes crashing down.

One brief public announcement from the Linton Police Force and all of those meticulously crafted conspiracy theories come crashing down to the ground:

Astronaut Frank Hanson is not the Linton serial rapist and occasional murderer!

As a matter of routine procedure, the DNA profiles of all personnel attached to the Space Programme are kept on file; and a comparison has established that Frank Hanson's DNA profile does *not* match that of the Linton assailant!

Hot on the heels of this announcement, the inevitable backlash to the previous conspiracy theories kicks in.

Well, *of course* Frank Hanson isn't the culprit! Frank Hanson is 200 million miles from Linton, joy-riding around the asteroid belt in his space capsule! And as for that theory about the Asteroid Belt Mining Project being a huge put-up job: Baloney! A hoax of that magnitude would have cost about as much to put into place as actually going out there for real would have cost! And what would be the point of it anyway? What is there to gain from fooling the public into thinking we're mining the asteroid belt when really we aren't?

The vitriol flies back and forth across cyberspace. People

who, only a few hours before, were staunchly supporting the conspiracy theories, are now amongst the first to pour scorn on them. Things move fast in cyberspace, and the traditional nine days' wonder can become a nine hours' wonder.

Fiona Lassiter loves her big brother. Her big brother is the best big brother ever! He's so handsome and manly, funny and charming, and so completely selfish and ruthless! There's no one like her big brother!

Fiona—Little Fee—sits on her brother's unmade bed, leafing through a naughty magazine she has found amongst the bedclothes and waiting for her big brother to come home. Fee often likes to sit in her big brother's room when he is not at home; she feels closer to him by being here. She loves this room cuz it smells of big brother's sweat and his gooey stuff. It's a manly room. And although Fee is a tidy girl herself, she loves the room's messiness; it reflects big brother's relaxed and unorthodox attitude to life!

Big brother has gone out this evening to see some naughty people who didn't do something that big brother had asked them to do! Just think of it! Not obeying her big brother seems preposterous to Fiona; unforgivable! Everyone should do exactly what her big brother wants them to do. Big brother doesn't like it when people don't do what he tells him to do; it makes him upset; and when big brother gets upset, then Fiona gets really angry! She hopes that big brother will really sort out those disobedient people he has gone to see.

There's an additional reason for Fiona having sought the refuge of big brother's bedroom; the whole house smells of poo! And nasty, stinky, big sister poo at that! But the bad smells can't get into this room! No nasty big sister smells can never get past manly big brother smells.

And the cause of this intolerable aroma? Norma, Fee's detestable big sister, has gone and pooed on the living room carpet! Imagine doing something like that! Yes, it's true that dear Daddy had ordered Norma to poo on the carpet and had quite rightly started hitting her when she'd at first refused. But then she had gone and pooed this absolutely vile and stinky poo! Clearly this was done with malice aforethought. No wonder dear Daddy had hit her even more after that and then rubbed her nose in the poo for good measure. And quite right too! The impudence of that girl!

Fee hears the front door, and a radiant smile lights up her cherubic face as familiar footsteps mount the stairs. Big brother is home!

But then the door opens and she sees that her big brother is not in a good mood.

'What are you doing here?' he demands. He can be like this sometimes.

'Did things not go well when you met those people, darling brother?' she inquires solicitously.

'No, they did not. And why does the house stink of shit?'

Lassiter sits down heavily on the bed, snatches the magazine from his sister's hands and makes a pretence of being interested in it.

Fee knows that big brother had told these people—some silly little gang who call themselves the Gentlemen—to beat up Murray Leinster, a boy from big brother's class at school. The reason for this is that there's this new girl in big brother's class, and this Leinster insect has started going out with her, even though big brother wanted to have the girl first. The nerve! Now of course big brother is strong and manly enough to beat up a dozen Murray Leinsters all by himself, but he didn't want to get in trouble and get expelled from school, so he had hired these 'Gentlemen' to do the job instead. They were meant to have done it over the weekend; so you can imagine how annoyed big brother was when Murray Leinster walked into class this morning in the best of health and not a mark on him!

'But what happened, big brother?' persists Fiona. 'Why didn't they do what they were supposed to do? Please tell me!'

Lassiter sighs. 'Eve Chandler is what happened.'

'Eve Chandler,' repeats Fiona. 'She's the new girl, isn't she?'

'Yeah. I wanted them to work him over in front of her, just to really humiliate the little shit, but that turned out to be a bad idea. Turns out Chandler is a one-girl army or something. She waded in to protect Leinster and really did a number on the Gentlemen. You should've seen those guys! They looked half-pulverised! Chandler must have a blackbelt in kicking the crap out of people.'

'Even so, they shouldn't have let themselves be beaten by a girl,' argues Fee. 'How many are in this gang anyway?'

'Six.'

'Six? Six against one and they still lost? Well, I hope you didn't pay them after that, big brother darling.'

'Not pay them?' echoes Lassiter scornfully. 'I had to pay the bastards extra! Compensation, they called it.'

'You should have refused.'

'Yeah, right. You don't know these psychos. If I hadn't paid up, they would have done to me what Chandler had done to them. As soon as they were out of their wheelchairs, anyway.' He growls. 'All that money thrown away for nothing!'

'You'll have to just think up another plan,' says Fee.

'Yes, thank you for that, dear sister,' sarcastically.

'You want revenge against Murray Leinster and you want his girlfriend Eve Chandler for yourself,' summarises Fiona. And then: 'I know how you can do this! Yes, I've got a lovely idea!'

'Oh yes? And what does this idea involve?'

'It involves me, big brother; it involves me!'

'You? What can you do?'

'I'm a little girl, aren't I? So I can get any older boy into as much trouble as I want!'

Lassiter looks at his sister, a smile of comprehension and approval spreading across his features. 'Yes...' he says slowly. 'I see what you're getting at...'

'Of course you do, big brother mine!' from Fiona, triumphant. 'That's because great minds think alike!'

Picture a queen-sized bed in a sumptuous boudoir. Picture soft colours and soft lighting. Picture three naked goddesses reclining on the bed; two of them enjoying post-coital cigarettes, the third deep in post-coital slumber. From left to right: Dodo Dupont, psychologist and spy: a robust Juno; and then Lady Jane Richmond, high-class prostitute and subversive: a regal Minerva; finally, Mayumi Takahashi, erotic photographer and sometimes assistant spy: a petite Hebe.

Dodo and Lady Jane are the smokers, reclining against the pillows. Mayumi, having been thoroughly put through her paces by the two larger women, lies on her side in a foetal ball, sleeping it off. Even her snoring sounds cute!

Lady Jane exhales a reflective cloud of cigarette smoke. 'There's something I'd like to talk to you about,' she says.

'I thought there might be,' answers Dodo. 'I mean, *you* practically picked *us* up! And I'm guessing that's not how you normally go about your business.'

'Correct,' confirms Lady Jane. 'I never tout for custom. My clients are usually men; they do the soliciting, not me.'

'Well, how's this for an idea?' says Dodo, smiling impishly. 'Since you pretty much forced us to hire you because you've got something you want to say to us, shall we just consider this session a freebie?'

'Not a chance,' declares Lady Jane, returning the smile. 'I couldn't sacrifice my principles; not even for two such delightful ladies as yourselves.'

'Fair enough,' agrees Dodo. 'Usual rates, is it?'

'Double. There were two of you last time I counted.'

'But there's only one of you,' argues Dodo, tipping the ash from her cigarette.

'Two clients, two bills,' is the response. 'But we can

settle up in the morning. Let's move on to what I have to say to you.' She glances to her left at Mayumi's sleeping form. 'Although I did want both of you to hear this…'

'Oh let her sleep, bless her!' says Dodo. 'Say what you've got to say to me and I'll clue her in later.'

'Agreed. I take it you two enjoy an open relationship, then?'

Dodo looks scandalised. 'No, we do not! We're tight, thank you very much. No playing away from home. We might occasionally invite third parties to join us, but we'd never do anything behind each other's backs.'

'I apologise for my misconception,' says Lady Jane. 'But, to the matter in hand. First of all, I ought to tell you I know what you're doing here in Linton; I know it's not just your student pep-talks and your girlfriend's book signing. I know of your association with Mark Hunter and that he is here on official business.'

'Okay, so you know,' replies Dodo, unconcerned. 'It's not that much of a secret. What about you, Jane? I'm guessing you've got more than one string to your bow?'

'Quite right. I do have other interests aside from my day-to-day occupation,' says Lady Jane. 'And as representative of a certain organisation I'm affiliated with, I'd like to make the both of you an offer…'

'It's like a bird, a flower, a flame… It flickers and it flutters… It is black, like the door to eternity… It is a shape, it is a void, a jagged tear in the fabric of reality… It is a giant's teardrop… It has eyes. The eyes are yellow, they are narrow, they taper upwards… They are bird-like, catlike eyes… They have small black pupils… The pupils are fixed against the upper lids… The pupils never move… The eyes glare with malevolence… They burn into your very soul…

'Sometimes the shape appears against a cloud of green fog… Sometimes it appears against a craggy, twilit alien landscape—the creature's home world, or just some place it has visited... It is drawing nearer, closer to us here on Earth... The dreams are harbingers of the creature's arrival on this world... The dreams will become real, the creature will be among us...'

'There! Was that poetic enough for you?'

'Yes, but now you just went and killed the mood.'

'I know! But I didn't want you getting all melancholy.'

The speakers are Rose Gardener and Jenny Jones, and the location, the bedroom of the former. Rose's facial injuries have by now disappeared, as have the floral offerings that were previously swamping the room.

The two girls are in night attire and sitting on Rose's bed. A sleepover, you might think; and in a way it is, but this sleepover has become an extended affair. As has been mentioned before, Jenny's disapproving parents have forbidden their daughter from seeing Rose outside of unavoidable school hours; and this injunction had not even been lifted or relaxed to any degree in the wake of the assault upon Rose. Jenny, furious at her parents' callousness, openly defied the injunction which had previously only been covertly defied. The result: Jenny's expulsion from her own parental abode and Rose's mother taking the girl in and accommodating her with the spare bedroom; Rose's mum being much more sympathetic, in spite of her insistence that 'It's all just a phase!'

(Rose's mum likes to remind her daughter and her houseguest of this cynical belief at regular intervals. Even once, during an act of cunnilingus, when Rose was being perhaps too vocal in her appreciation of Jenny's ministrations, her mum had put her head round the bedroom door to say "It's only a phase, you know!")

'Never mind about me getting melancholy,' says Jenny. 'You're the one who has to endure these dreams every single night.' 'Yeah, it is a bit sucky,' agrees Rose, readily.

'And nobody can explain why, can they?' proceeds Jenny. 'Why it is that you and Rachel and Vanessa keep having the same dreams...'

'Because we were raped by the same astronaut,' replies Rose. 'He must have picked up some weird kind of space virus.'

'But you *weren't* raped by an astronaut,' disputes Jenny. 'They announced on the news—'

'They got it wrong,' interrupts Rose firmly. 'The DNA test, or comparison or whatever they call it; they got it wrong. I'm telling you, Jen. It was *him*. Frank Hanson. When I saw those pictures of the guy, I knew it was the man who raped me. You don't mistake something like that. I mean he was even wearing the same flight suit in some of those pictures; the same one he was wearing when he attacked me. Like I said before, the only difference is that the Frank Hanson in those photographs was smiling and looked human, but when he attacked me he was more like a zombie or something.'

'I know,' sighs Jenny. 'But DNA comparisons are not normally something people just "get wrong". It's a very precise process.'

'Then maybe someone's telling fibs,' suggests Rose. 'And what about Scarlette in school today? You saw her face. She looked guilty as hell when she saw us walking up to her with Vanessa and Rachel. She legged it right out of school, didn't she?'

'Yes, but she might have been scared rather than guilty,' argues Jenny. 'With all the rumours flying around that she was the instigator behind the assaults, she may just have feared physical violence when she saw the three victims coming towards her.'

'Y'know what?' says Rose. 'As my woman, you ought to be agreeing with me not arguing with me. Enough of the scientific detachment.'

They kiss, and with no scientific detachment on either side. 'I'm sorry, my love,' says Jenny. 'I know my clinical objectivity must be an annoyance to you. My infuriating insistence on examining both sides of a proposition or argument. But my heart is always with you.'

More necking in confirmation of this fact.

'Yeah, I know Frank Hanson's the guy, and I know that cow Scarlette is the one making him do it,' says Rose. 'What about that old chapel that Eve and Murray followed her to? Eve reckons that Frank Hanson might be hiding out there, somewhere underground, maybe. Now, Professor Smarty-pants, can you think of one other good reason why Scarlette would've gone all the way out there if it wasn't to see her brother?'

'As a matter of fact I can,' answers Jenny smoothly. 'She might have discovered she was being followed by Eve and Murray and just led them on a wild-goose chase.'

'You always have an answer,' complains Rose, pouting. 'Too fucking clever by half. Still, I know one way of shutting you up! Don't I?' She pushes Jenny down onto the bed.

'You do,' concurs Jenny, solemnly.

'Ha! I always win in the end! You always have to submit!'

'I do,' solemnly.

'Y'know I'm glad you're around here with me,' says Rose, planting a kiss on Jenny's polished forehead. 'I mean, apart from being able to get my wicked way with you, I can keep an eye on you.'

'And why do you want to keep an eye on me?'

'Cuz I worry about you.'

'About what?'

'I worry that Scarlette might send her pet monster out after you. I mean, I know she always hated my guts the most, but she ain't that fond of you, either.'

'Agreed.'

'Right. So at least we're safe together here, right?'

'Possibly not,' cautions Jenny. 'Remember that Vanessa was attacked in her own bedroom. And they still don't know how the assailant got into the house.'

Speak of nightmares and most people visualise horror stories—a child's haunted house dream. Rose's dreams of the alien entity are more or less nightmares of that kind. But a dream doesn't have to have a horror film plot to constitute being labelled a nightmare. Any vivid, bizarre and generally unpleasant dream is a nightmare. And to experience nightmares on a regular basis is usually an indication of a troubled mind.

Our down-and-out friend Stavro enjoys this experience. He has nightmares every single night; nightmares he will awaken from in the small hours of the morning, racked with dread and self-loathing.

And tonight is no exception.

He lies awake now, paralysed with fear, and he thinks of McKearney the plumber. Although not a participant in the chaotic dream he has just emerged from, McKearney preys on Stavro's mind and has done for several days now.

He should never have let that man stay for drinks.

He should have listened to that internal monitor that was telling him to have nothing to do with that man. In his perverse policy of only mixing with the lowest of the low, Stavro now realises he may have taken a step too far when he invited that man to stay for drinks.

Yes, 'drinks' in the plural. That cold, relaxing beer had become a second and then a third. And after the beer had been exhausted, they had turned to Stavro's supply of spirits and had drank on into the evening. They hadn't left the flat. They had just talked. Actually, it was McKearney who had done most of the talking and Stavro most of the listening. Stavro had become so inebriated that he now doesn't remember the end of the evening and he doesn't remember everything that McKearney said to him. But he remembers enough of that monster's conversation to absolutely terrify him.

The conversation had started innocuously enough, with McKearney talking about all the odd-jobs he had performed over the years. Not just a plumber by trade, he had done other things, including working as a bouncer, which had confirmed Stavro's belief that the man wasn't as flabby and out of condition as he looked. Yes, McKearney had talked on, obviously testing the water, seeking to determine how far he could go with his present auditor. And by making himself out, as always, to be worse than he really was, Stavro had only encouraged the man to open up more and more. (And of course the drink had helped this process along.) Stavro could stomach the talk about Peeping Tom activities and even the boasts of statutory rape; but then McKearney had started to talk about the dark net and the groups to which he belonged therein. Stavro had always drawn the line at those dark net sites; the very idea of websites devoted to displaying the torture of animals, horrific assaults upon children, the live streaming of prolonged murders, etc., had always repulsed him, and he had never sought to get himself connected to the dark net. But McKearney *was* connected, and he had told tales of his experiences that had turned Stavro's stomach...

And there was something else. It must have been right at the end of the evening, because Stavro retains only tenuous, disjointed memories... He can see McKearney's ugly, alarming face; can see him relaxing in Stavro's armchair and telling him... telling him... When Stavro tries to recall this part of the conversation, his mind switches to a particular event; a news story of a famous local unsolved crime, one that had happened two, maybe three years ago... A family, mother and kids, taking a walk in the countryside had been attacked and murdered in broad daylight; bludgeoned to death. The crime had shocked the whole of Linton, had become that talk of the town... And the killer had never been apprehended.

Could it be... Could it be that McKearney had confessed to that crime? Is this why the story always appears in Stavro's mind when he tries to remember the plumber's words?

(The morning after this event, Stavro had awoken in his

own bed as usual. Of McKearney there was no sign; he had left presumably at the end of the evening, and Stavro has not seen the man again since that day.)

Had McKearney confessed to that crime? The thought of it appals Stavro. And not just on account of the crime itself; he is worried about his own neck. What if McKearney remembers what he told Stavro? What if he regrets having told it? He might think of Stavro as a liability; as a witness to be silenced...

Is this what his lifestyle has led him to? Has he become the target of a sociopath?

Chapter Seventeen
You Don't Look Very British!

The butler answers the door.

'Ah, good afternoon. I was wondering if Lord Parker is at home?'

The inquiry seems a very reasonable one to Mark Hunter, given that he is calling at Linton Hall, the country residence of the aristocrat just mentioned. And so he is quite struck by the butler's reaction—the functionary's eyes widen, and he stares mutely at the caller with something approaching a look of utter disbelief.

'This is Linton Hall, isn't it?' asks Mark, wondering if he has somehow driven to the wrong stately home.

'Yes, sir, this is Linton Hall,' answers the butler, seeming to recover himself. 'I take it you are not personally acquainted with his lordship?'

'Never met him in my life,' replies Mark, cheerfully. 'I'm calling on behalf of a mutual friend.'

'And who would that be, sir?'

'Sir Philip Chambers of the Foreign Office.'

'I see, sir.'

'Well? Is his lordship available?'

The butler glances over both shoulders and then looks back at Mark, his expression now displaying urgency and alarm.

'Listen, I—'

'And who might you be?' breaks in a new voice.

Mark looks round. A teenage girl of Oriental provenance, wearing shorts and a vest top, advances up the portico steps. The girl has bobbed hair and she favours Mark with a languid smile as she studies him with calculating eyes.

'Ah, your ladyship—' begins the butler.

'That will be all, Parker,' is the firm interruption. 'I will attend to our visitor.'

Crushed, the butler departs.

'Who might you be?' repeats the girl.

'I'm Mark Hunter,' replies Mark. 'I'm here to see Lord Parker, although as I explained to the butler, I'm not actually acquainted with him.'

'Are you acquainted with any of the family?'

'No.'

The girl's smile is renewed. 'I am his daughter, Lady Harriet. Please step inside.'

Mark follows the girl (and let's call her Misaki, because I'm sure the sagacious reader has discerned that it is actually her) into a spacious drawing room. He is invited to take a seat.

'I couldn't help noticing your surprise when I told you who I was,' says Misaki, taking a chair facing her guest.

'Well, yes,' confesses Mark. 'You weren't quite what I was expecting, I'll admit.'

'The explanation is quite simple,' says Misaki. 'My mother, now sadly deceased, was a Japanese lady. I don't see why this should be such a surprise to you. Many English men marry Japanese females; we seem to be popular.'

'Yes, you are,' agrees Mark. 'It's just not so common for an English hereditary peer to marry someone of a different race. I've always thought they were rather precious about their blue blood, and didn't care to have it diluted.'

'Is that so?'

'Well, it's the best excuse I can give you for being surprised at your appearance,' says Mark, with a smile.

'I like you,' declares Misaki, returning the smile.

'Thank you,' says Mark. 'Now about your father—'

'Of course! It was him you came to see! My apologies for not explaining sooner, but my father is very busy at the moment, so I don't think he will be able to see you. One of his hobbies you see, is taxidermy, and right now he is stuffing a rhinoceros.'

'A rhinoceros?'

'Quite so. Father was recently big-game hunting in Kenya.'

'Kenya?' questions Mark. 'I didn't think they allowed big-game hunting in Kenya anymore; and even if they did I wouldn't have thought rhinos would be on the menu, they're an endangered species.'

'This is true, but when you have money, these rules can be waived,' explains Misaki. 'Money, allied with rank, can purchase anything. And so, my father has shot a rhinoceros, and now he is stuffing it.'

'Just the head, I assume?'

'No. The entire beast.'

'Really? I thought big-game hunters just kept the heads as trophies.'

'A common misconception. People believe that the heads of the beasts are mounted on the walls, in fact the heads are projecting through the walls. The animal's body is in the adjoining room.'

'I see...' says Mark slowly, studying Misaki's face.

'What was it you wished to speak to my father about, Mark Hunter?' she asks. 'Perhaps it is something I can help you with.'

'Well, as I told your factotum, I'm actually here on behalf

of a mutual friend, Sir Philip Chambers. He was concerned about Lord Parker because it seems that he—and a number of other people—haven't been able to get hold of his lordship of late. His friends were becoming concerned, and so, knowing I happened to be in this neck of the woods, Sir Philip asked me to pay a call, see if everything was alright.'

'Well, you can see that I am alright, and I can assure that my father is also in good health—'

'Yes, but it's odd that he should be not replying to all his friends,' insists Mark. 'So if I could just have a quick word with him—'

'I have already told you he is busy.'

'Yes, I know, but this really won't take a minute—'

'Out of the question. Father hates to be interrupted when he is engaged in stuffing something.'

How Mark Hunter would have responded to this statement is unfortunately lost to history, because at this moment an interruption occurs in the form of another young Japanese woman, more robust in build than Misaki, with glasses and very long hair, irrupting into the room.

'Hey Misaki!' she cries, speaking in Japanese. 'Look what just arrived from Japan! My new figurine! It's "Karin Miyamoto in Alpine Schoolboy Disguise"!'

Smiling with a collector's pride, the girl holds the plastic figurine aloft. But then she belatedly notices that her friend is not alone, and the smile vanishes.

'Oops. Am I interrupting something?'

Misaki turns from her friend to Mark. 'My apologies. This is my cousin who is a guest here at the moment. As you can see, she is an otaku.'

'You know...' says Mark, 'I don't speak much Japanese, but I did catch that she addressed you as Misaki. You're not Lady Harriet Parker at all, are you?'

Misaki shoots a weary look at her friend.

'You needn't blame her,' continues Mark. 'I'd guessed already.'

Misaki looks genuinely surprised. 'You had? How so?'

Mark smiles. 'Well, apart from a dozen other things, there's the matter of your English. Although you speak it very well, I can tell from the accent that it's not your first language, which it ought to have been if you were born and raised in this country.'

Misaki bows. 'I concede. It was amusing while it lasted. Let me introduce myself. I am Misaki Morishita, and this is my friend Ren Hoshino. We are from Japan and are currently vacationing in your country. Lord Parker and his daughter are at present overseas; they have kindly granted us the use of their house while they are away.' 'Who is this guy?' asks Ren.

'I'm Mark Hunter,' says Mark, introducing himself.

Ren's face lights up. 'Ah! The spy!' 'How do you know that?' frowns Mark.

'I make it my business to know everything that is going on in the town of Linton,' answers Misaki. 'For instance, I know that you have been in Linton for some days now, and you have been interesting yourself in the affair of the serial attacker.'

'You certainly are well informed,' acknowledges Mark. 'You spend a lot of time in Linton then?'

'Oh yes. We go into Linton every night. It is only surprising our paths have not crossed before today. We have seen your friends Dodo Dupont and Mayumi Takahashi; we attended the latter's bookshop appearance on Saturday.'

'She sign my copy of *Multitask Lady*!' announces Ren proudly.

'Very nice,' says Mark. 'But just to clear up a couple of things before I take my leave, what exactly is your connection with Lord Parker? I'm assuming there must be one; I can't imagine him letting complete strangers have the run of his house.'

'You are correct, although my connection is not with Lord Parker, but with Lady Harriet. We have long been internet friends, but this is the first time I have actually travelled to England to see her.'

'Yes, but you're not seeing her, are you?' points out Mark. 'You're house-sitting for her while she's away.'

'True, but we did enjoy some time together before her departure.'

'Yes, about that departure, just where precisely have they gone? None of Lord Parker's friends seem to be aware that he's gone abroad. They think he's still at home. It seems funny that they should just head off like that without telling anyone.'

'I cannot answer for other people's actions,' replies Misaki. 'For reasons of his own, Lord Parker did not care to reveal to me his holiday destination. It would seem he has told no one.'

Mark rises from his chair. 'Well, that seems to be all I'm going to learn here today,' he says. 'I'll leave you both to…' He looks at the two smiling faces, '…whatever it is you're doing…'

'I am sorry we could not have furnished you with more information with regard to Lord Parker's current location.'

'Oh, I don't suppose it matters,' says Mark lightly. 'He's probably off shooting rhinos in Kenya.'

Misaki bows her head in agreement at this very plausible explanation.

Chapter Eighteen
Mysterious Night for Getting Laid

Night. South of the equator it falls with tropical suddenness. In the temperate zones it takes a bit longer. And if you happen to be in one of the polar regions you might have to wait up to six months for it, depending on the time of year.

Here in Linton night falls this evening right on schedule. I believe the rotation of the Earth and its yearly orbit around the sun have something to do with this.

Tonight promises to be a very special night for our hero Murray Leinster. For tonight he will be popping over the road to lose his virginity! His Mysterious Girlfriend is no longer menstruating and is ready to assist him in misplacing this item which is still perceived by many as a girl's most cherished possession, while for a boy is an embarrassment to be got rid of as soon as possible.

Murray stands in the hallway of his home, with his mother fussing over him as though he were about to attend an awards ceremony or some other gala event.

'Fingernails.'

Murray holds out his hands for inspection.

'Yes, they're clean. Nothing spoils the moment like dirty fingernails. Now, let me check that your ears are clean. She might want to stick her tongue in them and it won't be nice for the poor girl if they're waxy.'

'I've cleaned my ears!' groans Murray. 'I did everything on that list you gave me!'

'Let's look at you... Hair's alright. Good thing you had it trimmed on Saturday... Clothes are alright. Not that it matters; you won't be wearing them for long...'

'Mum...' protests Murray, embarrassed.

She sighs. 'Just look at you. My little boy, and you're

about to become a man! They grow up so fast!'

With his slight build and that baby-smooth face with its permanently bewildered expression, if anyone bears the hallmarks of being 'about to become a man', it is not Murray Leinster.

His mum pats his crotch. 'You scrubbed down there, I hope...? That's the most important part of all... And yes, your tanks are full; nice and heavy...'

'Can I go now, Mum?' pleads Murray. 'I don't want to be late...'

'You're right! Never keep a girl waiting!' She puts her hands on her son's shoulders, regards him solemnly. 'Now don't *worry*.'

'I'm not worried, Mum.'

'Good! Because worrying can lead to—although at your age that's not likely to happen. Anyway, just you go round there and act like it's a normal visit. You don't have to do anything; just let things take their natural course. Your girlfriend's the experienced one, so you just do whatever she tells you to. Unless of course she starts saying things like "No! Please don't!" in that particular tone of voice I told you about; then you've got to do the *opposite* of what she says.'

'I *know* all that, Mum,' insists Murray. 'You've told me enough times! Can I just go now?'

'Of course you can, sweetie!' says Mum. 'Mummy's just making sure you've remembered your lessons!' She kisses him.

But then she keeps on kissing him, and Murray has to forcibly disengage himself.

'Mum!'

Mum pouts. 'I just wanted to make sure your kissing was up to scratch,' she says. She turns her back and folds her arms pettishly. 'Fine, then! Go! Go, if you don't need me anymore!'

'I don't need you for *that*.'

And Murray hurriedly exits the house before any further

delays can occur.

He breathes in the air of the warm spring evening. He crosses the street, the familiar street with its cosy-looking bungalows, the street he has known all his life. And he knocks at the door of the opposite bungalow, the place where his Mysterious Girlfriend lives all by herself like a proper grown-up.

Eve Chandler seems to be positively glowing when she answers her front door. Her eyes are sparkling, her smile broad and genuinely welcoming. His heart leaps in response and he remembers that day— only last Monday but so long ago—when she first walked into 9-C's classroom and he instantly fell in love, feeling—just like James Bigglesworth—that he had found the person 'he'd been looking for all his life.'

'Come on in then!'

She leads Murray into the front room. Eve is dressed casually in jeans and t-shirt, her feet bare; her face, he notices, is more carefully made-up than usual.

She sits Murray down on the sofa.

'Stay right there,' she says. 'I've got a little surprise for you.'

And, winking, she disappears into the kitchen. Murray is afforded little time to speculate as to the nature of this 'little surprise,' as Eve returns almost instantly, carrying a dessert bowl. She presents it to Murray.

'Ta-da! Treacle tart and cold custard!'

'Wow! My favourite!'

Eve drops onto the sofa beside him while Murray, having taken the bowl, stares appreciatively at its contents.

'Well, tuck in then!' urges Eve. 'It's not just for looking at!' Murray does as he is urged.

'Wow!' he says again. 'This is great! It tastes exactly like Mum's treacle tart!'

'Ta, but I can't take the credit for it,' confesses Eve. 'I got that treacle tart from Lorrington's over in Bradford Court.

I'd've liked to bake you one meself, but what with everything, I just haven't had time.'

(There is a very good reason for this treacle tart tasting like his mum's—Murray's mum's 'home-made' treacle tart actually hails from the very same bakery!)

Murray polishes off his dessert, gauchely wipes his mouth with the back of his hand.

'How did you know I like treacle tart and cold custard?' he inquires. 'Did Mum tell you?'

'Nope,' replies Eve. 'I just knew.'

'How did you know?'

Eve smiles enigmatically. 'Same way I know a lot of things about you.'

Murray frowns. 'How come is it so many people know things about me. I mean, one of those Japanese girls said she even knew the size of my... my...'

'Your cock, yeah,' agrees Eve. 'Yeah, it's funny that. It's like you're a secret celebrity or summat. Actually, I'm pulling your leg, love. Your mam *did* tell me about the treacle tart. She gave me this big list of all your favourite things to eat.' She strokes Murray's face. 'So how are you doing? Any more memories come back to you?'

Murray shakes his head.

'And what about your mam? Have you asked her? I mean about that feller Carson?'

Another negative.

'I reckon you should. Like I told you, if anything bad went down between you and that feller when you were a kid, your mam most likely knows about it.'

'I don't like to ask her...' says Murray uncomfortably.

'Why not? She won't get mad at you.'

'She might. I mean, she might not want to talk about Carson... Y'know, she might... It might...'

Eve sighs. 'Look, if you've still got any daft ideas that that feller might be your dad; forget 'em! I'm telling you, he's too young!' 'Yeah, I know...' says Murray.

'I reckon you should try and get the full story,' continues Eve. 'Whatever happened, you must have buried it away in your mind, and if it had stayed buried that would've been fair enough... But now that you've started remembering, you'd be best off knowing the rest of it; otherwise you're always gunna be wonderin' about it.'

'Yeah...' says Murray. 'But it might... you know... it might be something... embarrassing...'

Eve squeezes his arm. 'I know what you mean. But y'know, if there is summat like that in it, you don't have to tell the whole world about it, do you? We'd keep it all between the three of us: me, you and your mam.'

Murray manages a smile. 'I guess so...'

'Good!'

'Are we going to go back to that place in the woods? I mean, because of Scarlette?'

'I'm thinking that we ought to. She were giving me a lot of smug looks in school today, was Scarlette... Yeah, she might've just been looking smug cuz she'd led us on a wild goose chase, but it might also be cuz she knew that we'd lost her trail at those ruins.'

'So you think she could be hiding her brother somewhere around there?'

'Yeah...' Specially seeing as Rose and Rachel are both so dead sure that Frank Hanson *was* the guy who attacked them...'

'Isn't Vanessa sure?'

'Vanessa never saw the guy's face. Poor lass, the whole world seems to know she got done from behind.' Eve's expression changes. 'Hey! Let's stop talking about that stuff! Tonight's meant to be for love and romance! Time to change the channel!'

'The TV's not on,' says Murray.

'It's a figure of speech, sweetheart,' says Eve. 'And we're not having the telly on; telly's for folks that haven't got anythin' to talk about; and us, we've got loads to talk about!'

'Have we?'

'Yeah! Let's talk about sexy stuff! To get us in the mood, like,' says Eve, winking a decorated eye. 'Let me see... I know! I'll tell you the story of me first sex experience! That's a really good one.'

'No!' objects Murray, affronted. 'I don't want to hear about the person you had before me!'

Eve ruffles his hair. 'No, silly! I don't mean the time I lost me Vcard; I mean the first time I saw people having sex! As a spectator, like. This were back when I were about eight or nine.'

'You mean you saw people having sex in real life? Not on the internet?'

'Yep, this were in real life. Real outdoor sex in the woods it were. Shall I tell you?'

'Okay.'

'Right. Well, like I say, I were about eight or nine and it were the summer holidays.'

'This was in Rotherham?'

'Aye; well, just outside. I was best mates with this lass called Laura back then. She was a shy girl, a bit backwards for her age. Always sucking her thumb, she was. Anyway, it was the summer holidays and we were out in the countryside, exploring, playing games. It were one of those really hot, sunny days, like they always are when you're remembering summers from back when you were a kid. Me an' Laura were under the trees in some woods where it was shady; I think we'd wandered off further than we were supposed to, that day; right off the beaten track.

'Well, we heard these voices. It was a feller and a lass. I think I guessed right off from what I could hear that something sexy might be going on, so I tell Laura that we ought to creep up on them and have a gander at what they're doing. Laura was kind of scared, but she followed me like she always did. So we followed the sound of the voices and we came to this clearing in the woods and that's where they were. The couple were right in the middle of the clearing and the sun was shining right down on them. I still don't know who they were; we'd never seen them before. They were grown-ups, in their twenties or thirties.

'Me and Laura were crouched behind these ferns. I whispered to her that we had to keep dead quiet, cuz if we got found out, it'd spoil the show. And what a show it was! Things were already well past the point of no return when we got there, cuz they were all over each other this couple, and the feller was helping the lass out of her summer dress. It was what you'd call a sexual frenzy, and I don't reckon either of us had seen the like of it before; not even on the telly.

'After he'd got the girl naked, the guy starts getting out of his own clothes. He already had his cock out (and *that* was a sight for our virgin eyes!) and so he was already ready for action, but the feller was obviously so horny that he just had to get himself naked. So there they both were, under the blazing sun. *Her* tits, ass and bush; *his* cock; that's what we were looking at. We were a captive audience.

'But there was still the main event to come. After another bout of trying to eat each other up, they get down on the ground. The lass, she knows how she wants to do it; she lies herself facedown with her big fat bum up in the air and all glowing in the sun. And of course the feller moves right in, buries his cock in her and starts fucking. Me and Laura, our eyes were glued on those two. Him pounding away and her crying out. We could see her face cuz she was lying with head looking our way. I know some young kids, when they see sex and don't really understand it, they sometimes think that the feller is hurting the girl. But I could tell that all that noise she was making was cuz she was happy, not hurting. I tell you, she was so full of joy that me and Laura were picking it up, like she was transmitting it to us.

'You get these kind of puritan feminists who say that women shouldn't have sex, cuz they say the whole business is degrading for women. Well, I say that's stupid. How can a lady look undignified if she's enjoying herself? That's what matters. (And anyhow, if anyone looks silly during sex, I reckon it's the feller; thrusting away like that, in and out, in and out, like a bloody oil pump!)

'Anyway, this guy must have known how to pace himself, cuz it seemed like they were at it forever. Not that it ever got boring for us who was watchin'. But they must have still been in a hurry or summat, cuz as soon as they'd come—and they *both* made a lot of noise when that happened—they were up and getting their clothes on. No lying back and lighting up ciggies; once they were dressed, they were off like they were late for a meeting or summat. We never did find out who they were or anything; but I've always liked to think they were part of a picnic group or summat and that they had to rush back before *her* feller and *his* wife started getting suspicious! That's how it seemed—a sudden, spontaneous fuck under the summer sun.'

'Why didn't you follow them to see where they went?' suggests Murray.

'Ah, well that's cuz there's a bit more to the story. After the couple had gone, we just looked at each other, Laura and me, and we were both all flushed and bright-eyed, as if we were the ones who'd just been serviced. And then we walked out into the clearing, right up to where they'd been, on the grass right under the sun. It was like we felt like this was some sacred spot or summat. Leastways, it must have had some effect on us, cuz you know what we did? We went and copied what we'd just seen! We kissed each other, we took our clothes off and then we got down on the grass, right where they'd been. Laura, she laid down with her bum in the air, and me, I was the man. Didn't have the right equipment of course, but I glued my crotch to her bum and then I started ramming away at her just like I'd seen him doing, and we both started making noises like that lady had! Monkey See, Monkey Do, eh?

'But sex is nature, isn't it? So it's just natural to want to do it outdoors and especially out in the countryside. Only drawback is you might get yourself an uninvited audience like those two did! Sometimes I like to think that lady could see us there, behind those ferns. Cuz like I said, she was facing right in our direction. So yeah, I like to think she could see us and she was pleased, cuz she wanted us kids to see, to see how much she was enjoying herself.'

'You think she really could see you?'

Eve shrugs. 'I dunno. It was really dark where we were, under the trees, so... I dunno. It's just nice to think that us three girls were all sharing summat that the feller wasn't in on, y'know? All Girls Together!'

Eve sighs reminiscently. Then she turns to Murray, strokes his face. 'So, how'd you like that little childhood story of mine?'

'It was nice,' says Murray.

'Aye, I can see it went down well,' says Eve, with a significant look at Murray's crotch. 'It's got me feeling all frisky, an' all. Tell you what—'

And she proceeds not to tell Murray anything at all but to show instead. Standing up, she first pulls off her t-shirt and then steps out of her jeans and reveals to Murray that she *has* dressed up for this evening after all. She now stands before him wearing a black lacy bra and a pair of black lacy knickers to match. Now, courtesy of a lifetime of being witness to his mother parading around the house in various states of undress, Murray has, all but unconsciously, become something of an expert on female undergarments; consequently, he does not have to be told that the lingerie his Mysterious Girlfriend has chosen for this occasion comes from the luxury end of this most interesting area of the clothing industry.

With her raven hair and creamy complexion, black is the perfect colour for Eve. She gives Murray a twirl, performs a brief hip-thrusting dance. Then she drops back down onto the sofa close to Murray.

'So what do you think?' asks Eve, in the confident tone of someone sure of a favourable response.

'You look beautiful,' says Murray simply, pronouncing the word 'beautiful' somewhat awkwardly. ('Beautiful' is not a word commonly found in the masculine lexicon, and as a consequence, it can sometimes trip rather clumsily from the male tongue.)

And beautiful she is. More than just beautiful for Murray Leinster— Eve Chandler represents to him the literal embodiment of physical perfection. Every instinct, every emotion contained within this boy's skinny body yearns for this girl. She reclines on her side, smiling at him, and his eyes devoutly devour the strong curves of her glowing, healthy body. The smooth expanse of her powerful thighs, the ripe heavy breasts, even the fold of fat just above the swell of her raised hip... An arousing, protecting, comforting body.

The tears well up in his eyes.

Eve slides close to him, enfolding him in her arms.

'You are so gone on me, aren't you?' she says, kissing him. 'So fucking gone. You love me more than anything, don't you?' 'Yes,' says Murray.

Another hungry kiss. 'And know something? I'm crazy about you. I'd do anything for you; and that almost pisses me off.' She strokes Murray's granite crotch. 'You're about to explode in your boxers, you horny cock-monster. Well, I'll just do summat to help you out there...'

She slides down to the floor, unzips Murray's jeans and pulls out his aching penis.

'Look at you,' she says, imprinting a tender kiss. 'Y'look like butter wouldn't melt, but just look at you.' More kisses. 'My sweet sexy cockmonster...'

She takes him in her mouth.

This is like last week in the Pavilion, only much better this time because it's just him and Eve; Eve's strong hand holding him tightly, Eve's hot mouth around him, Eve's strong teeth gently gripping... Along with the intense pleasure, a feeling of unreality floods over Murray Leinster. Why is she here, his Mysterious Girlfriend? What has he done to deserve her? He's just... He's nobody... Why would she choose him of all people? This beautiful girl who has taken him by the hand and out of his narrow life into a world of adventure. This larger than life girl who embodies all the confidence and charisma, all the boldness and animal vigour he sees as lacking in himself. This warrior goddess who can disable a whole gang of opponents with highly skilled savagery. Why would she choose him? Him of all people! It seems so preposterous that suddenly feels that it just can't be real at all. He must be living in a dream, in a world of his own creation. But if that is true, if this is all a dream, then please don't let it end... Oh please don't let it end...

He reaches white-hot climax. Light flashes before his eyes. The floodgates open, and it doesn't even stop then; he is caressed to such a state of pleasure he moans... And then the ecstasy starts to recede, he feels himself sinking...

And then Eve's smiling face is before him, an irrefutable reality.

'You're a naughty lad, aren't you?' she purrs.

'Did I... do something wrong...?'

'Only nearly drowned me in it,' she tells him. 'But that's okay cuz it just shows how much you love me...'

She kisses him, returning to him a taste of his love.

Another white flash and Eve is suddenly on her feet, facing the window.

'What the hell's going on out there?' she demands.

'I don't know,' says Murray. 'It's been going on for a while.'

Eve marches over to the open living room window and looks out into the street. Then her eyes turn downwards.

'You!' she exclaims.

Eve's living room—as I failed to mention earlier when I should have been setting the scene—is in partial darkness, with only a standard lamp in the far corner lighting the room.

The curtains are open and Murray has no trouble in identifying the figure that rises from its place of concealment beneath the window as being that of his own mother.

'Oh, Mum!' groans Murray.

'I hope I'm not interrupting anything,' she says. 'I just happened to be in the neighbourhood...'

'You *live* in the neighbourhood,' says Eve. 'What are you doing in my garden?'

'Well, you are both still minors,' points out Miss Leinster. 'So I just thought I should be the responsible adult and check up on you kids.'

'And is that why you were taking pictures of us?'

'Pictures? What pictures?'

'The pictures you were taking with the digital camera you've got in your hands.'

'Oh, *those* pictures!' says Miss Leinster. 'Just something for the family album.'

'Yeah, I reckon you've got enough snaps for the family album now,' says Eve. 'So... you can be going now, can't you? Please? Pretty please?'

'Oh, *all right*,' says Miss Leinster, in the tone of someone being unfairly imposed upon. 'I'll leave you two lovebirds to it.' To Eve: 'And don't you go holding back on my boy, young lady.'

'Does it look like I was?' retorts Eve. 'Good night, Miss Leinster.'

Murray joins Eve at the window and they watch Mary Leinster cross the road and re-enter her own house.

'Sorry about that,' says Murray.

'No worries,' replies Eve. 'She just cares about you.'

However, she firmly closes the window and draws the curtains.

'Come on,' she says. 'Let's take this to my bedroom.'

She takes Murray by the hand and leads him to that desirable room. Here the curtains are already drawn and the room cosily lit by a muted bedside table lamp. A scent of perfume pervades the air. Eve sits Murray down on her bed. Standing before him she unclips her bra and slips it off. Leaning close, she offers her breasts to Murray.

'Kiss,' she says.

Murray kisses. When his lips fasten around her erect nipple, the kiss instinctively becomes suction. Eve strokes Murray's hair.

And then she steps back, turns and presents her posterior to Murray. She peels off her knickers.

'Kiss,' she says again.

Murray leans in and kisses the warm buttocks, feeling the urgent heat and breathing the comforting aroma issuing from the deep cleft between.

And then Eve turns around and presents a dense growth of long pubic hair. She gently guides Murray's head towards her.

'Kiss,' she says.

Murray kisses, his nose and mouth buried in the dense pubic thatch. A new aroma assails him, unfamiliar and inviting.

Suddenly a cry of alarm, the sound of tearing fabric and something heavy impacting with the bedroom floor, and the mood is destroyed.

Eve jumps back, prepared for attack. Murray just looks alarmed. A figure lies on the floor beneath the bedroom window, tangled amongst curtains that have been torn from their tracks. For a split-second Murray thinks it must be his mother again, gone back on her word and returned for more espionage. But then he sees long black hair, and when the girl staggers to her feet he recognises her as the bespectacled one of the two Japanese girls they have met before. The same girls who ruined the moment of his first kiss with Eve!

The second Japanese girl, the smaller one with the bob, now appears at the window and climbs into the room.

'My sincere apologies for disturbing you,' says Misaki. 'My friend here is rather clumsy.'

Ren grins with her overbite and holds up a telephoto-lensed camera. 'Yeah, I trying to get good shot between curtain, and I kind of overbalance... Whoops!'

She taps her head and projects her tongue from the corner of her mouth.

Eve confronts these new intruders, arms akimbo.

'And what were you doing in my garden in the first place?' she demands.

'Well, we'd heard that you would be taking Murray Leinster's virginity tonight,' replies Misaki smoothly. 'So naturally we wanted to witness the occasion. Unfortunately, we discovered that someone with the same idea had arrived before us, forcing us to withdraw. But then she was caught and dismissed by yourself and so we were able to take over.'

'You got one major bush!' observes Ren, literally drooling at the sight of Eve's thatch. Hunkering down, she starts taking some shots of the area in question.

'Pack that in!' snaps Eve. 'In fact, shove off, the pair of you! This is getting like a ruddy circus! Out! And off my property!'

'Of course.' Misaki bows her head. 'We shall withdraw at once. And again, my sincere apologies for the disturbance.'

The two girls exit as they arrived, through the window, with Ren pausing only to deliver a final injunction to Murray:

'Hey, you! You rape her real good, okay?'

Eve slams the window shut behind her. Thanks to Ren's destructive entry, she can't do anything about drawing the curtains.

She exhales a gusty sigh and turning to Murray: 'What a palaver, eh? Now—'

She stops mid-sentence, her rueful smile transformed to look of horror.

'Murray, get over here right now!'

And it is here that Murray Leinster makes the mistake that almost ends his young life. Forgetting his mother's sage advice about doing everything that Eve Chandler tells him to, and perceiving that Eve's expression of alarm is directed not at himself but at something over his shoulder, instead obeying Eve, he turns to discover the cause of her alarm.

In the bedroom doorway stands astronaut Frank Hanson. Tall, broad-shouldered, he wears his grey astronaut's flight suit; the insignia on chest and sleeves depicting the logo of the Asteroid Belt Mining Project. The face, seen in so many photographs, is certainly his, but it is a face drained of all emotion, all personality. The eyes of this implacable visage are fixed on Murray.

Murray barely has time to panic before arms spring like snakes and two vice-like hands grip his neck in a crushing embrace.

After this it's all a bit of a blur for Murray.

Unable to breathe, his vision clouds over, head-splitting pain and dizziness assail him. He sees a pink shape which must be Eve smash into his assailant and the hands squeezing the life from him now pick him up and hurl him across the room. Murray collides with a chest of drawers and lying stunned on the carpet he hears splintering wood and breaking glass as something large and heavy crashes through the window. Murray perceives it to be a man dressed in black. A brief but intense struggle follows and then a figure—it must be Hanson—exits through the broken window.

And then it's all noise and confusion, people appearing from everywhere, looming over Murray… Then the police arrive, an ambulance crew, and finally a weary and wretched Murray Leinster is consigned to bed in his own familiar bedroom, his virginity still firmly intact.

Chapter Nineteen
Eve Scoffs All the Apples and Gives God the Finger

Scarlette Hanson had always idolised her brother Frank.

The two siblings were the only children of astronaut Colonel Joseph Hanson and his wife Eileen Hanson née Ballantyne. There was a surprising gap of fifteen years between the births of the two children, with not even a miscarriage or cot-death to mark the intervening period. And of course people would gossip about what the husband and wife had been doing during this period of childlessness, putting forth all the obvious suggestions: a rift in the marriage, a period of mutually agreed infidelities, or that too much time in space had interfered with the Colonel's fertility. And then, with the advent of the belated second child there were even (false) suspicions that it might not even be the Colonel's at all.

But whatever the reasons for the fifteen-year interim, Scarlette Hanson grew up with just one elder brother who was already an air force cadet while she was still in kindergarten. And to her young eyes this brother of hers had appeared such a handsome heroic figure, with his movie star good looks, his smart uniform, his ready smile. Of course, he was away from the family's Texas home a lot of the time while Scarlette was growing up; but how eagerly she would look forward to his every homecoming! And not just because he would always return well-supplied with toys and candy for his little sister, it was *him* she yearned to see; her heart raced whenever he walked into the room; she would run to embrace him on each homecoming; and she was never so happy as she was when he was spending some quality time with her, playing games with her, teasing her, telling tall stories about his exploits as an astronaut.

As she grew older, Scarlette would become increasingly self-conscious about her appearance when the time for another visit from her brother was drawing near. She wanted to look her best for him when he arrived and for him to notice how fast she was growing up. And being blessed with good eyesight, Frank Hanson certainly *did* notice that his little sister was growing up fast. And Scarlette, a slyly perceptive young lady, *noticed* that he was noticing.

And then, just three years ago, Frank and Scarlette Hanson, during the former's last furlough, had been discovered in bed together by their astounded mother. The resultant explosion in the Hanson household had led to the parents agreeing to separate, father and son remaining in Texas, mother and daughter moving to England; one reason for this split being that the Colonel blamed his daughter for the incestuous relationship, while Eileen blamed her son.

And actually it was the Colonel who was right, at least in so far as identifying the instigator. As the adult involved, Frank was the most culpable, but nevertheless Scarlette had been the seductress.

And so Scarlette and her mother had settled in the unremarkable Southern English town of Linton, where the daughter had started at the local school, and the mother had started to drink even more than she had before. As we know, Scarlette had hooked up with Lassiter, Malcolm and Sasha; three classmates she had discovered to be on the same wavelength as herself: intellectual and depraved. As three kindred spirits, they were amusing companions and she had happily participated in their various evil schemes. But try as she might, she could not forget her brother. That one night of forbidden love had left her panting for more; and now she couldn't even contact him. Her parents had placed a steel wall between the siblings; and in spite of her best efforts, Scarlette hadn't even been able to discover an email address by which she could speak to Frank. Was he yearning for her as much as she yearned for him? Or had he come to regret their night of passion? Perhaps even blaming his sister for what might have been a scandal that would have ruined his career had the story not been so effectively suppressed?

She just didn't know. Her selfish heart told her that he must be pining for her; that she had made herself indispensable to her brother; that thoughts of her fuelled his onanistic fantasies.

And then one night, just three weeks ago, her brother had returned to her.

She had awoken from a dream to find him just standing there in the darkness of her bedroom. She knew it was him instantly. She wasn't even surprised. Yes, he had come to her, drawn to her by a compelling attraction of souls which defied time and space. She had leapt from her bed and thrown her arms around him. Her first surprise was when he had not reacted to her embrace. He just stood there, warm and alive yet passive and inert. She had looked into his face and found it devoid of emotion, the eyes fixed and staring. At first she had been alarmed by this change that had come over her beloved brother, perhaps the result of his impossible journey. But then she had made a discovery which had turned her misgivings to boundless joy. She discovered that her brother responded to her commands. Like a robot he would move when and how she instructed him. He would look into her eyes if she so ordered him. He would kiss her if she so ordered him. He would strike her if she so ordered him. He would obey every physical command save for the speaking of words. In his new form he appeared incapable of uttering a sound. He could perform any task, obey any command; therefore his intelligence and understanding had to be functioning to some degree; yet he had lost all personal volition and free will. Her brother had returned to her as her puppet, her slave, her pet.

It was everything she could have wished for.

Naturally, the first use to which she had put her brother was that of serving her own pleasure and gratification. He proved an indefatigable lover, as gentle or as brutal as she commanded him to be. His new body required neither sleep nor sustenance; never tiring, he seemed able to draw on limitless supplies of energy. But he made love to her with no display of emotion, no manifestation of pleasure. It began to dawn on her that he just could not experience pleasure, that even an orgasm triggered no response; which then led her to wonder if this was also true in the case of pleasure's opposite number, pain. Some experiments performed with a knife soon confirmed this theory. Her brother's body could be injured, but his mind did not register the pain. Her brother had become an automaton, his brain still functioned but was devoid of emotion; he was numb to all feeling, be it mental or physical.

In the wake of her first intimacy with her brother, she had started to have the visions; those dreams of the Dark Lord, the Nameless One; the glaring-eyed spirit whose features were engraved upon the wall of their safe haven. It was coming; it was returning to Earth and its arrival would herald a new Dark Age of chaos and fear. Scarlette sensed these facts without their ever being put into words, just as she sensed the names by which the creature should be called. The Dark Lord; The Nameless One. It had been here before, long, long ago, in those dark spaces of prehistory; and by those names had the creature been known.

Scarlette had begun to despise more than ever the people around her, those poor fools, living their stupid mundane lives; she even began to despise those three classmates who were the nearest thing she possessed to friends; she had at first considered sharing her secret, her power, with them, but had then decided they were unworthy; their evil was too petty, too small scale.

And she resolved that to express her contempt and to afford herself pleasure, she would unleash her brother upon some of these fools with whom she went to school. Of course they all annoyed her, every single one of them. But some of them annoyed her more than others and she started to select those students; the ones who pissed her off the most; unwitting students who might even be unaware that they had ever incurred the malice of Scarlette Hanson; and she sent her brother out to assault them. It was a vicarious pleasure, as she did not accompany her brother to witness these assaults, but it was always gratifying when the news broke that they had been successfully carried out.

But then, last week, when she had fallen out with her friend Sasha Distel, her selfish friendship for that girl had turned to the most spiteful malice; Sasha who had always treated her like some sidekick or follower; Sasha who had thought she was better than Scarlette just because she looked like a fucking fashion model… Sasha would be the next target and this time Scarlette wanted to witness the assault in person. And so, she had accompanied her brother when they had waylaid their target, and Scarlette had watched with joy and savage satisfaction as he violently raped her; the only problem was that Sasha had inevitably seen her former friend looking on and of course this necessitated that Sasha be silenced. And so she had ordered her brother to strangle the girl.

Scarlette had now crossed the Rubicon; she had taken a human life, and now, far from feeling any remorse, she thirsted to take more. More blood must be shed, not just for her own pleasure, but in the name of her Dark Lord.

But now she was under suspicion and those busybodies, Eve Chandler and Murray Leinster, had started sticking their noses into other people's business. Well then, they would be the next targets. Her brother would kill the both of them. It didn't matter that Frank had been identified; no-one could stop him, and no-one could stop her, either.

Scarlette doesn't know it yet, but this latest attack has not panned out so well.

Eve Chandler, dressed for school, knocks on the front door

of the Hanson residence. The street is quiet. In consequence of the announcement which has seemingly exonerated Frank Hanson of any involvement in the serial attacks, the besieging journalists have dispersed.

The door opens, answered by a woman, thin-faced and fiftyish, dressed in a loose wrapper. Her hair is dishevelled, her make-up smudged. She regards her caller with bleary-eyed truculence.

'Whaddaya want?'

'Good morning, Mrs Hanson!' greets Eve brightly. 'Is your son Frank at home?'

'Frank? Oh gee, lemme see... Frank... Oh yeah, Frank can't come to the door right now cuz he's in outer space. Don't you people ever get the message?'

'I'm not a reporter,' Eve tells her.

Mrs Hanson looks at her again, absorbs more detail. 'Oh, yeah; you're a kid. You been in a catfight or somethin'?'

(Eve is sporting a swollen lip and a bruise above her left eye.)

'Kind of,' says Eve. 'What about your daughter? Is she at home?'

'Scarlette? Yeah, she's here,' replies Mrs Hanson. 'Leastways I think she is. She comes and goes as she pleases, that girl. Day or night, she just does whatever the hell she wants. So yeah, I think she's in; but I can't promise anything.'

'Could you check for me?' asks Eve. 'There's something important I need to talk to her about.'

Mrs Hanson snorts. 'Look, honey. I may be her mother, but I got no control over that girl, that angel of mine who's really a devil. She won't answer if I holler out; not unless she wants something. So if you got somethin' to say to her, then you just go on up to her room. I ain't stoppin' you.'

And so saying, Mrs Hanson turns away from the door and shuffles back inside on slippered feet. Eve follows her into the large open front room which seems to occupy most of the ground floor of the house. Mrs Hanson drops onto a sofa in front of a large screen TV, switched on but with muted volume. She picks up a tumbler of whisky and points with it to the staircase across the room.

'First door on the left,' she says.

'Thanks,' says Eve.

She ascends the stairs and knocks on the first door on the left. There is no immediate response, and not standing on ceremony, Eve just walks into the room.

Scarlette lies sprawled on her bed, one arm stretched over the pillow, twisted bedclothes only half covering her, suggesting a night of troubled sleep. A sticky rivulet of drool has escaped from her open mouth.

Standing on even less ceremony, Eve wakes the girl by the simple expedient of grabbing her by the collar of her pyjama shirt and shaking her violently.

Scarlette's eyes open, focus on Eve.

'What the fuck—' she begins. 'You?'

And then incredulity replaces anger. '*You!*'

'Yes, me,' says Eve firmly. 'You weren't expecting to see me today, were you? So was I supposed to be dead, or just raped?' 'I dunno what you're talking about,' says Scarlette.

'Don't give me that,' retorts Eve. 'You sent your brother after me and Murray last night, didn't you? Didn't you?'

She punches Scarlette in the face. Blood spurts from her nose.

'You fuckin' bitch!' screams Scarlette, quickly recovering from the shock. 'You can't do that to me!'

Eve pounces on her. She hits the girl again and again.

'I'll show you what I can fucking do!'

She tears open Scarlette's pyjama shirt, exposing her breasts. Scarlette screams invective. Eve throws the bedclothes aside and pulls the pyjama pants from the other girl's furiously struggling legs.

'For Christ's sake you fuckin' psycho!' screams Scarlette. She tries to escape, tries to rise from the bed. Eve drives a fist into her stomach, knocking her back.

'How about I give you a taste of your own medicine?' snarls Eve. She grabs a round hairbrush from the bedside table. 'How about I shove this inside you?'

Scarlette blanches, a look of horror on her battered face. 'You wouldn't dare!'

'Wouldn't I? It's what you fuckin' deserve, you bitch! After what you've done!'

Brandishing the hairbrush, Eve renews her assault. Scarlette struggles wildly, desperately; kicking and writhing, spitting and screaming. Remorselessly, Eve pins the girl down, grinding the hairbrush into her crotch.

The screams become shrieks of pain...

And then Eve finds herself violently pulled from the bed, and there are police officers all around, and Mark Hunter, holding her firmly, snatches the hairbrush from her hand.

'I think we'll take over from here,' he tells her.

Chapter Twenty
Mysterious Missive

PE this sunny afternoon is football; and with Murray Leinster and Kenneth Spacey in defence, and Pornboy keeping goal, victory is assured for the opposing team!

At the moment we join the trio, the action of the game is concentrated at the other end of the pitch, so the three boys are just standing in their positions and talking. Not about the game; Murray, Spacey and Pornboy are three people who couldn't be less interested in football or any other sporting activity and are numbered amongst those students who consider PE lessons to be an ordeal. So no, they are not talking about football, they are talking about the previous night and how Murray very nearly got strangled to death when he should have been getting laid.

'Well man, what doesn't kill you makes you stronger,' says Spacey philosophically.

'Yeah, but it was a waste of good Viagra,' remarks Pornboy in his usual sneering tone.

'Viagra?' echoes Murray, not understanding.

'It's an erection pill,' explains Spacey. 'It's for guys who can't... y'know, rise to the occasion.'

'Oh,' says Murray. 'I didn't use that. Should I have?'

'Nah! You don't need it, do you, man?' says Spacey. 'That girl of yours gives you a boner just by looking at you, right? Just shows she's the girl for you.'

'Yeah, right,' scoffs Pornboy.

'It's guys like you that need Viagra,' Spacey tells him. 'They can get it up when it's porn they're lookin' at, but then, if ever they find themselves with a real lady, they like fall to pieces. That's your future, my friend.'

'Shuddup!' snarls Pornboy.

'Y'know, you should lighten up,' says Spacey. 'You're gettin' more and more uptight these days.'

'Spacey...?' says Murray, hesitant.

'Yeah?'

'Do you like girls?'

'Sure, I like 'em,' answers Spacey, casually.

Murray has been wondering about this since seeing Spacey in town with that older boy; the one Eve had said looked like he was more than just a friend.

But now, conversation is suspended; the game is suddenly heading rapidly in their direction, leaving the boys with little choice but to start taking some interest in it.

After the match has been successfully lost, the boys return to the changing rooms. Murray discovers that during his absence a letter has been slipped into his bag—a letter in a girlish pink envelope with just his first name written on the front in an equally girlish hand.

Could this be from Eve? Is this part of some new

Adventure? Or is it just that her distrust of mobile phones has made her turn to old-fashioned hand-written communication?

Or maybe it's nothing to do with Adventures; maybe it's a juicy love letter! Murray has never had a love letter from his Mysterious Girlfriend. Love letters tend to happen at the tentative beginnings of a relationship, and in Eve and Murray's particular case, the rapid progress of their courting had by-passed letter-writing and had jumped straight to them actually talking to each other. So yes, perhaps Eve has written him a really naughty letter to make up for things going wrong last night! Murray likes the idea of that.

As soon as he has changed, Murray exits the changing rooms and, finding a quiet spot behind the PE equipment room, eagerly opens the letter. The note, written on cutely patterned paper, is unsigned, and Murray soon realises that it is not from Eve! It reads:

Dear Murray,

I just had to write this letter to you. I can't hold it in anymore! I'm in love with you, Murray Leinster! Every time I see you my knickers get wet! (Not with wee.) And I always think about you when I'm playing with myself. I know that you have a girlfriend, but I just have to see you and tell you how I feel! Please meet me in the Acorn Grove in Peter Street Park after school today! I'll be waiting for you!

Your Secret Admirer.

Secret Admirer! He has a Secret Admirer. Only two weeks ago Murray had been pretty much resigned to his status as one of those boys that 'girls just don't like in that way'; but now, he not only has a Mysterious Girlfriend, but he has a Secret Admirer as well! Just as well it isn't going to his head.

Harriet the maid stands primly just inside the doorway of Ren Hoshino's bedroom.

Picture a spacious bed chamber in a stately home; a room with ornate, antique furniture, rich carpets, curtains and upholstery; and then imagine that someone has lifted up the ceiling and dumped the contents of one of those Japanese shops devoted to retailing otaku culture into said room: graphic novels, art books, blu rays, computer games, figurines and toys; now you have an accurate picture of Ren Hoshino's bedroom at Linton Hall. Finally, add the girl herself, sitting on the floor surrounded by all this clutter.

She looks up at the maid who has just entered the room.

'I lose something,' she announces, ungrammatically.

'Really, miss?' responds the maid, unconcerned.

'Yeah...' continues Ren, looking—and feeling—more like the defendant than the complainant. 'My new figurine. Karin Miyamoto in Alpine Schoolboy Disguise. I put over there,' (pointing to an antique chiffonier graced with a collection of anime figurines) 'and now I can't find.'

'Really, miss?' repeats Harriet.

'Yeah...' says Ren, wilting under the maid's studied lack of interest. 'You haven't... see it around...?'

'No, miss, I haven't "see it around",' replies Harriet.

Ren scratches the back of her head. 'And... It not just that... I lose other things recently... Computer disc, manga, DVD...'

'Really, miss?' says Harriet once again. 'Perhaps you should speak to the maid who cleans your room?'

'I don't have maid,' answers Ren. 'I like to keep my own room tidy.'

'That fact is plainly visible, miss,' says Harriet, scanning cluttered the room with ironic admiration.

'So... you not see my stuff?'

'How could I have seen your belongings, miss? You surely don't suspect *me* of having taken them?'

Harriet looks straight at Ren, an insolent, challenging

smile on her face.

Ren looks away.

'Well, miss, if that will be all?'

Silence.

Harriet turns, opens the door.

'Oh, I almost forgot!' she says, having done nothing of the sort. 'A message from Lady Misaki: she wishes to see you in her room.' The maid departs.

Now, I'm sure that you have already worked it out by now (because I cannot but assume that anyone with taste and discernment enough to have picked up this book, will also be blessed with a correspondingly high intellect and perspicuity), that Harriet the maid and her father Parker the head butler, are in fact none other than heiress Lady Harriet and her father Lord Parker, rightful tenants of Linton Hall, who have been usurped from their places by their (invited) guest Misaki Morishita, and her (uninvited) Yakuza entourage, and compelled to assume menial positions in their own home. You all know this? Good! I would hope you do because I have scattered a number of clues along the way and not the least of them being the fact the two sets of people in question have the same names.

And as we know, Harriet has chosen to revenge herself by victimising the weak-willed Ren Hoshino, while her father seeks more long-term solutions to their dilemma. When an opportunity had allowed him to answer the ringing of the front door bell, he had been on the verge of revealing his own and his daughter's plight to the caller (Mark Hunter, as you will recall), but Misaki Morishita's untimely arrival on the scene had prevented this.

The above exposition would be an ideal set-up for us following Harriet to re-join her father in the pantry; which is a shame because we are doing nothing of the sort and are instead staying with Ren as she responds to Misaki's summons.

Into the Yakuza daughter's bed chamber Ren bursts as noisily as always, although on this occasion more through habit than from any excess of enthusiasm. She can't help brooding over the loss of her lovely 'Karin Miyamoto in Alpine Schoolboy Disguise' figurine.

Misaki sits up in bed eating her breakfast, which this afternoon happens to be a pot of instant ramen noodles, another delicacy to which the commoner Ren has introduced her during the time of their acquaintance. Misaki is eating her noodles with chopsticks, daunting utensils for the uninitiated, but the Japanese method for consuming cup noodles is if anything even more easy than the Western method of twirling them round a fork: You just grab a length of noodles between your chopsticks, put them in your mouth and then just slurp them up like a suction pump!

(Misaki's cup noodles are the genuine Japanese variety purchased from a UK-based wholesaler of Japanese grocery products; the instant noodles available in most domestic English supermarkets being, in connoisseur Ren's opinion, 'Gross'.)

'And how are you today?' Misaki greets her friend.

'Okay, I guess,' is the reply.

'Quite an eventful night wasn't it? It seems that for once I have to thank my father for his over-protectiveness.'

Misaki refers here to the fortuitous presence of her chief bodyguard, Kondou, at the time the violence had broken out at Eve Chandler's house. It was he who had come flying through the bedroom window to help Eve fight off the homicidal astronaut; and Misaki and Ren had been as surprised to see him as anyone else. It turned out that Kondou, or one of his subordinates, had been in the habit of tailing the two girls on all of their nocturnal expeditions into Linton. This on the instructions of Misaki's father, who wanted his daughter kept under observation and out of harm's way. But to his credit, Kondou had chosen to reveal his presence last evening in order to assist in combating the murderous intruder.

'Yeah, we were lucky Kondou was there,' agrees Ren. 'I mean Eve Chandler's a good fighter but I dunno if she could have fought off that guy by herself.'

'But didn't she dispatch a gang of about six people all by herself on Saturday?' Misaki reminds her.

'Yeah, but they were ordinary guys,' contends Ren. 'That guy last night wasn't ordinary. He was like a zombie; nothing seemed to hurt him.'

'I've been thinking,' says Misaki.

'About the attacker?'

'No, about Murray Leinster.'

'Oh, he's okay,' says Ren, holding up her tablet. 'I checked. He's even gone to school as usual today.'

'Yes, but I've been thinking that I would like to be the one to steal that boy's virginity.'

Ren looks surprised. 'But isn't Eve Chandler supposed to be doing that?'

'Yes, and that's why I'd like to steal him from her and take the prize myself.'

'You can be really mean, Misaki-chan,' says Ren.

Misaki wipes her mouth with a napkin. 'You don't approve?'

'Well…'

'You can watch.'

'I'm in!'

'Good. Then we'll have to set wheels in motion. Is Eve Chandler planning a repeat performance this evening?'

'I dunno, but I can find out.'

'Good.'

Ren turns to leave.

'Ren,' Misaki calls her back. 'Come here.'

Ren approaches the bedside. Misaki takes her hand. 'Are you all right? I thought you looked morose when you first came into the room.

Tell me if something's bothering you.'

Ren looks down. 'Oh, it's nothing...'

Misaki tugs her hand. 'Clearly it is something, Ren-chan. Tell me what it is. You're not allowed to have secrets from me.'

She sees the tears welling up behind Ren's spectacles.

'It's Karin Miyamoto in Alpine Schoolboy Disguise!' she blubbers. 'She's missing!'

And with tears and snot running down her face, she explains to her friend about the disappearance of her beloved possessions.

'Right,' says Misaki. 'First of all, you Ren must make a list of all the items that have gone missing from your room. I will have replacements airlifted from Akihabara straight away. And then,' she says, her face assuming a dangerous expression, 'and then, we shall take steps to discover who the culprit is...'

And the look on Misaki's face does not bode well for the culprit in question.

Chapter Twenty-One
Mysterious Assignation

Murray knows Peter Street Park; it is a Park on Peter Street. One of the town's smaller parks, not on the same scale as Fairview Park or Riverside Park, most of the available space is occupied by a kiddies' play area and on account of this is generally regarded as being just a kiddies' park. Murray himself used to play there when he was a younger; so he knows the park and he also knows the 'Acorn Grove' specified in the love letter: It is a grove of acorn trees (or 'oak trees' to us grownups) situated in a corner of the park. Moreover, there is a small clearing in the middle of this grove; an ideal location for an illicit rendezvous!

But surely (I hear you cry), Murray Leinster cannot intend to keep this assignation with his Secret Admirer? Surely not! Not when he has a Mysterious Girlfriend blessed with a posterior you would kill to get your hands on and whose perfections of mind and body had Murray Leinster literally in tears but three short chapters ago?

Yes, he is keeping the rendezvous, I regret to say.

But perhaps (I hear you desperately surmise) he has shown the letter to his Mysterious Girlfriend, and she has advised him to attend at the appointed time and place in order to gently inform his Secret Admirer that his heart is already engaged and that he can, therefore, not reciprocate her feelings?

Like heck he has.

The reason for this seemingly inexplicable behaviour on the part of Murray Leinster lies in the fact that he is, in his own quiet and unassuming way, actually incredibly selfish. And at the current time he happens to be rather annoyed with his Mysterious Girlfriend and so attending this rendezvous is by way of being his petty revenge.

In fairness to the lad, he did originally have every intention of showing the letter to Eve, with whom he had fully expected to be walking home from school. But then Eve had told him that she was off to see Mark Hunter and Dodo Dupont about the whole Scarlette and Frank Hanson business and that this would detain her for the remainder of the day. And if *that* hadn't been bad enough, she had gone on to inform him that an out-of-town conference involving that vague and shadowy organisation to which she belonged would keep her away from school tomorrow and that she wouldn't be getting back until late in the evening!

And with this she had given him a quick Frenchie and then rushed off.

And this is what has put poor Murray in a huff. For a start he doesn't see why he couldn't have gone along with Eve to see the two spies. Isn't he involved in the case just as much as she is? They're treating him like a kid, leaving him out like this! So thinks Murray, as he makes his way from school to nearby Peter Street and to the assignation in the park. He feels that he is entitled to do this by way of recompense for his grievances.

Howsoever, far from entertaining any ideas of two-timing his Mysterious Girlfriend, he doesn't actually intend to even meet his Secret Admirer! And as for talking to her, that would be completely out of the question! Cast your mind back, gentle reader, it was only a couple of weeks ago that Murray could barely speak to a girl without breaking out in a rash; and while he has undoubtedly gained a respectable quantity of life experience in the intervening time, he still hasn't actually changed that much! So, no, his plan is to surreptitiously approach the place of rendezvous, ideally arriving before the other party, and then from the concealment of the bushes, observe just who his Secret Admirer is! His curiosity on this point is understandable.

He arrives at the park. A lot of kids are playing on the swings and slides and climbing frames, with the mums keeping a weather eye on their offspring while they sit chatting with each other. Murray follows the path that skirts the recreation area. He nears Acorn Grove. No one in sight. He looks back, but sees only the little kids and the mums. He steps off the path and into the trees. The grove is not a large one, and the clearing is almost immediately in view. There appears to be no-one there. He approaches circuitously, quietly. No, there is no-one here. As he has hoped, he is the first to arrive. He finds a convenient bush and hunkers down. Yes, from here he has a direct view of the clearing through the interstices of the foliage. Perfect. Now all he has to do is wait. And it shouldn't be for long. He takes the letter from his bag to remind himself of its contents. Yes, 'after school today' it says. And that must mean *straight* after school, mustn't it? If they'd meant like two hours after school, they'd have said so.

Yes, soon a girl is going to walk into that clearing; a girl from his school. But who could it be? Someone from his class? But who? Perhaps a shy girl. Yes, that might explain why they wrote a letter instead of just going up to him. But then, maybe not. His Secret Admirer knows he already has a girlfriend, so maybe she just didn't want to be seen talking to him in school; maybe that is why she has arranged this rendezvous... Wait! The snap of a twig. Rustling foliage. She's coming!

Murray holds his breath, his eyes fixed on the clearing. A girl appears.

False alarm. It's just some kid; not as young as most of the kids playing on the swings, but still only a primary school girl; about seven or eight by the look of it. The girl wears a frilly dress and a straw hat. Her hair is very long and very straight. She doesn't look like she's just come out of school because she doesn't have a bag or satchel. What's she doing here? She's clearly alone, but she's just standing there in the clearing, looking around. Has *she* also arranged to meet someone at this location? This could mess things up! If his Secret Admirer comes now, she might turn back again when she sees there's already someone in the grove, might turn back before Murray even has a chance to catch sight of her...

Annoyingly, the girl starts to pace around the clearing, walking with exaggerated steps, humming a nursery rhyme. What is she doing? Playing some silly, solitary game?

The girl stops and she stops directly in Murray's line of sight and facing towards him. She inclines her head and assumes a thoughtful expression, tapping her lip with a forefinger.

'Now this is very strange,' speaks the girl. 'I *know* I saw that big-school boy walk into these trees, I *know* I did! But now, I can't see him *anywhere*.' She pirouettes on the spot. 'Where can he be? P'raps he's hiding in the bushes somewhere? But why would he be doing that? What would a big-school boy be doing on his own in the bushes? Is he having a poo? Hmm... I can't smell anything... Well, if it's not that then the only other thing I can think of is that thing big-school boys like to do on their own and that *I'm* too young and innocent to even know about.'

The girl performs another pirouette. 'This is *very* strange,' she repeats. 'I can't see him and I can't even hear him... What if something bad has happened to him? He might have fallen down a hole or been eaten by a bear or something! Why, if he *has* hurt himself, I must go and call an ambulance at once!'

This is too much for Murray. This little brat is going to spoil everything! He stands up. The girl sees him.

'There he is!' she exclaims.

Murray advances, casting glances towards the edge of the grove, nervously expecting the arrival of his Secret Admirer.

'I'm *so* glad you're alright,' says the girl. 'I was starting to worry.'

'Yeah, I'm okay, so can you—'

'You haven't been eaten by a bear?'

'No, so can you—'

'And you haven't fallen down a hole?'

'Look, I'm fine, okay!' says Murray. 'So just shoo, will you?' He makes the appropriate 'shooing' gestures.

'You want me to shoo?' asks the girl. 'Why's that?'

'Cuz I'm meeting someone here,' Murray tells her. 'So you need to clear off. Go'n play on the swings or something.'

'Who are you meeting?'

'Just someone.'

'What someone?'

'Look, I don't know, okay? Just go!'

'You're meeting someone and you don't know who they are?' The girl giggles. 'That's silly!'

'Will you just go?' urges Murray, getting more and more vexed.

'But your friend isn't here yet,' points out the girl. 'I know! I'll just stay here and keep you company until they arrive; then I'll go!'

'No!' groans Murray. 'If she sees I'm not on my own, she might go away again!'

'Oh, so you're meeting a girl, are you? Why would she go away just because I'm here?'

'Because she might!' retorts Murray.

'But why should she?' repeats the girl.

Murray, exercising his usual level of determination and perseverance, throws in the towel. Turning his back on the girl, he sits himself down under a tree, hugs his knees and buries his face in them.

After a while he looks up. The girl stands close before him, studying him with interest.

'What's your name?' she inquires.

'Murray,' is the sulky response.

'I'm Fiona,' the girl informs him. 'My friends call me Fee.'

'Great.'

'I like you, so *you* can call me Fee.'

'Yeah.'

Fiona makes a show of scanning the clearing. 'It doesn't look like your friend's coming,' she sighs, as though lamenting this unfortunate circumstance.

'That's because you scared her off!' snaps Murray.

'Why would she be scared of me?'

'Because,' says Murray, 'this was supposed to be a *secret* meeting, and it couldn't be secret if someone else was here, could it?'

'Why were you having a secret meeting? Are you a spy?'

'No.'

'Hmm...' Fiona ponders. 'Oh, I know! You got a love letter, didn't you? And you're here to meet your Secret Admirer! I'm right, aren't I?' 'Yes,' admits Murray.

Fiona subjects Murray to another searching scrutiny. 'You know, you don't look like the type of boy that girls would send love letters to,' she decides.

'What's that supposed to mean?' hotly.
'Well, *you* know,' says Fiona.
Murray *does* know, but even so...!
'Well, I *did* get a love-letter,' he insists.
'Don't believe you,' is the firm response.
'Alright, I'll show you!' says Murray. He produces the pink envelope from his bag, shakes it under the girl's snub nose.
'Oooh! Let's see!' and she snatches the letter from his hand.
'Hey!'
Fiona skips off across the glade. She takes the letter from its envelope and starts gleefully reading aloud. '"I can't hold it in anymore!" "My knickers get wet!" "I think of you when I play with myself!"'
She giggles with childish delight.
Murray has sprung to his feet. 'Give me that back!'
'What for?' returns the girl. 'You don't think this letter's real, do you? It's *obviously* a fake! Someone's just pulling your leg!'
And she proceeds to tear the letter—envelope and all—into little pieces and scatters them like confetti.
'Why did you do that?' demands Murray, horrified at the loss of his first ever love letter.
'You silly boy!' says Fiona, still grinning. 'I've told you, it's a *fake*. Someone was playing a trick on you! They were probably going to make you wait here for ages, and then they would come along and laugh at you for waiting so long!'
Murray's heart sinks. The possibility had never occurred to him before, but on hearing this explanation, it seems all too appallingly plausible.
Of course the letter is a fake! Murray has never been popular with the girls at school; it's always been like that! Only Eve loves him, and she's a transfer student from Yorkshire and she's different to other girls. The love letter is a practical joke; of course it is. And he almost fell for it!

And it serves him right. This is his punishment for not being true to his Mysterious Girlfriend.

Dejected, Murray sits back down under the tree and hides his face again.

And once again, when he looks up the girl is standing before him, this time with a concerned look on her round face.

'I'm sorry,' she says contritely. 'I didn't mean to laugh at you.' 'That's alright,' says Murray.

'Don't be sad.'

'Yeah, I know...'

Fiona brightens. 'I know what! To make it up to you I'll show you my knickers!'

And she starts to lift the skirt of her dress.

'Stop that!' orders Murray, alarmed.

The girl giggles. 'I was only joking!' she tells him. 'I wasn't *really* going to show you my knickers! I couldn't do that cuz I'm not wearing any!'

And this time she lifts her skirt up all the way and demonstrates the truth of this assertion.

'Stop doing that!' cries Murray. He springs forward and, grabbing the hem of the girl's skirt, struggles to cover her up, while she resists him, giggling gleefully.

Murray finally prevails. Fiona dances away from him across the glade.

'You shouldn't do things like that!' Murray tells her. 'If I'd been a bad man, you could have... Well, you could have been in a lot of trouble!'

'Yes, but you're *not* a bad man, are you?' replies Fiona. 'You're a good boy.'

'Well yes, but you can't always tell. You should always be careful around strangers,' says Murray, with the air someone offering profound advice.

'You're right!' declares Fiona. 'I shall certainly remember that advice of yours, Murray Leinster. Thank you *so* much.' She approaches Murray. 'But I think that since I've shown you my naughty bits that you ought to show me yours. It's only fair, isn't it?'

She reaches for the fly of Murray's trousers.

'Stop that!' protests Murray. 'What's wrong with you?'

He pushes the girl away. She resists. A struggle ensues. Murray falls backwards. The girl lands on top of him. She renews her assault, unzips Murray.

'Oooh! You've got a big willy!' she exclaims, brandishing her prize in triumph. 'Make it go hard!'

And Murray actually complies with this request, albeit entirely against his will.

'Get off me!' he yells.

By now desperate, he grabs the girl and hurls her away from him. He leaps to his feet and painfully zips himself up. And then, grabbing his school bag, he runs for it.

This is what he gets for believing in that stupid love letter!

Chapter Twenty-Two
Vesta Control Does Not Respond

'We didn't quite give out the whole story,' says Mark Hunter, 'about the DNA test.'

A swan drifts along the river, white plumage bright against the soft gloaming, seeming to float without effort, but whose frenetic paddling beneath the surface has long served as a metaphor. Along the opposite bank, a number of houseboats, floating tax havens, brightly painted. Eve Chandler, leaning against the railing guarding the embankment, feels the cool air rising from the rippling water.

'You lied?' she asks, seeking clarity.

'Not exactly,' is the reply, delivered with a stream of cigarette smoke. 'The assailant's DNA profile did *not* match that of astronaut Frank Hanson; that was true enough. What we *didn't* mention was that it was astonishingly similar.'

'Then they must have made a mistake,' asserts Eve, also carcinogenic. 'The rapist *is* Frank Hanson. We know it's him.'

'There was no mistake,' says Mark. 'That's what they thought themselves at first and the comparison test was repeated, several times. But the result was always the same: the DNA profiles did not quite match.'

'So you still think it's not Frank Hanson?'

'No, I'm as certain as you are that it's him. But something has happened to that man; something that has subtly altered his DNA profile.'

'Is that even possible? I mean, if you changed someone's DNA pattern, even if it was only a bit, wouldn't it change how they looked?'

'You'd have thought so, wouldn't you?' agrees Mark, smiling. 'But then we're dealing with a number of impossibilities here, aren't we? Like a man somehow being able to traverse 200 million miles of outer space in less than a week.'

'A week?'

'Yes. Between the time Hanson disappeared and the time of the first assault.'

'Okay, you've lost me again. Hanson disappeared from what? And where?'

Another smile. 'Ah. Now, that's a story that *was* covered up. Frank Hanson disappeared three weeks ago while on a space flight within the asteroid belt. A mysterious green cloud had appeared in the belt; it didn't drift in; it was just suddenly *there*. The thing defied analysis. Every signal they fired at the thing just came back scrambled. The cloud was an enigma. The only solution that offered itself was an on-the-spot analysis. Frank Hanson was sent out in a space capsule to perform the analysis; it was a one-man mission. Everything was fine until he entered the cloud. Apparently he saw something in the cloud; something that terrified him. One of the last things he said, or screamed, was "Those eyes!

Those eyes!"'

'Eyes! Like the thing Rose and the others have been seeing in their dreams!'

'So it would seem. After those words they lost contact with Hanson. And then, before any sort of rescue mission could get there, the cloud just disappeared.'

'So why wasn't all this on the news?'

'It was deemed advisable to suppress the story. Don't look at me! I'm not that high up, you know! I'm not the one who makes those kinds of decisions. There will be some kind of announcement very soon, though. There'll have to be. Things have deteriorated so badly, that it can't be kept back any longer.'

'What do you mean? What's deteriorated?'

'The situation in the asteroid belt. You see, Frank Hanson's disappearance was only the beginning. Since that time, over the past few weeks, the Mining Project has been beset with a series of "accidents". Gas explosions in mine tunnels. Equipment failure. Life support systems malfunctioning. Accidents invariably resulting in loss of human life. All of these disasters were withheld from the press. But now things have reached a critical point. Two days ago all radio and video contact with the Asteroid Belt Mining Project was lost. And it has not been reestablished. It's not that signals are being jammed in any way; it's just that no-one's answering.'

'Then they're all dead,' says Eve, simply.

'That's what they call the Worst Case Scenario,' Mark tells her. 'But, considering the known facts, it's also the most plausible explanation. And if it is, we're talking about over 300 people dead.'

Eve looks at him. 'Unless,' she says, 'the whole asteroid belt thing is a great big hoax like people are saying it is! If that's really true, then this whole contact lost story could just be their way of closing it down! Y'know, if they say everyone's dead, then that's the end of it; no-one can prove anything!'

'There are several holes in that theory. First of all Frank Hanson and the thing in the green cloud. Was that all part of the hoax?'

Eve thinks about this. 'Maybe... Okay! Maybe this weird alien thing has appeared, but not in the asteroid belt; instead it's turned up right here on Earth, wherever the fake Mining Project is!'

'Yes, that almost adds up,' concedes Mark. 'You know, I was talking about this with Dodo, when all those rumours started flying around... And I wondered, could even *I* have been fooled into believing in a great big hoax? And it *would* be the most staggering one in history.'

'Maybe you have been fooled,' says Eve.

'Either way, we've still got this alien ghost or whatever it is to deal with...' ruminates Mark. '"The Dark Lord is coming..." But what does it want? It takes over an astronaut, and by altering his DNA turns him into some kind of robot predator... And there's the sister... Was she controlling him somehow...?'

'Haven't you found out?' asks Eve. 'Is Scarlette not talking or summat?'

Mark smiles ruefully. 'Oh, she's talking alright. But it's nothing we can use in court. Something's happened to that girl. When we first took her in this morning she was spitting and swearing, saying we didn't have anything on her and that it was you we should have arrested, not her (which was a fair comment, by the way.) After we'd got her to the police station, cleaned up her wounds and put her in a cell, she quietened down. So we left her to cool her heels and mull things over... But then, this afternoon, things took a rather bizarre turn...

'The constable who was bringing some lunch for the girl found her sitting on her bed, and she was talking in the most extraordinary voice; kind of like the gravelly voice you hear when a woman impersonates a man's voice. She was talking in this voice, spilling out all these words. It was like an invocation or some bizarre religious sermon. She talked of her "Dark Lord" or "Nameless One" and how it was coming soon, drawn here by some "pillar of light." That was the most comprehensible part. The rest was gibberish, albeit deeply disturbing gibberish.

'The girl wouldn't reply when the police officer questioned her; she ignored him and just kept reciting her bizarre mantra. When she'd talked herself out she fell silent; refused to say a word. And then a couple of hours later she started up again; repeating more or less the same thing all over again. And that seems to be the pattern—delivering her set speeches in that gravelly voice, followed by intervals of silence...' 'Sounds like she's possessed,' remarks Eve.

'Possessed or just wants us to think she is,' says Mark. 'It's too early to tell.'

'And what about her brother? I'm guessing you haven't found him yet, otherwise you'd have said summat.'

'No, we haven't found him. Which brings us nicely to my next point. This ruined abbey, where you suggested we might able to find him: it isn't there.'

'You mean *he* isn't there?'

'No, my dear, I mean *it* isn't there. The ruined abbey. There isn't one.'

'There bloody is!' retorts Eve. 'Me and Murray were there the day before yesterday! An' I told you how to find the place—the tunnel through the brambles—'

'Yes, we found that patch of brambles you described. Trouble is, there ain't no tunnel. The thicket is solid; not a single gap in it. So then we tried going the long way round, following the bushes right to the end. This led us to a stand of trees, but there wasn't anything in 'em. The hollow you described; the wall, the ruins; they just weren't there, my dear.'

'But that's impossible!' declares Eve. 'Murray and me were both there! We—'

'And another thing,' interrupts Mark. 'If those ruins were anything more than just a couple of bricks, the National Trust would know about the location. They don't.'

'But we saw the place,' insists Eve. 'And Murray, he even remembered it, like he'd been there before, a long time back.'

'I'm not accusing you of lying, Eve,' Mark assures her. 'You see, Dodo decided to pay a visit to your town's main library this afternoon; she did some digging and discovered that there was once an abbey just to the south of Linton; and in fact there's even still an Abbey Road at that end of town. But the records do not speak of any trace of the building still remaining today.' 'So we went back in time?'

'Well, you certainly went somewhere. And if that place is Frank Hanson's hiding place, then it's going to be a job to extract him from it. Maybe you need some kind of occult "key" to get in; maybe Scarlette has this key, and you were only able to get in the other day because you were following her. That's one possible explanation…'

'But Murray… He thinks he was there a long time ago…'

'Thinks? Can't he remember?'

'No, he…he's got some kind of block. Summat bad must have happened to him back then, and I reckon there's a big part of him just doesn't want to remember it…'

'Another mystery,' murmurs Mark.

He turns from the river to face the park. Eve does the same, leaning back, her elbows on the railing. People pass back and forth in the gathering dusk. Others sit on the park benches. The owner of an ice cream kiosk, doubtful of any more custom at this late hour, is closing up shop. Lights are on in many of the windows of the polytechnic building across the park.

'So where is Frank Hanson?' wonders Mark. 'And if it is his sister who's somehow pulling his strings, can she do this from a distance, or does she have to be with him? Has he become inert now that we've got the girl in custody, or is he still active? And this entity, this "Nameless One"; assuming it was responsible for Hanson's transformation, can it take control of him? Is it perhaps also in control of Scarlette? She seems possessed, but her words are those of a high priest, an acolyte; she doesn't seem to be speaking the words of the creature itself... And where is the creature precisely? Is it drifting in from the asteroid belt or is it already here on Earth? Scarlette talks of its imminent arrival; your fortune teller hinted at something similar. And the destination, the point of arrival, seems to be right here in Linton. Drawn by a pillar of light. Why here of all places? Why in this insignificant small English town...?' He turns to Eve. 'Any comments? Is there anything you know that I don't?'

'Why would I know anything?' asks Eve.

'Because you're a bit of a mystery yourself, young lady,' Mark tells her. 'You live on your own, you're connected to some vague society, an occult matriarchy or something... Oh, don't worry! I don't want to pry into your group's secrets. I've heard vague rumours about you people, but even the rumours are fairly few, which is surprising in itself in this day and age... But you don't seem to be doing any harm... And now it seems you've even inducted my friends Dodo and Mayumi into your little association...' He smiles. 'You know, I could almost start to feel left out... So, your people don't have any additional information regarding this situation?'

'No,' answers Eve, simply. 'I reckon we know less about it than you do.'

'It wasn't what brought you here to Linton, then?' 'No.'

'May I ask what did? You obviously didn't just move here by chance.'

'It was Murray,' says Eve. 'Murray's why I came here.'

'Ah, Murray Leinster,' says Mark. 'He's the biggest mystery of all. Or rather, the mystery is why everyone seems to think he's so significant. Can you answer that one?'

'No...'

'And what's your job? To keep him under observation? To keep him out of harm's way?'

'Something like that.'

'And it was it also part of your job to fall in love with him?'

'Well, I was supposed to get as close to him as I could,' admits Eve, strangely bashful. 'I wasn't really meant to fall in love with him; I just did.'

'Yes, it often happens like that,' agrees Mark. 'Shall we have another look for that ruined abbey of yours? We can pick up Dodo and Mayumi and head out there right now. Who knows? Maybe with you along with us, we might have more luck!'

Chapter Twenty-Three
Murray Leinster: Paedophile!

North Linton stinks of shit this morning.

At first people think it must be the smell of manure drifting in from arable farmland to the north, but then the story gets out that a sewer has backed up somewhere and people wrinkle their noses in disgust because it somehow seems much worse, knowing that the stench pervading the air is that of human excrement and not the animal variety.

The smell accompanies Murray as he wends his solitary way to school this morning; the first morning since that memorable Monday that he has walked to school unaccompanied by Eve Chandler, who has gone off to that conference.

The first indication for Murray that something is amiss comes when, approaching the school gates, he encounters Pornboy. Murray greets him in the usual friendly tone, expecting the customarily surly or sarcastic response; but instead, the rotund boy looks pointedly away from Murray, and without saying a word, he increases his pace to a fast waddle, leaving a hurt and confused Murray behind him.

What was all that about?

Fearing a second rebuff, Murray does not run to catch up with his friend. He enters the schoolyard; students stand chatting in groups or running around as usual. But as he passes between them, Murray receives the uncomfortable feeling that many looks are being directed at him; looks of animosity, even disgust.

The hostile atmosphere becomes even more apparent when the bell rings for registration and, making his way through the school corridors to his homeroom, Murray finds himself deliberately jostled by other students, and at one point pushed into the wall with some force. Murray, by now seriously alarmed, submits to this treatment without comment or protest.

And it's the same when he has sat down at his desk. All the students look at him as they walk into the room. Some look disdainful, some even look fearful, while others look at him with something approaching wonderment, as though he has suddenly grown a second head. Pornboy, two desks to his left, keeps his eyes resolutely averted.

Murray knows enough about the workings of the school environment to realise that he has become the subject of some malicious rumour; he just cannot for the life of him think what that rumour might be.

And for this to happen on the one day when Eve Chandler isn't here to back him up...!

One of the last students to arrive is Spacey. When his eyes settle on Murray seated at his desk, his normally relaxed expression transforms to one of wide-eyed alarm. He hurries up to Murray and says:

'What are you doin' here, man?' His voice is low, his words urgent.

'What do you mean?' asks Murray, adopting the same low tone.

'Haven't you heard what they're saying about you?'

'No! What is it?'

Spacey exhales a deep breath. 'Look, you're my pal and I don't believe the stories for one minute; but you've got to get out of here, man! Before Lassiter shows up!'

'Lassiter?'

'Yeah, Lassiter! He maybe won't come in today, but if he does, he's gunna murder you, man! So please: just get outta here!'

'But what are they saying about me?' demands Murray, keeping his voice quiet with an effort. 'What's it got to do with Lassiter?'

'They're sayin' you've been messing with his kid sister,' Spacey tells him. 'Y'know, molesting her. They say it happened in Peter Street Park, yesterday, after school. And like I say, I don't believe it, but Lassiter sure does and he's gunna kill you, man! So I'm beggin' you, just get the fuck out of here while you still can!'

Panic seizes Murray. He leaps to his feet. He has to escape; not just from the threat of Lassiter, but from the horror of what everyone is saying about him; about what they think he is. His only thought is to run to someone who will protect him from all this. Crimson-faced and trembling he makes his rapid way to the door. All eyes are on him, but nobody attempts to impede his progress.

The moment he is through the door, he breaks into the run. He runs frantically down the corridor, turns a corner—
And collides with Lassiter.

Murray Leinster, a plaster on his chin, a patch over one eye, sits in an austere interview room, faced by two grim-visaged police officers. The senior of the two, Sergeant Brent, conducts the examination.

'Look, did you or did you not sexually assault Fiona Lassiter in the Acorn Grove of Peter Street Park, yesterday afternoon between the hours of 15:30 and 16:00?'

'No, I d-d-didn't!' wails Murray.

'Well, the girl says you did,' Brent tells him.

'Sh-sh-sh-she's l-l-l-lying!'

Murray's speech impediment, all but cured by the healing presence of Eve Chandler, has returned with a vengeance. This is not surprising— poor Murray is absolutely terrified; he feels like he has stumbled into a waking nightmare.

'So, you did not force that seven-year-old girl to perform any indecent sexual acts?' pursues Brent.

'No!'

Brent sighs wearily. 'For the record, I am now showing the suspect one of the photographic prints which were delivered to this station by an anonymous member of the public.'

From an envelope on the table before him, Brent extracts a number of photographs. Selecting one, he slides it across the table for Murray to view.

'For the record, I am showing the suspect the photograph which appears to show himself forcing a young female to perform the act of... of...' He turns to his colleague. 'What's it called again?'

'Fellatio,' supplies the constable.

'...perform the act of fellatio upon him,' concludes Brent (for the record.)

Murray stares at the picture. It captures the moment during his altercation with Fiona in which he had fallen to the ground and the girl had extracted his member and applied it to her mouth.

It is an image which, taken out of context, undeniably affords ample scope for misinterpretation.

'B-b-b-b-but it d-d-didn't h-happen like that!' stammers Murray.

'So, you admit that it's you in the picture,' challenges Brent.

'Y-yes, b-b-but it w-w-w-was her!' blubbers Murray. 'Sh-sh-she was d-doing it to m-m-me!'

'She was doing it to you?'

'Yes!'

'So you're saying that a seven-year-old girl was the one initiating the blow—the fellatio?' sneers Brent.

'Yes! She attacked me!'

'Oh, she attacked you, did she? The poor defenceless fourteen-year-old boy, savagely assaulted by the seven-year-old girl. Now why didn't we realise that sooner?' And he sits back in his chair, folds his arms and trades a sardonic grin with his colleague.

He leans forward again. 'Listen, sonny. We've got the girl's testimony. We've got witnesses who place you at the scene. And if that wasn't enough, we've got all these pictures of you caught right in the act!'

And, like a dealer flourishing a winning hand, he spreads the remaining photographs across the table for Murray to see.

And Murray does see them and he feels like curling up in a ball and dying. Just like the picture already shown to him, they are images of himself and the girl in the Acorn Grove, and just like the first picture, each photo seems to have been carefully taken with a view to presenting a distorted view of that fatal encounter; photos which all appear to depict himself as the instigator, as the assailant.

'I want my mum,' declares Murray, the tears streaming down his one exposed eye.

'Well, she ain't here yet,' snaps Brent. 'Now how about you stop with this crap about the girl being the assailant and confess that you assaulted her!'

'I d-d-didn't,' blubbers Murray, looking down.

Another sigh. 'Then why were you in the Acorn Grove in the first place?'

'I was meeting someone there!' says Murray, feeling like he has struck an alibi.

'Meeting someone?'

'Yes! I got a love letter in school yesterday. She said she wanted to meet me after school in the Acorn Grove!'

'Who said? What was the girl's name?'

'I don't know. She didn't put her name on the letter.'

'You don't know her? So she didn't show up for this alleged meeting?'

'No…'

'And can you produce this document?'

'Yes, I—' Murray's face falls. 'No, I can't. She tore it up…'

'What, the girl you didn't see tore up the letter?'

'No! That girl Fiona tore it up!'

'Really? And why would she do that?'

'I dunno. She just grabbed the letter from me and she tore it up.'

'Did she now? Well, that's very convenient, that is. So, let's get this straight: You went to the Acorn Grove to meet some girl from your school who had sent you an anonymous love letter. She didn't turn up, but the girl Fiona Lassiter turns up instead, and she tears up your love letter and she then proceeds to assault you. Yes?' 'Yes…' says Murray, mouse-like.

Brent exchanges another wry look with his colleague. 'That's your version of events, then,' he says. 'Well, how about this one: You go into the Acorn Grove to jerk yourself off because your teenage hormones are so out of control you can't even wait till you get home. But then this seven-year-old girl shows up and you decide you might as well make use of her instead of just working the hand-pump because you're a depraved little sexual deviant! How about that one, eh? That's more like the truth, ain't it?'

Brent positively glows with triumph after this summing up. He is feeling immensely pleased with himself; and not just because he is a natural bully enjoying the process of terrorising his youthful crime suspect. No, on this occasion he has another reason to congratulate himself; and this is because he knows Murray Leinster to be the same boy who was once suspected of having being abused in some way by Brent's former schoolfriend and now hated enemy, Carson.

Deciding on the spot that this case can only be a textbook example of an abuse victim growing up to become an abuser, he looks forward to seeing the blame for this incident being ultimately brought home to the aforementioned Carson.

This is why Sergeant Brent feels so pleased with himself.

However, his feelings of self-congratulation are somewhat dampened when the suspect he has so successfully intimidated now proceeds to throw up all over the photographic evidence.

The smell of shit still lingers in the air.

Stavro stands on a street corner, nervously surveying a particular house. The house is one of a terrace here in one of the most crime-ridden estates of which North Linton has to boast. Number fifteen. To Stavro this house has a fatal importance; it is the house of the plumber McKearney.

A perverse desire has compelled him to track the man to his lair. For days he had hesitated as to whether or not he should even attempt to do this. He had seen no more of McKearney since that awful day; perhaps he should have left well alone. But he couldn't just leave things like this. The uncertainty was driving him insane. So he had contacted the local agency through whom he had booked McKearney to fix his radiator, mendaciously saying he required the man's services once more. In reply to this he was told that McKearney was no longer on their books, but that they could provide him with a different plumber. Stavro asked to know *why* McKearney was no longer on their books; had he been arrested? No, McKearney had not been arrested to the best of their knowledge; he had simply ceased working as a plumber, presumably having found a better job elsewhere. So, he had moved away from Linton? No, they did not believe he had relocated.

Stavro had then demanded McKearney's home address and had been reluctantly supplied with this information when he had, again mendaciously, claimed that he suspected the man of having stolen something from his flat while working there.

And now here is Stavro, staking out McKearney's address. He can't help but associate McKearney's sudden decision to quit plumbing with himself and his hazy memories of the crime to which McKearney had—possibly—confessed. But if he has left his job from knowing or suspecting he said too much to Stavro, has he also left Linton? From surveying the house, Stavro just can't tell. True, there is no house agent's sign on the miniscule patch of front garden, but that means nothing; McKearney might have fled without giving notice, or the house might be the property of the council or a housing association... He can see curtains in the windows, but again that signifies nothing in the case of McKearney having decamped in a hurry or the property being let furnished.

What should he do? Should he keep watching in the hope of seeing someone enter or leave the house? Should he ask a neighbour or passerby for information? Or should he take the bull by the horns and just knock at the door?

Seeing someone approaching along the pavement, he decides to try the second option first. The pedestrian is a young man wearing a baseball cap. Stavro walks up to him.

'Excuse me?'

The man looks at him suspiciously. 'Yeah?'

'I was wondering if you could tell me who lives at number 15 here,' says Stavro, indicating the property in question.

'Number 15?' repeats the man. 'You wanna know who lives at number 15?'

'Yes, if you know...'

'Yeah, I'll tell you who lives at number 15,' declares the man, 'None of your Fucking Business, that's who lives at number 15!'

And having imparted this useful information, the man passes on.

Linton Police Station keeps its holding cells and drunk tank out of sight in the basement. The cells are of the cage variety and the whole chamber is suitably dank and dimly lit.

Each cell is provided with a truckle bed, a toilet innocent of seat or lid and a washbasin. Murray Leinster, relieved of his school tie and shoes-laces (just in case he entertains any ideas of escaping justice via self-immolation), has been deposited in one of these cells. Our wretched hero has thrown himself onto the bed and covered himself with the standard itchy grey blanket provided by these establishments. (He has compelling reasons for making use of the lavatory to evacuate his bowels, but the complete lack of privacy has deterred him. At least one of the neighbouring cells looks to be occupied.)

Having successfully shut himself off from the disagreeable reality of his current predicament, he lies curled in a foetal ball and imagines himself being embraced and comforted by soothing feminine hands. Sometimes it is Eve Chandler with whom he lies. Sometimes it is his mother. And, alarmingly, sometimes it is both of them.

At present it is his mum who seems the closest source of help. Eve is out of town and unreachable, but his mum is just at work at the science park. She will come, won't she? As soon as she hears that he's been arrested and put in prison; she'll come and rescue him, won't she?

'The Dark Lord is coming,' croaks a voice.

Murray pulls the blanket from his head. He lies facing the barred partition between his own cell and the next. A figure sits cross-legged on the bed in this adjoining cell. The light is dim and the voice of the speaker unfamiliar, but he soon comes to realise that his fellow gaol-bird is none other than Scarlette Hanson! She sits perfectly still, her face half obscured by her dishevelled hair.

'The Nameless One shall soon be with us,' she says.

Murray, not having seen Eve after her interview with

Mark Hunter the previous evening, has heard nothing of Scarlette's behaviour since her arrest the day before. Why the girl sounds so unlike herself is a mystery to him.

'Who's the Nameless One?' he tries asking her.

'Stare into the Eyes Without a Face,' proceeds Scarlette. 'Stare, if you dare to look upon the true way of things. Stare, if you would face pitiless eternity. Stare, if you would revel in the chaos. Stare if you would know your true self. Stare, and the eyes of the Nameless One will burn into your soul.

'Rejoice that the Dark Lord returns to us. Rejoice that the ivory tower calls out to our redeemer. Rejoice that the Dark Lord will cast its dark shadow over this world. Rejoice in the consummation of forbidden things. Rejoice in the delirium of blood. Rejoice in the breaking of shackles. Rejoice, for our Dark Lord is come again!

'The razing of temples shall come to pass. The spilling of seed shall come to pass. The overthrow of reason shall come to pass. The devouring of all things shall come to pass. The Nameless One returns and a dark flame of redemption shall burn strong.'

Murray, listening with attention and incomprehension in matching proportions, wonders if Scarlette has gone New Age. Is she trying to convert him with this speech of hers? She ought to do something about that creepy voice she's putting on. She's never going to attract the right sort of person talking like that!

He peers into the semi-darkness of the adjoining cell. He can see one of Scarlette's eyes, the one eye unconcealed by her falling hair; a shining eye that stares... at him? ...Or into infinity?

The lurid sermon continues: 'Let loose the maelstrom! Hurl the children from the ivory tower! Flay the unbelievers! Let their torments be endless...!'

'Oh, I'm not interested!'

Wishing he could slam the front door on this sermon, Murray retreats under his itchy blanket.

He had been online to re-familiarise himself with the events of that notorious crime.

It had happened two years ago, during the August heat wave of that year. A family had been taking an afternoon walk through the countryside to the north of Linton; an average, middle class, middle-income family, unremarkable in any way. The family consisted of husband and wife and two children; a boy, eight; and a girl, six. They lived in a detached three-bedroom house on one of the main thoroughfares of North Linton. (In North Linton, these more prosperous areas are never far away from the grubby estates; the better houses lining the main streets, and the estates tucked away out of sight.) Supplementary to the human contingent, there were two pets, a dog and a rabbit, completing this happy household. Only the father and the rabbit survived that fatal day, and this because they did not participate in that afternoon walk, the father being at his office, the rabbit in its hutch.

The victims were the mother, the two children and the dog. They were walking familiar and well-trodden paths through the countryside. Unfortunately for the family, there were very few other excursionists abroad on that particular day; the oppressive heat being a deterrent to many. One shady avenue, protected from the sun by lofty trees rising on either side, must have seemed a very pleasant location to the family during the course of their stroll. And it must have been a pleasant spot for the killer as well, because it was here that he had been waiting for his victims.

The family had no known enemies, so it was concluded that the attack was entirely opportunistic and unpremeditated. Motiveless unless you accept the simple desire to take the lives of your fellow human beings as a motive in itself. This family had just happened to be in the wrong place at the wrong time. According to the coroner's report, they were bludgeoned to death with a heavy mallet;

the mother, the children, even the dog. The same weapon was used against each of the victims, and this was one of the reasons why the investigating authorities deduced that the killings were perpetrated by a lone assailant. There were some who argued that three people couldn't have been subdued by one man; that one of the victims should have been able, if not to retaliate, at least to flee the scene. The experts suggested that this was not necessarily the case; that if, for example, the mother had been attacked first, the children, witnessing this horror, would most likely have gone into shock.

When the story broke, it quickly became a local sensation and with it being one of those summertime 'slow news' periods, even the national press and TV news stations gave it top-billing. A manhunt was instigated; but in spite of the police's best efforts, the killer remained elusive. Several solitary males residing in Linton—including Stavrogin— were hauled in for questioning, but all were released without charge. The *modus operandi* of the killings bore no resemblance to any past homicides in the region, although there were similarities with one or two unsolved slayings perpetrated elsewhere in the country.

Some maintained that the killer must have been a local man who knew the area; others contended he could have been a wandering sociopath, just passing through.

Without a suspect, without a lead and without any real developments, the story inevitably started to die down, superseded in the media by more pressing news, national and international. Locally, it was talked about for a longer period, but even here, for want of fuel the flames finally began to dwindle.

But now, two years on, there is one man who might just have had his beard singed.

Murray emerges from his blanket when he hears the sound of footsteps descending the concrete stairs from the station house above. A jangling of keys and the door opens to admit first a uniformed officer and then a woman in a white lab coat and with long blonde hair and a determined look on her face.

Mum!

He calls her name. She sees him and runs to the door of his cell.

'Your face!' she shrieks. 'Police brutality!'

'It wasn't the police,' Murray tells her. 'It was Lassiter at school did this.'

'My poor darling!'

And Murray feels like everything is going to be alright now. His mother is here, and she's obviously come here from work in such a tearing hurry that she's forgotten to even take off her lab coat. And on top of that, she doesn't believe those stories about him! She knows that he's innocent!

The cell door is opened by the policeman. Mary Leinster rushes in and embraces her tearful son.

'How long have they been keeping you here, my pet?' is her first solicitous inquiry. 'To think they'd dare to arrest my sweet, innocent boy!'

'I didn't do it, Mum,' snivels Murray.

'I know you didn't, sweetie,' replies Mum. 'And even if you had done it, Mummy would forgive you.'

'*Mum!*'

This is not *quite* the kind of maternal support Murray really needs at the moment!

Deciding at last to take the bull by the horns, Stavro walks determinedly up to the door of number 15 and knocks. He can't keep living in this agonising uncertainty. He has to find out if McKearney is still there or not. If he isn't there, then presumably he has skipped town and good riddance to him. And if he *is* there, well then, he will have to feel his way carefully; try and determine where he stands with the man. *Did* McKearney confess to that crime? And if he did, does he even remember making the confession himself? Or has he perhaps counted on him, Stavro, not recalling it? Either seems possible. It had been the tail end of a long drinking session and they were both very drunk.

Having knocked, Stavro waits. A large part of him wants there to be no one home. Even though he would have to come back and repeat this ordeal on several more occasions to know for sure that McKearney has gone, he prefers to avoid confrontation.

Nothing happens, and Stavro is about to leave, when he hears bolts being withdrawn. His guts churn with anxiety.

And then comes the anti-climax; the door opens to reveal the vacuous round face of his friend the Wheezer. 'You? What are you doing here?'

The Wheezer replies with his trademark laugh, clearly amused by the other's surprise. Other than this he offers no response; the Wheezer has never been one for talking.

'Do you know McKearney, then?' asks Stavro. 'I thought this was his place.'

The Wheezer turns from the door and leaving it open, shuffles back down the narrow hallway. Accepting what seems a tacit invitation to enter, Stavro follows him. He notices that the Wheezer wears slippers. Stavro follows him into an untidy living room. No one else is present, but the television is switched on and tuned to the afternoon horseracing. The Wheezer, looking very much at home, drops into an armchair, picks up a can of white cider, retrieves a lighted cigarette from the ashtray sitting on one arm of the chair and is soon rapt in the events of the turf.

Still confused, Stavro clears some room on the sofa and sits himself down.

'You look like you're quite comfortable here,' he remarks to the Wheezer. 'Are you house-sitting for McKearney, or has he moved out for good?'

The Wheezer turns his stubbled face to Stavro, smiles vacuously, then turns back to the television.

'See, I'm trying to find McKearney,' proceeds Stavro.

'So, if you could tell me where he is...? I dunno, maybe he's left an address or something? A contact number...?'

The Wheezer looks at him again and wheezes briefly.

'Yeah, that doesn't really help me, Wheezer,' says Stavro.

Another wheezing laugh.

'You know, I sometimes forget how difficult it is to have a decent conversation with you,' reflects Stavro, his voice tight. 'The thrust and parry of a satisfying verbal exchange is not something I've ever really experienced with you. You tend to just fall back on laughter in favour of verbiage, don't you? And while you're free to respond to everything that's asked of you with that meaningless laugh of yours, I feel that a lesser person than myself could become a tad annoyed at times.' Pause. 'Especially when he's trying to find out where the hell McKearney is
and what the hell you're doing in his fucking house!' Response as before.

'You can't take him home. We haven't finished our inquiries yet.' Sergeant Brent sits uncomfortably at the table in the interview room. Mary Leinster stands facing him, hands thrust in the pockets of her lab coat, her anger cool, controlled. A strong smell of disinfectant rises from the surface of the table.

'What do you mean you haven't finished?' she demands. 'Surely even someone as slow-witted as you can see that my boy has been framed!'

'Framed?' sneers Brent. 'Where'd you get that one from?'

'Christ, you *are* stupid, aren't you, Brent?' retorts Miss Leinster scathingly. 'Well, where do you want me to start? How about the letter? The anonymous letter enticing him to the Acorn Grove and which that little brat conveniently tore up so that my boy couldn't produce it as evidence!'

'Yeah, convenient for *him*,' contends Brent. 'Easy to say

there was a letter when it's been torn up. And anyway, we questioned the girl about it. She says she didn't tear up any letter; she says there wasn't any letter.'

'Well *of course* she'd say that, you fucking moron!' explodes Miss Leinster. 'That little brat is part of the frame-up! She was put up to doing what she did! Let me talk to her; I'll soon wring the truth out of her!'

'You're not going anywhere near that girl,' Brent tells her. 'She is a severely traumatised abuse victim, and you're trying to say she's the villain!'

'She *is* the villain! She might not be the main one, but she's one of them!'

'Yeah. Funny that, cuz she didn't look like the villain to me in those pictures we've got.'

Miss Leinster growls. 'Those pictures, you prick, are the biggest evidence of all that this is a frame-up! Firstly, the fact that there happened to be a witness there at all. Secondly, the fact that instead of video-recording the entire incident they just took a few isolated shots. And thirdly, the fact that this witness didn't even intervene to stop what was happening!'

'Sometimes it can be unwise for members of the public to intervene in the case of assaults,' says Brent, answering the last point first. 'There's always the danger of the assailant turning on them.'

'Yeah, right. The "assailant" in this case being my eight stone, five foot three, fourteen-year-old son. Yeah, most people would be scared of tackling *him*, wouldn't they?'

'He might have had a knife.'

'He *didn't* have a knife!'

'The witness might have been a little kid.'

'A little kid would've run off and told its parents, not stopped to take pictures. And there's the fact that those photos were delivered to you anonymously. That's pretty suspicious, isn't it?'

'Not when everything they show is backed up by the victim's testimony.'

'Stop calling that little bitch the victim!' spits Mary Leinster. 'My son is the victim here. He just wouldn't do anything like this. He's growing up well; I've seen to that. He's even just got himself a girlfriend.'

Brent looks at her. 'I don't think I need to remind you about what happened nine years ago,' he says quietly. 'Abuse victims sometimes grow up to be abusers.'

Mary Leinster takes a deep breath. 'There was no evidence my boy was actually abused,' she replies calmly. 'That's why I never pressed any charges. And I might add that the suspect in *that* business was an old crony of yours.'

Brent frowns. 'Carson's no friend of mine. Not anymore. I'm the one in charge of this inquiry and I'll be the one to decide when your kid can be released.'

'They must be really overworked at this nick if they're putting you in charge of anything,' says Mary Leinster, scornfully. 'I know you, Brent. You're just a stupid small-town lout and that uniform you're wearing doesn't change that one bit. There's somewhere I have to go right now, but I'll be back very soon, and when I come back, I'll be taking my son home with me.'

Mary Leinster leaves the room.

Chapter Twenty-Four
Muscular Lady

The story broke at 09:00 hours Eastern Standard Time: All contact has been lost with the Asteroid Belt Mining Project. No warning was given; no emergency situation had been reported that might account for this sudden loss of contact. Nor was there interference blocking communication; the mining colony just stopped answering. Neither the press release nor subsequent conference overtly stated that they feared the worst, but the perceived tone of both was suggestively ominous. Only one clear detail has emerged: a gas cloud, of unknown origin and composition, had appeared in the vicinity of the mining colony previous to the communication breakdown. And while the experts insisted that the cloud could not be interfering with radio signals, people on online were soon suggesting more terminal scenarios: the cloud was poisonous and had gassed every last one of the colonists; or else it was flammable and had caused an explosive chain-reaction that had wiped out the entire colony.

The conspiracy theorists who insist that the whole Asteroid Belt Mining Project is a hoax declare that this is the final proof of their assertions: This alleged disaster is just a story enabling its instigators to bring to a close a deception that they had come to realise could not be sustained for much longer.

And what about the personnel of this alleged fake mining colony; over three hundred in number? Well, they were supposed to be dead, weren't they? Then dead they would have to be. Even if the personnel were unaware themselves that they were part of a hoax, you couldn't have them just popping up here on Earth, could you? Those people had become liabilities.

The girl who walks into Dirty Dick's, Linton's infamous underworld hangout, draws upon herself a great deal of attention not only because she is a complete stranger to the establishment's regulars, but also because her appearance is in any case striking. She is tall above the average and powerfully built. Her hair is long, falling onto her shoulders and down her back in raven black waves. Her skin is a light brown, her rather stern features good looking in an androgynous way; her mouth is wide, thick-lipped, her nose prominent, her eyebrows heavy. But the face, however, retains the freshness of youth; the girl looks to be no older than nineteen or twenty.

Is she Indian? wonder the patrons. Or maybe from the

Middle East…?

She wears a black jacket, camouflage pants, heavy boots, and carries a hold-all over her shoulder. She crosses the aisle from the door to the bar at a brisk, military pace, glancing left and right at the tables, but as someone merely absorbing the scene, rather than searching for a particular person.

At the bar she orders herself a Southern Comfort (her voice is deep and husky) and she takes her drink to a vacant table. After depositing her bag under the table, the girl removes her jacket. A simple action, but one which prompts eyes to goggle and jaws to drop in disbelief.

Now, the muscles of some athletic women only become visible when being put to use; when not being flexed the muscles conceal themselves; but this girl's muscles are of the kind that are on permanent display. Her arms and shoulders exhibit the adamantine muscles of a bodybuilder and an equally taut and toned abdomen is also visible courtesy of the cut-off vest top she wears.

Some are impressed, some are repulsed by the girl's physique, but the young woman reacts not to the looks directed upon her, or the murmured comments passing around the room. Her features composed, she calmly sits herself down and takes a sip of her drink.

Amongst the patrons observing this newcomer, and undoubtedly her most ardent admirers, are our good friends Misaki Morishita and Ren Hoshino. After a brief conference, the two rise from their table and walk over to that of the newcomer, who watches their approach, calmly assessing them.

'May we join you?' inquires Misaki. 'It looks like we're the only girls here, so we should stick together, don't you think?' The girl looks from one to the other of her applicants.

'Be seated,' she says.

The Japanese girls eagerly comply.

'I'm Misaki Morishita and this is my friend Ren Hoshino,' introduces Misaki.

'I am Sabella,' responds the girl.

'You must be new in town,' continues Misaki. 'I know, or at least know of, everyone worth knowing in this town, but you I don't know.'

'You are correct,' replies Sabella. 'I have just this evening arrived in Linton. Why does your friend look at me so?'

'Ah, well Ren has a liking for muscular ladies,' explains Misaki. 'You put her in mind of our Japanese lady wrestlers.'

'Lady Sumo wrestlers?'

'No, Western wrestling. Ladies' wrestling is a much-loved sport in our country.'

'And you are attracted to these women?' queries Sabella of Ren.

'Not exclusively,' Misaka answers for her. 'Ren has a very broad range and likes females of many kinds, both 3D and 2D ... May we ask where you are from, Sabella? From your appearance and your name I am unable to hazard a guess.'

'I come from the Deserts of Araby,' replies Sabella.

'Where that?' wonders Ren.

'She means the Middle East,' translates Misaki. She smiles at Sabella. 'You make your background sound romantic, but I would imagine that your life has been anything but that. In fact, just from looking at you, I think I can surmise your back story. Shall I try?' 'Proceed,' acquiesces Sabella.

'Well, let me see... You are a war orphan. Your parents were killed when you were still a little girl. Growing up in a war zone, you had to live on your wits. You learned to trust no one. You had to fight just to survive. You would often be raped by soldiers and insurgents.' (A dirty laugh from Ren.) 'You became tough and self-sufficient, sacrificing your femininity. It was either that or go under. When you were twelve you entered a terrorist training camp, where you developed your physique and became lethal in unarmed combat and the use of firearms. But you had no ideological sympathies with the terrorists, who anyway also used you for sex.' (Another dirty laugh.) 'So you escaped from them. You then proceeded to utilise your newly-acquired skills to gain resources and reputation, and now you earn your living as a lone wolf mercenary, taking on any job that does not conflict with your personal code of ethics...'

Misaki sits back, pleased with herself. 'So, how was that?'

'That was amazing!' Sabella congratulates her. 'You managed to get not a single thing right! I am lost in admiration!'

Misaki's face falls. 'I got everything wrong?'

'Everything!' confirms Sabella. 'You are correct that I am proficient in unarmed combat and use of all firearms, but all of the biographical events you hypothesised are completely inaccurate. I am not an orphan, and my childhood was a happy and uneventful one. I am not terrorist-trained, nor do I earn my living as a mercenary. So you see, you are wrong in every particular! I applaud the fertility of your imagination!'

'What you said would be good plot for action manga,' Ren tells her friend by way of consolation.

'So, what brings you to Linton?' asks Misaki. 'Business or pleasure?'

'Perhaps both,' answers Sabella. 'I have some acquaintances in this town...'

Two women in white coats sit in a waiting room at Linton Police Station.

One of them is Mary Leinster, who we have already seen thus attired; the other is her employer, Doctor Fifi Fleetwood, head of Fleetwood Laboratories, who we last saw dressed much more casually. Both women sit with legs crossed, arms folded and fingers drumming upper arms with controlled impatience.

They have been waiting for some time, and finally their patience is rewarded when Sergeant Brent walks into the room, a sour expression on his face. Fifi and Mary Leinster bring their silent double act to a climax by springing from their chairs in white-coated unison.

'Well?' demands the latter.

'We found some of the girl's fingerprints on the fragments,' announces Brent with obvious reluctance.

'I knew it!' rejoices Mary Leinster.

'Thank goodness!' sighs Fifi. To Brent: 'Now you can release her little boy from that nasty prison cell.'

Yes! The anonymous love letter which drew Murray Leinster to that fatal spot has been found! And the finder is that crusading parent Mary Leinster! This is what happened: On leaving the police station, Mary first returned to the science park; she needed a witness for what she was about to do; she had to make sure there would be no loopholes; not a single one. Mary's employer, Fifi Fleetwood, on being informed of the situation, insisted on being that witness herself. The two women had then driven straight to Peter Street Park and had made their way to the Acorn Grove. Here, Mary Leinster had set about examining the clearing for the torn fragments of the anonymous letter, while Fifi recorded the event on her phone. The fragments had been found; first one or two, and then several; but Mary had pursued her painstaking examination until she had recovered every fragment she could find; each fragment being picked up with tweezers and placed in an evidence bag. Armed with this evidence, of which Mary had never doubted the existence for one minute, they hastened to the police station where Miss Leinster had demanded an immediate examination of the fragments. First, the fragments had been reassembled like a jigsaw and had proved to comprise both the letter and the envelope almost in their entirety, and with more than enough of the former to see that it had been worded just as Murray had claimed.

Then had come the more laborious process of analysing the fragments for fingerprints. And it is for the results of this examination the two women have been waiting. And Sergeant Brent, much to his chagrin, is the bearer of that report.

'Look,' he says, his tone surly. 'Just because it turns out there was a letter, doesn't prove he didn't assault the girl.'

'It proves she's a fucking liar!' retorts Mary Leinster, hotly. 'And if she lied about the letter, she could be lying about the rest of it. Which she is!'

'This case isn't closed yet,' says Brent.

'Yes, but you're going to release my son,' asserts Miss Leinster. 'From that look on your face, I'm guessing you haven't got any choice.
You've been *told* to release him, haven't you?'

'Oh, let's get it over with,' snaps Brent; he leads them to the cells.

All conversation abruptly ceases when the Boy walks into Dirty Dick's. Even the jukebox falls silent.

Flanked by his two bodyguards, Alf and Fred, the Boy swaggers across the room as though he owns the place (which in fact he does), occasionally shooting derisive glances at the quailing patrons, most of them his minions in one way or another. The Boy's usual sharp suit is complimented with a snap-brimmed hat. The thugs, as always, are dressed in black.

'Alright, I ain't 'ere ter make a speech,' says the Boy. 'Get back to yer natterin'.'

The conversation and the jukebox music resume, as though switched back on from the same source.

The Boy stops before the table at which Misaki and Ren are seated with Sabella.

''Oo's this?' he demands, glaring at Sabella.

Sabella is a stranger to the Boy, and to the Boy all strangers are objects of suspicion.

'This is Sabella,' Misaki informs him. 'She comes from the Deserts of Araby.'

'Oh, a wog bird,' translates the Boy. 'Is she a dyke or somethin'?' 'I am not familiar with her sexual orientation,' says Misaki.

'Oh, likes sexy Orientals, does she?' says the Boy. 'Then you two've got yer evenin' sorted out, 'aven't yer?'

And with a snort, the Boy moves on.

Our friends Carson and Drubble are seated at their usual corner table. And if both of them look ill and uncomfortable, this will be on account of the accelerated course of vitamin-C they have been enduring over these past few days.

The Boy swaggers up to their table.

'An' 'ow are we today?' he inquires. 'All nice 'n regular, are we?'

'A bit *too* regular,' says Carson, who has become intimately familiar with the pattern of his bathroom tiles; there's one man with a pipe in his mouth and a dog on a lead with whom he is almost on speaking terms.

'And we've both got these lousy headaches,' he continues.

''Eadaches, eh?' says the Boy. 'That'll be from too much thinkin'. Now I've warned you about that, ant I? You two and thinkin' just don't get along.'

Carson wearily indicates the two glasses of tap water sitting on the table before them. 'Well, we're ready for our next dose,' he says.

'Yeah, abaht that,' says the Boy. 'I'm feeling generous today, so what say we call time on the 'ole vitamin-C treatment, eh?' Carson and Drubble's faces brighten.

'Seriously?'

'Well, I ain't givern to jokin', am I?' points out the Boy. 'Thing is, I've attcherly found me a buyer for the stuff. Feller in Croatia wants ter take it off my 'ands. Seems they don't get enough vitamin-C over there.'

'So, we don't have to scoff any more of them pills?' says

Drubble, relieved.

'That is what I'm sayin', yeah,' confirms the Boy.

The two crooks sit back in their chairs, relieved that their present discomfort will be coming to an end.

As the Boy turns away, Drubble says, 'And if you've got any more jobs for us...?'

The Boy looks at him. 'Whenever I 'ave a job needs doin' what is worthy of yours an' 'is particular talents, you will 'ear from me directly.' And with this avowal, the Boy departs, followed by his goons.

Drubble turns to Carson. 'You hear that? He still needs us! Says he'll give us bell as soon he has a job goin' that's worthy of our talents!'

Carson shoots his friend a look that would have annihilated him had it been understood correctly.

'I wish someone would come and take that bloody girl away,' says PC Pike, just come up from the detention cells. 'She's driving me up the wall with her "Dark Lord is coming" speeches.'

Sergeant Brent looks up from the tabloid newspaper he is perusing. 'And where would they take her to?'

'Home. The funny farm. Borstal. Anywhere! I don't bloody care!' replies Pike, at the coffee machine.

'Well, you'd have to ask Mister High-and-mighty Mark Hunter about that one,' observes Brent. 'Seems like we can't do anything around here at the moment without getting his say-so.'

Pike, armed with caffeine fix, sits himself across the table from his colleague. 'You don't like that bloke, do you?'

'What's to like about him?' retorts Brent. 'Thinks he's James fucking Bond.'

'Well, he is, isn't he?' reasons Pike. 'I mean he's a spy, isn't he?'

'So, does that give him the right to boss us around in our own nick?'

'I wouldn't call him bossy,' says Pike. 'He seems alright to me. I just wish he'd do something about that psycho-bitch downstairs.' Suddenly the room is plunged into darkness.

'What the fuck?' exclaims Brent.

'Power cut,' replies Pike. 'Either that or we've both just gone blind.' 'Ha-ha.'

Brent goes to the door. The corridor is likewise in darkness. Someone rushes past him.

'What's going on?'

'Power cut!'

'No shit, Sherlock!'

'And it's just us, an' all,' reports Pike, at the window, peeking through the Venetian blind. 'Lights are on in the windows across the street. Streetlights are working, an' all.'

'How can we be the only ones having a power cut?' demands Brent.

'Dunno,' admits Pike. 'Maybe someone forgot to put enough fifty pees in the meter.'

'Stop, you're killing me.'

'What's going on?' comes a new voice, entering the room.

'What do you think?' retorts Brent. 'It's a power cut. And somehow it's only us that's affected.'

'Maybe it's our special generator,' suggests the newcomer, one PC Bailey.

'What special generator?' demands Brent.

'Well, we're emergency services, aren't we?' reasons Bailey. 'So we should have a special generator, shouldn't we? I mean, hospitals have got to have 'em, otherwise what would happen to all the people on life-support or in the operating room when there was a power-cut? They must have their own generators. Must have. So maybe we've got one an' all, at this station.'

'Y'know, that idea would make a lot of sense if the electricity was out for everyone except us,' says Brent. 'But in case you hadn't noticed, it's the other way round!'

'Who the hell's that?' blurts Pike, still at the window.

'Who the hell's what?'

'Just saw three people run across the street,' he tells them. 'Looked like they were in fancy dress, or something. They were wearing these robes with hoods over their heads. You know, like monks wear.'

'Probably just some people collecting for charity,' says Brent, dismissively.

'Yeah but—and now there's more of 'em!' exclaims Pike. 'They're in the car park! They're coming here!'

'Maybe they've come to check the fuses,' suggests Bailey.

Nobody answers him.

A commotion breaks out down the corridor; shouting and screaming. 'Now what?'

'That sounds like front desk!'

'But listen to it! It's like a fight's broken out!' 'A fight? Sounds more like a massacre!' Bailey races off down the corridor.

'Come back, you twat!' Pike joins Brent.

'I think we should get out of here!'

More screaming, closer.

'That was Bailey!'

'Let's get out of here!'

'Oh Christ! Oh Jesus fucking Christ...!'

'I'm not saying I *believe* the stories per se,' says Dodo Dupont. 'I'm just starting to think there *might* be something in them.'

Dodo guides her car through the lamp-lit streets. Her friend Mark Hunter occupies the passenger seat. Under discussion: the conspiracy theories surrounding the Asteroid Belt Mining Project.

'If there's *something* in the stories then there's *everything*,' argues Mark. 'Either the Mining Project is a hoax or it isn't.'

'Well, it would be one explanation as to how Frank Hanson, who was supposed to be 200 million miles away, turned up here in Linton.'

'You mean if we accept that the location of the fake mining colony is here in England; perhaps even close to where we are now. That's one I find hard to believe. To house such an elaborate deception would require a huge complex of buildings; it'd be hard to hide something like that on this small island of ours. You would expect them to put it somewhere really out of the way: the Arizona Desert, the Russian Steppes; somewhere like that.'

'You could hide the place in any country if you just put it underground,' reasons Dodo. 'I mean, we've known more than our fair share of underground bases, haven't we?'

'True,' agrees Mark; 'but how do you account for the green cloud and Hanson's disappearance? I mean, even if we accept the version that says the mining colony personnel have been conditioned into believing they are really in the asteroid belt, why would the people behind the deception manufacture the appearance of this green gas cloud?'

'Because they wanted to shut down the project,' answers Dodo. 'They shoehorned the appearance of this space anomaly into the script and then guided the story up to the complete loss of contact with the colony, leaving the public to assume the two events must be somehow connected.'

'But why the monster in the cloud?' questions Mark. 'Wouldn't the anomaly by itself have been enough?'

'Maybe the creature *wasn't* in the script,' replies Dodo. 'Just as Frank Hanson's escape and subsequent activities are presumably not part of the script.'

'So you're saying the fake mining colony complex was actually invaded and taken over by this thing...?' Mark ponders. 'Yes... That would almost tie everything up... You know, one thing that's always struck me: Frank Hanson's terrified words "Those eyes! Those eyes!" And they were more or less repeated by the first girl he attacked, in her sleep.

I can't help recalling that it was similar words that were spoken by that alien abductee Barney Hill, when he was under hypnosis, describing his close encounter.'

'Yes, but he was talking about the eyes of aliens who were more or less humanoid. I don't think that any alleged abductee has described seeing anything like this ghost creature that those girls have been seeing in their dreams. This is something new.'

'Yes, this Nameless One or Dark Lord, as Scarlette Hanson keeps calling it,' says Mark. 'Did she invent those names or did they already exist somewhere? Well, let's see how our patient is tonight...'

Dodo steers her F-type into the forecourt car park of Linton Police Station. The building before them stands in darkness.

'What's going on?' exclaims Mark. 'Whoever heard of a police station closing up for the night? I don't like this.'

Dodo parks close to the main entrance. They both get out. The silence, the building wreathed in darkness, are ominous. The main entrance doors stand open.

'Something's happened here,' states Dodo. 'Those doors shouldn't be open like that; they're automatic.'

Mark unholsters his gun. 'Come on,' he says.

As they approach the main entrance a smell reaches their nostrils; the smell of blood. Both Mark and Dodo have enough experience to know that for the blood-stench to be this strong, there has to be a lot of it.

They step through the open doorway into the foyer. Light enough filters in from outside for them to see the bodies. Sprawled on the floor, slumped against the reception desk, over the waiting area chairs... There must be at least a dozen. Most of the corpses are in police uniform, but there are a number in civilian attire as well.

'Jesus Christ,' breathes Dodo.

'A massacre,' says Mark. 'And judging by the complete absence of sound, I'm thinking we're going to find the same story all over this station house. How were they all killed? Were they all shot? Let's have a look.' Mark hunkers down beside the nearest body; a policewoman huddled on the floor. 'Pity we didn't bring a torch…'

'Hang on a minute, I'll use my phone,' says Dodo. So saying, she activates the light on her smartphone and directs it over the hunched body.

Mark turns the woman over onto her back. Her neck, jaw and chest are saturated with blood. 'Her throat's been cut!' he exclaims. 'Look how deep the wound is. It would have to be a dagger or a machete that did this; no street-thug's flick-knife could have done this damage.'

A rapid examination of more of the corpses reveal a similar picture: deep cuts or stab wounds that could only have been inflicted by a large-bladed weapon. There are no survivors; all have been efficiently killed.

'This wasn't the work of some demented spree-killer,' declares Mark. 'Everyone here has been dispatched thoroughly, professionally. This bears all the hallmarks of a commando raid, not a lunatic's rampage.'

'Yeah,' says Dodo. 'But was the object of the raid just to take out everyone in this police station? Or did they have some other objective?' 'Scarlette Hanson!'

'That's what I was thinking.'

The two friends make their way through the station. As anticipated, the corridors and rooms they pass are littered with corpses. Relentless death has swept through the entire building. They descend the stairs to the detention cells. Dodo's light traces a path across the inky darkness of the chamber. Three more uniformed bodies and, yes, one open cell door.

Dodo sweeps her light over the cell. It is empty.

'A gaol-break,' murmurs Mark. 'There's no way Scarlette broke out of her cell and did all this herself. This was a rescue operation.'

'Her brother?'

'You would have thought he could be the only suspect,' agrees Mark; 'but what we've got here doesn't match his *modus operandi*. And I just can't believe that one person could have massacred everyone in this station. It has to have been a group attack.'

'But what group?' wonders Dodo 'And what did they want with Scarlette Hanson...?'

Chapter Twenty-Five
Candy Is Dandy

Murray Leinster awakens from deep slumber with the sensation of a heavy weight pressing down on him. His eyes open and he sees that the heavy weight is supplied by his Mysterious Girlfriend, who sits straddling his recumbent form and grinning down at him. The still visible injuries on her face remind Murray of his own wounds and with them, all the attendant circumstances.

'And how are we this morning?' is Eve's cheerful inquiry.

'Okay, I think,' says Murray. 'What time is it?'

'Half eight.'

'Half eight! I'm late!'

Panicking, Murray struggles to rise, but with 150 pounds of uncooperative Eve Chandler pinning him down, his efforts are in vain.

'You're not late,' Eve tells him. 'Cuz you're not goin' into school today. Your mam thinks you should stop at home, and I'm right with her on that one.'

'So you know about what's happened...?'

'Aye, your mam's filled me in on the whole sordid business. I dunno...' She shakes her head in mock weariness. 'The one day I'm out of town an' all that has to happen to you! Can't leave you alone for five minutes, can I?'

Murray looks uncomfortable. 'So you know about the

anonymous' (he doesn't say 'love'!) 'letter and everything...'

'Yes, and you don't have to feel bad about going to that rendezvous,' Eve tells him. 'You just wanted to find out who your secret admirer was, didn't you? Anyone would. It's not like I think you would have dumped me for some other lass! I've got too high an opinion of meself to think summat like that could ever happen!'

'Yeah, but I didn't tell you about the letter when I could've...'

'Yeah, but I didn't really give you a chance, did I? I remember how I made my apologies and rushed off at the end of school that day. Bet you were a bit pissed off wi' me, weren't you? I don't blame you!'

She strokes his face. 'Poor boy... Been in the wars, haven't you?'

'That was Lassiter. He thought I'd...'

Eve scowls. 'Yeah but did he, though? I'll be having words with that feller today.' She brightens. 'Still, you were dead lucky your mam managed to get you out of the cop shop when she did! A couple of hours later and you'd've been dead!' 'Dead?' questions Murray.

'Aye, it's all over the news today: ten o'clock last night that police station was raided, an' they killed everyone in the place! "A Major Terrorist Incident," they're calling it. And I suppose it was, but it wasn't the Islamic State or anyone, cuz the whole point of the attack was to get Scarlette Hanson out of jail!'

Murray struggles to take all this in. 'But... who would do that...? I mean...'

'Well, we don't know who it were,' says Eve. 'But we know what they look like, cuz they were caught on CCTV cameras all over town. They were all like wearing these hooded robes and carrying long knives. I reckon they must be some kind of secret cult; but Christ knows where they popped up from!'

'A secret cult...' echoes Murray. 'Y'know, when I was in the cells I was next to Scarlette, she was talking like that; like she was in some cult or something...'

'Yeah, I've heard about that,' agrees Eve. 'But like I say, I just don't get where those people showed up from... I mean, before it seemed like it were just her and her brother...'

She looks at her watch. 'Well, I'd better be getting a shift on.' She leans in, close and confidential. 'So, how about tonight, love?' 'Tonight?' says Murray, red-faced.

'Yep. You rest up today, and then tonight you'll be all ready to impale me on your manhood and have your wicked way with me! How about that?'

Murray, though naturally embarrassed by the choice of words, can see no objections to this proposed table of events.

Eve finds the opportunity for those 'words' she wants to have with Lassiter.

She discovers that worthy with his remaining crony Malcolm outside the school gardens during first break. She could've quite easily spoken to Lassiter during registration, but it seems these proposed 'words' of Eve's require a degree of privacy for their telling, and it is only now that she discovers her target in a suitably out of the way location.

Lassiter looks visibly troubled when he sees Eve walking purposefully towards him, a look that a sickly version of his trademark smile fails to obliterate.

Malcolm, immediately sensing that three is going to be a crowd on this particular occasion, taps out the contents of his pipe, pockets the same, and with a cheery 'I'll leave this one to you, old son,' takes his leave.

'Hiya there,' says Eve, stopping before Lassiter. 'I wanted to have a quiet word with you. Nice of your friend to leave us in peace, like.'

Lassiter brazens it out. 'If this is about me hitting your boyfriend, I know I shouldn't have done it, but you've got to admit I had a good reason. I thought he'd been messing around with my kid sister, didn't I?'

Eve shrugs. 'I dunno: did you? I know that's what folks were saying yesterday before the truth came out, but y'see I can't help having this feeling that you already knew Murray hadn't done anything.'

'How could I have known that? I only knew what my sister told me, didn't I?'

'What she told you? Or was it what you told her?'

'What are you on about?'

'Well, you see, the whole thing seems like it were a set up to me,' proceeds Eve calmly. 'The fake love letter that made Murray go to that place. Your little sister being there. And someone else there, conveniently hiding in the bushes with a camera to take the snaps when your sister started throwing herself at Murray... Yeah, it looks like it were a trap to me; like someone just wanted to drop Murray right in it.'

'Meaning me, I suppose?' challenges Lassiter. 'And why would I want to do that? I've got nothing against Murray; I never had. I've always stuck up for him. Ask him yourself if you don't believe me!'

'Oh, I believe you,' Eve assures him. 'You never used to have it in for Murray; but things change, don't they? And I reckon you might have got yourself a grievance with him recently. Say after the day I first arrived here; when I gave you the brush-off and started going out with him.'

'Like I care about that,' snorts Lassiter.

'Don't you? Not just a little bit jealous of 'im?'

'Don't flatter yourself. And even if I was, d'you think I'd go to the trouble of making him look like a paedo just to get even with him?'

'You might,' says Eve. 'Depends how much of an evil bastard you are, doesn't it? Some folks'll do anything, just to get their revenge... Y'know what happened to me and Murray in town last weekend? We got set on by this gang of psychos who call themselves the Gentlemen. Seemed pretty clear to me that they didn't just happen on us by chance; someone set them onto us. First off, I thought it were me they wanted beaten up or raped, but now I'm starting to think that it was really Murray they were after.'

'And I suppose you think I set this gang on you?'

'Yeah, I do. And when that one didn't work it was time for Plan B, wasn't it? Make Murray look so bad that I'd dump him on that spot. That was your idea, wasn't it?'

'Bullshit,' retorts Lassiter. 'You can't prove any of that. And anyway, my family's dropped the charges against Murray. He's not in trouble any more. What else do you want?'

Eve ponders this. 'Hmm... How about you being kicked out of this school? I reckon that'd be nice.'

Lassiter looks worried in spite of himself. 'You couldn't do that,' he says. 'You can't just accuse me of things. They wouldn't expel me without proof.'

'I could probably dig up some proof,' says Eve. 'But, y'know? You're not worth it. This time I'll let you off with a warning. Leave my boy alone from now on.'

Eve turns to leave. And just as Lassiter has allowed himself to relax, she turns back and drives her fist into his stomach. '*That* was your warning.'

We once again find Carson in the driveway outside his house, engaged in that Sisyphean task of repairing his motorcycle. It has become an obsession with Carson; he dreams of the moment that the inert engine will erupt into smoke-spewing life, and he will be able to take to the roads, proud in the knowledge that he and he alone was the one who succeeded in making the machine roadworthy.

And we can only applaud Carson for his perseverance, his determination in this endeavour. A lesser person than he would have just called in a garage mechanic and have been enjoying the freedom of the roads long ago.

Two newcomers step into the driveway from the street.

Carson looks and is surprised to see Misaki Morishita and Ren Hoshino.

'What are you two doing up and about so early?' he asks. 'It's not even tea time.'

'Pressing business has brought us into town earlier than usual today,' answers Misaki. 'And I've also come to bring you some good news.'

'Oh yeah?' says Carson. 'What would that be?'

Misaki leans her elbows on the saddle of the motorbike, smiles at Carson. 'Your old enemy Brent is dead.'

Shock, swiftly followed by comprehension are pictured on Carson's face. 'So he *was* in the nick last night! I wondered about that, but they hadn't mentioned his name...'

'Yes, they still haven't released a full list of the victims,' says Misaki. 'But of course, I have my own sources of information.'

'So Brent's dead...' murmurs Carson.

'You don't look very pleased,' accuses Misaki. 'I was hoping for more of a reaction.'

'You want me to jump for joy or something?' inquires Carson. 'Well, I don't feel like that. I mean yeah, I didn't like the guy, but... I dunno...'

'You used to be friends.'

'That was a long time ago... A lot's happened since then...'

'Yes, it has,' agrees Misaki. 'While you're in this reflective mood, there's something else I want to talk with you about. I would very much like to know what exactly happened between you and Murray Leinster nine years ago.'

If Misaki is hoping for more of a reaction this time, she gets it. Carson looks horrified, the colour ebbing from his face.

'How do you know about that...?' he asks, his voice tight.

Misaki renews her smile. 'I know everything, don't I? In fact it was because I knew of your connection with Murray

Leinster that I made myself acquainted with you in the first place.'

'Why?' demands Carson. 'What's Murray Leinster to you?'

'That's my business,' is the smooth reply. 'I just want to hear from you precisely what transpired back then.'

'Forget it,' snaps Carson, turning resolutely back to his engine maintenance.

'No charges were preferred,' continues Misaki. Although Murray's mother placed a restraining order on you. She didn't want you being allowed anywhere near her boy again. This being the case, you probably don't know that soon after that time, Murray was able to banish every memory of those events from his conscious mind. He came to forget that he'd ever known such a person as Carson...'

Carson looks at her, his expression ghastly. 'He forgot...?'

'Yes. But now he's starting to remember again...'

'Chocolate?'

Mary Leinster offers the selection box to her son. Murray realises she must have bought these chocolates just for him; his mum is not someone who regularly eats chocolates. An extra treat they must be, after his ordeal of the day before.

Mother and son are seated in the living room, Mary Leinster having just made them both mugs of afternoon coffee. Murray senses something in the air; some serious announcement to be made. From his mum's demeanour and the fact that she's wearing all her clothes, he senses that she is in one of her more serious, parental, moods; one of those moods when she actually acts like a proper grown-up.

Having studied the menu, Murray selects the strawberry crème, pops it in his mouth.

'And how's my boy this afternoon?' commences Mary Leinster.

'Okay,' replies Murray, mouth full.

'This has been a bit overwhelming for you, hasn't it?' continues Mum. 'You getting arrested and taken to the police station... If I hadn't got you released from that place when I did—'

'I'd be dead!' says Murray cheerfully.

'Yes, darling... So I don't know if today is the right time to be bringing this up... But I've been talking to Eve about this...'

'About what?'

'About that man Carson,' says Mary. 'You've started to remember him, haven't you?'

So it's this that Mum wants to talk to him about!

'Yes, but not much,' says Murray. 'I've just remembered his name. It was when me and Eve were at the ruined abbey on Monday.'

'The ruined abbey,' repeats Miss Leinster, reflectively. 'You know, at the time we'd all pretty much decided that ruined abbey was just some place you'd invented between you. We searched and searched and we couldn't find the place...'

'...I tried to show the fuzz where the ruins was,' says Carson. 'But I couldn't find the bloody place. You had to go through this tunnel through the bushes to get to it, but the tunnel wasn't there! It'd gone!'

'And of course they just believed you invented the place,' surmises Misaki.

'Yeah. They kept on and on at me, the coppers did. They wanted me to admit there was no ruined abbey; that it was just something I'd made up and made the kid believe was real...'

'...But now Eve tells me the place is there after all! That you and Eve were both there on Monday and that that was where you started to remember...'

'Why did I forget, Mum?' asks Murray. 'Did you make

me forget about what happened?'

Mary Leinster smiles sadly. 'No, sweetheart. I'm sure most parents would like to be able to make their children forget all the bad things that happen to them... But no, you did that all by yourself.'

'How? I mean, was it straight away?'

'No, I think it was gradual. At first, you just didn't talk about it. It was like you were pushing it to the back of your mind and thinking about other things... But then, it must have been about a year later, I asked you if you'd run into Carson recently. I wanted to make sure he hadn't been trying to contact you. But when I asked you, you just looked up at me with this puzzled look and you said, "Who's Carson, Mummy?" And that was it: you honestly didn't remember him. You'd managed to block the whole thing out of your mind...'

'But blocked out what, Mum? I still don't really remember anything.
What happened? What did Carson do to me...?'

'...I didn't do anything to that kid! I swear I didn't. I mean, yeah I was hanging around with him a bit. But we was just pals, that's all! No harm in that, was there?'

'A lot of people would think it was wrong,' says Misaki. 'It might have been okay if you were a relative or friend of the family, but as you were not, people would naturally suspect your intentions. But I don't mind! If you sodomised the boy, you can tell me and Ren! We won't judge you!'

'I didn't bloody touch him...!'

'...So they examined you, but there were no signs that you had been subjected to pederasty...'

'Pedder-what?'

'He hadn't put his willy up your bum, sweetheart,' explains Mary. 'Of course he could have abused you in other ways that wouldn't have left a mark, but Carson insisted he hadn't molested you at all, and you... well, you weren't saying anything at the time. You were in shock.'

'Why was I in shock?'

Miss Leinster shrugs helplessly. 'That's what we could never find out. We thought maybe Carson had been playing mind games with you; but he said something happened to you when you were out of sight. He said you disappeared while you were playing amongst the ruins...'

'...He vanished! I looked everywhere for him, I did. But I couldn't find him... In the end I decided he must have just run off; you know, just to play a trick on me. Thought he'd probably just gone back home...'

'...But he hadn't gone home?'

'No. They found him later. He was just lying in a field, scared half to death they said...'

'...And that's all we know...'

'Maybe I'll start remembering more of it,' says Murray. 'If I go back to the ruined abbey—'

'You should stay away from that place,' says his mum. 'Something very bad happened to you there, precious. And if it wasn't anything that man Carson did to you, then it was something else; something that might still be there. Don't go back there, sweetheart. Even with Eve; don't go back there...'

Mary Leinster responds to a knock at the door to find two smiling Japanese girls standing on the doorstep. It is now early evening.

'Herro,' speaks the bespectacled of the two girls. 'We come to ask about our friend Murray Reinster. We hear he have bad time. We come to see if he okay.'

'You know my boy?' says Mary. 'Oh yes! I remember he said to me he'd met two strange Japanese girls in town.'

'That us,' replies the girl. 'We two strange Japanese girl.'

'Well, it's nice of you to call,' says Miss Leinster. 'Would you like to see Murray?'

'Very much like to see. He at home?'

'Yes, he's in his room.' She calls over her shoulder, 'Murray! Two friends here to see you!' No answer.

'Come on in,' she invites them. 'He's going to see his girlfriend in a bit, so he might be in the middle of getting ready.'

'Oh! We not want to interrupt if he going out…'

'Don't be silly! You've come all this way. Come in.'

The two visitors follow Miss Leinster into the hallway. She taps on the door of Murray's bedroom.

'Sweetheart, are you decent? Two friends are here to see if you're okay. Those nice Japanese girls you told me about.'

No answer.

She calls again, frowns. 'He's not gone and fallen asleep, has he?' she mutters.

'We not know,' answers the bespectacled girl. (The question was a rhetorical one, but Miss Leinster happened to be looking at the two girls when she uttered it.)

She cautiously opens the door.

She opens it widely.

The room is empty.

'Where's he got to?' wonders Miss Leinster.

'Perhaps he in *toire*?'

'Well no; the bathroom door's open,' indicating the door in question.

To the house in general: 'Murray! Where are you?' No answer.

Mary Leinster puts her hands on her hips. 'Has he just gone out without saying anything?' she mutters. 'Did he think I was going to follow him again…?'

'Most regrettable Murray not home,' says the Japanese girl. 'We go now. Please to give Murray our regards.'

And the two girls bow and make a hasty exit.

Chapter Twenty-Six
Liquor is Quicker

Since the days of the Penny Dreadful (and anyone who says that this book is the modern equivalent can go and stand in the hallway), one of the storyteller's most convenient devices is that of consigning his or her hero or heroine to temporary oblivion at the end of one chapter and then having them return to consciousness at the beginning of the next. Back then, if the protagonist was male, he would usually receive a blow to the head; if the protagonist was female, she would faint.

And while Murray Leinster is just as capable of fainting as the best of Victorian heroines, on this occasion it is neither a swoon nor a cosh on the head that has rendered the protagonist insensible: instead it has been that other useful device, the cloth soaked in chloroform.

And this is why his mum finds Murray missing from his bedroom: he has been abducted!

We will now re-join him as he returns to consciousness.

A Japanese nurse.

This is what Murray sees when he opens his eyes. A very young, good-looking Japanese nurse: a starched white tunic-dress hugs her ripe curves; her hair is clipped up and tucked under her red-cross-emblazoned nurse's cap, and she wears large, thick-lensed glasses.

She looks familiar.

'You awake,' says the nurse. 'How you feel?' Murray blinks as she shines a light in his eye.

'Okay...' he says.

Groggy and disorientated, Murray struggles to collect his thoughts. His mind latches onto the nurse. Those glasses, that broken English: he knows he has met her before. But where? He hasn't been in hospital for years, and there are no

Japanese nurses at his local doctors' clinic. In fact, the only Japanese girls he has ever known are—

'I know you!' he exclaims. He tries to sit up, but the nurse pushes him firmly back down.

'Must not move,' says the nurse. 'You been in bad accident.'

'No, I haven't!' retorts Murray. 'And you're not a real nurse!'

'Am real nurse,' is the sharp reply. 'And you must stay in bed. Much hurt.'

'But I'm not in a bed! This is a sofa!'

This is true. Murray has assimilated his surroundings: he is stretched out on an antique *chaise longue* in a large wood-panelled apartment, which looks to Murray more like a room in a stately home than a hospital. He sees paintings on the walls, antique vases, a carved fireplace. Drawn curtains and electric lighting suggest that night has fallen.

'I know you!' repeats Murray. 'You're that girl! With that other girl! And that big Japanese man in the black suit who's your bodyguard or something: he kidnapped me! He climbed into my bedroom through the window and knocked me out with a wet cloth! I remember it! So where am I now? Where is this place?'

'Doctor, patient talking crazy-talk!' calls out the nurse. 'You better come! Patient need sedative!'

In response to this, the doors at the far end of the room open and a white-coated physician, the usual stethoscope hanging around her neck, walks in. She is another young Japanese woman.

'How is the patient, nurse?' she asks as she briskly crosses the room in her high heels.

'And you're that other girl!' accuses Murray.

(Murray has forgotten their names, but I'm sure the perspicacious reader has recognised the nurse as Ren and the doctor as Misaki.)

'Delirious,' replies Nurse Ren. 'That car smash knock

him up real bad.'

'I wasn't in a car crash!'

'I shall examine the patient,' says Doctor Misaki.

She sits primly on the edge of the settee, takes Murray's wrist. Then she raises his t-shirt and, placing the stethoscope in her ears, listens to his heart. Murray opens his mouth to voice another protest, only to receive a speech-inhibiting thermometer. Doctor Misaki studies the patient dispassionately while waiting for the thermometer to do its work; she then extracts the device and holds it up to the light.

'Yes... He needs a dose of the medicine, nurse,' reports Doctor Misaki. 'Prepare the mixture.' 'Yes, Doctor.'

Nurse Ren moves out of Murray's line of sight. He hears a clink of glass.

'Look, will you tell me where I am?' demands Murray. 'Is this where you live?'

'Please do not excite yourself,' answers Doctor Misaki. 'You were very badly injured in that earthquake.'

'Earthquake? You just said it was a car crash!'

Nurse Ren returns with a glass beaker containing some fizzing brown liquid.

'Take this.'

Murray takes the glass, sniffs cautiously. 'It smells like coke,' he says. 'Funny coke.'

'It is your medicine,' Doctor Misaki tells him. 'It has been diluted with coke for ease of swallowing. Please drink it in one go.'

'I won't,' retorts Murray, sullenly. 'There's nothing wrong with me.'

Nurse Ren shakes her head sadly. 'Poor kid. He don't know what he saying.'

'You must drink your medicine,' insists Doctor Misaki. 'It is the only treatment for victims of lightning-strike.'

'Lightning-strike?' echoes Murray, incredulous.

'Drink.'

'No!'

'Drink!'

'No!'

'Nurse!'

Nurse Ren tilts Murray's head back, firmly squeezes his nose. Murray's mouth opens to inhale oxygen and Doctor Misaki deftly pours the contents of the glass down his throat. Murray swallows the concoction, this being the only alternative to choking on it.

Misaki and Ren now help the spluttering youngster to sit up, the latter assisting him in his difficulties with a couple of generous slaps on the back.

Upon recovering from this treatment, Murray sits back.

'And how do you feel, Mr Leinster?' inquires Doctor Misaki.

'Okay, actually,' confesses Murray. This seems funny, considering what he's just gone through. So funny, in fact, that he laughs.

'Yes, you look much improved,' concurs Misaki. 'What do you think, Nurse?'

'He look much better,' affirms Nurse Ren.

'Yes, you wouldn't think he had been savaged by a bear,' agrees Misaki.

'A bear?' repeats Murray. He laughs again.

'Still, I think a second dose of the medicine would help him even more.'

'Sure. I fix more medicine.'

Ren moves off to do this.

'Can I go home now?' inquires Murray, red-cheeked, a silly smile fixed on his face. 'Cuz, Eve, she'll be wondering where I am...'

Nurse Ren returns with the second draft. This time Murray swallows it without demur.

'Yeah, I feel much better now. So I better be going...' He hiccups.

Misaki rises to her feet. 'I am afraid you cannot go anywhere just yet,' she says. 'It is time to commence the second stage of your treatment.'

Murray gawps at Misaki as she unbuttons her white coat and lets it drop to the floor. She now stands dressed in a lacy lingerie set: a bustier, panties, stockings and suspender-belt; all in black.

Murray looks at her curiously, pouting his lips, tilting his head from side to side.

'Whassat all about?' he asks.

'The second stage of your treatment,' says Misaki. 'Copulative therapy.'

'Copu-whattative?'

'Copulative therapy,' repeats Misaki.

She steps forward, places one spike-heeled foot on the sofa, looms over Murray.

'We must check your sexual functions.'

Murray shakes his head firmly. 'Not doing it,' he says flatly. 'You're not my girlfriend—that's Eve, an' it's only Eve's allowed to check my sexy functions and not you. So there.'

'You have to do what your doctor tells you,' coaxes Misaki.

Another resolute headshake. 'Shan't. 'Sides, you're not even a proper doctor.'

Misaki looks down at him. 'Are you sure?'

''Course I'm sure. Proper doctors don't wear what you're wearing.'

'I mean are you sure you would not like me to test your sexual functions?'

'POSSERTIVE.'

'Let's see shall we?'

Misaki removes her shoe, and with her foot on the chaise longue next to Murray, unclips her stocking. She starts to slowly peel off the garment. Murray follows the slow, sinuous course of the stocking down that shapely leg with polite but drunken attention.

And then the smooth leg has shed its artificial skin.

'Now…' says Misaki. 'Are you sure you don't want me?'

Taking Ren's hand to aid her balance, Misaki raises her leg and presents the sole of her foot to Murray's face, close enough for him to feel the heat it radiates, to smell its odour.

'Go on,' invites Misaki, scrunching her toes.

'Lick it.'

'Don't wanna,' says Murray, vehemently shaking his head.

'Go on… It's such a hot foot, isn't it? You can resist it, can you? Lick it.'

'Don't wanna,' repeats Murray.

Misaki is nettled. Her naked foot is scant centimetres from Murray's face but the boy is clearly unmoved.

She wriggles her toes some more.

'Go on… Just one little kiss…'

'Shan't.'

'Er, Misaki-chan,' interjects Ren. 'I don't think foot fetish is as big with Westerners as it is back home.'

'I see,' sniffs Misaki. 'Well then, let's see… How about this?'

She lowers her cruelly rejected extremity and places it on Murray's crotch. She starts to slowly rub the area, provoking an immediate and satisfactory response.

'Stop it!' says Murray, trying to move Misaki's foot. 'Only Eve's allowed to do stuff like that.'

'But you're aroused,' purrs Misaki. 'That means you want me.'

'No! You're cheating! Stop it!'

'You know you want me,' insists Misaki. 'Forget Eve Chandler. She doesn't love you.'

'She does!' retorts Murray. 'She said so!'

'And you believe her?' jeers Misaki. 'You can't trust that girl. She is an enigma. No records, no past. Where does she come from? Where are her parents? Don't you think she's suspicious?'

'No! She's not shu-shupicious! She's a spy! Spies have

to keep secret about stuff.'

'She's a spy? You mean she works for Mark Hunter?'

Murray shakes his head. 'No. She's not an official spy. She's a secret spy.'

'Is that what she told you?'

Murray reacts to the mocking tone. 'She's showed me,' he declares firmly. 'She's showed me their headquarters. The Garden of Cats.'

'Garden of Cats?'

'Yep, it's a Shecret Garden. It's right in the middle of Linton but no-one knows about it. Only Eve and...'

'...and...?' questions Misaki.

'...the others...' says Murray, even in his befuddled state he starts to realise that he might be saying too much.

'What others?' Misaki footsies Murray's crotch vigorously. 'Speak. I want to know about this. I dislike not knowing things. Where is this Garden of Cats? Who are Eve Chandler's associates?'

'Not telling!'

'Tell me!'

'No!'

'Tell me!'

'NO!'

Murray grabs the leg attached to the insistent foot and pushing Misaki backwards with surprising force, he springs from the sofa and runs for the doors.

Only Ren's presence stops Misaki from falling over. The two girls give chase, Misaki awkwardly at first until she remembers to remove her other shoe.

Through the doors and Murray finds himself in a hallway, with an ornate staircase at one end, imposing doors at the other. He runs towards the imposing doors because they look to him like the building's entrance (and therefore also exit) doors. But he has covered less than half the distance when doors open from without and in walks the same man with the black suit and shades who had chloroformed him in his bedroom. The man is followed by two others, similarly attired. Behind them he sees night sky.

His escape blocked, Murray spins around on the tiled floor and makes instead for the staircase, shooting past Misaki and Ren who are just emerging from the drawing room.

'Come here!' orders Misaki.

'Noooooooooooo!' replies Murray, trailing the word behind him as he runs up the stairs.

'Morishita-san!' speaks Kondou. 'If I might just—'

'Not now, Kondou!' snaps Misaki. 'Can you not see I am busy?'

With her mismatching legs she pursues Murray up the stairs, followed by Ren, jiggling in her tight tunic-dress.

On the landing, Murray speeds across a gallery and then along a corridor, fizzing like a shaken-up champagne bottle. His buzz, however, does nothing to improve his poor athletic skills, and his pursuers rapidly close in on him.

Seeking cover, he darts into a room, which happens to be Misaki's own bedchamber. Seeing the sumptuous bed, Murray's first thought is to collapse onto it and catch his breath.

Too late he remembers why he was running in the first place.

Misaki springs on top of him.

'Got you!'

'Nooo!' whines Murray. 'I'm not telling you anything!'

'That can wait,' replies Misaki. 'My thirst for information made me temporarily forget the real reason why I brought you here! I am going to steal your virginity!'

And she sets about unzipping Murray.

'No!'

'Yes! You will be mine!'

'No! Lemme go!'

Ren produces her smartphone and sets the camera to video mode.

'It okay,' she assures Murray. 'In Japan we don't mind rape scene, as long as is work of fiction.'

'But this isn't a work of friction!' protests Murray.

Unzipped and flying at full mast, poor Murray despairs of preserving his chastity for his Mysterious Girlfriend. But then suddenly the room is full of people, Misaki is dragged from on top of him. He sees his Mysterious Girlfriend, he sees Mark Hunter, he sees Dodo Dupont and he sees numerous Japanese men in black suits; and, his head spinning, he just wishes they couldn't all see so much of him!

Chapter Twenty-Seven
Mysterious Green Fog

Lady Harriet Parker, currently working as a maid (unpaid) in Linton Hall, her own ancestral home, is becoming more and more anxious about her father. He has been missing since yesterday. (Her father being Lord Parker, who, like herself, has been forced to assume a menial position in his own household, courtesy of the usurper Misaki Morishita.)

Harriet first missed her father at lunch yesterday. He did not turn up for this meal, and none of the servants could locate him. Hearing the news, Harriet's first reaction had actually been one of joy, hoping that his non-appearance augured well. For this reason she had refrained from raising a hue and cry over his absence. Being prisoners on their own estate, and constantly on the look-out for means of escape, the father and daughter had come to an arrangement that, if one of them should chance upon an avenue of escape, a moment that would pass irrevocably if not taken advantage of immediately, then they would seize that moment and make their escape; the idea being that whoever escaped would then contact the relevant authorities and return with the necessary force to have the intruders evicted from their home.

This is what Harriet had first hoped had happened to her

father: that a means of escape had presented itself, and escaped he had. She had even thought the cavalry had arrived when there was all that commotion at the gate last night; all those people demanding to be let in. But it had turned out these people were only interested in rescuing some Linton boy Misaki had abducted that afternoon; and once they had achieved this rescue, these people had just left! No police involvement, no charges preferred; nothing! And this in response to an abduction! What was going on?

And now a day has passed, Harriet is once again wheeling the trolley bearing Misaki's afternoon breakfast, and still no word from her father.

Where can he be?

She knocks on Misaki's door and is bade enter.

'You're late,' is Misaki's greeting. 'I've been kept waiting and I don't like being kept waiting.'

'Very sorry, your ladyship,' replies Harriet. She knows that she has not been tardy, therefore Misaki must be in a bad mood, and Harriet is well enough acquainted with her mistress to know better than to contradict her when she is in a bad mood.

She's probably still annoyed at having had her toy taken away from her the previous evening.

Harriet wheels the trolley up to the bedside, fluffs up Misaki's pillow, pours out her usual cup of green tea and serves her her breakfast. Today's breakfast is a bucket of fried chicken legs, and Misaki, in the accepted Japanese style, sets about devouring the bread-crumb coated skins and discarding the rest.

'Your ladyship…?' ventures Harriet at length.

Misaki looks at her narrowly. 'Yes…?'

'I was wondering…'

'What were you wondering? Just say it.'

'I was wondering what has become of my fath—of Parker, the head butler.'

'What do you mean "What has become of him"? Can't

you find him?'

'No, your ladyship. No-one can. He's been missing since yesterday.'

Misaki tosses the last flayed chicken leg back into the bucket and delicately wipes her mouth with a napkin.

'Missing?' she says. 'How strange. Where could he have got to, I wonder?'

'Then your ladyship doesn't know…?'

'How would I know? I don't keep track of the menials,' replies Misaki, wiping her greasy fingers with a second napkin. 'That would be the head butler's job. But of course, he's the one who's missing, isn't he?'

She throws aside the napkin.

'You know, it's an interesting coincidence that you've lost your father,' she continues. 'Because recently my friend Ren has lost some of her possessions; some of her most cherished anime merchandise has been disappearing from her room. You wouldn't happen to know anything about that, would you?'

Harriet blanches under her mistress's sly, accusing look.

'No, my lady,' she answers.

'Hmm. Well, perhaps there is some connection here. Perhaps whatever has happened to Ren's belongings has also happened to your father…'

'I don't… see the connection…' falters Harriet.

'No? Well, I'm sure your father will turn up sooner or later…. You can take the things away.'

Once out of Misaki's room, Harriet orders a passing maid to take charge of the trolley, and she rushes to her own quarters, seriously alarmed.

She had enjoyed stealing Ren Hoshino's belongings. She has always detested that girl and had taken great pleasure in snapping those game and Blu-ray discs in half, in tearing up those graphic novels and especially in dismembering that stupid plastic figure of the schoolgirl in alpine shorts. (The latter had proved to be sturdily constructed; she'd needed to employ a hacksaw in order to fully dismember it.) And she knew that Ren was so gutless that even if she suspected Harriet of being the thief, she would never dare openly accuse her!

But of course, that wouldn't have stopped Ren from telling Misaki about the missing items... And maybe even passing on her suspicions as to the culprit...

Reaching her small chamber in the servants' wing, she goes straight to a cupboard built into the wall. In this cupboard, underneath some boxes, she has hidden the remains of the stolen items. She hurriedly moves the boxes.

The floor underneath is bare. The torn books, broken discs, the dismembered figurine: all have gone.

Keith Lassiter, actor (currently out of work) and co-star of the cult film classic *Shadbolt & I*, is chairing a family conference in the living room of the Lassiter domicile. Facing him are his son and Fiona, otherwise Fee, his youngest daughter. His wife and eldest daughter are not present. Having no say in the running of the household, the presence of these two would have been anyway superfluous.

Holding forth in his usual measured tones, an observer would think that Keith Lassiter is calm and untroubled; his two children know better; they know that their father is very, very angry.

'...And now we have the social services knocking on our doors. At the moment they are only inquiring about you, Fiona, but what if they start inquiring about your sister, or about your mother? This could be very awkward for us. We've all worked very hard to make this home of ours a happy one, to get things running the way we want them; running to our mutual satisfaction. And now all of this is in danger because of that silly prank you pulled; pretending this boy had interfered with you...'

Fiona sits pigeon-toed, looking at her clasped hands. 'It was big brother who wanted to get that boy in trouble,

Daddy...'

'Thanks!' snaps Lassiter. His stomach still smarts from that punch Eve gave him, and is doing nothing for his mood.

'Yes, but it was your idea, wasn't it, Fiona?' responds her father. 'You were the one who concocted this silly frame-up, and because you didn't do a very good job of it, the authorities now believe that you were the instigator, and that in turn has made them turn their attention to this household. They want an explanation as to why you are apparently so sexually precocious. Now do you see the ramifications of this, Fiona? Our comfortable domestic situation is in peril; we needs must put up a front, establish a cover story, in order to screen ourselves and fend off these inquiries. They will want to question all of us. They may become curious as to the condition of your bed-ridden mother. All this trouble, and you are the one who has brought it down on us, my dear...'

'I'm sorry, Daddy!' blubbers Fiona, the tears coursing down her cheeks.

'I'm sure you are, child,' sympathises her father. 'But apologies are never enough. The system I have perfected for the running of this household demands stringent enforcement of discipline. Mere words do not serve as adequate atonement. You have to be punished, my dear.'

Fiona looks incredulous. 'Punished? You mean you'll hurt me?'

'Of course, my child. Pain has to be administered in these cases. I wouldn't feel that you have adequately atoned for your crimes unless you experience pain.'

'But, Daddy... I thought only Mummy and Norma...'

'You thought that only your disobedient sister and her mother have to endure pain in this household?' says Mr Lassiter. 'Under normal circumstances that would be the case, but don't you see, dear? You have brought yourself down to their level, and now you must suffer as they always have to suffer...'

Fiona looks helplessly from her brother—who stolidly

ignores her— and back to her parent. 'But I don't want to be punished!' she wails.

'I'm sure you don't, child,' replies her father. 'But there is no other way. To ensure the well-being of this family unit, I must inflict punishment on you. I shall have to hurt you a great deal.'

Fiona knows too well what her father does to Norma not to be terrified at this announcement.

'But, can't big brother punish me?' pleads Fiona.

'Now that wouldn't be punishment at all, would it?' reproves her father. 'No, dear. I must ask your brother to leave us now. I fear that his
presence would only lend you moral support.'

Without a word, Lassiter rises from his chair and makes for the door.

'Big brother!' cries Fiona.

Lassiter exits the room.

Mr Lassiter, smiling benignly, rises from his chair.

'Now, my dear...'

The woman pauses at the top of the stairs. Her parents are talking in the room below.

'Is she going out again tonight?' asks the father.

'I think so,' replies the mother.

A sigh. 'Just what is she doing when she goes out like this all the time?'

'Going to the pub, dear.'

'Yes, but who with? Who are her friends? She never mentions any. They never come round here. How do we know she even has any friends?'

'She must have *some* friends...'

'But does she? What if she hasn't got any? What if she's going to the pub on her own?'

'What's wrong with that, dear? She's a grown woman...'

'Everything's wrong with it! Women only go to pubs on their own when they're hoping to get picked up by some man.'

'What do you mean by that?'

'I'm talking about desperate, lonely women, who think that even a one-night stand, letting themselves be used by some man, is better than nothing.'

'But Clare wouldn't do that! She not the type!'

'How do you know? We've got no idea what she gets up to. If she's socialising, where are her friends? If she's meeting men, why doesn't she ever bring any home with her? She never stays out all night; she's always back before sunrise…'

'Is that so bad?'

'Yes! Yes, if it means she's just having sex with men in their cars or up against walls!'

'Arthur!'

'Well, it could be that, couldn't it? Clare's shy and timid; she always has been. People like her, when they start going out and trying to mix with people in pubs and what have you, they just get taken advantage of.'

'But she's just looking out for a husband, dear…'

'Well, she won't find one like that. She'll only be meeting the wrong kind of men that way. And what about her drinking? You know the state she comes home in sometimes!'

'So, she has a few too many now and then. We've all done that, dear.'

'Yes, and that might be alright when you've got friends with you, but not if you're drinking on your own.'

'But you don't know—'

'She hasn't got any friends, I'm telling you! We would've seen them if she had!'

'But what do you want us to do? We can't make her stay in if she wants to go out!'

'I know that. Maybe it would be better if we just washed our hands of her completely…'

'Arthur! We can't just throw her out!'

'She needs to be independent, Mavis. It would do her good to have a place of her own, even if it's just a bedsit. A woman her age shouldn't still be living with her parents.'

'But—'

The sound of footsteps descending the stairs puts a stop to the conversation. The parents, seated before the evening television, watch as their daughter appears. The daughter is someone we know: no less a person than Miss Clare Forbes, form teacher of class 9-C at North Linton Comprehensive.

'You off out, dear?' asks her mother.

'Yes,' replies Miss Forbes.

'When will you be back?'

'Not sure. Late, I think.'

'Well, have a nice time.'

Miss Forbes crosses the living room and exits through the front door.

'Prostitution as a profession has enjoyed a varied reputation over the centuries,' says Lady Jane, studying the glowing tip of her cigarette. 'At different times and in different places prostitutes have variously been regarded as degraded or divine, have been treated as celebrities or as pariahs. The current climate is equivocal. There are those who choose to equate the voluntary pursuance of the profession with female emancipation, others see it as an impediment to complete sexual equality. It is much like pornography in that regard; always a contentious issue.

'For myself, I feel that it depends upon how the profession is conducted. First and foremost it has to be entirely voluntary; an act of free will; a career choice. Forced prostitution is nothing more than a combination of rape and slave labour. But a woman can be forced by circumstances as well as being physically forced by violence and intimidation. Primarily, this will be the urgent need for money, perhaps to keep herself and her children from starvation. If a woman takes up the profession out of desperation and against her personal inclinations, then she will likely despise herself for it and will fear being despised.

'But prostitution, like any other retail service, exists because there is a demand; and there has always been a demand for prostitution because the world is full of sexually voracious men. They may be men who cannot form relationships and acquire sexual partners through social interaction, or they may be promiscuous men who seek variety, or itinerant men whose calling takes them away from their normal partners; it doesn't matter. They are men, they crave sex, and they are willing to pay for it. Men possess testicles, and those testicles are constantly manufacturing semen which urgently demands to be discharged into a female womb; this desire for release is constant physical urge and mental preoccupation. Prostitutes offer the service of relieving men in this regard.

'Of course historically, prostitution was the only career open to women; at least, prostitution and domestic manual labour. Until recent times women were prevented from developing their intelligence and barred from all professions which required intellectual skill or training. Now that this is no longer the case, there are those who consider that a woman using her body to earn her living is outdated and that she should be using her mind. But it is really a matter of preference. Women no longer have anything to prove regarding their ability to excel in artistic, academic or corporate arenas; so whether to utilise her body or her brains to earn her living is a matter of personal choice. For myself, I found employment in the business world for many years before electing to change my career to prostitution.

'I am a courtesan, a high-class whore. My place of work is this hotel bedroom. To some, this would seem more noble, more "respectable" than the situation of a working-class prostitute who pursues her calling in the back alleys of housing estates or at truck-stop cafés. But the profession has to adapt itself to different environments, different clienteles.

'There are some who maintain that the intrinsically male pursuit of war would somehow be noble if conducted in a particular way, obeying a certain etiquette, certain restrictions; but this I cannot agree with. War is slaughter and should not be regarded as a noble and inevitable part of life, regardless of what the Greek philosophers had to say on the subject. War is the sanctioned taking of life, fuelled by masculine avarice, bloodlust, desire for power and intolerance. No authorised taking of human life should be tolerated in a humane society... Having said that, I'm afraid it has still become necessary for me to kill you. You see, the people I represent find these isolated executions sometimes necessary. You may not have been the world's worst sexual predator, serial killer or misogynistic corporate executive, but sometimes we find that a certain individual needs to be written out of the script, to be removed from the equation, and in the present case, that individual unfortunately happens to be yourself... This is why you were granted a final opportunity of satisfying your primary male impulse before your termination... Although I will of course still be posthumously debiting your fee for my services from your credit account. After all, business is business. So you see... Oh, you're already dead, aren't you? The injection seems to have taken effect more rapidly than I anticipated...'

The service station and diner located just to the east of Linton is a notorious hangout for prostitutes; as such, the locality can be said to provide more than one 'service' for the lorry drivers who frequent the place. Picture a vast apron of macadam, with the filling station on the right and the diner as the centrepiece. Off to the left are the toilet cubicles. The service station stands alone, facing the busy Linton bypass; behind it rises a tract of woodland. Night has fallen, and inviting light emanates from the plate-glass windows of the diner. The forecourt of the filling station is also illuminated, while lampposts shed pools of pinkish light over the vacant spaces of the parking area. For the girls who work this beat, it has so far been a disappointingly quiet evening.

There they are, gathered at the back of the parking lot, close to the treeline and away from the nearest lampposts. While the owners of the service station tacitly tolerate the presence of the prostitutes, they prefer that they should keep out of sight as much as possible; although the station is for the most part patronised only by haulage drivers, the occasional commuting family does call in, and would most likely drive straight back out again on catching sight of loitering females in tight skirts and stiletto heels. But standing back here is actually convenient for the girls, it being close to both where the drivers park their trucks and close also to the path through the woods which takes the girls to and from their homes in Linton.

Our friend Liz Drubble is amongst the group of girls hoping for custom tonight. Her friends, like herself, all retail sexual favours to fund their heroin addictions. Scrawny Sally, boss-eyed Chloe, Sonia the Scouser, Jamaican Gwen, fat Jilly and Sindi the Serb. All seven girls totter on heels and smoke cigarettes as they chat away with each other.

Scrawny Sally is holding forth: '...And he's like "repent your sinful ways and embrace the bosom of God". And I'm like "Bosom? So has God got tits, has he?"'

Appreciative laughter.

'Those Christian groups really creep me out, man,' says Gwen. 'I mean like, why are they always tryin' to convert you? I mean I don't go around tellin' people to do what I do, y'know?'

'Yeah, we should start goin' round people's houses,' says Chloe, 'and get more people on the game. It's better than cleanin' bogs.'

'Well, I wouldn't be doing this if I had money, like,' says Sonia.

'That's a no-brainer,' retorts Liz. 'None of us 'ud be here if we had money.'

'Yeah, we'd be snorting coke with rolled up fifties,' says Gwen.

'Speakin' of,' says Liz. 'I've really gotta go'n shoot up. Back in five.'

She heads off across the car park towards the toilets.

The facilities here at the service station have been thoughtfully adapted for junkies, with 'Bin the Pin' notices and the appropriate secure receptacles for doing just that. The ladies' room isn't actually too bad in terms of maintenance; the lights all work, the place has been cleaned within the last month, and none of the bogs are clogged up and making the place stink of shit. Liz seats herself in her usual cubicle and, while taking the opportunity to relieve her bladder, she reaches into her handbag for her needle. She has an ampoule of liquid heroin, which she feeds into the tube of the syringe.

She rolls up her sleeve (all of the girls always wear long sleeves) and injects the drug directly into her bicep muscle.

She sits back on the toilet seat and waits to come up.

That brother of hers! Doesn't even realise she's got a habit; doesn't even realise what she does to pay for that habit! Thinks she stays out at nights because she's a party animal. Thinks her withdrawals are just hangovers. And no-one's ever set the poor guy straight. They're just laughing at him; laughing because he doesn't see what's right under his nose. All except Carson. He just doesn't tell Drubble the truth about her because he knows how much it'd upset him. That's why she doesn't tell him, either. Her brother took her in when Mum chucked her out. He's a decent bloke. Carson's a decent bloke as well. Liz remembers that she went with Carson once, years ago. Proves he does like girls; that he's not into little boys like they were saying that time. When she was in Year Eleven, that was when she went with Carson... Or was it Carson that time? Maybe it was Boonie... Or Ferris... It's all so long ago (three years) that her memories get confused...

As high as a stray thought floating through the ether, Liz

sets off back across the car park. She sees the girls still standing and gossiping... She locks her sights on them and heads towards them... And then she can't see them... They're starting to fade in and out... Smoke... There's smoke or something wafting past them... A fire in the woods? She can't see any flames, any orange haze lighting the horizon... Fog? Funny time for fog to be drifting in...

'What's going on?' she calls out.

They've gone again. She can't see the girls... Now it's starting to billow around her... It *is* smoke; but it doesn't smell like smoke; doesn't smell like anything at all... And... It's green! Green smoke! What does it mean? Where do you get green smoke from?

Liz wades through the billowing mass... Is she still heading towards the girls? She can't tell. It's all around her... Like pea soup... Pea soup fog! Do they call it that because it's green, like this...?

She's lost all sense of direction now... She calls out again.

She hears the girls... Laughing... They think it's funny, do they? Funny that she can't find her way back to them? The bitches... No! They're not laughing; they're screaming! Screaming like they're being murdered or something! Jesus Christ! What's happening to them?

Liz calls out. She rushes towards the sounds... But the screaming is drawing away from her, fading out...

Silence... The fog, or whatever it is, starts to thin. The aureoles of the lampposts become visible again.

The fog disperses. Everything is back to normal: the vacant parking lot, the lights of the diner... Everything is normal except for the girls. They're not there. Gwen, Sonia, Jilly and the others: they've all vanished.

Chapter Twenty-Eight
Mysterious Eyes Without a Face

McKearney!

Dutch courage isn't infallible, and the drunk though he is, Stavro feels fear lance through his body when he sees that face, illuminated by a street lamp up ahead. But then the approaching figure draws closer and he sees that it isn't McKearney after all.

Stavro stumbles on through the high street, weaving his inebriated way through the evening pedestrians.

This isn't the first time this has happened; this thinking he has seen McKearney; not by a long shot. It's been getting worse these past few days: day or night, drunk or sober, he keeps seeing McKearney's face. Everywhere he goes, he thinks he sees that man; and every time it turns out to be a false alarm, the features always resolving into those of someone else. They say that if your distance vision is bad, your mind will always interpret objects you see ahead of you as whatever it is you most want to see. In Stavro's case, the reverse is happening: he keeps seeing the thing he particularly *doesn't* want to see: McKearney.

That round, stubbly head; the heavy, flabby features; those deep-set eyes with the threatening gleam. The face that had started alarm bells ringing in Stavro's head the moment he had set eyes on it; the day that McKearney the plumber had come to his apartment to fix his radiator. Why hadn't he listened to those alarm bells? Why had he followed his pathetic urge to wallow in the mire and associate only with the worst people he can find? Now look where it's got him!

It's the uncertainty that's driving Stavro up the wall. He just doesn't know if the man has jumped town or if he is still here somewhere, lying low. The man has quit his plumbing job. He has apparently left his former address. Both of these moves suggest to Stavro that McKearney remembers confessing his crime to him. But has he left town, fearing that Stavro will have informed on him? Or is he still here? And if he is still here, the only reason Stavro can think of for the man to still be here, is to keep an eye on *him*, to see what he does. Why else would he hang around? And it is this idea that McKearney must be dogging his steps that has resulted in him starting to see the man's face everywhere he turns.

And why *hasn't* Stavro informed on McKearney? Stavro can boast a fair number of convicted and unconvicted criminals amongst his acquaintance, and his embittered nature allows him to be unmoved by the knowledge of their offences... But this is different; this is a horrific, notorious mass-murder: a woman and her two kids (not to mention the dog) bludgeoned to death while on a bucolic stroll on a summer's day... This is not something that Stavro, jaded though he might be, can just shrug his shoulders about and dismiss.

He should have reported the man. True, at first he wasn't sure if his mind was playing him false; wasn't sure if McKearney had really confessed to the crime; his memories were the hazy, disjointed memories of the tail end of a long drinking session. But by now Stavro is convinced; the man's apparent disappearing act seems to confirm his culpability. So why doesn't Stavro just go to the police?

There are a number of obstacles: his reputation is one. The police regard Stavro with suspicion and might not believe him. They might even start to think once again that *he* is the culprit and is attempting to incriminate someone else in order to cover for himself. And then there's McKearney himself. If he learns that a warrant is out for his arrest, McKearney will know who the informer must be, and he may come looking for him, looking for revenge. If Stavro thought the cops could just collar McKearney straight away, it might not have been so bad; but he doesn't know where McKearney is to be found; he cannot lead the cops straight to him. (And add to this the fact that the Linton Constabulary has just had its numbers decimated after being the target of some kind of ritualistic *Assault on Precinct 13*.)

Faced with all these problems, Stavro has turned to his usual source of consolation, booze. And as usual the booze isn't really consoling him at all; unless he drinks himself into complete oblivion, the alcohol just aggravates his condition.

Some company might have helped, but Stavro's circle of acquaintance are not the most regular of people in their habits, and this evening, a trawl of his usual haunts has turned up a big fat zero in the way of drinking buddies.

Now he has given up on finding solace in the form of company and he wends his lonely way home, walking as steadily as his currently impaired motor-functions will allow.

He leaves the brighter streets behind and enters the maze of back streets forming one of the dodgiest residential areas of Linton. Stavro has no choice but to enter this dodgy residential area because he happens to live in it. He has never been overly concerned at walking these streets by night; experience has taught him that any danger there might be usually announces itself with a lot of noise; if you hear the sounds of angry or even boisterous male voices coming your way, and/or the sounds of property being violently assailed, you know that it will be a wise career choice to make a detour down another street, even if doing so does take you out of your way.

Tonight, or at least right at this moment, the neighbourhood is reassuringly quiet. Perhaps it is this quietness, or perhaps it is just Stavro's presently paranoid mental state, that causes him to glance over his shoulder. Whatever reason prompts the action, look back he does and is rewarded with the sight of a shadowy figure advancing along the path in his direction. The figure is too far off for Stavro to even imagine he can discern the facial features of McKearney, but he can see the outline of the figure and that outline is broad and stocky, and McKearney is broad and stocky.

Stavro ducks into a convenient alley. Pinning himself against the wall, he waits.

The figure appears. It is the Wheezer.

Stavro's relief turns to anger. He grabs the Wheezer and drags him into the alley.

'Were you following me?' he demands, shaking him. The look of fright soon passes from the Peeping Tom's face when he sees who his assailant is. He laughs his wheezing laugh.

'No, of course you weren't,' says Stavro, answering his own question. 'No-one would set you to tail anyone. You don't even know what day of the week it is. No, I don't suppose you're actually in cahoots with McKearney; but you know where he is, don't you? So tell me! Tell me where he is!'

The Wheezer just laughs.

Stavro shakes him some more. 'Where is McKearney? Where's he hiding? I'm fucking serious here! Tell me where he is, you bastard!' The Wheezer sniggers, eyes wide and aggravatingly vacant.

'You—' Stavro punches him. The Wheezer flops about like a broken doll. Stavro punches him again. He collapses to the ground.

After giving him a kick for good measure, Stavro turns and leaves him.

A Southern Comfort on the rocks for Room 319.

Daphne's heart pounds as she exits the lift. She grips the tray in hands whose unsteadiness pose a distinct threat to the contents of the glass.

Room 319 is the current abode of Sabella. Sabella Whatshername, the Muscular Lady.

Daphne had been working reception two nights ago when Sabella checked in. And it was love at first sight. The Indian (or is she Middle Eastern?) girl had been bare-armed, carrying her jacket over her shoulders, and the combination of her regally beautiful features, her flowing black hair and those toned, muscular arms and abs had set her heart aflutter.

She knew that the starry-eyed admiration must have been written all over her face, but if Sabella had noticed this she had not reacted, remaining cool and aloof as she booked her room.

Since then Daphne has been able to do nothing but think of the girl in Room 319. This preoccupation has been seriously interfering with the performance of her job, an unfortunate fact because her job performance had been pretty poor to start with. At 19 years of age, Daphne is a recent recruit to the hotel's staff, and although never lazy, unmotivated or tardy, she is unfortunately a complete klutz, invariably leaving a trail of disaster in her wake.

Daphne would almost certainly have been fired before now, except that she has become a favourite of the hotel's resident prostitute in room 510. And although she's grateful for the patronage, Daphne is somewhat in awe of Jane Richmond. Not only is she a very elegant and classy lady, but she's so good at her job that her clients sometimes expire from it!
Only this evening they have had to dispose of another body.

Here it is. Room 319. She knocks timidly on the door.

The door opens, and there is Sabella, wrapped in one of the white towelling bathrobes supplied by the hotel, her hair lank and wet from the shower. The robe is short-skirted, affording Daphne a view of Sabella's long, athletic legs.

'Enter,' she says, holding the door wide.

Trembling, Daphne follows her inside, through the hallway and into the main room of the suite.

'Please to put the drink on the table,' instructs Sabella.

A simple instruction, but one which Daphne still manages to botch. Perhaps we can blame the rug because it is on this that she trips, and she 'measures her length on the floor,' or, in other words, falls flat on her face. The tray goes flying and one perfectly good Southern Comfort on the rocks gets soaked up by the carpet.

Daphne bursts into tears. Not because she has fallen flat on her face; she is used to this; but because she had to fall flat on her face now of all times. On her journey from the hotel bar to Room 319, she had concocted all kinds of fantasies of the events that might transpire when she arrived at her destination; surprisingly, making a complete fool of herself hadn't figured among them.

Hands, strong but gentle, help Daphne to her feet. She finds herself pressed close to Sabella, looking up into her aristocratic face. The white bathrobe, loosely knotted, has fallen open, revealing the Arab girl's taut abdomen and heavy breasts.

'I'm sorry...' blubbers Daphne, aroused and ashamed and a hundred other things.

'It was a simple fall,' says Sabella. 'There is no need for apologies.' 'I feel so stupid...' says Daphne.

'There is no need,' Sabella tells her. 'Your misadventure has not impaired my opinion of you. You care about how I regard you because you are in love with me, yes?'

Daphne's eyes open wide with surprise and delight. 'I... I didn't think you'd noticed...'

'There is nothing that I do not notice,' is the simple reply. 'You developed feelings for me immediately upon our first meeting one another two nights ago. These feelings have intensified since that time, yes?'

'Oh, yes!' gushes Daphne, throwing her arms around Sabella, burying her face between her breasts. 'My heart's bursting! My body yearns for you! Just take me! Please!'

She directs eyes of sweet surrender into those of Sabella.

'This I will do,' is the cool reply. 'I cannot promise to return your feelings of love. Perhaps this will come later. But for now, yes, I will accept this offering of your body and make you mine.'

The bathrobe drops to the floor and Daphne sighs as she caresses the smooth-skinned, granite-hard muscles of Sabella's arms.

Is that...?

Yes, it is! It's Miss Forbes, his homeroom teacher! And she looks totally wrecked!

Wait a minute.

Is he really seeing her there? Or is it just part of his trip?

Spacey turns to his friends.

'Is there a lady sitting on the floor there?'

'She's sitting on the pavement, yeah,' confirms Gary.

Spacey walks up to her, leans forward to look more closely.

'Whadda you staring at?' demands the woman.

It is Miss Forbes. Drunk, glasses askew, speaking in a louder voice than usual; but it's her!

'Hey, Miss Forbes,' he says. 'It's me, Kenneth Spacey. I'm in your class, remember?'

'Sho what?' she retorts. 'You're not the bosser me!'

'I'm not bossing you,' says Spacey. 'I'm just like seeing if you're okay, cuz you're sittin' in the middle of the street, y'know...'

'No, I'm shitting against a wall,' replies Miss Forbes. 'Sho what? It's not your wall, is it? Ish not your street!'

'Yeah, you can sit anywhere you want,' agrees Spacey. 'But, y'see, I don't think you should chill right here, cuz y'know if you fall asleep, well, somethin' bad might happen. You should head on home; that's what you should do.'

'Too tired to walk home,' mutters Miss Forbes.

'Take a taxi!'

'Too tired to take a taxi...'

'No problem,' says Spacey. 'I'll help!'

He takes one of Miss Forbes' unresisting arms, hooks it over his shoulder.

'Someone help me out here!'

Gary takes the other arm and they haul her to her feet and start walking her down the street.

'Where're you takin' me?' demands Miss Forbes.

'To the taxi rank,' replies Spacey. 'So we can get you home nice an' safe.'

'Who're all these people?' asks Miss Forbes, looking blearily around.

'My friends!'

'Huh. They look too old to be your friendsh. And who's that girl?
She looks like a guy in drag.'

'He is,' Spacey tells her. 'That's Sean.'

'Huh. You a fag, then? Always figured you were.'

'And I like *never* figured you were a binge-drinker, Miss Forbes,' parries Spacey.

Miss Forbes bridles at this. 'Who shays I am? Who shays I'm a dringe-binker? I can have a little drink outta school time if I wanna! You're not the boss of me, you pansy!'

'Sure, sure,' Spacey soothes her.

They arrive at the taxi rank and decant Miss Forbes into the back seat of a cab.

'What's the address?' asks Spacey.

'Whose?' retorts Miss Forbes.

'Yours!'

Miss Forbes pronounces her address and the taxi departs.

This good deed performed, Spacey and his friends resume their interrupted journey. They are heading to Gary's place to chill and watch a movie.

Eve Chandler's suspicions are correct of course. Spacey is gay. But he has sound reasons for not having officially come out as of yet. First and foremost, no-one in their right mind comes out while they're still at school. Section 28 may have been repealed, and the school rules might be politically correct these days; but it doesn't mean the kids are! There's also the problem of Spacey's mum and dad. They would totally flip if they found out he was gay! Spacey isn't sure if they could legally evict him before he turns sixteen, but they could still make his life hell for him!

But Spacey is not one to worry himself about these things;

he's very much a 'one day at a time' person. He likes his life. LSD has opened his mind to a reality he finds much more appealing than the old, workaday one. He vaguely remembers how things were before—there was something flat about life, something missing. LSD made him realise what the problem was; it wasn't reality that was wrong, it was his perception of it; the hallucinogenic has changed his worldview, painting it in bolder, more vivid colours. Spacey sometimes thinks everyone would be better off seeing the world through an acid haze. Then maybe people wouldn't be so uptight.

He'd once been told about this book that depicted a future world drenched in LSD, where life was one big trip. Unfortunately, the book had turned out to be lousy. Even reading it under the influence of the drug in question hadn't made it any better.

Yeah, Spacey likes his life. He likes the people he hangs with and he likes the flawed but beautiful world around him. He likes hitting the streets at night with his acid-head friends; and he likes going to school in the daytime and hanging out with people like Murray Leinster and Pornboy. Two totally different crowds, but he likes them both.

A green haze starts to drift across Spacey's vision. He has let himself fall behind his friends; the haze starts to obstruct his view of them. The drifting green barrier rapidly thickens, and Spacey realises it isn't part of his trip at all. Smoke? He can't smell anything. Must be fog. Fog seen through LSD-tinted glasses.

'Hey, guys!' he calls out. 'Wait up!'

There is no response. Spacey lurches forward to catch up with them, but the green fog coils all around him, growing denser all the time. He quickly loses all sense of direction; he stumbles blindly on. With nothing to anchor him to his native environment, he feels like he has been disconnected from it, plunged into a new world of endless swirling fog. He can't even tell what type of surface he is walking on, man-made or natural.

He sees a light ahead. Two lights. He rushes towards them.

Two lights. Burning like beacons through the green fog. Two lights that stare back at Spacey with unspeakable malevolence.

Two lights that are actually a huge pair of eyes.

Chapter Twenty-Nine
Mysterious Concatenation of Events

What with all the nerve-shatteringly exciting events which occurred in the town of Linton on Saturday night, as detailed in the previous two chapters, there was one other notable event that evening which was completely overlooked by your unreliable narrator: Murray Leinster and Eve Chandler finally had sex!

Yes! That much postponed and interrupted landmark event has finally come to pass! Murray Leinster is no longer a virgin and Eve Chandler is even less of one! (And speaking of, I really think there ought to be some sort of 'statute of limitations' attached to being designated a non-virgin. I feel it would be fitting that anyone who remains sexually inactive for the length of say fifteen or twenty years ought to have their virgin status officially reinstated!)

Don't feel bad that we weren't there to witness the consummation of Eve and Murray's love. It happened round Eve's house, so basically all you have to do is imagine a replay of Chapter Eighteen minus all the comical and violent interruptions, a replay in which everything goes according to plan and events come to a satisfactory climax. ('Come.' 'Climax.' I can almost hear Ren Hoshino's adolescent sniggering.)

And if you're annoyed that this momentous event was not described in graphic detail, well I'm sorry, but that's not what I'm here for. If you want something to read with one hand then pick up a copy of *Fanny Hill* or *The 120 Days of Sodom* or something, and then when you've got it out of your system, you can come straight back here where it's now Sunday morning, and Eve Chandler, the first to awaken, lies on her side, elbow on pillow, head propped up on arm, regarding her still sleeping boyfriend with a smile which indicates that she has found our hero to be satisfactory in the execution of his carnal duties.

Murray finally stirs. His eyes open, he turns his head, sees Eve smiling at him and blushes.

Back in Chapter Six, and just before she got raped, Rose Gardener had wondered if the loss of his V-card would significantly change Murray Leinster. We are always being told that the acquisition of a sex life is beneficial in many ways; that it imparts a healthy glow to a woman's face; that it makes a man more confident and assertive... So, do we see any immediate change in Murray Leinster? Has he suddenly developed a muscular physique, started chugging cans of beer and manifesting a desire to watch football on the telly? None of these things are evident. He still looks the same wet-behind-the-ears, permanently bewildered youngster to whom I introduced you in Chapter One.

'And how are we today?' asks Eve, stroking Murray's downy (facial) cheek.

'Okay,' says Murray, gazing into her eyes.

'Just okay?' Eve affects a gently offended tone.

'No! I mean... more than okay...' offers Murray, unsure what to say.

'That's alright, love,' Eve tells him. 'You don't have to say anything. We were good together; that's all that matters, eh?'

Murray agrees.

'Tell you what,' says Eve. 'I'll go'n make us both a

cuppa. You stay where you are; I'll bring it in to you. You've earned yourself a lie-in.'

Eve is about to get up when the bedroom door opens, and into the room breezes Mary Leinster, very much at home.

'Only me!' she greets them brightly. 'Just being the responsible adult and checking up on the kids. And how are we both this morning?'

She crosses the room and sits herself on Murray's side of the bed.

'And how's my little man today?' she inquires, tweaking his nose. 'More of a man than you were yesterday?'

'Mum!' protests Murray.

Miss Leinster turns to Eve. 'So, how did everything go with you two lovebirds?'

'Everything was fine, thanks,' replies Eve.

'No embarrassing mishaps?' pursues the concerned parent. 'A bad first experience can be very harmful to a sensitive boy like Murray; I don't want him going through life with any hang-ups.'

'Nothing went wrong,' smiling Eve assures her. 'In fact it was perfect! Fantastic!'

'Fantastic, was it?' Mrs Leinster glances at her boy with pride. 'So tell me more. What was it like? Was his stamina good? What about his recovery time?'

Eve proceeds to launch into a detailed description, while poor Murray just hides his head under the duvet.

Pornboy's mum, curly-haired and tremendously fat, occupies her usual place in front of the television, surrounded by her brood, who, when not running hyperactively around the room, sit squalling, fighting and breaking toys. She divides her time between swearing at her offspring and watching the screen.

Pornboy, eldest son of the house, walks into the room.

'Mum, I can't find the laptop!' he yells.

'And you won't find it, will you?' shouts back his mother.

'Cuz I've sold it, haven't I?'

'What did you go'n sell it for?' demands Pornboy, aghast.

'Because we haven't got enough money, have we?' retorts the mother. 'I've got bills to pay and all you greedy gannets to feed, haven't I?'

'Couldn't you have sold something else?' wails Pornboy.

'Like what? The TV? The cooker?'

'But I need the computer! I need the internet for… school and stuff…'

'Well, you've still got your smartphone, haven't you?'

'But that's got a much smaller screen!'

'Well, of course it's got a smaller screen! It wouldn't fit in your bloody pocket otherwise, would it?'

Crushed, Pornboy retreats upstairs to his bedroom.

We all know that the advent of the internet, and the fact that said internet was quickly filled up with porn, has made it all too easy for kids to view this equivocal material. Amongst the many reasons that people insist that it is harmful for juvenile eyes to view this material is the belief that it will interfere with an adolescent's sexual development, or send it off at a tangent, resulting in the of viewing pornography becoming a primary instead of ancillary sexual focus; in other words that they will prefer looking at other people doing it to actually doing it themselves.

To declare that this will be the inevitable result of prolonged exposure to porn by a minor would be a gross exaggeration; youngsters can and do view and enjoy porn while at the same time developing a normal healthy appetite for what Aldous Huxley termed 'the carnal reality' (as opposed to the vicarious pleasure of viewing the dirty postcards which an Arab had been trying to sell to him at the time.) So it would be a rank untruth to say all that teenagers exposed to pornography will inevitably become porn-addicted masturbaters.

However, it does happen to be true in the case of

Pornboy.

Yes, and I know the cynical amongst you will say that Pornboy in any event is not the kind of person who was ever likely to have much of an actual sex-life; not unless he either payed for it or sent off for a mailorder bride from Thailand; but nonetheless, he has become so completely addicted to online porn that at the moment it doesn't even look like he'll ever even try to experience the real thing. Sure, he's got enough of the human instinct of sexual jealousy to be resentful of his friend Murray having landed himself a girlfriend; in fact he feels that Murray has become a traitor and that the two of them can no longer be the friends they once were. But for himself, not only does Pornboy not think himself ever likely to be as fortunate as Murray, but at present he doesn't even want to try and find a girlfriend. His craving is to keep trawling cyberspace looking for that perfect porn scenario; because however good a porno film he views might be, he always feels that there's something lacking, something not quite perfect, and that there must be a better film out there somewhere; the ideal porno, the porno of which every other porno is just a pale reflection.

And of course his quest, although grounded in sound Greek philosophy, will be as futile as it will be unending, because he never will find that perfect porno.

And right now he's reduced to watching the stuff on his piddling smartphone screen! He might as well not bother!

But he does bother anyway.

Sitting on his bed, he logs on to one of his favourite sites. (He prefers the ones that don't come with built-in viruses.) One of these sites features a 'Sexy Schoolteacher' series that he really likes. It seems to be genuine because the woman's face is always pixelated over, and whether it's just acting or not, she occasionally seems like she's a somewhat reluctant participant in some of the group sex scenes, and this in itself is an additional turn-on.

Pornboy's eyes goggle behind his glasses as he reads a

new announcement: 'Revealed at Last! The Face of the Sexy Schoolteacher!'

For real? Have they removed the pixelation? Why would the woman agree to do that? If she's okay for her face to be seen, why couldn't it have been seen from the start? Does it mean she's not really a schoolteacher at all? Or is it going to turn out to be some kind of trap? Like she's really a rough looking dog or something?

Pornboy taps the screen to bring up one of the videos.

Yes! You can see her face! The pixelation has been removed! And she's not ugly, either! She looks really sweet, she—hang on a minute! He knows her! He's seen her before...

It can't be! No fucking way! But it is! It's her! It's her!

'So this is where the youth of Linton like to hang out?' says Mark Hunter, cigarette in hand, admiring the panorama from the platform of the tower. An orange band along the western horizon, a remembrance of the vanished sun, gives way by gradations to the darkness encroaching from the east. The streets below, the landscape of roads and buildings, are at the moment still visible, but lampposts and car headlights are now being lit against the deepening twilight haze.

'Not all of them,' answers Dodo Dupont, lighting one of her occasional cigars. 'It seems only certain privileged people are in on the secret of how to get up here. Some sort of word-of-mouth thing.'

'Yes, that makes sense,' says Mark. 'If all the kids were coming up here all the time, someone would have noticed by now and put a stop to it. Well, the view's certainly worth the trekking up all those stairs... But what's the thing for?' He looks up at the tower's spire. 'This was never a bell or a clock tower, and we're past the age of watch-towers; this whole structure seems completely pointless. Like some urban Victorian folly.'

Mark sounds vaguely annoyed by this enigma of the

tower's purpose.

'But the view's nice,' Dodo reminds him. 'I thought you might appreciate the change.'

'I do,' Mark assures her. 'The town, the sunset, the fresh air; couldn't be nicer. I just wish this change of perspective could help shed some light on what's been happening around here.'

'What's the latest on that boy?'

'Well, he *was* on drugs. They found lysergic acid diethylamide in his system; seems this boy was a regular user. But that isn't what killed him. A teenage boy wouldn't have a cardiac arrest from taking LSD. He died of fright. You saw the look that was frozen on his face. And while I'll admit the drug may have aggravated his response to what he saw, I don't believe he was scared to death by a hallucination. It was something very real that he must have seen.' Mark draws on his cigarette. 'Like I said before, I can't help thinking of that gipsy fortune teller. She had the same look of absolute terror frozen on *her* face.'

'So you think it's finally showed up?' asks Dodo. 'The thing with the eyes?'

'Well, knowing what we know, I can't help equating this green fog people have seen with the green cloud that appeared in the asteroid belt. This creature seems to live in it. And anyone who sets eyes on it either gets scared to death or disappears. Frank Hanson disappeared, possibly along with the rest of the asteroid belt personnel. Now the cloud appears in Linton. Six prostitutes disappear. The lucky seventh who escaped says she heard her friends screaming; we can hazard a guess as to what it was they were screaming at. And then, a few hours later a bunch of kids were seen to walk into a green cloud. One of them was found dead and his friends are still on the missing list.'

'So now we've got to ask ourselves what this thing wants and where these people are being spirited away to,' muses Dodo. 'And then there's that girl Scarlette Hanson. She said her "Dark Lord" was coming, and it looks like he's here. So where is she hiding herself?'

'Yes, we haven't seen anything of her, or those hooded acolytes or whatever they were, since the night of the gaol-break. And we still don't know where they sprang from in the first place.'

'Some sort of cult,' suggests Dodo. 'Worshipping this eye creature.'

'Yes, but that doesn't explain where they sprang from,' points out Mark.

'Well, from what Scarlette was saying when she started talking like some mad high priest, it sounded like this thing has been on Earth before and it had its worshippers. Maybe fragments of this cult have survived up to the present day. Passed down through generations by certain families or communities, maybe.'

'That might be it,' agrees Mark. 'Only I'm surprised such a cult could have survived without anyone getting wind of it. There ought to be some stories about this cult of the "Nameless One" in circulation, even if only as vague legends...'

'So, what's the next move? Since those incidents last night, it's been pretty quiet. No other manifestations of this green fog have been reported.'

'Yes, but it's getting dark now,' says Mark, his eyes on the streets below. 'I think this thing likes the darkness. The darkness of night; the darkness of outer space... I think we'll be hearing something soon...'

Eve finds Murray in his bedroom that evening. She looks downcast. She is the bearer of sad news.

Murray reads her look.

'What's wrong?' he asks.

Eve sits next to him on his bed, puts an arm around him.

'I've got some sad news for you love, love,' she begins. 'It's your friend Spacey. He died last night.'

'Spacey?' echoes Murray, grinning feebly. '*He* can't be dead; he's...'

'He is,' answers Eve gently. 'He collapsed in the street last night. They're saying it was drugs, but, I dunno... It might be something else. I'm starting to hear that a lot of weird stuff happened in town last night...'

Murray looks at the floor. Spacey. One of his two oldest schoolfriends; the one who was actually nice to him... Spacey...

Eve hugs him close when the inevitable tears start to come.

Another Monday morning for class 9-C. Most of the students have arrived and taken their seats. Murray and Eve have not appeared, for reasons which will be explained shortly. And of course the desk occupied by Kenneth Spacey is vacant.

A tearful Miss Forbes walks into the classroom. She has a sad announcement to make.

'Quiet down, class,' says Miss Forbes, taking her seat behind her teacher's desk.

Surprisingly, her request is for once obeyed.

Miss Forbes scans the faces of her students. Every one of them is looking at her, and nearly all of them are grinning. Salacious grins, grins of disbelief, grins of many kinds; all directed at herself.

Alarmed, Miss Forbes looks behind her. No, nothing rude has been written or drawn on the blackboard. She knows there is nothing amiss with her appearance; she routinely checks this before leaving the staffroom.

So, what are they all grinning about?

'I have a very sad announcement to make,' she begins, pushing back her vague fears. 'Our good friend Kenneth Spacey has passed away over the weekend.'

Miss Forbes does not receive the reaction she was expecting. No murmurs of surprise. No distraught looks. Those unsettling grins remain in place.

'I know this must come as a shock to you all,' she proceeds, feeling even as she makes it, that her claim is unsubstantiated. 'This is the second student we have lost from this class in as many weeks...' An outbreak of sniggering.

'What are you all laughing at?' demands Miss Forbes, with as much stern authority as she can muster. 'Two of your classmates are dead! This isn't anything to laugh about!' The laughter increases.

'You heartless people!' protests Miss Forbes. 'Everything they say about teenagers is true! You're so callous and unfeeling!'

More and more laughter. Smartphones appear in student's hands, the speakers projecting sex noises.

'Put those phones away!' orders Miss Forbes. 'You shouldn't be viewing that kind of material in school! You shouldn't be viewing it at all! Do you all want to end up sex maniacs?'

An explosion of laughter, completely out of control.

'What's your excuse, then?' someone calls out.

'What's that supposed to mean?'

Miss Forbes hears her own phone bleeping.

'Better answer that!' someone advices.

Miss Forbes activates her phone. An email. Someone has sent her a link. She clicks on the link and finds herself watching a porno. This must be what they're all watching! The dirty wretches! How did they know her email address...?

And then she recognises the leading lady of this amateur production.

Herself.

The class are expecting a flood of tears. Miss Forbes has always been quick to burst into tears. But this time, when she looks up at her laughing students, there are no tears; her face is blanched and she looks absolutely mortified, completely crushed.

She looks to the back of the class, sees insolent grins on

two male faces; faces cruelly triumphant, pitiless.

Miss Forbes rises from her chair. She doesn't run but walks deliberately towards the door, followed by laughing comments from her class.

The door opens before she reaches it. It is one of her colleagues, Mr Hayles. He looks embarrassed.

'Ah, Miss Forbes,' he says. 'Mrs Pritchard would like a word with you. I'll just take charge of the class for you...'

Miss Forbes passes him without a word of acknowledgement. Mrs Pritchard is the school's headmistress. Miss Forbes does not obey the summons; instead, anticipating the result of the conference, she walks straight for the exit and leaves North Linton High School for the very last time.

Eve and Murray never do make it to homeroom that morning. This is why:

'I saw it,' says Rose Gardener, strangely subdued. 'That thing with the eyes.'

'You dreamed about it again?' asks Eve.

They stand at the school gates. First bell has not rung yet and students are still filing in. Eve and Murray have joined Rose and Jenny, the latter two looking downcast and undecided as to whether or not to enter the school precincts.

'No, I mean I *really* saw it,' clarifies Rose, firmly. 'When I was awake.'

'Or she *thinks* she was awake,' adds Jenny.

'I *know* I was awake,' insists Rose. 'I wish you'd believe me.'

Jenny hugs her. 'I'm sorry. I suppose I just want it to have been a dream. Otherwise it could mean that thing's really after you...'

'Okay, let's have the full story here,' says Eve, business-like. 'When did this happen?'

'Last night,' answers Rose. 'Well, early this morning really. I woke up from a bad dream; the usual bad dream, about that thing. But this time I woke up feeling totally parched. I was covered in sweat; it was like I'd sweated so much I'd dehydrated myself or something. So anyway, I got out of bed to go'n get a glass of water.'

'I wish you'd woken me up,' pouts Jenny.

Rose pats her shoulder. 'I would've done, sweetie, if I'd known what was going to happen. But normally I'm quite good at getting a glass of water in the night on my own.'

'So, what happened?' asks Eve.

'Well, I went down to the kitchen. I poured myself a glass of water and I drank it. I was standing in front of the sink. The blind was down, but it looked like there was some bright light on outside. I thought maybe the outside light had come on, so I pulled the blind. And there it was. The thing. Those huge yellow eyes, right outside the window, staring in at me.'

'Christ,' says Eve. 'That must've scared the shit out of you.'

'Oh yeah,' confirms Rose. 'Might have done that literally if I hadn't had a crap before I went to bed.'

'Too much detail,' says Jenny.

'So, what did you do after that?'

'Well, I was kind of paralysed for a bit. But then, soon as I could move, I ran straight back to the bedroom and woke Jenny up. You can probably guess the rest. I dragged her to the kitchen and the thing wasn't there anymore.'

'Christ,' says Eve again. 'It looks like this creature has really arrived. I've heard that a load of other weird stuff went down in town over the weekend. A green fog and people disappearing... And then there's poor Spacey...' To Rose: 'So, what does it look like, this thing? I'm trying to picture it in my head. You girls who've seen it, you say it's like a flower or a bird or a flame or summat. It can't be all of those, can it?'

'Ah,' says Rose, rummaging in her school bag. 'Jenny asked me the same thing, so I scribbled a picture of it in my notebook.' She extracts a battered exercise book, flips through it. 'I wouldn't hand it in for Art class, but it'll give you an idea.'

Sketched on the lined paper, a pair of tapering, malevolent eyes, with a black elliptical shape shaded in behind them.

'Weird,' says Eve.

She hears Murray catch his breath. Turning to him she sees that he has turned deadly pale, eyes fixed on the drawing, a horrified look on his face.

'What's wrong?' demands Eve.

'I've seen it,' croaks Murray. 'I've seen it before!'

Chapter Thirty
Tales from the Crypt

They take the bus this time.

The bus drops them on Abbey Road, and from Abbey Road they find their way to the wasteland on Linton's southern periphery, following the same path they had followed previously. They have come to pay another visit to the ruined abbey; if those ruins are even there to be found. Everything, even the weather, is the same as it was a week ago.

The tunnel through the briars is the only way in, and apparently that tunnel only appears at certain times or for certain people. Only through this tunnel can the hollow and its adjacent ruins be reached; if the tunnel is not there and the location is approached from any other direction, there will be no hollow, no ruins; there will only be a copse of trees. This is what Eve had discovered one evening last week, when she had come here with Mark Hunter and Dodo Dupont; the tunnel had not been here and neither had the ruins. She hopes that today the tunnel will present itself; it didn't appear for her, but perhaps it will for Murray. Murray has strong connections with this hidden place.

Murray Leinster. Carson. Scarlette and Frank Hanson. And now that eye monster. They all have some connection with those ruins.

'So you've seen this creature before?'
'No. Not in real life. I mean I've seen the picture before.'
'This sketch? How can you have seen that before?'
'Yeah, I only bloody drew it this morning!'
'No, I mean I've seen another drawing of the same thing. It was on a wall.'

Following the footpath, the thicket comes into sight, off to the left. They even discover the vaguely defined track through the long grass which Scarlette must have made on her frequent visits to the location. Would they find her there today? Has she been hiding out in the ruins since being sprung from the police cells? And if she is there, who will be with her? Will she be alone with her brother, or will those hooded figures who had left a trail of death at Linton Police Station also be there?

Eve finds it hard to imagine a large group of people hiding out in such a place as the ruined abbey. But then there is a connection, of kinds, as well: from all accounts, there had been something monastic about the way those raiders were dressed. Do they somehow belong to the abbey?

'No, I don't mean graffiti. It was—what do you call it—like drawn on a stone wall…'
'Engraved, you mean. And where did you see that?'
'I'm not sure…'
'Is this one of your memories coming back?'
'Yeah. I saw it in my mind as soon as I looked at Rose's drawing. The same shape, drawn on a stone wall. Very old…'

The tunnel is there.

They both see it as they cross the trail of trampled grass towards the hedgerow; that low, dark cavity amongst the tangled wall of brambles. The hidden dell is going to let them in this time. Is this because of Murray? Is this place always open to him? Or are they perhaps expected?

Eve wonders if she should even be bringing Murray back to this place. Even his mum has asked Eve not to do this unless the matter is urgent. Eve has been taking Murray out on Adventures since the day she met him, and she has always warned him that no Adventure comes without an element of danger. But things are getting weirder here in Linton, and more and more the element of danger is starting to take the form of the Unknown.

'Did Carson see this? Was he with you when you saw it?'

'I'm not sure... He was there, I think... It's still all muddled up...'

'Can you remember where it was that you saw this engraving? Is it on one of the walls of the ruins?'

'I think... I think it was in a room... Not out in the open... Somewhere hidden...'

'Somewhere hidden? Like a cave? Or underground?'

Eve and Murray emerge from the tunnel into the green twilight of the dell. It looks just as it did the week before: the carpet of moss, the spreading foliage of the trees arching overhead; and that one tilted, lightning-blasted tree striking a jarring note, like a rotten tooth.

A pregnant atmosphere hangs over the scene, an atmosphere of quiet menace, of things unseen.

'It's real enough this place,' says Eve. 'We're here and we can see it. But sometimes, somehow, this place isn't here. It's like it hides itself or summat. Well, it looks quiet enough, but it's like I'm getting bad vibes this time. But maybe that's just cuz I know more about this place than I did when we came here before... What about you, love? Are any more memories coming back to you?'

'Not really...' replies Murray. 'It's still all jumbled up... There's gaps... I know I came here before, though... And that man Carson was here...'

'And that engraving of the alien thing,' says Eve. 'Do you reckon you can take us to it?'

'I think... We have to go to the ruins. It's... It's somewhere there...' 'Come on then.'

They traverse the hollow and reach the old stone wall with the arched doorway. Through the door they wade uphill through the dense undergrowth to the walls of the ruined abbey.

A branch snaps. A rustle of disturbed foliage.

'Someone's here,' says Eve.

Followed by Murray, Eve passes through the gap in the wall, into the overgrown and rubble-strewn interior space of the building. The sounds came from somewhere around here, but there is no one in sight. Nothing moves.

'Someone was here,' repeats Eve. 'And we didn't hear that much movement so I'm guessing they're still around. Probably watching us from out of sight.'

'Maybe it was just a rabbit or something,' suggests Murray hopefully.

'No. That were something much bigger than a rabbit we heard,' replies Eve. 'It were a person.'

They step forward into the shell of the abbey, stepping amongst the fallen masonry, skirting the denser patches of foliage. They venture further than they had on the previous occasion, reaching the far wall of the building. Beyond the ruins a belt of thick undergrowth gives way to a stand of trees, the trees that guard and surround this place.

Another branch snaps, off to the left.

'Something's over there!' cries Murray, alarmed.

'Nothing to fret about,' answers Eve easily, guiding Murray back into the abbey. 'You know, you might've been right; maybe it was just a rabbit!'

And then suddenly she turns and springs over a broken wall, crashes into the shrubbery. Murray hears a brief struggle behind the bushes and then Eve reappears, leading a captive she has secured. The captive, held in an arm lock, is Carson!

'Lookee who I found,' says Eve.

Murray is looking. And as on those previous occasions, the sight of this man prompts no happy feelings within him.

'Let go of me!' yells Carson.

'If you promise not to run off,' responds Eve.

'Yeah, alright,' acquiesces Carson.

Eve releases him from the arm lock.

'Right. Now you can answer some questions,' says Eve.

'Like what?'

'For starters, what are you doing here?'

'Why shouldn't I be here?' retorts Carson, rubbing his arm.

'Well, for one thing, this place can be very tricky to find; but then you know about that, don't you? When they arrested you nine years back, you couldn't find this place again, could you?'

Carson assumes a sulky expression. 'How do you know about that?'

'From Murray's mam, stupid. So, next question: what were you doing here with Murray back then? Why were you messing around with a five-year-old kid?'

'I wasn't messing around with him! I never laid a finger on him!' He looks at Murray, looks away again.

'You must have been doing summat,' says Eve. 'But look, we're not after a confession. So how come you're here today?'

Carson shrugs. 'I dunno. I just started thinking about this place. It's been years since I last tried to come back here. And then today... Well, I just got this urge to come here and have another look... So I did, and there it was: the tunnel through the bramble bushes, staring me in the face. Nine years since I last saw it... It was like walking into the past...'

'So you did come here with Murray back then?'

'Yeah, two or three times, I reckon. It was Murray who found that tunnel first. Neither of us'd seen it there before...'

'And it was just the two of you?'

'Yeah, we never came here with anyone else.'

He darts another look at Murray. 'You started rememberin' all this, have you?'

This is the first time he has addressed Murray in nine years. Murray doesn't reply.

'He's just remembering bits,' Eve answers for him. 'Not much about you. Just that he was here with you, and that summat bad happened.'

'Is this the first time you've come back an' all?' Carson asks Murray. 'Funny we both came here today...'

'It is funny,' agrees Eve. 'But it's not the first time for Murray. Him an' me came here last week. We were following Scarlette Hanson.'

'What, that astronaut's sister? What's she got to do with this place?'

'That's what we'd like to know,' says Eve. 'Y'see it looks like there's some connection between this place and everything that's been happening lately. That's why we're here. Murray's just remembered something: a weird engraving on a wall. He thinks he saw it back then, somewhere around here. Underground maybe.'

'Underground?' jerks out Carson, alarmed.

Eve looks at him. 'Yeah. A crypt or a cellar or summat, under these ruins. D'you know if there is one?'

Carson pauses before answering. 'Yeah, I know... There is a crypt.' He looks at Murray. 'He went down there. That day. That's when he disappeared.'

Both Eve and Murray look surprised. 'He disappeared in the crypt?' demands Eve. 'Murray's mam never mentioned that. I thought she said—'

'I didn't tell them about the crypt, that's why,' cuts in Carson. 'I've never told anyone about it. I told the cops it all happened out here in the open. I said I just turned round for a minute and he vanished.'

Eve frowns. 'Why'd you lie about that?'

Carson looks shifty. 'I dunno… I just didn't want them to know I'd let him go down there on his own, I s'pose…'

'I remember!'

These are Murray's first words since Carson's advent. They both look at him. Murray's eyes are fixed on Carson, accusing.

The stone steps descend into darkness. A square hole in the ground, bordered by weeds and brambles. The boy looks down into the hole with fear and wonder in his wide blue eyes.

'What's down there?' wonders the boy.

He turns to Carson. The same Carson we know, a few years younger, but still in dress polo-necked, wide-lapelled and flared. The boy is Murray, and you can recognise him as well; much smaller but with the same blonde hair, big blue eyes and cherub face.

'Who knows?' replies Carson. 'There might be treasure down there.' 'Or ghosts,' suggests Murray.

'Come on, you don't believe in ghosts, do you?' chides Carson.
'There's no such thing as ghosts.'

Murray looks at him. 'There's not?' he asks.

'Course not,' Carson assures him. 'So there's no need to be scared of them, is there?'

'But Kenny's mum said she—'

'Lots of people say they've seen ghosts,' interrupts Carson. 'But they're telling lies. Either that or they just thought they saw a ghost when it wasn't one.'

'Ohhh…' says Murray, comprehending.

'Right,' says Carson. 'So why don't you go down there?

See if you can find any treasure.'

'Are you coming too?'

'Yeah, but you gotta go down first,' Carson tells him. 'You gotta prove you're a man, an' that you're not scared of ghosts, see?' 'Is it a dare?' asks Murray.

'Yeah, that's right,' agrees Carson readily. 'It's a dare. So go on then.'

Murray looks down the hole.

'It looks scary,' he says.

'What's to be scared of?' remonstrates Carson. 'Unless you're scared of ghosts, scared of things that ain't even real. Are you?' 'I'm not scared of ghosts,' says Murray.

'Then go on then,' urges Carson, leaning in close to Murray. 'Do the dare. Prove that you're a man and not a big sissy.'

'Do I have to?' says Murray. 'It looks scary.'

'Just go on!' snaps Carson, shaking the boy by the scruff of the neck.

Tears well up in Murray's eyes. 'You can't do that!' he wails. 'You promised you wouldn't shout at me like that anymore...'

'Then just do what I tells you,' says Carson. 'Go on. Just go down them steps, and I won't shout at you ever again.'

'Okay...'

Hesitantly, Murray puts his foot down onto the first stone step...

'So that's it!' Eve glares at Carson. 'You were bossing him around! Playing mind games with a little kid!'

'It wasn't mind games!' retorts Carson.

'Yeah? Well, that's what I'd call it,' says Eve. 'Making a little kid go down into that crypt like that.' She turns back to Murray. 'And you don't remember what happened after that?'

'No,' says Murray. 'I know I went down the steps, but I can't remember what happened after that...'

'You disappeared, that's what happened,' says Carson. 'You went down. I asked if you was okay, and you said you was. You said there was light coming in from holes in the roof and you could see what was in the room. You said there was a big stone box in the middle of the room. That was the stone coffin. I suppose you'd never seen one before back then. Anyway, I was just coming down to join you, when you yelled out. Yelled like you were scared out of your wits or something. So I came down after you quick as I could; but the place was empty; there was no sign of you. I looked all around that bloody crypt but you'd gone, vanished.'

'And what about the engraving on the wall?' asks Eve. 'Did you see that?'

'Yeah… yeah, there was this weird drawing on one of the walls, but I didn't pay it much mind; I was more worried about where Murray had got to. I couldn't find him, and there was no other way out of that room; no door, no hole he could've fallen down; nothing.'

'So that was it until they found Murray lying in a field?'

'Yeah. It was in the long grass back over there. He was in shock or something when the cops found him. Couldn't remember anything.'

'We need to have a look at this crypt,' declares Eve. 'Could you find it again, either of you?'

Carson answers. 'It was just over there, the entrance,' he points to the area in the ruins most thickly overgrown. 'There weren't as many bushes there before, but even back then it was pretty well hidden.'

'Let's take a look.'

It takes some doing, but they finally locate the entrance to the crypt. They have to penetrate the thick underbrush and tear away the encroaching weeds and creepers; but finally the entrance and the stairs are revealed.

'No one's been here for donkey's,' observes Eve. 'So unless there's another way in, I reckon I've been wrong thinking that Scarlette and her brother were using this place as a hideout.'

She turns to Murray. 'How do you feel about going down there, sweetheart? You don't have to; you haven't got anything to prove. Forget this twat and his mind games. I can just nip down and have a look for meself if you like.'

'No, I'll come with you,' says Murray.

Eve smiles, chucks his cheek, then leads the way down into the crypt.

Dim light filters down through weed-choked holes in the ceiling, illumines a small, vaulted chamber, a sarcophagus standing on a pedestal in the centre. Almost immediately Eve notices the light glinting from an object on the floor. She crosses the chamber and picks up what proves to be a bracelet.

'This is new,' she reports. 'A girl's bracelet. I bet it's Scarlette's.'

'But how did she get in here?' wonders Carson. 'I mean, like you said, no one's come down those stairs for years. They were all blocked up.'

'Then there's got to be some other way in,' says Eve. 'Got to be.'

'Well, I couldn't see no other way back then, and I looked all over the bloody place.'

'So what? That just means it's well hidden.' And then, seeing that Murray is looking past her shoulder, eyes wide: 'What's up, love?'

She turns to follow his gaze, and there it is. Graven on the wall and picked out by a shaft of diffused daylight, a disturbing image that does indeed strikingly resemble the one sketched by Rose Gardener; the creature from her nightmares. Two narrow, slanting eyes against an irregular elliptical shape that could be a flower or a flame.

'Nice thing to put in a crypt,' snorts Carson. 'Look at it! The monks what lived here must have had some funny ideas about interior design.'

'I don't think those monks made this,' counters Eve.

'Look, you can see the slab it's engraved on is totally different to the rest of the wall. It's older than the rest of the crypt; a lot older. I reckon the monks may have put it here, but they didn't make it.'

'I remember seeing it now...' says Murray. 'I think the light shining on it was stronger before... I just stood there looking at it...'

'Y'know...' says Eve. 'The size of that slab; it goes right from the floor to the ceiling. Maybe *this* is the other entrance...'

Eve walks forward with the intention of examining the block more closely.

'Don't touch it!' cries Murray suddenly, stopping Eve in her tracks. 'That's what I did! I remember now! If you touch it something bad will happen!'

Chapter Thirty-One
Losing Face

Lady Harriet Parker, heiress of Linton Hall, currently reduced in the ranks to position of maid in her own home, has just delivered Misaki Morishita's afternoon breakfast. She found the Yakuza daughter to be in an unusually buoyant mood. Harriet now repairs to her chamber in the servants' wing to rest herself and ponder once again the perplexing mystery of her still missing father, Lord Parker, head butler of the establishment.

She is about to be favoured with the resolution to this troubling enigma.

The charnel-house smell greets her the moment she opens the door. Her first thought is that the nauseous smell, whatever it is, must be coming in through the open window; but on crossing to the window she discovers the air outside to be clear. The source of the stench can only be somewhere inside the room. She finally traces the odour to the built-in cupboard, the cupboard from which the broken remains of the belongings she had stolen from Ren Hoshino had been abstracted.

She opens the door.

Harriet has no difficulty in recognising her father: the corpse has not been divested of its butler's clothes before dismemberment, and anyway the head is lying on the top of the pile of body-parts.

When the first moment of paralysed horror passes, Harriet flees the room and is violently sick. She then slumps to the floor, moaning and rocking herself.

In the turmoil of her mind, she manages to resolve her horror and devastation into a basic need for finding someone to blame and on whom to revenge herself. And Harriet does not have to look far for such an individual.

Ren Hoshino.

She is the cause of all this. All this has happened just because she purloined and broke up that girl's stupid possessions. It doesn't matter to Harriet that it is Misaki who would have ordered the sick joke that is this act of reprisal. It doesn't matter that it would have been Kondou and his black-suited thugs who carried out the hideous crime. Ren is the one to blame. That fat-arsed, flat-footed, four-eyed bitch Ren Hoshino.

Harriet's seething mind locks onto this one conclusion. Ren Hoshino is to blame and she's going to make that girl pay. She looks no further forward than the consummation of this act; revenge is the only thing that matters to her now.

Galvanised by this resolve, she climbs to her feet and bends her steps towards the kitchens; here she avails herself of a carving knife. With this weapon concealed behind the apron of her uniform, she re-ascends the stairs and reaches Ren's bed chamber. She finds it vacant.

On the landing she encounters Kondou.

'Excuse me, where might I find Miss Ren?' she inquires,

keeping her voice calm. 'I have a message for her.'

'Is that so?' Harriet can feel the eyes behind those inscrutable shades. 'I think she's out in the garden doing her morning callisthenics.'

Harriet bobs a curtsy and goes down to the back gardens. The sound of recorded Japanese music draws her to the spot where Ren, dressed in shorts and t-shirt, her hair gathered in a ponytail, is performing (rather late in the day) her Japanese callisthenics (which look to Harriet's eyes more like dance than exercise.)

The girl breaks off when she sees Harriet approach.

'Hi,' she says. 'You have message for me?'

'Yes,' growls Harriet between clenched teeth. 'I have message for you.'

She produces the carving knife.

Ren's eyes goggle.

'I'm going to carve you into little pieces, you fucking Japanese bitch,' announces Harriet.

'Hold on minute!' says Ren, extending an arm, palm outwards. 'Not ready!'

'Not ready to be carved into pieces?' echoes Harriet, with more than a trace of irony. 'And when do you think you will be ready? Shall I wait or come back later?'

'No! Just wait!' Ren rushes over to a sports bag lying on the grass beside the cassette player from which still issues the gentle exercise music. Ren starts frantically flinging items out of the bag. 'One minute! One minute!' she says. 'Where is? Where is?'

Harriet seethes. This is supposed to be her long-awaited moment of revenge against the girl she has hated from the day she first blundered into Linton Hall; the girl who has now been the cause of her father's brutal murder. The girl should be quaking in her boots, vainly pleading for mercy. Instead she's just acting stupidly and pissing Harriet off like she always does!

Wondering why she has even waited for one second,

Harriet advances towards the girl, knife raised.

'Ah! Here is!'

Ren leaps to her feet and points what looks very much like a plastic water-pistol at her advancing assailant, grinning like someone who is expecting praise.

Harriet stops in her tracks. Her annoyance boils over. A water-pistol! Does this stupid girl think this is some kind of joke?

'What's that supposed to be?' she demands.

'Ah!' says Ren. 'Misaki-chan warn me that you might wanna kill me. So she give me this as self-defence.'

'What? A water-pistol?'

Ren nods eagerly. 'Yes! Fires special knock-out spray! Send you to sleep!'

Misaki bursts into sardonic laughter. 'A knock-out spray? You really believe that?'

Ren looks confused. 'Sure. Why not?'

'She's set you up!' declares Harriet. 'Don't you get it? Your mistress has finally got fed up with you and hung you out to dry! Knock-out spray! Even if that was true, that toy you're holding has probably got a range of about half a metre; I could slice your hand off before you could even squirt me with it!'

'No no!' insists Ren. 'This knock-out spray! I don't wanna hurt you, see? Even though you steal and break my stuff and I real sorry about your dad, I don't wanna hurt you!'

'Oh, shut up!'

Harriet springs forward, face convulsed with rage.

Panicked, Ren squeezes the trigger. The gun's range proves to be a lot more than half a metre. The spray ejects with surprising force and catches Harriet directly in the face.

She screams, dropping the knife.

'It okay!' Ren assures her. 'Just knock-out spray!'

But then, when she sees Harriet's face starting to bubble and melt, Ren realises she may have been deceived by Misaki after all…

The desk sergeant is a stranger to Mark Hunter.

'Can I help you, sir?' he inquires, his words as expressionless as his face.

'I'm Mark Hunter,' says Mark, displaying his ID card to substantiate this fact. 'I've been working with the constabulary during this current crisis. You must be part of the relief squad, I take it? Have you just arrived this evening?'

'Yes,' says the desk sergeant.

'Does this include the new chief superintendent? Has he or she arrived?'

'Yes.'

'Can I have a word with them?'

'No.'

'No?' Mark is surprised. 'Are they not in the station?'

'The superintendent is in his office.'

'Then can I just pop in and—'

'No.'

'No?' Mark looks in vain for some kind of explanation in the sergeant's stolid refusal. 'Look, I don't want to throw my weight around here, but you know who I am, and I—'

'No-one can see the chief superintendent,' says the desk sergeant. 'He is engaged.'

'Alright, can I speak to Detective Inspector Preston?'

'No.'

'No? But—'

'Detective Inspector Preston is off-duty.'

'Well, is there anyone I *can* speak to?' pleads Mark. 'I only want to know if any new incidents have been reported this evening.'

'Incidents?'

'Yes. Any more disappearances. Any outbreaks of that green fog.'

'There have been no incidents.'

'None?'

'None.'

'Well… I suppose that's good news…'

Mark becomes aware that he has become the focus of attention. There are several other officers in the foyer, all of them strangers to him, and all have stopped whatever they were doing and are regarding him with faces as devoid of expression as that of the desk sergeant.

He suddenly feels like he is standing on very thin ice.

'Well,' he says, sounding as nonchalant as possible. 'If there's nothing requiring my attention, I suppose I might as be off then.' 'Yes,' says the sergeant.

Mark exits the police station.

It will be all over town by now.

The knowledge that she, the apparently meek, timid even, schoolteacher Clare Forbes, is actually a dirty whore, a nymphomaniac porn star. That's what they'll call her. She will be reviled by respectable people, propositioned by the licentious. The tabloid newspapers will trumpet her story with their usual combination of prurience and censure.

People will now probably never know the real truth behind it all: the fact that she had never sought this double-life of hers; that it had been forced upon her. She had never possessed any hidden vices, any desire to wallow in depravity behind her respectable schoolteacher façade; she had had no choice in the matter. Her worst crime had been that of allowing herself to give in to intimidation and blackmail.

There is just one person responsible for everything that has happened to her; her descent into vice, her consequent descent into alcoholism and self-loathing, and now her humiliating exposure and the loss of her career; only one person is responsible for all this: Lassiter, one of her own students.

Oh, how she hates that boy! His cocksure attitude, his self-love, his air of being the good-humoured, easy-going ladies' man. Most of all she hates the way he has always pretended to be her champion at school; calling the class to order when they ignored her instructions; standing up for her when she was addressed impertinently by any other student... All an ironic deception, a rubbing of salt in her wounds, this support from the monster who was actually the author of her corruption, her degradation.

It had started with her being lured into the school gardens, the place Lassiter and his friends had somehow made their own. There he had seduced her, or he had raped her, or something between the two. Right there in broad daylight and with his friends looking on, he had disrobed and deflowered her. (Yes, it had been her first time. She had managed to emerge from her school life, even her time at university, without having had a boyfriend or even a one-night stand to her credit.)

And when Miss Forbes had told Lassiter she ought to report him for taking this liberty, he had calmly replied that if anyone was in a position to report anyone it was himself. He could spill the beans about the oh-so-respectable maths teacher who actually had a secret craving for adolescent boys. And he had three witnesses here to back him up; to confirm that she had been the instigator.

She knows now that she should have called his bluff there and then. She should have reported Lassiter and defended herself against his counter-accusations. When the boy involved was someone of Lassiter's sexual reputation, there was every chance that she would have been the one to be believed, that hers was the account that would have been credited with truthfulness. But she had been scared; scared of losing her career, her reputation. She had capitulated.

After this, she had become a frequent unwilling visitor to the school gardens, and she had had to surrender herself not just to Lassiter but to Malcolm as well, with the two girls either looking on and jeering at her or else participating themselves. Everything that happened in those gardens had been geared towards her humiliation, to depriving her of every vestige of her dignity, her self-esteem.

Later, the venue had changed to the house of a local pornographer; a friend of Malcolm's older brother. Lassiter longed to put her shame on public display; to disseminate her indignity over the information highway. Posting recordings of those school garden sessions would have been too risky; the location and the school uniforms might have been identified, and consequently, Lassiter and his friends themselves. Enslaving Miss Forbes to the Adult Entertainment Industry was the happy alternative that offered itself. She would be billed as the prim school marm with the double life; the teacher who did porn on the side just to satisfy her own depraved tastes. But even in the midst of her filmed orgies, her 'other' side would sometimes surface, and she would seem reluctant to perform particular acts, or remonstrate against what was being done to her.

And again, Miss Forbes had given in. She felt completely hopeless; as if she had gone way too far to ever turn back. The only concession she had succeeded in having granted was that her own face would be off-camera as much as possible, and when on-camera, would be pixelated. There was always the chance that someone who knew her might view the material, and Lassiter not wishing things to end too soon, it had suited himself to allow this favour.

But it seems that with his usual wilfulness Lassiter has gone back on his word. Or perhaps he has just become bored with the whole thing, because now those videos have been reposted without the censorship, and links to these videos obligingly sent to students (and presumably teachers) all over the school. She knows from Lassiter's triumphant look in homeroom this morning that he is the one responsible. He has brought about her ruin and he's loving every minute of it.

In one way, this explosion comes as a relief; a relief that it is all over at last. It's not that she had ever started to like the things she was being forced to do, but she had become resigned to doing them, accustomed to doing them, and that in itself had been an additional source of self-censure.

But even with the resignation, she had still turned to alcohol as a means of support. And as she was still living with parents, that has been one element of her new life that she has been unable to conceal from them.

At first they had actually been pleased that she was going out at nights, assuming she had acquired a social circle of friends, and that maybe she might find herself a boyfriend, a husband even. But no boyfriends had been forthcoming and she had been unable to hide how inebriated she sometimes was when she returned home from those nights out. She knew that her parents had started to suspect her of having a dissipated lifestyle; drunken sex in dark alleys... But they were wrong about that. Her nights out have always been for solitary drinking. She would sit alone in pubs, and if any man approached her—which of course happened all the time—she would drive him away with a barrage of drunken bitterness and imprecation.

This had always been the relief for her; drinking herself into a state where she could vent her frustrations verbally, and where she could turn away as many sex-hungry men as she wanted to.

But now... Now the dam has burst; the whole thing has come out into the open. Her career is over. Her life is over. She doesn't know if her parents have heard the news yet, but if they haven't, it won't be long before the story reaches them. And she knows what their reaction will be; she knows that they are already getting impatient with their grownup daughter for not having flown the coop, and this scandal will be the one excuse they need to throw her out of their house.

Except that Clare Forbes has pre-empted her parents, just as she pre-empted her dismissal from school by walking out of her own accord.

When her father eventually breaks down the bathroom

door, he will see his daughter slumped in the crimson water of the bathtub, and he will know that she has taken matters into her own hands.

Chapter Thirty-Two
Mysterious Green Day

Everything that has transpired in the town of Linton over the past couple of weeks is nothing compared with what will happen today. An astronaut serial rapist? Happens all the time. The massacre of almost an entire regional police force? Wake me up when something interesting happens. A boy like Murray Leinster actually having sex with a girl? Okay, that's a bit more unusual.

However, all of that pales in comparison with what happens next. And yet, all those previous events have been leading up to today; today, the day in which law and order, science and sanity all get thrown out of the window.

It first becomes apparent that something is seriously wrong when the sun fails to rise at what should be, according to the inevitability of planetary rotation, dawn. This is not to say that the night doesn't end; there is an increase in visibility, but this increase only serves to show that something is horribly wrong.

The sky above Linton is green.

Weather anomalies have been known to create skies of just about any colour you care to mention, but no weather anomalies have been forecast for today. Yet here it is, a thick blanket of murky green lowering over the town of Linton, leaving everything beneath it in a depressing grey semidarkness.

It's just wrong, this green sky, and everybody in Linton feels this. It's more than just the enigma of it, and the fear of the unknown engendered by this, but there is also a profound sense of menace, of looming, unseen danger.

But the panic really starts to kick in when people find out that they are offline. The internet is inaccessible. No signals are available. In a society in which the internet has become as essential to many people as a generous supply of oxygen, this development is even more alarming than the absence of the sun.

And it's not just the internet. It soon becomes apparent that all electronic signals have been affected. Telephone communication is down. Terrestrial, satellite and cable TV signals are all unobtainable. Radio wave-bands pick up nothing but static.

People get in their cars and try to leave Linton, hoping to ascertain how far this atmospheric phenomenon has spread.

And it is then that they discover that they *can't* leave.

The green sky, or rather gaseous formation, descends like a wall, blocking off the road. It is not a solid barrier, but it has the appearance of solidity, as well as being completely impossible in its immobility. Gaseous formations should not be able to shape themselves like this. They should not be able to remain in place like this.

East Road is one of the main thoroughfares leading in and out of Linton. It will take you to the Linton bypass, or else over it and to neighbouring villages. But today this road, like all other roads leading out of Linton is closed; blocked by the green cloud which has covered the town like a huge dome. A crowd of people has gathered at the edge of this green barrier, standing on the roadside, while the road itself is congested with stalled vehicles. There have been a number of collisions at the meeting-point of the road and the barrier; the reason for this being that any vehicle attempting to drive into the wall of gas finds itself inexplicably deflected and drives straight back *out* of it the way it came.

At this moment a man steps out of the fog and looks a lot more surprised than the crowd of people observing him. The man is Mark Hunter, and he had just ventured into the fog moments before.

'I'd swear I was walking in a straight line,' he declares. 'But here I am, back where I started. Somehow I made a 180° turn without feeling a thing.'

'It's like walking into a mirror or something,' says Dodo Dupont. She stands at the front of the crowd, her girlfriend Mayumi Takahashi beside her.

'Yes, some kind of instantaneous deflection,' agrees Mark. 'Everyone who walks, or drives, into the fog comes straight back out again.'

'My husband didn't!' one shrill voice contends. 'He walked into that muck and he *never* came back out.'

'Then he must have got through!' declares a bald, pot-bellied office worker.

'Yeah, it must let some people out!' eagerly agrees a harassed-looking woman with a brood of squalling infants.

'We shouldn't assume that anyone who doesn't come out again has got safely through to the other side,' cautions Mark.

'Why not?' retorts the woman. 'What else could have happened to them?'

'They might have disappeared completely,' answers Mark. 'You must have heard the stories of the appearances of this green fog over the weekend, and the people who walked into it and just vanished? Well, this is the same green fog, but now it's covering the entire town.' 'How can a fog do that?' protests someone.

'And how can it make people disappear?' adds the bald man.

'Because this fog is alien,' replies Mark. 'And there's something in it.'

Noises of derision.

'Look,' says Mark, firmly. 'This green cloud first appeared out in the asteroid belt; and you know what has happened there, complete loss of contact with the mining colony. It was all over the news, so you should all have heard about it. And now this gas cloud has come here to Linton. I don't know why, but it has. The assaults committed by Frank Hanson, an astronaut for the mining colony; the massacre at the police station; these are all connected with the cloud.'

Howls of protest.

'There isn't any mining colony! It's all a fake!'

'Yeah! And now someone's tricking us!'

'This is a put-on!'

'And who are you anyhow?'

'Yeah! You can't stop us leaving!'

'I'm a government agent!' replies Mark, raising his voice. 'And no, I can't stop you from trying to leave; but if you walk into that fog, you'll either come straight back, or you won't come back at all!'

'How do we even know there's anywhere to escape to?' asks a new voice.

All eyes turn to the new speaker; a bearded, down-at-the-heels man in his late thirties. Our old friend Stavro, no less.

'What's that supposed to mean?' demands someone.

'I'm saying, even if you do get through that fog without being turned back, how do you know what's on the other side?' says Stavro. 'We may not be where we used to be. This whole town might have been transported to another planet.'

'That's bullshit,' retorts one man.

Other voices are raised in agreement.

'Well, what about the people like this woman's husband?' persists Stavro. 'The ones who went into the fog and didn't come back? Maybe they *did* get through, only to find that the atmosphere on the other side of the fog isn't even breathable! Maybe this barrier is the only thing keeping us safe, keeping our atmosphere in. And that would also explain why we can't pick up any signals like TV and radio; we can't pick them up because they're not there anymore!' An uneasy silence greets this sally.

Mark Hunter is the first to speak. 'That's an interesting theory,' he says. 'But it *is* just a theory. You haven't actually got any evidence to back it up, have you?'

'Maybe not,' allows Stavro. 'But you've been putting forward a lot of theories yourself.'

'Yes, but my guesses have been based on facts, on previous events,' argues Mark. 'Yours are just pure speculation. I won't say it's out of the question that you're right, but I think it much more likely that we're still on Earth, still where we always were; we've just been isolated from the outside world.'

'But why?' demands the bald man.

'That I don't know,' confesses Mark. 'Some kind of alien entity has descended on this town. I'm not sure what it wants. Perhaps it doesn't know. Perhaps it's just curious.'

'Curious!' sneers Stavro. 'You just said the thing was tied in with those rapes and the massacre at the police station!' Noises of concurrence.

'I know,' says Mark, firmly. 'This being, whatever it is, certainly has an alarming effect on the people it encounters, but the effect might not be intentional. Those rapes were committed by astronaut Frank Hanson, but not, it would seem, at the behest of the alien; he was being controlled by his own sister, and the girls he attacked were classmates of that girl whom she disliked. Those assaults were all an act of petty spite.'

'Oh yeah? Why would an alien care about some schoolgirl's private vendetta?' demands Stavro.

'That's just what I'm saying!' replies Mark. 'It doesn't care. The alien may be the catalyst for these violent outbreaks, but by accident rather than design.'

'I'd say *you're* the one just indulging in pure speculation now,' responds Stavro.

Mark shrugs, allowing that this might be the case.

'Here comes the fuzz!' yells someone.

Everybody looks. A police car, having mounted the verge to pass the tailback of traffic, is approaching them. This advent is hailed with relief by the crowd of townspeople.

'Now we'll find out what's going on!'

'Yeah, the cops should have some answers!'

'I don't think we can rely on the police right at the moment,' cautions Mark. He is ignored, apart from by Dodo and Mayumi.

'So you reckon this relief force are fakes?' asks Dodo.

Mark nods. 'Either they're imposters, or they've been... affected somehow,' he says. 'Let's move quietly away. I'd rather they didn't see us.'

'What, you think they could be after us?'

'They could be. I'm not sure what their agenda is yet.'

The squad car pulls up just short of the crowd and thus becoming the centre of attention, Mark and his two friends are able to retreat unnoticed.

Two officers, a man and a woman, step out of the vehicle. Mark is still close enough to observe that they have the same blank faces he had observed at the station house the previous evening. And there's something else he observes...

The police officers are greeted with a volley of questions and demands from the anxious crowd. Their faces remain impassive.

'Return to your homes,' speaks the male officer.

'But what's going on?'

'When will the internet be back online?'

'When will this fog go away?'

'Return to your homes,' repeats the officer. 'The situation is under control.'

Mark and his friends have gained the cover of some nearby allotments.

'You're right about those coppers,' says Dodo. 'They're acting like zombies.'

'Yes, and that's not all,' says Mark grimly. 'I recognise that police woman, and she's not a police woman at all.' Dodo and Mayumi look at him.

'At least, not unless she's opted for a sudden change of career,' proceeds Mark. 'That woman happens to be Professor Marta Sandström, chief scientist for the Asteroid Belt Mining Project.'

Chapter Thirty-Three
Last of the Lassiters

'There's no way out?'

'That's what they're saying. This green fog or whatever it is goes right round the town. It's like a wall keeping us in.'

The speakers are Lassiter and Malcolm. They have been making a quick tour of the neighbourhood. Residents wander around in the eerie green twilight, forming groups, exchanging rumour and speculation, hoping to hear something that will reassure them that this is not the end of the world.

'But it's a fog, isn't it?' says Lassiter. 'It can't be like a solid wall, can it?'

'Well, no,' replies Malcolm. 'You can walk into this stuff, but apparently you walk straight out of it again, back where you started from.'

'That doesn't make sense!'

Malcolm removes his pipe from his mouth. 'I hadn't noticed any of this making any sense.'

They reach Lassiter's house. It is a large house, purchased by Keith Lassiter's brief moment of big-screen stardom; a house set well back from the road and surrounded by a tall brick wall.

'Come in for a bit,' says Lassiter.

'Are you sure?' asks Malcolm, surprised. 'I thought your "special" domestic arrangements didn't really allow for house guests.' 'It's alright if it's you,' Lassiter tells him.

He opens the gate and leads Malcolm across the garden.

'The front door's open!' he exclaims.

'You probably left it open,' opines Malcolm. 'Other things on your mind.'

'I did *not* leave it open,' asserts Lassiter. 'I locked it when I went out; I know I did. Come on!'

He breaks into a run. Malcolm follows.

They burst into the hallway. The house is quiet. There are no signs of disturbance.

'Hello?' calls out Lassiter. 'Dad? Fee?'

'Come here, old son,' says Malcolm in an odd voice, standing at the living room doorway.

Lassiter joins him. There in the living room, his little sister Fiona lies on the floor in a pool of her own blood.

'Fee!'

He runs over to her, drops to his knees. The girl's face is ashen, and at first he thinks she is dead; but then her eyes flicker, settle on her brother's face. A weak smile forms on her pale lips.

'Big brother...' she says, her voice barely audible.

'What happened?' asks Lassiter, his voice thick with emotion. 'Who did this to you?'

'Oh, big brother... My time has come... My well has run dry... I can feel myself slipping away... I shall be going off to heaven...'

'Fee...'

'Will there be lots of big brothers with big willies waiting for me in heaven, dear brother...?'

'Yes...' sobs Lassiter. 'Yes. All the big brothers you could want...'

'Yes... I think I can see them now, just inside the pearly gates... They're all lined up in a row with their flies open; standing to attention and beckoning to me...'

'Who did this to you, Fee...?'

'Are you still there, dear brother...? It's hard to see... The lights are growing dim... But life has been good... I can die without regrets...'

'Who was it, Fee? Who did this?'

'I'll miss you, big brother... I'll miss you...'

'Who did this to you, Fee?'

And once more ignoring this vital question, Fiona Lassiter quietly expires.

'She's dead...' Lassiter wipes the tears from his face.

'I'm sorry and all that,' says Malcolm. 'But I think we'd better get out of here.'

'No,' dissents Lassiter, firmly. 'Not until I know who did this. They might still be here.'

Now this is precisely why Malcolm has suggested vacating the premises; but Lassiter is adamant.

Upstairs they find another door wide open; one that ought to be firmly closed—the door to Mrs Lassiter's bedroom; the room of the invalid or captive wife into which no-one has ventured for several years, save for that lady's devoted husband. Even his two accomplices, Lassiter and Fee, have been left to only speculate as to the true state of affairs in that forbidden chamber.

But the door is now open, and a hospital aroma issues from within.

The room is in heavy-curtained semi-darkness.

Lassiter approaches the door.

A body lies face-down on the floor close to the bed. Lassiter recognises it as that of Norma, his other sister. Blood has saturated her dress, the blood that has seeped from the wound in her back.

Lassiter crosses the room, steps over his sister's corpse and stands over the bed. A recumbent figure lies on the bed, completely shrouded. Lassiter pulls back the covers. The mummified, exsanguinated corpse he now sees is presumably that of his mother. She, at any rate, has been dead for a long time. Poor mum. She'd always let the rest of the family walk all over her and this is where it gets her.

'But who did all this?' wonders Lassiter, still looking at his mother but with reference to the two much fresher corpses of his siblings. 'Was it Norma? Did she kill Fee and then herself...? No, it can't be that; she can't have stabbed herself in the back...'

'Ah... I think I know who did it, old son...' says Malcolm, speaking in a strained voice.

Lassiter turns just in time to see Malcolm pitch forward,

toppling like a tree in the approved manner. Behind him, bloody knife in hand, stands Keith Lassiter.

'Dad!' gasps Lassiter.

'I had to do it,' says the father in his usual easy-going tones. 'You spoilt everything with that silly trick of yours... You and Fee... Now we've got social services knocking on the door. They're getting very nosy... Yes, we had things going perfectly here; just the way we wanted; and now it's all been ruined...'

Lassiter has always been more or less aware that his father's placid exterior has been the mask for complete mental derangement. But only now, now when it's far too late, does he realise just how psychotically insane the man is...

'I had to do it...' he repeats, advancing towards his son. 'No other choice, you see...'

A coil of black smoke rises into the green sky.

'That's coming from the centre of town,' declares Eve.

She and Murray stand in the middle of the road, viewing this latest sign of growing unrest. They have heard loud bangs, shouting and other sounds indicative of increasing disorder, but so far the neighbourhood of Meredith Way remains quiet; the activity seems to be focused further into the centre of Linton.

But this very fact is a cause for deep concern for Murray. His mother happens to be in the centre of Linton. She had set off by car three hours ago, when things were still quiet, with the intention of calling at her place of work at the science park, hoping her boss Doctor Fleetwood would be there and might have some information regarding the green sky and the electromagnetic blackout. Leaving Murray in Eve's care, she had promised to return as soon as possible.

'We've waited long enough, I reckon,' says Eve. 'Let's get going.' 'Yes,' agrees Murray.

They set off, following the route into town that Mary

Leinster would have taken in her car.

Murray is scared. The end of the world is hanging over them; he just wants to find his mum and then hide away somewhere safe with her and Eve.

'Do you think we'll find Mum?' he asks.

'Well, I don't know, do I?' replies Eve. 'We're going the way she would have gone, so if she comes back, we ought to see her. If we don't, we'll just have to see what's what when we get to the science park.' 'But what if we can't find Mum there?' presses Murray.

'Then I reckon we'd better go to the Pavilion,' replies Eve, referring to the haven in the Garden of Cats. 'I reckon we'll be safe there, and there should be some of my people there an' all.' She gives Murray an encouraging smile. 'You never know, Fifi might have taken your mam there!'

'Mum wouldn't go there without telling me!' retorts Murray.

'Yeah,' agrees Eve. 'But then, maybe summat stopped her from getting back home to you. And yeah, and they might have gone to the Garden knowing that's where I'd take you!'

This explanation sounds encouraging. Murray clings to it. He fondly remembers the Garden of Cats; the peaceful, protecting atmosphere of the place. Nothing bad could get to you there; it's like a place that's separate from the rest of the world.

'And you can't use your watch to speak to your friends?'

'No, it's not working.'

A car speeds past, driving recklessly. A second car follows, either in pursuit of or in company with it; it's hard to tell which.

'People always go mad, first chance they get,' remarks Eve. 'Doesn't matter if it's a natural disaster or a demonstration or whatever; people soon go off the rails, and they start smashing and burning and looting. It just shows you, don't it? We think we're all civilised and intelligent like, but we're only a step or two away from acting like a pack of animals. Well, you fellers are, anyway.'

'Me?'

'No, not you especially, love. I'm talkin' about fellers in general. As soon as all the controls go out the window, men just give into their two basic instincts; an' you know what they are? Killing and raping. You always see it going on in countries where you've got wars and social unrest and whatnot. Fellers start raping as soon as things are so they know they can get away with it.

'I mean yeah, us lasses can join in with the smashing and burning and looting in this day and age; equal opportunities and all that. But when things get really bad, the lasses only come together in gangs for self-protection; we have to protect ourselves from the male gangs that want to rape us.'

Murray is seriously alarmed by this discourse. 'And is all that happening in town right now?'

'Well, I doubt it's gone that far just yet,' replies Eve. 'But it's starting.'

They see a person ahead; the first pedestrian they have encountered for some time. Most residents have retreated indoors now that the streets are becoming unsafe.

'It's Stavro!' says Eve. 'He might know summat about what's happening.'

Murray looks. It's the dishevelled bearded man he remembers seeing in Fairview Park a couple of weeks before. Stavro...

'Hiya,' Eve greets the man. 'You been into town? What's it like?'

'Oh, it's you. What's it like in town? It's all going to hell in a handbasket, that's what it's like,' is the bitter response. 'If you two are heading that way I suggest you turn back right now.' He eyes them with disfavour. 'Unless of course you were both just planning to join the fun.' 'What fun would that be?' asks Eve.

'Oh, the usual. Looting. Fighting. Vandalism. The usual behaviour Homo Sapiens turn to the moment the shackles of law and order are broken… Look at us. We impose all these rules and restrictions on ourselves, because we know full well what we're like underneath. We try to keep the beast in check; whole religions are based around the idea of keeping ourselves under control. But why do we bother? Why do we bother? Why try and hide the fact that when it comes down to it all human beings do is kill and eat and reproduce just like the rest of the animal kingdom?'

'Well, if that's how you feel,' says Eve brightly, 'why don't you just go and "join the fun" as you call it?'

Stavro wrinkles his nose. 'I'm a lone wolf, not a pack animal,' he tells her. 'I know that's not much to hang my self-esteem on, but it's all I've got.'

'Can't the police stop the rioting and stuff?' wonders Murray.

'We haven't got many police right now,' Eve reminds him.

'Yeah, but others could come in from outside.'

'*No-one* can get in from outside,' retorts Stavro. 'Haven't you heard? This green cloud,' pointing upwards, 'it comes down like a curtain all around the edge of town. We're completely cut off; no one can get in and no one can get out.'

'Have you seen this yourself?' queries Eve.

'I have,' is the reply. 'I've been all over the place this morning. People have been trying to get out of town but they can't. If anyone walks or drives into that fog wall, they just come straight back in again. And no, I don't know how that happens; it just does. I've seen it.'

'So people are like deflected by summat inside the fog,' ruminates Eve.

'Yes,' says Stavro. 'And another thing, you were talking about the police. Well, you were wrong that we haven't got many, but you really should avoid them. A replacement force has arrived, and I don't like the look of them. They act like zombies or robots or something. They're probably aliens.'

'You reckon?'

'Yes, I reckon. You don't think this green muck is a natural phenomenon, do you?'

'No, I know it's not,' rejoins Eve. 'There's a monster in this cloud. If the cops are acting weird then they're probably being controlled by it.'

'Well, whatever they are, avoid them,' reiterates Stavro. 'They're armed and they're not friendly. They want everyone to stay in their homes, so my advice to you two would be to do just that.'

'Thanks for the heads up,' acknowledges Eve. 'But we can't go back home. Murray's mam here went to the science park where she works, so we've gotta go'n find her.' She turns to Murray. 'C'mon.' They set off.

'Hold it,' says Stavro in an odd voice, stopping them in their tracks.

They turn. Stavro, a strange expression on his face, stares intently at Murray.

'Your name is Murray and your mother works at the science park?' he asks. 'Is that right?'

'Yes...' says Murray.

'And what's your surname, Murray?'

'Leinster.'

Stavro smiles bitterly. 'Yes, she would have given you that name, although it's not the one written on your birth certificate.' 'What are you on about?' demands Eve.

'Your mother's name is Mary, isn't it?' continues Stavro. 'Well, I was once married to that woman, Murray. Now I'm sure this will not be welcome news to you, but I happen to be your father.'

Chapter Thirty-Four
A Very Brief Reunion

Yes! The man who calls himself Stavrogin is actually Murray Leinster's father.

Is this revelation a surprise to the reader? Or did you see it coming a mile off? I ask because it's hard for me to gauge these things. This is one of the drawbacks of being an omniscient third-person narrator: knowing everything in advance, it can be difficult to judge which hidden facts and plot developments can be foreseen by the reader and which cannot.

Let's take this particular case. There have been a number of pointers to this revelation: First we had Murray starting to speculate about his paternity and to question his mother on the subject. He had even at one point suspected that Carson might be his father. As for Stavrogin himself, I did refer to there being a broken marriage in this character's back-story, but this was way back in Chapter Twelve, so if your memory is as bad as mine is, you may well have forgotten this detail. (Unless of course you made the connection there and then; in which case you will have remembered it.)

But then, perhaps you weren't even expecting the question of Murray Leinster's paternity to be resolved; you may have considered it to be a peripheral issue and not at all the main object and focus of this history. And you would be right; it isn't.

Stunned, Murray stares at this scruffy and disreputable man who has just announced himself to be his father. Stavro in turn observes Murray's reaction with a bitter, ironic smile and nary a trace of parental affection.

'Have you got any proof that you're his dad?' demands Eve.

Stavro makes a show of patting his clothes. 'Surprising to say, but no I *don't* have any documentary evidence about my person,' he replies. 'But I'm sure I can supply you with enough circumstantial information regarding my marriage with his mother to satisfy you that I am speaking the truth.'

'Okay,' says Eve. 'For a start what's your surname? Stavro who?'

Another bearded smile. '"Stavro" is short for "Stavrogin", and it's not my real name. The name on *my* birth certificate is David Clark, and the name on *his* is Murray Clark.'

Eve looks at Murray. 'David Clark. Have you ever heard that name?'

Murray shakes his head. 'No. When Mum was telling me a bit about Dad, she didn't say his name…'

'No, she wouldn't have,' says Stavro. (We might as well keep calling him that!) 'She would have been very careful not to give you any information that might have led you to me. In fact, I'm sure she would have liked nothing more than to have erased me from history if she could. I even helped her out a bit in that regard by adopting this new name and persona. Wasn't that considerate of me?'

'Yeah, but you've still been right here in Linton all this time, haven't you?' challenges Eve. 'How come you've never tried to see your boy?'

'I suppose the main reason would be that I've never wanted to see him,' is the blunt reply. 'Why would I want to see him?' He points a finger at Murray. 'You see, that little piece of excrement ruined my entire life!'

'You can't talk to him like that!' snaps Eve.

'Can't I, now?' responds Stavro. 'It happens to be the truth. I was happily married to Mary until *he* came along. Yes, it was all perfect, or as near to perfect that things can be in this imperfect world. I had a career, a nice house and a beautiful and intelligent wife who loved me dearly. Yes, she did love me, then. I'm still convinced she did really love me those first three years. But then *he* came along.'

'You keep saying that,' says Eve. 'But how could Murray being born ruin your marriage? I mean you expect a mum to love her baby...'

'Yes, but that was *all* she loved. Don't you get it? It was like I was suddenly reduced to nothing. A zero. He was *her* baby, not *ours*. Oh yes, my sperm may have fertilised her egg, but once it had created that embryo, that was it: I got shunted out. All of my genes were completely overwhelmed by hers. I mean look at him!' pointing again. 'He's like a clone of his mother, isn't he? There's nothing of me in him, is there? Not a trace!'

'Well yeah, he does take after his mam,' concedes Eve.

'Of course he does! I bet there isn't a single atom of my DNA inside him! I bet it will all be hers! It was like... I don't know what it was... I mean there was nothing excessive about her maternal instinct before the event; we just quietly decided to have a child. But then, when he popped out, it was like he was suddenly everything to her; she would hardly even notice if I was in the room. It was just him him him!' He fixes Murray with a disdainful look. 'Do you know what she used to do when you were a baby? No? She used to suck your little penis, that's what she did. Sucked on it for all she was worth, she did. It was nauseating... The way she carried on like that, you must be hung like a bear by now!'

Eve coughs into her hand. 'Yeah, let's not worry about that. But if you were feeling left out, why didn't you just talk to her about it?'

'I *did* talk to her,' retorts Stavro. 'And a lot of good *that* did. She just wouldn't listen to me. Said I was being childish. She either honestly couldn't see how she'd changed, or she just didn't care. Either way, I told her I'd leave if she didn't start treating me with more consideration, and she just calmly replied that perhaps I *should* leave; that my "tantrums" were upsetting the baby. And so I did leave. I packed my bags and walked out. It was either that or wring the little bastard's neck.

'And after that, everything else just went wrong for me; I lost my job, my friends... And now, well now I'm what you see before you...' He smiles bitterly. 'My one consolation is that I've never had to pay any child maintenance. Mary never demanded any. She obviously didn't want my money any more than she wanted anything else from me. It was just her and him.' To Murray: 'Well, boy? What do you think of your dear mother now?'

'Oh leave him alone!' says Eve. 'Okay, she treated you badly, but it wasn't his fault, was it?'

'Yes, it was his fault,' insists Stavro. 'It was entirely his fault. He's not normal. He was some freakish abomination from the moment he was conceived!'

'Shurrup, will you?'

'And what's he to you?' inquires Stavro, looking at Eve. 'Classmate? Childhood friend?'

'I'm his girlfriend,' says Eve.

Stavro grunts. 'Well, in that case, he's probably got hold of you like he got hold of his mother. Got you thinking the whole bloody world revolves around him, hasn't he?' To Murray: 'Well, son, I'm probably not the father you wanted, but don't worry; I shan't be starting to impose my disreputable presence on you just because we've found each other out. But then, you don't need a father at all, do you? No... You're alright where you are. You just attach yourself to all these females you feed off, you little parasite!'

And with these comforting words of parental support and affection, Stavro, formerly David Clark of this parish, takes final leave of his son.

Liz Drubble compliments the untidy mess that is her bedroom, sprawled on her bed an untidy corpse. Her murderer, needle-tipped, lies by her side.

Carson looks down at her corpse with mingled feelings of pity and of guilt, wondering if he couldn't have done more to prevent this tragedy.

Drubble stands blubbering, devastated both by the loss of his sister and the revelations about her lifestyle. He had never had a clue. He had lived in the same house as her and he had never had a clue.

'You should have told me,' says Drubble, quietly.

Carson sighs. 'I know... I just always thought maybe you was better off not knowing. That's what she thought, an' all...'

'And all the time I thought she was going out clubbing when she was really... I bet you were all laughing at me...'

Now this as we know is perfectly true: Everyone *had* been laughing at Drubble for being oblivious to the fact that his sister was a smackhead whore; but Carson feels that now is not the time to be acknowledging this fact.

''Course we weren't.'

'If I'd known... Maybe I could've helped her...'

'What? Kick the habit?' Carson shakes his head. 'Easier said than done, mate... Look, let's just make her decent. We can't leave her lyin' like this, and we got no idea how long it'll be before we can get hold of anyone to take her away...'

Downstairs, Drubble says, 'This is Piggy's fault. He's the main dealer in Linton. It's his fault. And to think I've done jobs for him...'

'Oh come on,' protests Carson. 'You've always known Piggy's mob peddle drugs!'

'Yeah, but I didn't know he'd got my sister into the stuff!'

'But he didn't, did he? Not personally. And like I say, you've always known Piggy was a dealer, but you still took his money. It's a bit late to be gettin' all high and mighty about it now.'

'Well, I ain't workin' for him no more,' declares Drubble.

'Yeah, well maybe no one's gunna be workin' for anyone anymore,' says Carson. 'Look outside. It's bloody doomsday or somethin'...'

Stavro walks away from the meeting with his son feeling more agitated now than even the bizarre events of today have agitated him. To see his own son for the first time since he had been a baby... And to discover that after all that time he still only feels the same jealousy and resentment towards him that he felt back then. It all comes flooding back to him; that brief period of unalloyed happiness, with Mary and himself and a job and a house and a car... And then that squalling, milk-hungry parasite had come along and his life had turned to shit.

If Stavro has gone to the dogs, it has been pretty much through personal choice, but still he has to look for someone to blame. Until today he has always visualised that gurgling baby as his destroyer, but now he has to adjust the image to that of a fourteen-year-old boy; a boy who looks just like his mother.

Can he really blame that boy for everything? Has his downward fall been the inevitable consequence of his bitterness and his setbacks? Is he himself blameless? In spite of the bad reputation he succeeded in establishing for himself, he has never actually committed any crime, caused another person any harm...

Except there was this one incident; one event which always brings with it a stab of guilt whenever he recalls it: Stavro has always hated paedophile hunters, the male ones at any rate. These sad, solitary men, either jobless losers or ex-cons, who take up the vigilante crusade of tracking down and trapping child-molesters just to boost their own fragile egos; doing what they do more with the goal of making themselves feel good about themselves than out of any real concern for children. Stavro has always been deeply cynical of them as a breed; and there was one in particular, a local paedophile hunter of his acquaintance who conformed to this despised stereotype in every way. A common tactic of paedophile hunters is to entrap their prey by posing as kids online. Stavro managed to find out the online identity this particular man used, and he decided to use this knowledge to set the guy up, to entrap the trapper, just to teach him a lesson. And Stavro had succeeded in this noble endeavour; succeeded in luring the paedophile hunter to a rendezvous in which he had gotten very badly beaten up, to the extent of needing major dental surgery. As a result of this salutary lesson, the man had given up paedophile hunting and had taken up in its place the new career of being an alcoholic nervous wreck.

Now Stavro has felt some stabs of remorse about this one. Yes, he had not been personally involved in the working over the man had received, but he had undeniably been the catalyst of the event. Can he really blame his perpetration of this malicious act on the milksop schoolboy he has just encountered, the squalling baby of his memories?

He knows this is tantamount to absolving himself of responsibility for his own actions.

No, it's me, isn't it? I did this. I made myself who I am. I made the decision to wallow in the mire… And it was all out of bitterness and self-pity, wasn't it?

Oh, what's the point? What's the point of anything anymore?

Fighting the feelings of despair, Stavro tries to switch his focus back to the present crisis. Maybe he can do something for once—do something useful.

Yes! Maybe now is the opportunity to start turning over a new leaf.

But then he walks round a corner and finds himself face to face with McKearney.

'I've been lookin' for you,' he says, smiling with grim satisfaction. 'Y'see, I've been thinking that today might be a very good day for us to sort a few things out…'

He has something in his hand…

Chapter Thirty-Five
Last of the Last of the Lassiters

This may be a bit late in the day, considering how close we are to the end of the book, but I'd like to take the opportunity to formally introduce the reader to Mayumi Takahashi, or 'Sir Not Appearing in this Film' as she might as well be called, so shamefully neglected she has been thus far. I think she was first brought to the reader's attention on the night of her book signing, but as we never actually ventured into the shop, we didn't get to meet her. After that, she was present for that conference in Lady Jane Richmond's 'office', but being fast asleep at the time, she played no part in the conversation. And most recently she was one of the crowd gathered at the edge of town just a couple of chapters back, but again she had no impact on that scene.

Mayumi Takahashi is a small lady, thirty years of age, she has very long, straight hair and wears large glasses. She has what might be termed a 'Japanese figure'; i.e. a curvy lower body, but not so much up top. She has a tanned 'yellow' complexion and not the pale skin possessed by many Japanese women. When she smiles she reveals that pronounced overbite which Japanophile men find so appealing. (The stereotype of the buck-toothed Japanese person is not based on thin air: overbites are actually very common in Japanese mouths.) All in all, she is a remarkably attractive lady.

One notable characteristic of Mayumi is her love of hats. She has a large collection, hats of all shapes and styles, and she is rarely seen out of doors without one. Taciturnity would be another distinguishing feature of this lady; Mayumi is spare with her words, and all the more so when she is here in the UK, as her command of English is imperfect.

Mayumi is a renowned photographer. In her native Japan her name is mentioned alongside those of heavyweights like

Nobuyoshi Araki and Kishin Shinoyama. And as with those two worthies, Mayumi's photographic obsession is women and girls. Actresses, idols and cosplayers are amongst her subjects and her photography covers nudity, kinbaku (Japanese bondage), fetishism, etc. Her latest book, the previously mentioned *Multitask Lady*, has garnered much controversy in some places on account its content veering dangerously close to scat porn. But this proximity is of little account to Mayumi herself; in her country scat porn is not only a perfectly legal branch of pornography, but it is actually considered to be less explicit than regular sex porn!

Although revered on her own soil, Mayumi Takahashi only really achieved widespread attention in the UK when she published her book *Juno*, which showcased Dodo Dupont, her first European model. Mayumi had fallen in love with the TV psychologist's larger-than-life body the moment she had set eyes on it, and Dodo had in turn fallen reciprocally in love with the Japanese woman. Mayumi and Dodo are now an item, mismatched in size perhaps, but in every other way made for one another.

And through Dodo Dupont, Mayumi has of course also become friends with secret agent Mark Hunter and has even been involved in some of his adventures, including this current exploit.

And now that Mayumi Takahashi has been well and truly (although belatedly) introduced to the reader, we will now join her in a new scene in which she actually has a line of dialogue!

'Situations like this,' says Mark Hunter, 'reveal another tragic effect of the closure of high-street stores thanks to online shopping: there's a much poorer selection of goods for the looters to take home with them.'

Mark, Dodo and Mayumi are making their careful way through the streets of central Linton. They have passed widespread looting and vandalism, dodged gang fights and joyriders. So far they have been unmolested; but even if they were threatened, it's not as if this particular trio cannot take care of themselves. Being a spy, Mark has a handgun tucked in his shoulder holster, while Dodo can boast of having a black belt in karate. (Mark himself is no stranger to unarmed combat, but his fighting style tends to be more the Western saloon punch-up variety.)

'It's one thing for an invading army to indulge in all this looting and wanton destruction of property,' proceeds Mark. 'But for residents to be doing it in their own small town: seems too much like messing in your own back yard, doesn't it?'

'Like that landlord in Dickens who joined in smashing up his own pub during the Gordon Riots,' says Dodo.

'Oh yes; that was in *Barnaby Rudge*, wasn't it? Did he actually take part in the destruction, or did he just stand back and let it happen? It's a long time since I've read that one... People always call these outbreaks anarchy,' proceeds Mark, 'but in a way they're strong indicators that political anarchy just won't float. I mean even if you totally destroy the old system, after the inevitable period of violence and unrest, some dictator or crime lord will just rise up and take over, establishing their own brand of law and order. And then you're pretty much just back where you started from.

'Yes, it's all very nice on paper, this idea of abolishing government and laws, and introducing individual self-government, but the way human beings are at the moment, it doesn't seem like we're ready for it; we haven't evolved to that state of perfection, yet.'

'I'd be inclined to say "speak for yourself" there, Mark darling,' replies Dodo. 'I think political anarchy would work very well if it wasn't for you blokes and your violence. If it was just us women, I'm sure we could get along very nicely without governments and laws. Women are nature's anarchists.'

'Yes, you're probably right about that,' agrees Mark readily. 'Maybe that's what government and statesmanship is all about; satisfying a male lust for control.'

'And historically, at least, for controlling women most of all,' adds Dodo. 'That's what men wanted. It was all about female bondage.'

'Nothing wrong with that!' speaks up Mayumi.

'I was talking figuratively, sweetheart,' explains Dodo. 'I meant bondage as in the oppression of women, not your aesthetic Japanese bondage.'

The trio's destination is the Linton Police Station. Mark has now seen two members of the newly arrived police force whom he has recognised to be personnel of the Asteroid Belt Mining Project. First Marta Sandström when they were at the edge of town, and since then he has recognised another uniformed constable as being Don Taylor, an American astronaut attached to the mining colony.

'...And I don't think it's too much of a leap in the dark to assume from this that they're *all* from the mining colony. They appeared from out of nowhere, and we've all seen how strangely they're behaving.'

'So you think the entire crew of the Mining Project have been teleported here to Linton and are now acting as a zombie police force?'

'Well, yes. It's not that far-fetched, is it? Not when you put it alongside everything else that's going on at the moment.'

'So are we looking at an invasion here? A takeover? These cops are being controlled by that alien?'

'That I'm not so sure about. I still rather like my theory that the alien is not something we can understand or who can understand us, and that its effect on people is unintentional. No, I think we'll find that there's a human being behind this: our errant friend Scarlette Hanson.'

'Scarlette? Well yeah, it seems fairly certain now that she was controlling her brother... But all these other people as well? That's a lot for one teenage girl to do...'

'Yes, but those coppers we've seen aren't displaying

much in the way of individuality, are they? So I think there could well be just one person pulling their collective strings.'

'Okay, I'll go with that. But where do we look for her?'

'I'm hoping we'll find her at the local nick. I'm thinking that maybe she's actually that new chief superintendent I wasn't allowed to see last night...'

They now come to a shopping street, and the three friends witness both unhurried looting and the boisterous vandalism of some parked cars.

'Just like a family day out, isn't it?' observes Mark. 'The kids indulging their penchant for smashing things up while the parents help themselves to some new household appliances.'

Says Dodo: 'For all they know it could be the end of the world, but they still want to satisfy their desire for acquiring worldly goods. In some ways the kids' vandalism makes more sense.'

A police van appears at the end of the street remote from the three observers. Looters and vandals stop what they're doing and watch as the van pulls up. The rear doors are thrown open and about a dozen police officers pour out. They move like a well-drilled army unit, and they are armed. Heavily armed.

'Assault rifles!' exclaims Dodo. 'Where the hell did regional cops get those from?'

'I don't like the look of this,' says Mark. 'We need to grab some cover.'

There is no verbal warning, no order to cease and desist. The officers just open fire. Kids standing on the roofs of cars, adults with electrical appliances in their arms are all mown down by the fusillade of bullets.

Mark, Dodo and Mayumi dive for the cover of a parked car. Screams fill the air as people run to escape the deadly hail. The officers advance down the street, training their guns on every moving target, dispatching them with cold-blooded precision.

Hunkered down beside the parked car, Mark looks at his friends. 'So this is the next move,' he says grimly. 'But what's the objective of this slaughter? Restoring the peace? Or just stirring things up?'

'I think we ought to get out of here before pausing to reflect on the situation,' opines Dodo.

'Agreed,' says Mark. He unholsters his gun, peers over the bonnet of the car. It appears that the trio's presence has already been noted; two of the armed officers are moving purposefully towards them, rifles aimed and ready.

'Two of them coming this way,' he reports. 'When I start shooting, you two run for the next street. I'll be right behind you.' 'Got that,' says Dodo.

Mark takes aim at the approaching officers. He fires; two headshots in quick succession. Dodo and Mayumi break from cover. Mark sees the two officers fall, then takes off after his friends. Bullets pursue him, none of them reach him. He makes it to safety.

The trio keep running until they have put two streets between themselves and the death squad.

They pause to catch their breath.

'Still want to get into that police station?' inquires Dodo.

'More than ever,' replies Mark.

'Look, don't beat yourself up about this,' says Eve, consolingly. 'He's just bitter, is all. It's not your fault.'

'But it *is* my fault,' replies tearful Murray Leinster.

'If anyone's to blame, it'll be your mam,' Eve tells him. 'You have to admit she did treat the guy pretty crappily. But it's not your fault.'

'It is,' insists Murray. 'She wouldn't have acted like that if I hadn't been there. I made Mum act like that. So that makes it my fault, doesn't it?'

Eve sighs. 'You were a new-born baby, love. You can't blame yourself.'

The two are making their way into town, close to the

science park now, Eve with a comforting arm around Murray's shoulders.

'Like I say, the guy's bitter,' continues Eve. 'People like him always want someone to blame. When we find your mam, you can talk it through with her, okay?'

'You think I should tell her?' asks Murray. 'That I've seen my dad?'

'Yeah, I think you should.'

A new sound cuts through the air. Automatic gunfire.

'Machine guns!' blurts Eve. 'Who's firing them? Have the rioters got hold of 'em somewhere?'

'It might be the army,' suggests Murray.

'Where would the army have come from? Nobody can get in from outside, remember?'

They are close now to the town centre. The air around them suddenly starts to thicken; objects become hazy.

Eve looks upwards. 'The green cloud! It's coming down!' She takes Murray's hand, grips it firmly.

The green haze deepens and very soon visibility is reduced to zero.

Eve increases their pace to a fast walk. 'Come on. Let's keep going.'

'But we can't see where we're going!'

'I know, but we need to keep moving. The fog might not be as thick as this everywhere.'

Eve doesn't know how it happens. At no point does she relax her tight hold on Murray's hand. But, nevertheless, suddenly her hand is gripping thin air.

'Murray!' she shouts.

No reply.

'Murray!'

She runs blindly into the fog. She collides with something, something too solid to be a person. She lands on her backside, stunned.

And then, while she is still gathering her senses, the fog begins to dissipate. The air clears. Before her stands the lamppost with which she collided. She scrambles to her feet. The street is empty. No Murray.

She calls his name. She runs to the next street. She backtracks to the previous street. No sign of Murray.

The fog has taken him away.

For once Eve finds herself irresolute. She has lost Murray. Murray Leinster has been her assignment from the start. She moved to this town and enrolled at his school with the sole purpose of observing him. But she had fallen in love with her assignment, an eventuality both anticipated and accepted by the people for whom Eve works.

And now Murray has vanished; taken away by the green fog. And people who get taken away by the green fog have a habit of not coming back.

Tears forming in her eyes, Eve proceeds with fists clenched and dogged footsteps. Should she head for the Garden of Cats? Or should she carry on towards the science park?

She sees a man sitting on the kerb ahead, sobbing. No, not a man, a teenage boy. He raises his head as she approaches, and she sees that it is Lassiter. She is surprised. Lassiter is not someone she expects to see in tears. She is surprised, but she is not sympathetic. She would not have cared about Lassiter's woes at the best of the times, and she cares even less right now.

Her intention is to pass him without even speaking, but Lassiter stands up and blocks her path.

'You...' he says. Wiping away his tears and his look of dejection, his features harden into anger. 'Do you know what you've done?'

Eve sighs. She doesn't have time for this. 'No, and I don't fucking care either. Get out of my way.'

'I had to kill my own dad!' snarls Lassiter.

Eve is surprised, also confused. 'Okay. And how is that my fault?'

'Because it is!' roars Lassiter, his face growing redder.

'He killed my sister! He killed Malcolm!'

'Who did?'

'My dad!'

'Still not seeing the connection here,' says Eve. 'Have you seen Murray around? This fog came down—'

'Him!' spits Lassiter. 'This is all his fault!'

'I thought it was my fault.'

'Yours and his! I'll kill the both of you!'

Lassiter flies at Eve, locking his hands around her throat.

'Die, you fucking bitch! Die die die!'

Choking, Eve lashes out at her assailant. But then the murderous grip around her windpipe suddenly relaxes, and she feels Lassiter pulled away from her.

Eve staggers, struggles for breath. She looks to see who her rescuer might be and sees Lassiter firmly held by a tall, muscular, Middle Eastern girl.

'Sabella!' she croaks.

'Yes, it is I,' confirms that worthy. 'Shall I kill this male for you?'

Sabella is an old friend and colleague of Eve's. In fact, three years before, Eve had spent several months in a desert training camp, being instructed by Sabella in armed and unarmed combat.

Eve, massaging her throat, shakes her head. 'Nah… He's not worth it. Just a guy from my class…'

'What is his name?'

'Lassiter.'

'Ah! I hear of this one! He is the wretch who forces his teacher into performing in pornographic films.'

This is news to Eve. 'Did he? I'd heard he was the one who'd spread the news that Miss Forbes was doing those pornos. He got her sacked from her job cuz of that.' She looks at Lassiter with renewed aversion. 'But you forced her into doing that stuff in the first place?'

'This is so,' confirms Sabella. 'And furthermore, the shame of her exposure caused the woman last evening to take her own life.'

'What! I didn't know that!'

'It is true. Our people have learned of this.'

Eve glares hatred at Lassiter. 'You shit. You fucking shit.'

Lassiter smiles defiantly. 'I only blew the story cuz you and your boyfriend were pissing me off so much. Just a bit of revenge to make me feel better.'

Eve looks at Sabella. 'I've changed my mind. Kill him.'

Obediently, Sabella takes Lassiter's head and twists it. He has no time to even protest. His neck snaps with an audible crack. She tosses the corpse aside.

All the key members of the Linton underworld have been summoned to an urgent meeting at Dirty Dick's, at the behest of their leader Piggy. (I say the 'key members' have been summoned, yet somehow Carson and Drubble have been overlooked!)

The Boy stands on the bar counter, suited and hatted as usual, with Alf and Fred positioned before him in front of the bar. His assembled men (and they are all male) sit at the tables, facing their leader. This with the one exception of the Accountant, the Boy's elderly scrivener, who, taking advantage of the absence of the regular bartender, is behind the bar helping himself to the whisky.

'Now, yer all know why y've bin summoned 'ere,' commences the Boy.

A hand is raised.

'We *don't* know, Boss. We was just told to come 'ere, that's all.' Murmurs of agreement.

'Alright then,' says the Boy, teeth gritted. 'Let me tell ya all why y've bin summoned 'ere: As some of yer may've noticed, the fucking sky's turned fucking green and there's no fucking internet or telephones workin' and we can't get out of town cuz of the fucking green fog wot's surroundin' it. Some of you 'ave noticed that, right?'

Murmurs of assent.

'Good. Nah, we don't know wot this is all abaht, but while things is like they is, we need to take advantage of the situation. Good business-sense, that is. That's why y're 'ere. Got it?'

More noises of affirmation.

'Right. Now, we ain't gunna start emptyin' all the shops and whatnot, cuz the 'ole bloody town's already doin' that. But what we can do is take advantage of this mess to settle some old scores, right? To rub aht some people wot I says needs rubbin' aht. Anyone got any problems with that?'

No one has.

'Good. Now I've made a little list,' says the Boy, producing such a document from the inside pocket of his jacket. He unfolds it. 'Right. 'Ere's the names. I'll read 'em aht first, then we can decide 'oo's gunna take aht oo. Right: First off: Lenny Ferret. Yer all know 'ow 'e's been musclin' in on our turf, shiftin' gear and not cuttin' us in. Made a deal with the Albanians, or somethink, 'e 'as.' (For the Boy, it's always the Albanians. By his reckoning, any trouble can be traced back to them.) 'Well, we can't 'ave that. Then there's Boonie. We all know it was 'im wot grassed on Pete Brady. So 'e's got ter go. Next we got them socalled "Gentlemen". They really piss me off, they do, so they can go. Then there's Belinda Farrer wot runs the cat-'ouse on Silver Street. She's got a serious attitude problem, so she can go, an' all. Then there's Kylie Smith; check-out girl at Tesco's. Gave me a funny look last week she did; well she won't be doin' that anymore, I reckon. Then there's Kenny Dale, oo goes to East Linton Primary. When we woz nippers that little shit stole my Tonka JCB digger; an' if he thinks I've fergotten abaht that, then 'e's in for a surprise, ain't 'e? Next we got—'

The Boy's roll-call of miscreants is at this point rudely interrupted by the bursting open of the doors. Four uniformed policemen appear on the threshold, armed with assault rifles.

'What the bleedin' 'ell—'

The first stream of bullets cuts off the Boy mid-sentence

and sends him flying backwards from the bar counter. Alf and Fred are taken out by the same fusillade. As for the assembled hoodlums, they never have a chance. Each and every one is mown down by the relentless hail of bullets that sweeps the room. Some make it to their feet; the rest are just killed where they sit.

And then silence falls; silence save for the liquid dripping from smashed bottles on the shelves behind the bar. Not a single one of the assembled crooks moves. All lie dead, slumped in their seats, or sprawled on the floor amongst the splintered chairs and tables.

The four policemen study the results of their work with the same expressionless faces with which they executed it. Then, without exchanging either look or word, they turn and exit the pub.

About a minute passes, then, a white-haired head peeps cautiously over the bar counter. Determining that the coast is now clear, the survivor rises to his feet and sighs a gusty sigh. It is the Accountant. He extracts from under his jacket a half-bottle of scotch that, along with his own skin, he has preserved from the general destruction. He surveys the carnage in the room with an understandable feeling of satisfaction that he himself is not numbered amongst the corpses.

And then he looks at the Boy, lying behind the bar only a few feet away from himself, and he feels an additional sense of relief in the knowledge that he is no longer in that person's employ. He salutes the Boy's bullet-riddled body with the whisky bottle and takes a hearty swig of the contents.

'The inevitable end,' philosophises the Accountant. 'Those who live by violence invariably perish by violence. Or in prison. Well, I won't say it has been an honour to serve you, Master Piggy, sir, because it hasn't. But, in the interests of respecting the dead, I shall not verbalise my opinion of you at this time. But now, I have the freedom for which I have so long yearned. At last I can bask under blue skies…'

He breaks off, recalling the current absence of blue sky. 'Well, I can bask under the sky, at any rate, stretch my legs and breathe the fresh air, instead of being chained to that thrice-accursed office all day long…

'So, I shall bid you adieu. There is an unpleasant sanguinary stench permeating the air of this establishment which even the cocktail of alcohol fumes cannot entirely dispel. Yes, I shall remove myself to another house of refreshment, one in which the bottles are still intact.
Farewell, Master Piggy, sir.'

And with this, the Accountant takes his leave of the Boy.

Mark Hunter is by this time familiar with the layout of Linton Police Station, having been in Linton for nearly two weeks and basically having had the run of the place during that time. So now, having gained entrance, he bends his steps towards the chief superintendent's office.

The building is quiet, bearing out Mark's hopes that he would find the place undermanned, if not completely deserted. He makes his cautious way up to the second floor. So far he has encountered no one, confirming his belief that the bulk of the force are out on the streets, busy aggravating the current state of unrest. But just how many of them are there? He knows that the fake replacement force is composed of members of the Asteroid Belt Mining Project, but are they all here? That would mean a police force of over three hundred! Far more officers than a town the size of Linton would normally require; and a terrifying number if a general massacre is being planned.

Without encountering a soul, he gains his objective, the superintendent's office. He pauses a moment before the door. Will he find the author of this tragedy waiting behind this door? Or will he just find an empty office?

He opens the door. The room is dark. The blinds are down, and what with the murky light outside, the darkness in the office is almost that of night. But there is light enough to see that the desk facing the door is occupied. The chair is turned sideways, and Mark sees the profile of the seated figure—an unmoving figure and clearly too big to be that of Scarlette Hanson.

Mark pauses, adjusting his thoughts. It looks to be a man; and he sits as still as a statue. He has not reacted at all to Mark's advent. Is this superintendent just another one of the zombified colonists?

Drawing his gun, Mark walks around the desk and as he draws closer, enough light filters through the blind for Mark to recognise the man seated in the chair: Frank Hanson. Still clad in his astronaut's jumpsuit, he does not move; his eyes are open but they stare into vacancy, fixed and unblinking.

'Well, I had wondered where you'd got to,' murmurs Mark. 'But I was expecting your sister to be the one sitting in that chair. Isn't she the one pulling the strings around here? Yes, you're just a puppet yourself, chief superintendent. Where's that girl hiding herself?'

A rasping chuckle behind him.

Mark spins round, gun at the ready. A hunched shape detaches itself from the shadows in the corner of the room. Mark's first alarmed thought is that he is looking at some formless monster, but then the shape resolves itself into that of a hunched figure draped in the black, hooded robes of the raiders who attacked this station the week before. But the figure is somehow crooked, deformed, and Mark cannot shake his initial impression of being in the presence of something not human.

Having shuffled into the light, the figure halts, and again comes that sibilant laughter. The hood is drawn low over the figure's head; nothing of the face can be seen.

'Scarlette?' says Mark. 'Is it you?'

'The Nameless One is upon us,' rasps the voice. 'The ivory tower calls it forth. As it was in the old old time, now it will be again.'

The voice—it does sound like the voice in which

Scarlette started speaking when she was detained here at the station; but now there is something else, an insect-like buzzing at the edge of the words; a sound that no human vocal cords would be able to produce.

'The blood will flow,' continues the disturbing voice. 'The blood will flow in honour of the new age of darkness.'

'Scarlette?' says Mark. 'Is it you? Are you still in there? You've got to stop this. You've got to stop this slaughter. Do you hear me, Scarlette?'

Another chuckle, this one sounding even less human. The cowled head turns towards Mark; a light gleams from the shadows within.

No. Not a light.

An eye.

A blazing tapered yellow eye.

Chapter Thirty-Six
Murray Leinster is the Centre of the Universe!

Eve was wrong in believing that Murray had been spirited away.

At least, he hasn't been spirited any great distance. After losing Eve in the green fog, the fog rapidly clears for Murray, and he finds himself still in Linton, but now standing in a street right on the outskirts of town.

After recovering his scattered faculties and perceiving that he has been relocated and that Eve is not with him, Murray's first thought is to panic. Where's Eve? Is she still where they were before the fog came down? Or has she disappeared completely? Has she been taken from him?

He turns to the curtain of green fog forming a barrier across the road. Could she be somewhere in there?

'I wouldn't go in there,' says a voice.

Murray spins round. Misaki Morishita smiles languidly at him.

'You!' says Murray. And then, irrelevantly: 'You tried to get me drunk!'

'No, I *did* get you drunk,' Misaki corrects him. 'I *tried* to steal your virginity.'

'Have you seen Eve?'

'No.'

'I've got to find her! She might be back where we were.'

He tries to pass Misaki, but the girl's smiling, feline visage keeps blocking his way.

'Stop doing that!' protests Murray.

'No,' replies Misaki.

Murray searches for an avenue of escape.

'Where's your friend, anyway? That other girl.'

'Ren has gone. Kondou as well,' says Misaki. 'The fog took them away.'

'That's what happened to Eve!' says Murray. 'Or to me...' He explains.

'You won't find her,' Misaki assures him. 'She's gone.'

'But it was me who went!' argues Murray. 'Eve's probably still back where I was before.'

Misaki thinks about this.

'Yes, you might be right,' she decides.

'So that means your friends might still be okay as well,' says Murray.

'Maybe. But I think many more people taken by the fog have not come back. Maybe you are the one lucky one.'

'Why should I be the lucky one?'

'Because you're Murray Leinster.'

'What do you mean?'

'I mean you are you.'

'Well, I've got to find Eve,' says Murray, not understanding this philosophy.

'And how will you do that?' inquires Misaki.

'I'll go back to the street where we were when the fog

came down.'

'That's stupid. She won't still be there, will she? She'll be looking for you; she'll have moved on.'

Murray looks alarmed. 'How am I gunna find her then?'

'Well, where were you going when you got separated?'

'The science park, to look for my mum.'

'Then go there. You're more likely to find Eve Chandler there. I'll come with you.'

'Okay.'

They set off. The sounds of violent conflict reach them as they venture further into town. Presently, they come upon a street littered with bullet-riddled corpses.

'The police,' says Misaki, pointing to the bodies. 'They're enforcing a curfew or something; shooting everyone who's outdoors.' 'But why would they—'

And then it appears, blotting out half the sky.

From out of nowhere and within the blink of an eye: a nightmare, an insane impossibility. A huge shape, an immense ellipse of intense blackness; the darkness of the void but impossibly tangible; and glaring from this black void two inhuman eyes, tapered and of a vivid yellow hue, horrific to behold.

'It's here!' screams Murray.

He falls to his knees, horror-stricken. 'Those eyes! Those eyes!'

Casting no shadow, it looms over the town, this nightmarish impossibility strayed from some other plane of reality. And those appalling eyes, eyes which attract by their very repulsion. In spite of themselves people stare at them for just a moment too long before looking away.

The townsfolk who had taken to the streets are no longer looting and fighting and breaking things; they cower in fear, hiding from those awful inhuman eyes.

They are pouring from the doors of Claverings, the robed and hooded acolytes, running off in all directions like insane flapping phantoms. The Linton branch of a department chain-store may seem a strange place for these fiends to be emerging from, but recollect that the tower rises from this building; the tower whose internal stairwell descends several storeys below ground level. It is from these depths the acolytes have appeared. Eve had told Murray there was no door at the foot of the stairwell, but perhaps there is one now.

From the window of a public house across the street, Mark, Dodo and Mayumi observe this exodus of ghouls. The bistro has but one other patron, a white-haired old man with a goatee beard. The Accountant. Seemingly unconcerned with outside events, he sits at a table, sipping a mature Malaga, relishing his liberation from those endless stacks of paper, those additions and subtractions.

'Maybe they're more of the Mining Project personnel,' says Mark.

'Yes, and maybe that's where they're coming from,' suggests Dodo. 'Maybe the Asteroid Belt Mining Project is actually right beneath our feet.'

Mark looks at her. 'Is that a serious suggestion?'

Dodo shrugs. 'Why not?'

Says Mark: 'Even if we did accept that the Mining Project is a deception, based here on Earth, you'd expect them to have built the thing somewhere out of the way, not right underneath a population centre.'

'Well, maybe that's why they *have* put it here and not under a moor or something,' contends Dodo. 'You know: hiding in plain sight.'

'Goodness knows,' is Mark's weary response. 'Maybe the colony's even in both places at once: out in space where it should be and right
here beneath our feet. This whole situation is insane.'

'Any ideas on how to stop it?'

'Just one,' says Mark. 'Get rid of that tower. From what Scarlette says, that "ivory tower" she babbles about, I think it might be the lodestone.'

'Yes, but where is this ivory tower?'

Mark points. 'We're looking at it.'

'But that tower can't be much more than a century old!' protests Dodo. 'And it isn't ivory, in case you hadn't noticed!'

'Yes, but I think this tower is like an after-image, an echo of something that stood on that same spot a very long time ago. And there's something still there... something that's attracting that nightmare that's hanging in the sky... Why did anyone even build that pointless tower? Maybe they were compelled to, maybe some instinct told them to... Yes, perhaps there's always been a tower, a structure of some description right on this spot—always something here for thousands and thousands of years... I'm thinking that if we destroy that tower, it might be the solution... The only trouble is I didn't pack any explosives with me this trip, and I very much doubt we're going to find any lying around in Linton...'

'Fortune and Son,' comes a voice from across the room.

The trio turn from the window and look at the old man.

'Come again?' says Mark.

'Fortune and Son,' repeats the Accountant, studying his wineglass. 'A building demolition firm, based here in Linton—they have a yard over on Cutters Lane. They will have a supply of explosives. Of course, they won't just be sitting on a shelf for you to pick up; they will be safely and securely stored, you can be sure of that. You might not be able to get at them...'

'Yes...' agrees Mark, musingly. 'You wouldn't also happen to know where we could get our hands on some cutting tools...?'

Ren once told Misaki a funny story about something that had happened to one of her classmates in middle school. The classmate was this ditzy airhead of a girl, and she'd come home one tea time to find a turd—one of those curly "Mr Whippy" turds that seem to be peculiar to Japan— lying in the hallway just inside the front door. Outraged at this desecration of the family home, the girl had drawn her parents' attention to the turd, and the result was a family conference to determine the provenance of the excrement, with the offending turd placed, like a defendant in the dock, on the kitchen table before them. The shrewd mother discerned that the faeces contained fragments of corn kernels which could only have come from the cereal the family had eaten at breakfast that same morning; ergo, the culprit was someone in the house! It was only at this point that the airhead girl remembered that she was the one who had deposited the turd. Coming home from school a few hours before and with aching bowels, she had been in such a hurry and, unable to make it to the toilet in time, she had dropped her cargo in the hallway and then gone back out to play, promptly forgetting her misdemeanour. The anxious girl still hoped that she would escape without having to confess her crime, but then the father, who had been sniffing at the faeces on the table, suddenly blurted out: 'This is definitely schoolgirl turd!' at once incriminating his daughter and at the same time begging the question how it was he was able to identify this particular brand of excrement with so much authority.

Misaki had found this anecdote highly amusing, in addition to shedding intriguing light on the lives of the common folk; but when she inquired of Ren what the sequel of these events had been, Ren had been forced to admit that it hadn't actually happened to anyone she knew, it was just a story she had read in a manga. The final panel of the comic strip had shown the irate mother crucifying her daughter and husband upside down, her for defecating in the hallway and him for being a pervert.

Ren...

Even when you force yourself not to look at that monstrosity in the sky, you can still feel its presence, you can still sense those baleful eyes burning into your soul.

Murray needs Eve; Murray needs his mother; because Murray is scared and selfish and dependent and in spite of everything is still just a boy. True, he has a girl by his side: Misaki Morishita. But he doesn't understand Misaki and he doesn't entirely trust her. He feels she is someone who might lead him astray.

Misaki is better than nothing, better than being all alone, but he wants Eve or his mother, someone he can lean on and who will comfort him... And he's not even sure he's going the right way about finding them. He might discover neither of them waiting for him at the science park.

And then the landscape shifts. Literally.

The street around them suddenly becomes a valley in a plain of huge rocks. The sky becomes purple in hue. But yet, somehow it's still the same. A spire of rock points to the heavens just where the tower was a moment before and that awful creature still hangs in the sky. The visual details have altered but the atmosphere remains the same; it is as though they haven't moved at all, but that their eyes and brains are receiving fresh visual information; an adjusted perception rather than a change of location.

Of course, none of these conclusions occur to Murray's frightened mind, not now when he is right in the middle of it. He can sense the similarity, but the alteration of the landscape is incomprehensible to him and just an additional source of fear.

He grabs Misaki's arm for support. 'What's going on?'

'I don't know,' she answers. 'It's like we are in a virtual reality simulation that is starting to malfunction. New landscapes are mapping themselves over the old... We must keep going.'

'But where?' wails Murray. 'The town, the science park—they're not there anymore!'

'We must keep going,' insists Misaki.

They press on. The buildings, the street, swim back into view, the sky becomes murky green again.

'Come on,' says Misaki. 'Perhaps we can control this if we concentrate.'

'Oh no!'

Robed figures appear. Closing in from all directions, they surround Murray and Misaki and restrain them. The faces of their captors, framed by the hoods of their black robes, are lifeless, expressionless. Had Murray been familiar with the personnel of the Asteroid Belt Mining Colony, he would have recognised the black woman firmly holding his arm to be Dr Floella Benjamin, head physician of Vesta Base. Similarly ignorant on this subject, Misaki fails to recognise her own captor as Clayton Daniels, a mining engineer from Vermont.

Without a word, the acolytes move off with their prisoners.

'Where are they taking us to?' asks Murray.

'I don't know,' answers Misaki. 'But it won't be the science park.'

'Aren't these the people who attacked the police station? Weren't they supposed to be dressed like this?'

'Were they? Then if these are Scarlette Hanson's rescuers, perhaps they are taking us to her.'

Reality slews back and forth as they proceed, the town and the plain of rocks dissolving in and out of each other. Their destination soon becomes clear enough—the one constant, the finger in the sky, sometimes a square concrete tower, sometimes an irregular spire of rock. And behind that spire, looming on the horizon, the baleful-looking creature.

'It's the tower,' says Misaki. 'That's where they're taking us. The tower must be an important place for them.'

'But what do they want with us?' wonders Murray.

'Perhaps they only really want you, Murray Leinster.'

They arrive at the entrance to Claverings department

store. Murray looks up and descries a lone robed figure standing on the platform at the top of the tower.

'Who's that up there?'

'Someone waiting for us. I think "up there" is where we are being taken.'

'What are they going to do to us?'

'Who knows?'

Murray looks up again, and for just a moment the tower is not an ugly structure of bricks and cement, but a glowing ivory tower, it's architecture the dreams of a forgotten time...

Urged on, they troop through the glass doors of the department store and then start to ascend the rocky pathway which winds its way to the top of the spire of rock. As they proceed, they occasionally pass strange runic symbols, perhaps thousands of years old, carved into the flanks of rock: 'KILROY WAS HERE' 'POLEAX THE POLLTAX!' 'HAS ANYONE SEEN MIKE HUNT?' Abstruse symbols whose meanings have become lost in the oceans of time.

And then the ground starts to shake. An ominous rumbling, gathering in intensity, fills the air. Murray's arm is released as the acolytes stagger. Rocks and dust start to fall around him. He turns to Misaki but cannot see her. The ground beneath his feet lurches, he is about to fall, but then someone grabs him, pulls him out through the fire door and he feels himself flying...

When he was five Murray Leinster had gone on a summer holiday with his mother to Scarborough. One blazing hot day they had been on the North Bay, his mum, bikini-clad, lazing under the shade of a parasol, while Murray, closer to the sea, was building sandcastles. Working diligently, he had actually constructed quite an elaborate fortress—a structure of many levels with turrets and battlements; and he was now in the process of digging a moat, which he planned to feed with water from a nearby tidal pool.

A boy, a stranger, came up to him; a dark-haired boy with

a big, friendly smile and like Murray himself wearing only a pair of bermuda shorts.

'Hiya,' said the newcomer, and from his accent Murray could tell that he was from this part of the world, not a Southerner like himself.

'Hello,' said Murray.

'Great castle you've built here,' enthused the newcomer, squatting down.

'Thanks,' said Murray.

'What're you doing now?'

'I want to fill the moat with water,' explained Murray. 'So I'm digging a ditch from here to the water.'

'Who are you here with?' asked the newcomer. 'Your mam and your dad?'

'Just my mum.'

'Where is she?'

Murray pointed.

'Wow! She's your mam? She's really hot!'

'No, she's alright in the shade under the umbrella.'

'I mean she's good-looking, silly,' grinned the newcomer. 'She looks like a model or summat.'

'Does she?'

'Aye. And you're a handsome lad y'self. You get your looks from your mam, eh?'

'S'pose so,'

'You ever seen your mam naked?'

'Of course. When we're in the bath.'

'Woo-hoo! You go in the bath with your mam, eh?'

'Why not? Everyone does.'

'I don't reckon they do, y'know,' said the stranger. 'So, do you like all that, then?'

'What, having a bath?'

'No! I mean all that sexy, grown-up stuff. Naked stuff.'

'What do you mean?'

'You know! What grown-ups do. Naughty stuff!'

'I don't know about that.'

'Don't you! I mean stuff like this!'

And then the newcomer leaned in and kissed Murray!

'You can't do that!' exclaimed Murray, frantically wiping his mouth.

'Why not? Haven't you ever kissed anyone before?'

'But two boys can't kiss each other!' 'I'm not a boy, you wally! I'm a girl!'

'You can't be!' protested Murray.

'Why can't I be?'

'Cuz you're not wearing anything on top! Girls are supposed to wear something on top!'

'No point, is there? I 'aven't got anythin' worth hiding yet, have I? I'm not old enough.'

'Girls are still supposed to cover it up,' insisted Murray. 'I don't believe you, anyway. You've got short hair. You're a boy.'

'No, I'm not!'

'Yes, you are!'

'No, I'm not!'

'Yes, you are!'

'No, I'm not! An' I'll prove it!'

The newcomer stood up and literally right before Murray's down went the front of the bermuda shorts! Murray's eyes goggled. No willy! Just a line there! She really *was* a girl!

A blue sky.

Murray lies on his back, stretched out on springy turf. The air is warm, scented with the aromas of nature. He is in a clearing. The crowns of trees appear in the periphery of his vision, sharply-defined against the pale blue sky.

Murray has no need to get up or look around to know where he is. On the last occasion he was here by moonlight, but he recognises the tranquil, soothing atmosphere: he is in the Garden of Cats. What he cannot remember is how he comes to be here. Has he been lying here for long? Has he just awoken from deep slumber or has he been merely daydreaming?

He feels contentment, a kind of blissful lethargy. He doesn't want to move from this spot. He wants to stay right where he is for as long as this feeling lasts. Moving might spoil it all, the slightest motion of an arm or a leg might disperse this happy feeling.

A cat appears, its face close to his own. Looking down at him, the cat studies Murray with that look, peculiar to the feline visage, that seems to combine curiosity and alarm. The cat is purring, and the tranquil sound compliments Murray's own feeling of happy contentment.

The cat disappears and then, moments later, Eve Chandler steps into his line of vision, smiling down at him. She is naked but Murray sees nothing strange in this. It is just as it should be.

'Hello there, pet,' she greets him. 'Having a nice rest?'

'Yes,' says Murray. 'How long have I been here?'

'Ooh, a while,' answers Eve.

Murray watches the pendulous motion of her breasts as she kneels on the grass beside him.

'How did I get here? Did you bring me here?'

'More like you brought me here,' replies Eve. Even her smile, broad and large-toothed as usual, seems to have in it something of the tranquil satiety that flows through Murray. It flows through him and urges him to remain still, to just lie back and let time drift over him and pass without touching.

'I brought you here? How?'

He thinks of the door in the wall and its complicated electronic lock.

Eve shrugs, as if this is a matter of small importance. 'I guess you brought us here cuz this is where you wanted to be.'

'But I was at the tower…' says Murray, struggling with memory. 'The tower, but sometimes it was more like a tower of rock… It started to fall down…'

'It *has* fallen down,' Eve tells him. 'You were dead lucky you didn't go down with it.'

'I was with Misaki…!'

'She's okay. Don't worry.'

'Someone grabbed me… Everything was shaking and someone grabbed me…'

'Yeah, that were me,' says Eve. 'Just in the nick of time.'

'You saved me?'

'Course I did.'

'What about Mum? Where's Mum?'

'Relax, she's here; she's alright. Everyone's alright.'

'And the thing in the sky?'

'Gone. It's all back to normal now. Everything's just like it should be.'

'And Mum's here?'

'Aye.' Eve looks over her shoulder. 'She's coming now. They're all coming. Coming to see that you're alright.'

First Mum appears, naked also. She kneels down at his other side.

'And how's my little man?' she asks, her voice warm and milky.

'I'm okay,' says Murray.

More women appear. First Misaki and Ren. Then Dodo and Mayumi. Fifi Fleetwood. A dark, muscular girl he has not seen before. Lady Jane Richmond. Even Rose Gardener and Jenny Jones. All naked, all smiling at him.

'Y'see, you're the Centre of the Universe, Murray Leinster,' explains Eve. 'It's always been like that, hasn't it? Ever since the day you were born…'

They crowd around him these women, kneeling on the grass, smiling at him, touching him. Murray, caressed by the warmth of their bodies, the scent of their genitalia, feels himself drift…

Drifting like he's lighter than air or floating on water, quietly rising…

The last bolt in place, Carson throws down his tools, climbs onto his motorbike and turns the key in the ignition. He has performed this ritual a thousand times before. But this time something unexpected happens: the engine roars into life. No longer the inert creature it has always been, his motorbike is now alive, alive and champing at the bit.

Carson is flabbergasted. He can't for the life of him think what he has done to achieve this result. All he has just done is perform the usual ritual of stripping down and reassembling the engine. He can't recall doing a single thing he hasn't done a thousand times before. And yet somehow, somehow the machine is actually working! Somehow, he has actually fixed it!

He laughs. He gives vent to a feeling of elation the like of which he hasn't known in years.

His mother, equally disbelieving, emerges from the house.

'Where is he?' she demands.

'Where's who?' answers Carson, shouting over the noise of the engine.

'The mechanic who's fixed your bike! That's who!'

'There ain't no mechanic, Mum!' says Carson, laughing. 'I fixed it all by myself!'

'You never did!'

'I did, y'know!'

'What did you do?'

'Haven't a clue!' is the cheerful reply. 'Go'n get me helmet, Mum; it's in the garage. I'm going out for a spin!'

His mum makes a show of irritation. 'And what did your last slave die of? Get it yourself!'

'But I don't wanna have to cut the engine, Mum!' says

Carson. 'I'm worried it won't start up again! I've gotta go now, while it's working!'

'Alright, I'll get your bloody helmet!'

Mrs Carson waddles off to the garage and returns with Carson's crash helmet, the crash helmet Carson bought brand new to go with his newly acquired second-hand motorbike and has up until today been gathering grease and cobwebs in the garage.

It's one of the 'open face' helmets, the type with no lower section to project the jaw. Carson has always preferred this type, thinking that the other kind are too restricting. He wipes down the surface of the helmet with his sleeve, places it on his head, buckles the chinstrap.

'Right! Now I'm ready to go!'

Mrs Carson looks at her son's flared jeans. 'Shouldn't you be wearin' special boots or somethin'?' she asks.

'I ain't got time for those accessories,' says Carson dismissively. 'I'm off!'

Lowering his visor, he releases the handbrake and the machine moves forward. Liberated from the driveway that has been its home for many years, the machine accelerates noisily down the street.

His original idea was just a quick spin around the block; but, soon intoxicated by the freedom, Carson yearns for more. He feels like a caged bird suddenly set free. All these years, all these years tied down to this grubby little town, never going anywhere, never seeing anything new... But now, now he can go anywhere. With this machine he can go and he can keep on going, anywhere he likes. He can leave it all behind, this town, his past, his problems; he can just twist the throttle and take off like a bullet!

Carson powers along the streets, passing cars, turning corners. His machine; the one he has finally got working himself; this bike is going to take him away, take him forward to a new life. This is amazing! He's never felt like this in his life!

He takes the next corner with precision but way too much speed.

There's no time to slow, no time to swerve; he only has time to recognise the blond-haired boy crossing the road, to see the startled pink face, before the hurtling metal collides with flesh and bone. And he never laid a finger on the boy…

Samurai West

disappearer007@gmail.com

Printed in Dunstable, United Kingdom